The PEARLER'S WIFE

Roxane Dhand was born in Kent and entertained her sisters with imaginative stories from a young age. She studied English and French at London University, and in 1978 she moved to Switzerland, where she began her professional career in public relations. Back in England and many years later on, she taught French in both the maintained and private sectors. Now retired, she is finally able to indulge her passion for storytelling. *The Pearler's Wife* is her first novel.

To find out more about Roxane, catch up with her on Twitter and Facebook.

@RoxaneDhand
/roxane.dhand

The
PEARLER'S WIFE

ROXANE DHAND

A division of HarperCollins*Publishers*
www.harpercollins.co.uk

Harper*Impulse* an imprint of
HarperCollins*Publishers*
The News Building
1 London Bridge Street
London SE1 9GF

www.harpercollins.co.uk

This paperback edition 2018

First published in Great Britain in ebook format by HarperCollins*Publishers* 2018

A catalogue record for this book
is available from the British Library

ISBN: 9780008283926

Set in Goudy Old Style

Printed and bound in Great Britain by CPI Group Ltd,
Croydon, CR0 4YY

MIX
Paper from
responsible sources
FSC C007454

This book is produced from independently certified FSC™ paper to ensure
responsible forest management.

For more information visit: www.harpercollins.co.uk/green

For Harry

CHAPTER 1

FROM THE DECK OF the SS *Oceanic*, Maisie Porter looked down on the wharf. The bugle sounded, signalling that all guests should curtail their farewells and go ashore. Her father had already averted his face and was walking away.

This is it, then, she thought. As she watched him vanish in the distance she could not say if he would miss her. She hoped so but in her heart she doubted it. Over the week before setting sail, Maisie had felt she was being edged towards a precipice, that her days with her family were counting down like the number of nights until Christmas Day. And now here she was, off to Australia. The bugle sounded again, and the ship slid into the stream.

Her mother hadn't bothered to see her off. Up until the last moment she had wondered if her mother might have made the effort, if only for the pleasure of seeing her go, to give the final shove that propelled her over the cliff edge, permanently out of view.

A few weeks ago, Maisie hadn't even known her cousin Maitland existed. Now she was on her way to marry him.

She hefted the leather bag at her feet and stood staring at the dot that was her father in the distance, traces of panic rising inside her again. Her heart began to pump hard against her ribcage, like a fist.

When she was a child, Maisie had thought her father was like one of the old leather reference books that lined his library shelves – something to touch only when allowed and to consult on rare and weighty matters – but like the books, he was solid and dependable. Although he was never a man to show his affection, she felt his loss like an engulfing wave.

A steward, tall and portly in his dark uniform, appeared at her elbow, startling her. He looked at her closely, in a way that made her feel exposed, like a curiosity at the circus. She became instantly conscious of her unfashionable travelling clothes, the heavy shoes that rubbed against her heels, the felt hat that couldn't quite contain her disobedient hair.

Then he blinked and smiled: a tight smile that turned his eyes to slits. 'May I be of assistance, Miss?'

His grim reproval washed over her. She knew that her face telegraphed her discomfort. She felt colour flood her cheeks, like the sting of the face slap her mother had given her when Maisie tried to protest the arrangement. She swallowed the lump in her throat. 'Might you show me to my cabin? I am travelling without my family but am to share with a Mrs Wallace.'

He consulted his list and squinted in the gloom. 'Miss Porter?'

Maisie nodded.

'Mrs Wallace is already in the cabin. I'll walk you there.'

He took her bag and pushed open the door, leading her down a flight of carpeted stairs towards the first-class staterooms.

She held on to the handrail, thinking the ceiling was too low, that her feet hurt, that she wanted to run away. The steward steered her along a narrow corridor, until he stopped with a crisp click of polished heels at a sturdy door.

Somewhere within the ship, a woman began to scream.

The ship had started to roll, its sides creaking, the roar of the engine a deep unfamiliar resonance. For a moment, Maisie braced herself against the wall and clung to the handrail. 'The lady sounds very distressed. Do you think she might require a doctor?'

'Hysteria would be my diagnosis,' the steward said, matter-of-factly. 'Happens every voyage as soon as we set sail.'

'But aren't you going to check – just to be sure nothing is seriously wrong?'

He doled out his opinion. 'Not much point. There's no pill that can cure her of this ailment. When she realises she's not going to drown, she'll stop. Simple as that. Now, here you are, Miss.' He took a step forward and knocked on the door, his touch surprisingly light.

Maisie mumbled her thanks and tried to ignore the persistent screaming.

The door opened inwards and a stout, big-jawed woman with a helmet of crinkly platinum hair appeared in the doorway.

The woman raised her eyebrows over steel-rimmed spectacles as the steward loitered. 'No need to stand there, steward,' she said, her clipped English poorly disguising her Australian vowels. 'You have already received your tip.'

The man sniffed but held her gaze for a fraction longer than was strictly polite before stepping away.

Maisie's shock at his boldness shrank her voice to a croak. 'Mrs Wallace?'

'Pompous little pipsqueak,' Mrs Wallace said, loud enough for him to overhear. 'Put an ordinary man in a uniform and he thinks he commands an army.'

She stepped to one side and gestured Maisie in. 'Come on, dear. We may as well get acquainted. We are to be roommates for the next couple of months, after all.'

Mrs Wallace was, Maisie understood, related to a friend of her mother. She had a tone of address which might easily have rivalled that of a major general. Though the older woman had been paid handsomely for her chaperoning services, her connection to home was of some comfort to Maisie, and she very much hoped they would get along.

Maisie looked round the tiny cabin. The room was spare and had a strong, clean smell, like pine trees. She took in the white rivet-studded walls, the little handbasin and tap concealed in a coffin-like upright stand in one corner, and the crisp linen sheets folded flat on the bunk beds, which were separated by a short ladder hooked over the foot rail.

'What's the matter, dear?' Mrs Wallace asked. 'You don't look very happy.'

Maisie tried to rearrange her expression into a smile. 'It's just . . . Well, this is not quite what I was expecting.'

Mrs Wallace blinked several times. 'In what way exactly?'

'I've never shared sleeping quarters before. It seems a very small space for two people. Especially in first class.'

Mrs Wallace smiled. 'You can't buy something that is not for sale, Maisie. Not even your parents, for all their money and influence. There are very few single-berth cabins on this steamship and you were simply too late to secure one.'

'Oh dear.' Maisie faltered. 'And there is no window. How shall we get fresh air?'

Mrs Wallace wagged a finger. 'You'll be very pleased when the weather turns foul, just mark my words. You wouldn't want seawater sluicing you in the middle of the night. Now, buck up dear. You need to have a wash and change for dinner.'

Maisie froze as confusion overtook her. Was she supposed to undress there and then, in front of Mrs Wallace? Whom she'd only just met? Maisie stared at the floor, fingering the top button of her jacket, aware that her eyes had become slightly damp.

Mrs Wallace coughed two or three times, as if she understood the awkwardness of the situation. 'Would you like the cabin to yourself while you change your clothes?'

Maisie nodded, pulling out the sharp pearl-tipped pin from her hat and tossing it onto the bottom bunk. Almost before it had landed, Maisie snatched it back up again and glanced at Mrs Wallace.

'Put it on the chair, dear,' Mrs Wallace instructed. 'We are going to have to learn to dance round each other, aren't we?' the older woman quipped brightly. 'There isn't enough room to unpack everything, so you will have to use your trunk as a sort of auxiliary chest of drawers. It is already under the bed. I am afraid that I have filled up the wardrobe with my own frocks, so you will have to fold your things carefully.'

Maisie felt a flicker of annoyance as she watched Mrs Wallace pat her hair into place and then squeeze past to open the cabin door. 'I shall go up to the drawing room for half an hour or so and see if I can rustle you up a cup of tea. How does that sound? And don't worry about the sheets. They've already half made up my bed and they're going to do yours while we are having our dinner.'

When she left the cabin, Maisie stood looking at the back of the door for a moment. As soon as the heavy footsteps died away, she began to unbutton her jacket.

She pulled her trunk out from under the bed and ran a shaky hand across its pitted surface. Bound with brown, wooden ribs and fastened with two brass locks, it wasn't new. She traced a finger over the initials stamped in gold on the scuffed black lid. 'Maisie Porter,' she said aloud. *What on earth are you doing here?*

She fished out the key from her handbag and sprang open the catches. She managed a wash of sorts at the cabin's tiny basin, trying not to miss her evening bath nor the spacious London bedroom of which she'd had sole occupancy. By the time Mrs Wallace swooped in over an hour later – with no sign of the promised cup of tea – Maisie was changed into evening-wear and ready for dinner.

Mrs Wallace bustled her out of their cabin and down the cheerless corridor. When they reached the landing, they stopped at the top of a wide wooden staircase.

'We go down to eat, dear,' she explained, 'not up. The dining saloon is always situated on a lower deck, but everything else – for us – is above.'

Maisie peered over the bannister at the small knot of people below. 'That's interesting. Why down?'

'To be nearer the kitchens, I would imagine, although I've never really given it much thought. Come along, dear. People are already gathering and we don't want to keep them waiting. Unpunctuality is not attractive in a lady, and we are already later than I would like.'

As they went down the stairs, Maisie glanced across at Mrs Wallace. 'Do the second- and third-class passengers go down to their meals as well?'

Mrs Wallace tucked in her chin and at first gave a fair impression of considering the question. It was apparent, though, quite quickly, that her mind was elsewhere. She pointed a large finger. 'Look what has been prepared for us!'

Laid out on the side tables were plates bearing small rounds of toast covered with what seemed to be tiny black seeds.

Maisie's eyes widened. 'What are those?'

'That's caviar, dear,' Mrs Wallace explained. 'Fashionable with the wealthy. I'm surprised you don't recognise it.'

She processed this a moment. 'My mother says it's a delicacy from the Caspian Sea but I'm not sure I know what the delicacy actually is.'

'Sturgeon eggs.'

'Oh dear!'

'You should try some. Good for your education if you are to live by the sea.' She beckoned to a steward.

Maisie watched the waiter lift a plate and followed his progression to her side. She looked from the caviar to Mrs Wallace, hoping that by some miracle she would understand her silent plea. *Fish roe,* she thought. *How absolutely ghastly.*

'Pinch the toast between your fingers, dear,' Mrs Wallace said and gave her an encouraging smile.

'I don't care for fish.'

'For goodness' sake, Maisie, just eat the thing.'

Maisie frowned and picked up the small round of toast. She bit into the spongy roe, which had the texture of tapioca. The eggs burst on her tongue as the overwhelming taste of fish swelled in her mouth and into her nose. It almost made her retch.

'Nice?' Mrs Wallace asked.

She shook her head and pressed her clenched hands against her sides.

Mrs Wallace patted her shoulder. 'It's not everyone's cup of tea but it's good you've tried it. I don't especially like it either and have never understood why it's considered such a delicacy in English society. Personally it makes me think of mouse dirt.'

'Mrs Wallace!'

'What, dear? I can't believe you've reached nineteen years of age without coming across the mouse's particular calling card.'

Maisie looked into her inquisitive eyes, which seemed to expect a reply. 'I have, of course, Mrs Wallace, but never on a piece of toast that I was ordered to eat.'

Mrs Wallace chuckled as they moved away from the plates of fishy roe and joined the other passengers funnelling into the restaurant.

'Where shall we sit?' Maisie asked as they paused at the entrance, eyeing the tables that snaked round the room, white-topped and solid. 'Surely there must be a seating arrangement?'

'The staff will tell us, dear. No need to be quite so anxious. We shall be seated with people like us.'

As if on cue, a young officer, immaculate in his white uniform, appeared beside them and ushered them to a circular table set for eight. Stiff white napkins stood on empty plates like sails and a lone candle rose tall in a silver stick.

Mrs Wallace poured some water in a glass and handed it to Maisie. She lifted the half-filled tumbler and took a sip, resisting a very strong urge to gargle the taste of caviar away.

'We shall eat our meals here for the entire voyage, so best to get busy and befriend your fellow diners,' Mrs Wallace said.

According to the name cards, Maisie was placed next to Mr Smalley on one side and Mrs Wallace on the other, with the ship's second officer to Mrs Wallace's left. Maisie turned to her neighbour, a seedy-looking gentleman with a sweaty top lip and a flaky patch of skin on his scalp, and managed a faint smile. Mrs Wallace craned forward and introduced herself loudly to a newly married couple sitting across the table, which was so wide that even if they stretched out their arms as far as they could, their fingertips would never meet. The couple boomed back that they were travelling with the bride's parents, Mr and Mrs Jenkins.

A waiter was working his way through the dining room and arrived at their table to light the candle with a long taper. As he explained the menu, Mrs Wallace announced, 'I shall decide for us both, dear. You are too young to make sensible dietary decisions. I believe we shall both have the soused salmon tonight.'

Maisie dipped her head, lips sucked tight, and swallowed down her resentment. She had wanted the duck because she knew her mother loathed it, and had already told Mrs Wallace she did not care for fish. *At what point will anyone see I have a mind of my own? Good God!* She hugged the blasphemy and enjoyed it. *I am nearly twenty and considered old enough to get married. Why am I not permitted to choose what I want to eat?*

During the meal, she picked at her food and sipped her water, her eyes jumping from one diner to the next as if following a game of tennis.

The mother of the bride was rubbing her arms and complaining of the cold.

'I'm sitting in a draught, Harold,' the woman said to her husband, staring accusingly at the door. 'Could you ask them to close it?'

'Of course, my dear,' Harold said, getting to his feet. A moment later, a waiter pounced on his napkin like a cat on a ball of wool and replaced it by his plate.

Mrs Wallace covered her mouth with her hand and whispered, 'You should try to make conversation, Maisie. It will seem rude if you don't.'

'Are you looking forward to the warmer weather?' Maisie called across the table.

The mother of the bride cupped a hand behind her ear and shook her head.

Maisie leaned forward and tried again. 'Are you travelling to Australia for the better weather?'

The woman's new son-in-law, a handsome man with blond hair and a military moustache, said loudly from his side of the table, 'You'll have to crank up the volume, Miss Porter. The new mater is dreadfully hard of hearing.'

Maisie pressed a hand against her chest and said ironically, 'I'm sorry to hear that.'

'Don't bother yourself trying to shout tonight. There's going to be lashings of time to get to know her. Perhaps best though if you talk to someone else just for now, don't you think?'

The waiter cleared away her half-eaten bowl of consommé.

She was not in the mood for another culinary scolding. She glanced at Mrs Wallace who, happily, was chatting enthusiastically to the second officer and glowing like a lantern.

Maisie turned back to the seedy gentleman. He was stabbing at peas with the tines of his fork, stacking them up like beads on an abacus.

'Could I pass you anything, Mr Smalley? Salt or pepper perhaps?' *A shovel?*

'Wine bottle first,' he said, his mouth full. 'Then the bread basket.'

She resisted the temptation to pass comment, and lifted the decanter. 'Is your wife not with you on this trip?'

Mrs Wallace, who apparently had the hearing of a bat, leaned in close as though about to tell her a secret. 'Don't ask personal questions, Maisie dear. It's vulgar.'

Mr Smalley filled his glass and swirled it round, inspecting the amber liquid in the candlelight. He took a large gulp and chewed it a few times, as if consulting the wine for an answer, then began cramming wodges of butter into a roll. 'Never married,' he said, a spray of spittle flying from his mouth. 'But that's not to say I'm not open to offers.'

Course after course as the meal ground on, Smalley became more tiresome. By his sprouting eyebrows and the silver hair that hung in tufts round his ears, Maisie judged him to be in his sixties, give or take. That they were at least forty years apart in age seemed almost to encourage him. When desserts were laid before them in twinkling glass bowls, he was already too close, his liver-spotted hand inching purposefully towards hers across the tablecloth, trapping her palm between the cream and custard. Plump, deliberate fingers crept a little closer with the cheese and crackers, and when coffee was poured, his knee was banging against hers with the determination of a rutting ram.

'Let me tell you how I come to be on board, Miss Porter.' He took a handful of petits fours from an oval china plate. 'I'm taking the British Empire to the wilderness to enforce law and order in one of the gold-rush towns. I am to be Ballarat's new resident magistrate. What do you say to that, eh?' He stuffed a petit four into his mouth and started to chew. 'And you, Miss Porter? What takes you to Australia?'

Mrs Wallace straightened her spectacles across the bridge of her nose. 'Maisie is going to Australia to be married.'

'Oh!' Mr Smalley perked up. 'Going fishing?'

Maisie shrank from his remark and Mrs Wallace dived in. 'No, not fishing, Mr Smalley.' She waggled an admonishing finger. 'She is not fishing at all. She has landed herself a splendid prize. She is engaged to be married.'

Maisie felt a little queasy at the mention of the wedding, but hoped Mrs Wallace's forthrightness would bring Mr Smalley to heel.

He was not to be put off. He tipped some wine into a glass and pushed it towards her. 'Could I tempt you to a glass of wine, Miss Porter? To celebrate your good fortune?' He dropped his hand below the tablecloth and squeezed her knee, kneading her flesh with his hot fingers.

Unable to move without causing a scene, she felt his hand scrabble up her thigh like an agile weasel. She batted it away, shifting sideways in her seat to increase the distance between them. *If he does that one more time, I'll stab his hand with my fork*, she promised herself.

'No, you could not, Mr Smalley.' Mrs Wallace pushed the glass back across the tablecloth. 'But you may pour one for me.'

The steamer chugged slowly towards its destination. The warm air became hot and started to make clear the impracticality of Maisie's clothes. Away from all that was familiar, she felt herself changing in small rebellious ways. For the first time in her life, she was answerable only to herself. Although, of course, there was still Mrs Wallace to negotiate.

Her first defiant gesture happened quite unexpectedly one morning. In the cabin, the two women dressed and undressed mostly behind the bunk curtains. Mrs Wallace had laid claim to the lower berth and for Maisie, the novelty of negotiating the tiny wooden ladder several times a day soon lost its appeal. Lying or sitting on her bed, trying to lace herself into her corset with its steel boning in the gathering heat near the roof, proved too much of a trial. Even without the restrictive garment, she was as thin as paper, and it fitted snugly over her chemise and squeezed her hips and breasts into a shapeless column.

What must it feel like, she wondered as she plucked at the laces behind her back, *to belong to a native tribe who wear nothing at all?* So, in the privacy of the small, curtained space, she left the corset off and smuggled it down into her cabin trunk while Mrs Wallace was still asleep.

If Mrs Wallace noticed she had removed it, she didn't remark on it – indeed, she was constantly distracted from her caretaking duties by Mr Smalley. She seemed very struck with him, but he had taken to staring at Maisie with looks of overpowering interest. She would almost have preferred the groping.

Towards ten o'clock one evening, when they had been at sea for several weeks, the ship was nearing the Cape of Good Hope and Maisie was melting in her clothes, Mr Smalley badgered his female companions to make up a four for a rubber of bridge.

Beads of sweat trickled down her worsted-clad spine, her feet protested in pools of deliquescent silk stocking, and the blood pounded hot in her cheeks. She folded her napkin carefully on her plate. 'Would you mind very much if I give it a miss, Mrs Wallace? I don't understand bridge at all well and am so hot in these suffocating clothes, I would prefer to take a turn on deck, to try to cool down a little before bed.'

'You must not do that alone, Maisie. People will think you are fast. You must remember your position, as an *engaged* woman.' She accented the word, giving Mr Smalley a sharp look. 'I will forgo my game of bridge and accompany you, to safeguard your reputation. Western Australia has a very small English community and there will be gossip if you gad about by yourself. We must get you out of the habit quick smart.'

Maisie looked down at her hands. 'No,' she said quietly to no-one in particular but primarily to herself. She had put a smile on her face all evening until her muscles ached from the effort and she felt ill-disposed towards the loathsome Mr Smalley and his proposed game of cards.

Mrs Wallace blinked several times, very fast. 'I beg your pardon?'

'I may be engaged to be married but I am not about to enter a religious order and take my vows. I am quite able to take a walk by myself.'

'Don't be cheeky, dear. Have you no sense of propriety?'

'I'm sorry,' she said. 'I shouldn't have said that.' *Out loud.*

Mrs Wallace gave her a nod. 'Good. Now come along. I thought you wanted a stroll.'

The divide between decks was no more than a couple of wooden gates, but everyone was aware of their function: to keep the three classes separate and in their proper places.

That evening, Mrs Wallace had liquid courage pumping in her veins. 'What would you say, Maisie, if we were to take a turn through third class?' Her speech was a little slurred.

Have we swapped roles and I have now become the responsible adult in charge of what is right and wrong? She put a hand on Mrs Wallace's arm. 'I'm not sure that we are supposed to. Trespassing between the decks is not permitted. The captain was very clear on that point. Do you not remember that he said so, at dinner on the first night?'

'Of course I do, but he didn't mean people like *us*, Maisie. These third-class folk know their place – they have had centuries of observance to remind them. The comment was made for *them*.'

'They weren't at our dinner, Mrs Wallace.'

'Don't split hairs, dear.' Mrs Wallace clicked open the gate that accessed the lower deck and clattered down a flight of narrow wooden stairs, with Maisie a reluctant accomplice.

The night was overcast, but every now and then the clouds parted and moonlight filtered palely across the deck. Maisie saw they weren't the only trespassers from the upper deck: a man with a sun-mottled complexion and an excess of yellow teeth stood at the bottom of the steps, his back braced against a deck lamp. She recognised him from the first-class lounge, wearing what her mother would describe as 'new-money clothes', smoking a slim cigar and, by all appearances, having helped himself generously to the post-prandial drinks tray. He steadied himself on the handrail, his bony fingers clutching the smooth, rounded wood like an eagle perched on a branch.

'Is that you, Mr Farmount?' Puffed from the stairs, Mrs Wallace dragged air into her lungs and blinked several times.

He didn't bow. Maisie suspected that the gesture would have toppled him over.

'Ladies. What brings you down to the third-class deck?'

'Stretching our legs,' Mrs Wallace replied. 'And yourself?'

'Checking on my off-duty divers over there.' He took a puff of his cigar and let a cloud of dense, blue-tinged smoke swirl up out of his open mouth.

'What do they dive for?' Maisie had romantic visions of Spanish galleons and buried treasure.

'Pearl shell. They are going out to Australia to settle a bet.' He slid his eyes in her direction and then looked away again.

'What sort of bet?' Maisie followed the line of his arm. She half-expected his fingernails to be filed sharp, like claws.

'Maybe to prove a point would be a better way of describing it.'

'I'm not certain I understand.'

Mr Farmount swayed towards them, exhaling sour gouts of cigar-tainted breath.

'My boys are going to show that the pearl industry is better served by white divers.'

When Maisie shook her head, none the wiser, Farmount looked at her as if she were stupid. He dabbed at his face with a freckled hand. 'The industry imports a coloured workforce. Japs, mostly. Australia wants to kick them out.'

'And the English divers are going to help do this? To put them out of their jobs?'

'Precisely. They're no longer wanted.'

Maisie looked over at the group of ten or so men who were sitting under the deck lamps, playing cards for a pile of matchsticks. 'That doesn't sound fair.'

Mr Farmount picked a strand of tobacco off his tooth. 'That's not the point. The English boys are what the government wants. They'll give those imported fellers a run for their money.'

'Have they experience of diving for pearl shell?'

Mr Farmount waved his hand in a dismissive gesture. 'Details, my dear. Diving is diving when all is said and done. It doesn't matter at all what they are diving for.'

Maisie glanced across for a second time at the group of card players. One of the men, his cards held close to his chest in a neat fan, looked up from his hand and locked eyes with her. His stare didn't waver. With legs crossed, the stub of a cigarette glowing between his teeth, she saw he was dark-haired and lean, like a panther she'd once seen in a zoo. His fingers tightened on the cards and she sensed his concentration on her face, the animalistic coiling of a predator preparing to pounce on his prey. She bowed her head for a moment then looked again at his face, a vague, undefinable sensation stirring her stomach.

Without warning, it began to rain gentle, warm drops from the dark night sky.

Mrs Wallace turned away from Mr Farmount. 'Take my arm, dear. It's high time we went back up and got you off to bed.'

Maisie cupped her hand under Mrs Wallace's elbow and steered her back towards the dark flight of stairs. By the bottom step, the lamp cast a little patch of yellow light. She placed her foot in the centre of it and, for a reason she could not explain, turned back towards the card players.

CHAPTER 2

FEBRUARY WAS AN UGLY month in Buccaneer Bay.

The pearling magnates and town bureaucrats were crammed into a smoke-filled bar. Well oiled with drink and shiny with sweat, they nodded towards their civic leader, impatient to hear his message; it was stiflingly hot and they were not happy to have their drinking interrupted for long. It was going round that someone had set up a game later on in Asia Place and there would be the usual female attractions afterwards. The windows had been flung open but there was scant relief from the heat and humidity. One or two ran surreptitious fingers round the inside of their collars and slacked off the studded moorings. Standards of dress in the Bay had to be upheld even among groups of men. It was not the done thing to breach etiquette.

'Gentlemen,' the mayor began, standing atop a chair and waving his glass in a wide, embracing circle. Blair Montague was top dog in Buccaneer Bay, not only mayor but also acting president of the Pearlers' Association. He divided his time buying and selling pearls in Asia and Europe and overseeing his business interests. A sheepdog herding its flock, his voice was hard and flat. 'We have a delicate situation on our hands. On the very eve of a brand-new pearling season in Buccaneer Bay, our Australian government has issued a directive: we must expel all non-white labour from our fleets.'

He pulled a folded paper from his inside jacket pocket. 'I quote what is written: *White Australia will no longer tolerate the yellow-faced worker on its pearling fleet. The Japanese, the Malays and the Koepangers must go home.*'

He looked down at the sweaty faces. 'It seems our Asiatics are no match for the white-skinned Navy diver. To prove the government is right, we are to welcome a handful of English divers into the bosom of our community and employ them on our boats. There is to be no discussion.'

He watched as his words hit them as hard as a blow. They all knew what this would mean to their balance sheets.

Blair nodded. 'I agree with your sentiments, but these men are already on their way and there is nothing we can do to stop the process. I have had to spread them among us and we will have to bear the cost of their passage. When you do the sums you will see that these flash divers will cost us five times as much as we are paying our indentured crews. They will be a cause of discontent and trouble among our workforce and the means of huge financial losses for us.'

He produced another folded paper from his pocket on which he had recorded names and details in neat columns. He had chosen wisely. The men he had selected were rugged entrepreneurs – tough, demanding individuals who had made their pearl-shell fortunes through hard-nosed dealings in a perilous industry.

Blair got down from his chair and pushed it back against the wall with his foot, his legs stiff from standing. He scanned the room and found his man amid the town's grumbling elite, a faint smile softening his angular face. He nodded towards the door. 'Join me outside for a jar?'

Blair found a vacant table on the narrow verandah and motioned his guest to sit. A steward appeared, his drinks tray tucked under his arm, a foot soldier at ease, awaiting orders.

'Bring Captain Sinclair a single malt with some Apollinaris water. I'll have my usual.'

Maitland Sinclair looked Blair straight in the eye. 'How long have you known about this?'

Blair lounged back in a cane chair and crossed his legs. 'Dear me,' he said in a gravely mocking voice. 'Did I forget to consult you?' He reached over to the next table and stretched his fingers towards a newspaper threaded on a hinged wooden stick. Blair never sweated. There were no half-moons of damp fabric under his arms. His face and clothes were wrinkle-free. He tapped the headline with a long lean finger. 'Look at that. Captain Scott's reached the South Pole.' The newspaper was dated January 1912; it was six weeks old. Something else further down caught his eye. He smoothed out the page with the back of his hand. 'What's the surname of that overbred English girl you're bringing out here? Father's a judge, didn't you tell me?'

Maitland squinted at him, a pipe hanging from his bottom lip. The sullen line of his mouth relaxed. 'Good memory. Judge George Porter.'

'Seems he's trying that big Jew murder in London.'

'Let's see.' Maitland leaned forward and traced the words under the photograph with his finger. 'Yes, that's him.' He flicked the photograph of Captain Scott and his sled with his nail. 'Would be nice to escape from this bloody heat and feel the chill for once.

Wet's hardly half-through.' He wiped his brow with a white silk handkerchief as a streak of lightning flared overhead and silhouetted the lighthouse against the stormy sky. Seconds later, a blast of thunder muffled the blow of his fist hitting the table.

'Why didn't you tell me about the English divers?'

'Look, Mait, I didn't want to tell you about the government's directive until I'd had time to think.' Blair pulled the paper off the wooden stick and rolled it up like a cosh. 'This white diving thing's a bugger.'

Maitland shook his head.

'Stop sulking, Mait. You now know as much as I do. All you've got to do is help me make sure this thing fails.'

The steward arrived with the drinks and temporarily cut the conversation. Maitland stretched over to take his drink off the tray, took a sip and dabbed his lips with his handkerchief.

Blair drained his glass in two gulps without any pretence at restraint and thrust it back towards the steward. 'Another.'

The steward nodded. When he left the table, Maitland leaned in slightly and dropped his voice to a whisper. 'What do you want me to do?'

'You've got to get everyone on board with this. The local press, all them in there.' Blair waved his hand at the bar. 'Even the Japanese doctor.'

'Yes. He's popular. He's got gumption.'

Blair narrowed his eyes. 'He's got ambition. That's different. He showboated himself through that hospital-building project. He's a crowd manipulator.'

'Precisely.'

Blair squeezed Maitland's arm, his mouth thin with resolution. 'This is up to you, Mait. I'm doing the behind-the-scenes work but now I'm handing you the rope to strangle the venture. Get all our current divers on board. Offer them advances on their pay, better percentage rewards on the shell and pearls they bring up – whatever it takes. Get the tenders and shell-openers on side. Talk to Doctor Shin and offer him a donation for his hospital but make sure he's in our pocket. All you've got to do, Mait, is wind the rope of failure so tightly round those divers' white necks that they lynch themselves. Then I can get on with flogging my pearls and turning a decent profit, and you can get on with buying yourself some class. Do we understand each other?'

Maitland held his gaze. 'I've always been your man, haven't I?'

Blair slapped his hands together, as if he were shutting a book. 'As I have been yours. We must work together, Mait, and stamp on this bloody notion before we both lose everything we've built up. When those divers set foot on our jetty next month, they're already condemned men.'

A few weeks after the mayor dropped his bombshell, Maitland Sinclair sat at the scarred wooden desk in his office and scowled at the wall. Blair's words had been giving him headaches for what seemed like forever. The venture had to fail, but on paper he needed it to look above board. It was hot in the packing shed and he was already sweating through his shirt. He had risen early, and on his way to work had dropped by the Black Dog Hotel and eaten a substantial breakfast of fried steak, salted bacon and tinned tomatoes. There were no fresh eggs, which had made him cross. The hotel had run out and was, the Japanese proprietor apologised profusely, waiting for the next steamship from Port Fremantle to top up its larder. Maitland had sworn freely and pushed over the table, refusing to pay the bill.

Now he glanced through the open door onto the mudflats and allowed himself a moment's distraction. His hands coiled into fists. The girl would arrive on the coastal steamer all too soon from Port Fremantle. He had cabled the steamship, and once in the Bay, she would have a bed to sleep in. What else was there to do? He shook his head to clear the concern. She was a means to an end.

Back to work. He was tallying up the costs he had incurred to take on the white diver, William Cooper. He knew nothing about him, other than he was said to be the Navy's top man. By the time Maitland had learned that the diver was being dumped on him, there had been no time to write chummy get-to-know-you letters, and now the bloke was about to arrive. Blair was right, though. Putting white divers on the pearling luggers made no financial sense. He had personally had to pay the cost of two third-class passages from England: Cooper had insisted on bringing his own tender with him. Adding in half-wages during the two-month journey for both, he had forked out £24 just to get them to Buccaneer Bay – and he had no idea whether they would be any good at bringing up shell. It was starting to look like a very expensive exercise. He put down his pen and tamped down the tobacco in his pipe. A blob of nicotine dripped from the stem and flared onto his white trousers. He swore under his breath and hurled it to the floor.

What he did know was that Cooper would have to collect a hell of a lot of shell for Maitland to recover his expenses. He had more than a slight suspicion that he would be out of pocket, but if it meant that the government's white-diver experiment failed, then he supposed a few quid gambled on a good cause was a reasonable investment. He would write the money off against his profits somewhere else. After all, the whole point of living in the back of beyond was not having to play by the rules. Not one official had ever bothered to come to the Bay and police what was going on. And if he managed to pick up a pearl or two along the way, well, he would make a generous donation to the Pearlers' Association and buy himself a bit more leverage.

He swivelled on his chair and looked out at the murky water. Along the foreshore, the luggers were lined up, hauled up high on the beach by their crews to await maintenance and refits for the start of the new season. The thirty-foot ketch-rigged vessels looked spacious enough on the flat yellow sand, but once the boats were loaded up for the season there was barely room for a man to stand.

He pushed himself up from his chair and shuffled out of his office, lumbering round the back of the building, the momentary shade softening his mood. He picked his way along the crunchy shell path that snaked towards the lighthouse where the track petered out. Towering stacks of empty oil drums and wooden pallets lined his route. The stench of ozone, fish and stale urine was strong as he heaved himself up the steps towards the loading stage of his packing shed.

He heard the familiar sound of tomahawk striking shell from inside the large, corrugated-iron shed. At the entrance, it took him a few moments to adjust from the bright sunlight to the gloom of the interior. At the far end of the shed he saw a huge pile of pearl shell that two Manilamen were processing, squatting back on their haunches, sarongs tucked up between their legs as they sorted the shell into shallow floor bins according to size and condition. The gold-lipped shell sparkled in the light from the open doors as they tossed it through the air. A third man was stencilling letters onto a wooden crate destined for New York, where Maitland sold the majority of his shell to the button trade. Another man, his back to the door, sat cross-legged beside the bin containing the largest shell. Maitland watched him pick out a shell and hold it up, eyeing himself in the shining surface. He stroked the smooth surface with the long arc of his finger and then held it up against his cheek, caressing it like a lover. Something about the intimate gesture rooted Maitland to the spot. He glanced around. When he was sure they were alone, he spoke rapidly in Malay and the other man turned, the shell still pressed to his cheek. They held each other's gaze and Maitland flicked his head towards the door. The Malay threw the shell back into the bin and scrambled to his feet.

'I go your office,' he stammered in English.

Maitland strolled out into the sunshine, a sly smile tugging at one corner of his mouth. The Malay followed behind, dragging his feet in the dust.

CHAPTER 3

THE MORNING WAS SPARKLING blue as the SS *Oceanic* bumped onto its moorings in Port Fremantle. Soon, Maisie's six-week voyage from England would be a memory of deck tennis, quoits, concerts and endless meals dodging Mr Smalley's groping fingers. On deck, a dozen Englishmen gathered by the rail. They stood quietly, facing away from Maisie, looking towards the rotted jetty stumps. Clothed in heavy dark wool suits with white celluloid collars that looked stiff and unfamiliar, most were smoking. One of the men wore his trousers short to his ankles, his fancy patterned socks on display above the toe-pinching shoes. Maisie, sitting on a deckchair next to Mrs Wallace, flexed her swollen feet in sympathy.

A small engine-driven tugboat bounced alongside the ship, jammed with men waving pale-jacketed arms in the air. They were clutching notebooks, some with cameras slung on straps round their necks. The second officer had told Maisie that newspaper reporters would come aboard that morning to the first-class deck and would, regrettably, delay their disembarkation by an hour or two.

A brass band was blaring 'Land of Hope and Glory' from the quayside. Maisie caught the whiff of excitement that thrummed through the crowd and leaned forward in her chair on the upper deck to watch the scene. Shading her eyes from the bright sunlight, she saw that the first of the newspapermen had climbed up the ladder and was shaking the hand of Mr Farmount. By the time the tugboat's passengers were fully on board, Mr Farmount had the twelve Englishmen corralled and a photographer was arranging them, a few seated and the surplus standing behind. There they remained under the unrelenting sun, eyes on the camera box for some time, red patches blooming on tender exposed skin.

Maisie shaded her eyes from the blinding sun and considered for a moment retreating into the shade, until she saw that Mr Farmount had moved closer to the press party.

She patted Mrs Wallace's arm. 'I think Mr Farmount is about to make a speech.'

'Of course he is, dear. It's why the newspaper people have come. Now pipe down or we shan't be able to hear what he says.'

Maisie pressed her lips together, her cheeks burning.

Farmount consulted his notes and thrust his redundant hand in a pocket. Maisie saw that he was nervous; his face was spotted with perspiration and his other hand was trembling. He straightened his jacket and cleared his throat.

'Thank you all for coming,' he began, his voice just audible against the brass band's enthusiasm. 'The gentlemen to my left are all ex-Royal Navy Divers. I am here as their ambassador, and also to represent Siegfried and Hammond – the largest manufacturer of diving apparatus in the world. The company is the sole contractor to the British Admiralty and the Crown Agents for the Colonial and Indian Office.' He broke off and wiped a handkerchief across his brow.

'Their arrival on Australian soil marks the end of an era. Our divers are here to prove, once and for all, the superiority of the Britisher over the Asiatic.' Farmount looked up, his nerves seemingly forgotten. 'We cannot allow one of Australia's primary industries to be dominated by a bunch of brown-skinned foreigners! Let the Japanese, Malays and Koepangers take heed. Their stronghold over the pearling industry is about to end, and these men—' He waved a freckly paw at the sweating, wool-clad group. 'These men, gentlemen of the press, are the men to end it.'

His fervour ignited the crowd. Amid a flurry of enthusiastic applause, a spiky-haired reporter thrust up his hand and shouted, 'Mr Farmount! Ray Jones, *Perth Advertiser*. How long do you think it will take to drive the coloured fellers out?'

Farmount glanced sideways and nodded at the divers. 'We've settled on a year to do the job, but we anticipate that it won't take that long.'

'Well said!' a voice yelled from the crowd.

Maisie moved in her chair, looking from Mrs Wallace to Mr Farmount and back again. She knew so little about Australia – there had been no time to research – but she did know that this felt wrong.

'Surely they should show more respect towards the men they are trying to replace,' she said, not knowing anything about the white dominance of the coloured population. Mrs Wallace, padded in purple gingham, was nodding vigorously and banging her cotton-gloved fingers together in enthusiastic support of Mr Farmount's speech.

Another hand shot up. 'Pete Ramsey, *Fremantle Chronicle*. Can I get the names of all these brave English blokes, sir?'

Mr Farmount turned to the group and named the twelve men in turn, the last of whom was introduced as William Cooper, the most experienced diver in the team.

'Can we get a few words, sir?'

Craning forward for a better view, Maisie recognised the man who had pushed to the front as the panther from the card game. His hair was as black as coal and even with the sun on his face, his eyes were dark and proud. She thought again of a sleek cat, crouching in the long grass, prey between its claws, and shrank back, her heart banging against her ribcage. Its excessive beating seemed to throw her balance and she felt as if she might faint.

With one arm draped around the diver's neck, Mr Farmount slicked back his brilliantined hair with his free hand and wiped the excess grease down the side of his trousers. 'William Cooper is the British Royal Navy's finest diver. He has pioneered the use of my company's engine-driven air compressor on his deep-sea dives, which will further prove that the day of the darky hand-pump deck-boy is done! We have brought this wonder machine with us and will use it to great effect on the luggers in Buccaneer Bay. We will show you all just what English manufactured equipment and the white diver can do.'

William Cooper stepped forward and shook the hair out of his eyes, exuding the casual assurance of someone who was used to the limelight.

Maisie fiddled with her gloves. 'Have you heard of that diver William Cooper, Mrs Wallace?'

Mrs Wallace wedged her frame deeper into her chair and smoothed her dress over her bosom. 'Do you not read the newspaper, Maisie?'

Maisie opened her mouth and closed it again. She knew if she were patient there would be more. Mrs Wallace was like a bottle of beer – once shaken up and the cap released, the contents couldn't help but bubble out.

'Mr Farmount told me he's one of the Admiralty's top operatives and has dived throughout the Mediterranean, wresting lost treasure from sunken ships. He's unmarried – but has a keen eye for the ladies – and is reputed to be as tough as kangaroo meat, which is why he was wanted for this exercise. Now *do* be quiet, Maisie, dear. He's going to say something.'

William Cooper flashed a brilliant smile at the reporters, and shouted to make himself heard over the music. 'It is true. It is absolutely true what Mr Farmount has said. We are all British Royal Navy trained, and the depths in Buccaneer Bay are shallow compared to the depths we are used to. We have been given a challenge, and frankly, we can't wait to pick up the gauntlet that has been thrown down. We want to get started right away and prove that the faith the Australian government has placed in us is not misguided.'

'Hear! Hear!' Mrs Wallace boomed. 'Hear! Hear!'

Maisie wore her confusion on her face. 'Mrs Wallace, I'm not sure I understand. I mean, just because these men are white, will they really be able to do it better than the men who have been doing it for years?'

Mrs Wallace removed her spectacles, her expression turning serious. 'Maisie, you have a lot to learn, just as I did when I first came out here. The Australian government finds the reality of a coloured workforce unpalatable and is keen to seek a viable alternative. These English divers represent the answer to everyone's prayers. Your future husband will be thinking these exact same thoughts and I'm sure that, as his wife, you will realise this soon enough when you are trying to staff a house with Japs, Malays and Binghis.'

'Binghis?'

'Aborigines. The Indigenous population. The average black fellow is reasonably honest until he takes a fancy to your gin bottle, at which point he will most likely turn into a mad savage. He could come at you with a tomahawk!'

Maisie tried not to betray her anxiety. 'I thought that was what they used in the Americas.'

Mrs Wallace clicked her tongue. 'Keep your smart comments to yourself, Maisie, until you know more about what you are saying. The Australian nation needs protection from these people and the Asian hordes invading in their droves from the north. All those Japanese and Malays – it simply can't go on. Australia is a vulnerable island, Maisie. It is quite right that we try to keep our drawbridge up.'

Since that evening weeks ago, when the girl had come down to C Deck, William Cooper had been unable to put her out of his mind.

After that, sitting in the dark, night after night, he had looked up from his hand of cards and stretched his neck towards the first-class promenade deck.

He'd seen her for the very first time at the lifeboat drill. Even now, at the end of the voyage, that still bothered him. The SS *Oceanic* had been at sea for twenty-four hours before the passengers were shown what to do if the ship went down. Perhaps it was because he knew the sea that he found such negligence unfathomable. Cold, black water was no-one's friend. It wouldn't answer your cries for help or buoy you up when you knew you were sinking. He knew to respect the sea; everyone who earned his living from it did.

A good two hours had passed since the pressmen left the ship.

He leaned back against the metal chair, feeling the push of a bolt head against his spine. It was hot, holding the full day's heat. He shifted a little to the side, easing his weight off his back, and let his hands drop loose by his sides.

Seeing her today on the deck listening to his speech, he'd felt like he was talking to her. Explaining why he'd come to Australia. He'd watched her draw in a breath, though, a cloud coming over her face at something he'd said. She pursed her lips and narrowed her eyes slightly, a frown appearing over the bridge of her nose.

William Cooper wondered where she was going. Was this her final stop? What would he say to her if ever they were to meet? What would her voice sound like? Would she even notice him?

His shirt stuck in damp patches to his back.

Maisie picked at the rumpled fabric on the chair's armrest in the first-class lounge. 'I know we change ships here in Port Fremantle, Mrs Wallace, but shall we move onto the coastal steamer tonight?'

'Goodness no, dear. We shall stay in a hotel for a few days to gather our strength for the return to the north-west coast. I'm not quite sure if the coastal steamer even works on an exact time-table. Here we shall be ladies of leisure.'

Maisie dabbed at her face with the side of her hand. Although the portholes had been thrown wide open, the lounge was boiling hot and she was gently cooking inside her English wool travelling suit. She had already removed the long-line jacket but was still buttoned up to the neck in a silk blouse and tie. She parted her legs under the floor-length skirt and tried to subtly flap the fabric.

'Haven't we done that for six weeks already on this ship?'

'Don't be in too great a hurry to embrace your new life, Maisie. It might not be an exact replica of your home in England. Just make the most of your time at Port Fremantle and enjoy the cooler weather. And for goodness' sake, dear, do stop fidgeting. If you're that hot, go back up on deck and perhaps you'll catch a bit of a breeze.'

It was just as hot on deck.

The sun had burned the sky to white. Maisie paused at the door of the lounge, studying him before he saw her. William Cooper was sitting on a chair, on the exact spot he'd made his address earlier on. His feet were dangling over the rail, eyes fixed on something in the water, his concentration absolute. He had taken off his jacket and rolled up his shirtsleeves. His fingers, she noticed, were long and still by his sides.

Maisie stepped back into the shade and slid into a deckchair. She dropped her bag on the deck, took out her book and tried to concentrate on the words. She could see him out of the corner of her eye, his foot swinging back and forth, rhythmic. She fanned the book wide and leaned her forehead against the smooth paper.

A hot hand clamped down on her shoulder and squashed her mouth against the page. Her throat went tight with alarm.

'Miss Porter!' Mr Smalley boomed. 'I didn't mean to startle you. The purser says we'll be getting off soon, so I said I would come to fetch you.'

Maisie scrambled to her feet and knocked over her bag, the contents skittering across the deck. 'Thank you, Mr Smalley. I'll be there in a moment. Just let me . . .' She fluttered a hand at the scattered items. Smalley had the grace to look slightly embarrassed before he toddled off.

William Cooper glanced sideways and flicked a strand of hair from his eyes. He stood up, scraping his chair across the polished wood, and looked directly at her. Maisie felt perspiration collecting in beads on her forehead.

He stood motionless for a second, then bent to gather her fallen items from the deck, trapping them against his side with his arm. She stared at him, confusion rearing up in her chest like a horse.

'Forgive me,' she said, her cheeks stained with embarrassment. 'I am so sorry to have disturbed your reverie.'

He turned back and laughed, the skin twitching the soft edges of his lips.

'You're forgiven,' he said, placing her treasures on a table. 'For disturbing my "reverie".'

Maisie scrabbled her possessions back into her bag, her hands trembling as she wished she could claw the words back. *Why on earth did I say reverie? I sound like a nincompoop.*

When she moved to rejoin Mrs Wallace in the downstairs lounge, Maisie found that her legs were rather wonky.

It took a long time to disembark, but eventually, their paperwork secured in the hand luggage, they walked down the canvas-lined gangway; hands clutching the thick rope sides, swaying on sea-habituated legs. Their cabin luggage was to follow them to the hotel but the hold luggage would be stored in a warehouse on the dock.

Mrs Wallace seemed happy to be home. 'Welcome to Australia, dear. The hotel is scarcely a few minutes' drive from the quay so it is hardly worth seeking out a conveyance,' she said, pushing her damp hair from her eyes. 'I'm sure you agree it will be good to stretch our legs.'

Mrs Wallace was set on a path and Maisie felt a stab of dismay. She had learned, often, during the six weeks of their acquaintance, that contradicting Mrs Wallace was like trying to hold back the tide. There was absolutely no point because it simply couldn't be done.

The sun blazed down on the corrugated-iron sheds as they began their journey and there was no shade to be had. They paused where a single railway line bisected the wharf and a funny-looking little train let out occasional gasps of steam. A ferryman was tying up his boat, and other dilapidated vessels were bobbing on their moorings. Nothing looked new. She felt she had washed ashore at the end of the world.

'Pace all right, dear? You look a bit wrung out.'

'I'm fine, thank you, Mrs Wallace,' Maisie managed. 'I'm not quite used to the heat just yet.'

Mrs Wallace looked relieved and pushed on. They walked up the main street where a woman in a pale green dress was brushing the footpath to her shop and when they rounded the corner – two or three turnings further on – they stopped again. A battered sign nailed to a gum tree, handpainted in yellowing pink letters, read, 'The Garden of Eden Guesthouse'. The house itself was half-obscured by an overgrown garden behind rusty wrought-iron gates.

'What a dirty place,' Maisie exclaimed, as they climbed the narrow steps to the front porch. 'I imagined it to be white. Bleached, perhaps.'

She had also imagined a more intimate, inviting welcome to Australia. There was nothing in her future husband's manner of address in his telegram, nor the accommodation he had arranged for her, that dispelled a deepening sense of foreboding.

The two women waited several days in Port Fremantle for the Blue Funnel coastal steamer; there would be five ports of call, dropping passengers at intervals over seven days, and then, after almost two months at sea, Maisie would meet the man she had been exiled to marry. At the third stop, Gantry Creek, Mrs Wallace would leave her for the home where she lived with her husband and seven children. Her husband had built the sheep station – apparently the size of a small country – from scratch. He was Scottish and, at just twenty-two, had panicked his grandparents with a persistent, phlegmy cough. Fearful he could be developing tuberculosis, and scared for the life of their only grandchild, they dispatched him to Australia to ensure the longevity of the Wallace line.

Maisie was fascinated by the few glimpses she had been given into Mrs Wallace's life.

The first night, they had just finished their supper and were still sitting at the table in the dining room. She dropped a sugar lump into her coffee and gave it a swirl with her spoon. The sun was beginning to sink and glinted on the gold wedding band squeezing the flesh on Mrs Wallace's left ring finger. 'How did you meet your husband, Mrs Wallace? Were you already in Australia?'

Mrs Wallace leaned back in her chair, ran both hands round the square neckline of her dress and yanked it up over her cleavage. 'No, dear. We met on the ship when I was coming over to begin my nursing in Perth. We were seated next to each other at the same table.'

Maisie propped her chin on her hand. 'What happened?'

'It was a very turbulent night. The ship was ploughing through the Atlantic. Do you remember how rough it was?'

Maisie nodded. She would not easily forget the enamel basin, the weak, sugary tea and the days confined to the cabin feeling wretched.

'We were listening to the orchestra and talking a great deal. I remember – as clearly as if it were yesterday – that I was wearing a new black dress that was rather tight over the bodice and it was all covered with big shiny sequins and I had feathers in my hair. I loved that dress! Arthur leaned over to me and said I looked like an exotic princess and asked if I would take a chance on a waltz with him. He was so handsome with his hair slicked down, he made me tremble inside.'

'And did you dance and fall in love?'

'We danced for a bit, yes. The boat was rocking considerably, and it threw us together. Quite literally! And that was that.'

Maisie imagined the handsome Scotsman dipping down on one knee and begging for her hand in marriage. 'Did he propose straightaway?'

'Not precisely, dear.' Mrs Wallace adjusted her spectacles. 'We had only just met, but our fates were intertwined from that moment on.'

Maisie wondered idly whether there would be such a moment for her and her captain. Beyond the grubby balcony and peeling shutters of the hotel dining room, she could see the tall masts of the ships at anchor in the bay. She imagined him at the helm, singing a romantic solo of his own as he charted his course to claim her.

The next afternoon, Mrs Wallace put down her coffee cup and blotted her top lip. 'I'm off for my nap, dear. I think you should have one too.'

'In England, people never sleep in the afternoon,' Maisie said.

'That is irrelevant here. When you are married, your husband will come home for his lunch at midday and will, I am sure, lie down for an hour or so before he returns to his office. It's a common practice and one you should adopt too. After that, you will be free to socialise.'

Maisie wasn't certain if Mrs Wallace was implying that she would be joining him or having a private nap of her own.

'As a young English woman and a newcomer to the town, you will be screened by the ladies, ogled by their husbands and judged by your help. You must have an At Home Day once a month during which you will invite all the resident ladies of your social circle to tea, cards, pianoforte recitals – whatever you choose to host. You must serve afternoon tea off your best china. Tea is a formal occasion, so you must produce the lightest of cakes and instruct your help how to serve them.'

Mrs Wallace delved in her mending bag and from the depths produced a wooden darning egg as well as her scissors and an assortment of threads. A tan lisle stocking lay limp on the round table by her elbow. 'You must repay their visit on their appropriate At Home Day, leave two cards of your own and one of your husband's. You will be expected to attend all other At Home Days besides your own; it will be seen as the epitome of impoliteness if you fail to appear. The likelihood is that you will not care for the majority of these women. The old tabbies will want to get a look at you, and all the young unmarried girls will critique your appearance and scrutinise your wardrobe and probably gossip about you too. It is very important that you are sucked into the bosom of your new life from the start, or you will find yourself very lonely indeed.' She pushed her spectacles up her nose and squinted at the eye of her needle.

Maisie thought this sounded utterly ghastly. 'I must confess that I am surprised, Mrs Wallace. This sounds much more formal than England.'

'Of course it is, dear. It is all people have to hold on to. They have created a tiny replica of Home, and you must slot in and run with it.'

'But what if no-one likes me?' Maisie said.

Mrs Wallace began to stab her needle through the stocking. 'You must work hard to ensure that they do. Your husband will not give up his drinking, his clubs or his gambling for you, nor should you expect him to. It is your job to adapt to him and his lifestyle. If you don't fit in, he will simply carry on as he did in his bachelor days and leave you at home. Even though you might find yourself in a comfortable position financially, if you are isolated socially, you will be overwhelmingly alienated and unhappy.'

'But that's . . .'

'The way it is in frontier towns, my dear. You must ensure that you succeed. You are going to need to toughen up and develop a backbone. Think of your mother. That should starch your resolve.'

A few days after their arrival in Port Fremantle, Maisie slept in well beyond breakfast.

When she woke, she saw that Mrs Wallace had made good use of the opportunity to sort through her cabin trunk. She sat up in bed, a poor effort at a smile wobbling at the edges of her mouth. Slack facial muscles were not to her mother's taste. *I do hope you are not about to cry, Maisie.*

She pinched the insides of her wrists; the pain was distracting. 'Good morning, Mrs Wallace. Did you sleep well?'

Mrs Wallace looped the wide leather handles of her handbag over a fleshy forearm and patted the contents.

'Passably, thank you. A breakfast tray – rather desiccated, given the hour – is beside your bed if you are hungry. I thought we might attack the shops today. An indelicate question, I know, but do you have funds?'

With a quick up and down of her chin, Maisie confirmed that her parents had not cast her adrift without money.

'Good. We must spend some time at the shops while we are here. I have had a good look through your trunk this morning. I know you will think this a dreadful invasion of your privacy, but it had to be done. You need cotton dresses to keep you dry, loose underwear and silk stockings, a wide-brimmed hat and parasol to keep the sun off your face as well as gloves to protect your hands.

And you will need to do something about those dreadful shoes of yours. They are not suitable for this climate. Whatever can your mother have been thinking?'

Maisie picked a corner off a dry bread roll. 'But Mrs Wallace, if I wear any more garments, I shall die!'

'You cannot let your lovely white skin become tanned by the sun, dear. You must not turn brown like a coloured. That would be certain social suicide. I suggest you acquire a cotton kimono-style wrap to keep yourself cool when you are at home. You can wear it without any underclothes, provided you are alone and you keep the doors locked.'

Maisie stared.

'And don't forget, dear. If you are accepted wholeheartedly into the social fabric of Buccaneer Bay, you will need a range of evening clothes and ball gowns. I expect you have them already in your hold luggage or you will order them from Paris or London if you find that what you have brought is not in tune with what you need. Everyone dresses properly for dinner here, regardless of the heat.'

The day before the coastal steamer was to set sail, Maisie woke to a pain in her abdomen like a sword, skewering her to the bed. A ripple of queasiness rose from her stomach and sour saliva filled her mouth. The shared bathroom was a long way down the landing at the bottom of a splintery wooden staircase, and as she stood her legs felt achy and weak. The bedroom door had warped in the heat and she had to lean hard against it to push it open. She mistimed the manoeuvre and the door swung away from her, crashing her sideways into the wall.

'Is everything all right, dear?' Mrs Wallace called across the room.

'Oh!' Maisie said, sinking to the floor. 'I have The Visitor and I feel very unwell.'

Her mother had always discouraged discussion of the monthly event and refused to have any sign of it brought to her attention. If she had to mention it at all, it was to be referred to as The Visitor.

She heard rapid footsteps and in a moment Mrs Wallace appeared in the doorway with her own supply of Southall's Sanitary Towels for Ladies and hauled Maisie to her feet.

'Come along, dear. We'll have you fixed up in two shakes of a dingo's paw and then you can hop back under the covers while you ride out the worst of the cramps.' She picked up a rusty handbell from the nightstand by her bed and gave it a spirited rattle. 'I'll organise some morning tea with that dozy girl at the front desk. I always find a hot cup of tea does wonders when we are not at our sparkling best.'

Maisie climbed into bed and a short while later, a lumpy, dark girl with hunched shoulders and downy cheeks clattered up the stairs with the tea. She wore a faded blue dress that was too small around her hips and revealed the bulge of her suspender clips.

Mrs Wallace relieved her of the tray and set it down on a scratched wooden table – tutting loudly through her teeth – and pulled up a chair by Maisie's bed. She administered a spoonful of Mrs Barker's Soothing Syrup for Children in a cup of tea and swirled it round with a teaspoon.

'I'm no Florence Nightingale, dear, but I think we need to ensure you are stocked with medical essentials before we board the coastal steamer. If you are afflicted this badly every month, you must arm yourself accordingly. I have no idea what you might be able to purchase up in your backwater of a town, but we must assume that there will be very little in the way of ladies' supplies or medicines. You need to be prepared. Consider it a battle plan for a lifelong siege!'

Maisie reddened and sank down between the sheets.

'Have you not organised sanitary protection for yourself before?' Mrs Wallace leaned forward to the morning-tea tray and poured herself a cup.

Maisie shook her head, ashamed. 'I never visit shops by myself. I rarely go out alone. Sanitary napkins appear in a drawer in my bedroom, and I'm sure the maid must keep a note of how many I use each month because the supply remains constant. I can't think my mother would ask for such a private thing in a shop. I'm certain everything comes in the post.'

'How does your mother think you will cope by yourself?'

Maisie shook her head and pictured the brown paper packages on the hall table in London with their plain address labels. 'We never had that conversation.'

She found herself thinking back to a Christmas Eve when she was little. There was a large fir tree in the hallway, the topmost branches reaching almost to the third floor. Its boughs glittered with glass balls, lighted candles and small gifts wrapped in coloured paper. Underneath the spreading lower limbs were larger brown parcels with handwritten labels, tied up with curly string. On one of the lower branches she discovered a tiny teddy bear, a woolly blue scarf wrapped round its furry neck. Delighted, she reached up and tried to grab it.

'Don't touch!' Her mother had swatted her hand away, pulled the bear from the branch with a tenderness Maisie had rarely seen from her and cradled it in her arms, like a baby.

Mrs Wallace rattled her teaspoon against the inside of the cup. 'Do you know anything about your husband-to-be?'

Maisie felt the heat in her face. The shock of the memory had caught her out. 'I know nothing about him other than that he is a sea captain. I have no idea what he looks like or even how old he is. He wrote to my parents before Christmas saying he was in a position to offer me marriage and so here I am two months later in Australia.'

Mrs Wallace looked stunned. 'Did you not have any say in the matter?'

Maisie shook her head. 'I think it was all arranged before they told me. It seems as if Cousin Maitland sent over a shopping list and I was one of the items on it.'

Mrs Wallace laughed. 'I'm sure that was not the case.'

'No, really,' Maisie continued. 'In my hold luggage I have a twenty-four-place china dinner service, glassware, linens and silverware and all sorts of other things too. Mama and Father said nothing about the expense. I suspect they were glad that someone would remove me as far away from them as is geographically possible on this planet. I'm not exaggerating – I looked it up on the atlas.'

Mrs Wallace patted the back of her hand. 'Don't be so introspective, dear. You overthink everything. No parent would throw their child to the lions without being reasonably certain she would survive, and they would most certainly have sent you on your way with a substantial dowry. Every parent wants a good marriage for their daughter – a husband and place in society. But enough of that. On a practical level, for the monthly trial, you will find it impossible in the heat to wear the rubber protective apron you have brought with you under your dress. It will stick to you and give you prickly heat. You've probably had a bit of that already on the ship with all those garments you've been wearing.'

Maisie thought her own face must have stained as red as the counterpane on her bed, but Mrs Wallace said all this without a hint of embarrassment.

'You are going to have to manage with those sanitary knickers you have in your trunk. They are a boon in a hot country, provided you don't overexert yourself. We might try to find you a night tidy, though. We should be able to pick one up from the chemist here. It's made of muslin and has a waterproof lining. It will prevent accidents on the sheets and unnecessary extra laundry for your help. I'm glad also that you have brought the metal stock box to keep the towels dry. Otherwise they will go mouldy in the wet season and I am sure you don't want them infested with silverfish or moths. The best plan is to have a baby straightaway and have one every year for a while. That way, you won't need supplies for years. It's what I did.' Mrs Wallace poured Maisie another cup of tea.

'Does it hurt like this, having a baby?' Maisie ventured, knowing that she would never have asked this of her mother.

'Were you not given any indication of what to expect?'

Maisie cringed, pulled the sheet up under her chin and sank down further towards the foot of the bed. She knew the rudimentary facts of life, but her knowledge of the sexual act and its consequences was vague. As far as she knew, her parents did not undress in front of each other, and they slept in separate beds in different rooms. She hadn't really thought about the mechanics of procreation. She supposed that her mother must have lifted her skirts at least twice and invited her father in, but specific details hadn't seemed important. Ignorance had enabled her not to incorporate the physical reality into her romantic dream.

Mrs Wallace pushed her generously padded posterior towards the back of the chair and set about a lengthy narrative on the subject of the needs and desires of the gentleman and his insatiable 'boneless finger'.

'But I am sure your husband will be sensitive to your needs and will treat you with the greatest of respect. And you can always say you have a headache – it's an acceptable excuse that no decent man would contest. I have a copy somewhere at home of the *Physiology of Marriage*. I'll search it out and send it to you.'

Maisie slid down another inch beneath the sheets. 'What is that?'

'The last word in marital relations. Perfect for you, I would have thought, with a mother who . . .' Mrs Wallace bit her lip.

'Who what?'

Mrs Wallace refilled her teacup and took a noisy gulp.

'Who . . .' She balanced the saucer on the chair arm. 'I believe she was rather keen on someone else for a while.'

'Before she married my father, you mean?'

Mrs Wallace lifted the teacup and Maisie watched the blush wash over her face. 'Exactly, dear. Now you'll have to remind me what I was saying just now as I have lost my train of thought.'

'*Physiology of Marriage* and why it will be perfect for me, given my mother.'

'Oh yes! The newspapers here have been running advertisements for it, but you wouldn't have found it in England, as it is an Australian publication. It is only available here via mail order. As I said, I'll send it on to you straightaway so you will have it before your wedding night. It might make you less anxious.'

She dispensed another spoonful of syrup into Maisie's tea. 'Now, drink this down and have a little nap. I'm going to sit on the balcony and make a list of what you will need. When you wake, we'll have luncheon and then we will see about stocking you up with supplies.'

Maisie reached for the syrup bottle and squinted at the label, feeling faint as she studied the lengthy list of opiates, moving the black bottle backwards and forwards in front of her face trying to bring the tiny print into focus.

She gave up and sank back against the soft pillows, eyelids heavy, and in that brief moment she could not have cared less about Maitland Sinclair and his insatiable urges.

CHAPTER 4

ALMOST A WEEK LATER, just before sunrise, Maisie put on a new cream dress, revelling in its floaty freshness. She lifted her arms, testing the weight of the unfamiliar, soft, feminine fabric. She'd passed over a pick of her mother's from Peter Jones and shoved it to the bottom of her trunk. Thanks to Mrs Wallace, she now owned a wardrobe of loose-fitting clothes appropriate for the Australian climate. She went out on deck, her new shoes noisy on the planking, and settled herself into a deckchair, the familiarity of the hard wood beneath her skirts reassuring. The purpose of her dawn expedition was to see a glorious sunrise – her last at sea for a while. But the sun remained persistently hidden somewhere within an angry purple sky.

She had been aboard the coastal hopper for six days, the pace of which would have made a snail weep, and was set to arrive in Buccaneer Bay that evening. The ship inched along the flat, grey coast, which provided little of interest beyond rocks and endless scrubland. She shivered as she picked out a light winking beacon-like on the shoreline, hoping it was not a warning of danger ahead.

Mrs Wallace was no longer on board. Two days earlier, she had disembarked at Gantry Creek, in a hurry to get back to her husband, her boys and their sheep in the Pilbara.

Maisie had become uncharacteristically weepy in her arms as they said their goodbyes. 'What will I do without you, Mrs Wallace?'

The older woman pulled Maisie to her squashy bosom and said, with benevolent tartness, 'What on earth's got into you today? I am two days away. There are steamers every two weeks, and we will write. Don't whine, Maisie. It makes you look feeble.'

Maisie had clamped her jaw shut. She knew better than to make a scene.

The steamer ploughed on, making deep furrows in the turquoise sea. Lulled by the regular rolling of the boat, Maisie was rocked into dreams. Her father was wearing his judge's wig. She was in the dock pleading for mercy. Her mother was prosecuting and demanding that she be hanged from the neck until dead. Her father placed a black cloth on his head, shook his head and removed it. The punishment was too severe, he said, and commuted the sentence to life imprisonment in a penal colony. Australia, he declared, would be the perfect place for her to live out her days. She begged them to explain what she had done, but the judge banged his gavel on the bench. *It is the wish of this court.*

She woke in the grip of panic and for a moment couldn't think where she was. Voices floated up from the third-class deck. She recognised one: William Cooper, the English diver who had made the speech at Port Fremantle. The brass band had been loud but it hadn't completely drowned him out. She was glad she hadn't seen him since; he made her feel flustered. A huge fish leaped out of the water next to the steamer and fell back with a splash. It jumped again, dived deep and disappeared. She envied its freedom.

The arrival of a coastal steamer was apparently a big event at Buccaneer Bay. As the light began to fade and the steamer dropped anchor amid a dense woodland of naked masts, the handful of remaining passengers crowded the decks and peered out into the gloom. As the steamer lurched against its moorings, Maisie watched the commotion and scanned the waiting throng. On the wooden jetty below, a crowd had gathered – waving handkerchiefs and hats – all jostling to come on board. The men were spotlessly white, splendid in their immaculate tropical suits and solar topis. A European woman wearing an ankle-length dress was negotiating her way round a stack of boxes. Maisie couldn't tell her age, but Mrs Wallace had been right: a hat, veil, gloves and high-ankle shoes assured that the sun would never glimpse her skin.

The boarding party surged up the gangplank like a tidal wave. Men with waxed moustaches, some with burned complexions, elbowed their way on deck. The noise jangled Maisie's nerves and she looked around, unsure what to do. Was Maitland Sinclair in their midst pushing his way up the ramp, eager to claim his future bride? She started to panic. How would he know her? She followed the crowds into the first-class lounge, where the captain was dispensing complimentary drinks. She accepted a glass of lemonade from a steward and settled on a velvet banquette, her eyes trained on the doorway. Her heart was battering her ribcage like a parade-ground drum, her palms damp and clammy. Surely he would come soon? Or maybe he'd changed his mind and she'd travelled thousands of miles for nothing? She felt faint with misgiving.

Time passed and still he didn't come.

In the lounge, Mr Farmount started to make a speech. She looked up and tuned in to what he was saying. She couldn't avoid it; his voice was so loud it reverberated around the room. He was introducing the English divers to the four master pearlers who had agreed to employ them, his speech a poorly disguised sales pitch for the diving company he represented. He talked at length about a new, engine-driven air compressor, which had not previously been used on the pearling grounds of the north-west. It would transform safety on board, he said. Hands were shaken, contracts exchanged and start dates discussed. The master pearlers quizzed the Englishmen about their training, and their experience of diving at great depths. Toasts were made, backs were slapped and the drinks kept on coming. Maisie wondered how they could concentrate with so much alcohol coursing through their veins.

William Cooper was sitting by the bar, wiping his forehead with the back of his arm. She saw that there were dark damp patches under his arms and around his collar. His eyes lit up for a moment at something the barman said and she heard him laugh. It sounded joyous, and her heart dropped then. *When was the last time you were really happy?* She searched for the answer but it was nowhere to be found.

From feet away a voice said, 'Cousin Maisie?'

She started and turned her face towards the voice.

He was dressed in a cream linen suit, with a spiky-leafed flower she didn't recognise in his lapel. It was a stark contrast to the flabby outline of his jaw and the puffy pouches under his eyes. Short, bald and fair-skinned, he had a misshapen nose, ruddy flesh pitted with blackened pores, and clamped between his nicotine-stained teeth was a short-stemmed pipe.

She shot up, clutching her glass like a lifebelt, and spilt yellowish liquid down the front of her dress. 'Cousin Maitland?'

Pipe still in his mouth, he took her hand between both of his and pumped it up and down, then dropped it just as rapidly. He rubbed his palms together and peered at her with assessing eyes. She looked for a sign of approval but there was none. Disappointment settled heavily on them both.

He didn't introduce himself. He didn't ask, with the touching solicitude she'd imagined, if her journey had been bearable. If she was managing in the heat or was missing her parents. She turned her thoughts to her appearance, to lighter complications and concerns.

'I must look a mess.' She ran a shaky hand over her hair.

He was standing so close to her she could smell his sour breath. He took hold of her arm, pinching her flesh hard through the sheer fabric.

'Won't matter what you look like. No-one's going to care. Come. Everyone's waiting.'

She would have envied his lack of concern had she not been its collateral. She could see that there was nothing about her that raised his interest; that her presence seemed to annoy him. She tried to think where she had gone wrong.

'Waiting?' She pulled out her handkerchief and dabbed self-consciously at the stain on her dress.

'Yes. Waiting for you. Come on. No time like the present.' He bedded his free hand in the middle of her back and propelled her along the passageway into the stateroom. 'We need to get it over with. There's nowhere for you to stay if we don't. It's the lay-up.'

She had not the first idea what he was talking about.

The ship's stateroom was a bear pit, crammed with people she didn't know and smelling foreign: of alcohol, tobacco and stale sweat. She pressed a finger across the underside of her nose and tried to force down the fear. She could sense that all eyes were upon her, triggering a hot blush on her face. She couldn't be the centre of attention. Her mother would have whipped her for such presumption. She had been conditioned throughout her life to shun the limelight yet now all eyes were on her. Her knees began to wobble. She wanted to run, to leave as quickly as she was able. It had been the safest course at home. Frightened she would be scolded, she tucked her chin to her chest and began to apologise for her lack of manners.

The ship's captain held up a finger, snapping off her words, and twisted the strap of his watch. He stretched his mouth in a smile and pointed at a chair.

'If you would care to take a seat, we can make a start.'

Maisie turned to Maitland. 'I don't understand.'

'Dear little Maisie. You've travelled miles to be my wife. All my friends are here on this ship right now. It makes perfect sense to marry with everybody present, and make a party of it.'

'Are we not to marry in church?'

'No need. The captain can marry us. It's often done at sea.' He nodded at the captain, who squeezed out another smile.

'But we aren't at sea.'

'As good as.'

'Is it legal in the eyes of God?'

Maisie started as Maitland punched the back of the chair. 'Lord above, Maisie. Of course it's legal. Do you think I would do anything illegal?' He jabbed her in the ribs with his elbow. 'Now shut up. You're embarrassing me.'

Maisie watched him, trying to gauge what had triggered his reaction.

The captain shuffled his feet and said nothing.

Although her legs were trembling, Maisie felt she had to say, 'I should like to put on my wedding dress.'

'What for?'

'I've brought it thousands of miles for this occasion. I'd like to wear it on my wedding day. The dress I'm wearing is crumpled and stained and I should like to change out if it.'

A shadow of irritation crossed his face and Maisie saw him clench his fist. Instinctively she stepped back, and ducked her face once more into her chest.

The captain tapped the glass face of his watch. 'Are we able to proceed, or does the lady need a moment?'

'She's fine. She doesn't need to dress up.'

The captain checked his paperwork. 'Who are the bridesmaids?'

'Miss Locke said she'd stand in.' He indicated the woman Maisie had seen on the gangplank.

Maisie smiled across at the elegantly clad stranger. 'Are there no other ladies here?'

Maitland's lips tightened. 'Mostly in Perth. They go south for the Wet. It's too bloody uncomfortable for most females at this time of year. They'll flitter back in March, give or take.'

She tried to unravel her disquiet as, wearing a stained dress and with tears not far from surfacing, Maisie promised to love and obey Maitland for the rest of her life, her spirits as low as the hemline of her dress.

The party was in full swing by the time it was dark.

Maisie slipped away to her cabin. Lit only by the overhead lamp, the shadows dimmed the horror of her situation. No-one noticed she had left the wedding party. The event had not been about celebrating a marriage. Maitland had barked his responses during the ceremony, as if he were commanding a fleet of warships; she had responded in a wavering treble that Mrs Wallace would have despised.

Her husband – she shivered at the title – was now enveloped in a wave of backslapping and ribald well-wishing. She sank down onto the bunk, wondering where her great hope for happiness had gone. She lifted the lid on her trunk and fingered the princess gown of white duchesse satin that she would never wear. Her trousseau had been handmade in London and had cost a great deal of money. She ran her hand over the dress's silky fabric, which had been embroidered with pearls – a most appropriate and clever touch, the dressmaker said, being associated with brides and weddings and the profession of her future husband and all. For Maisie, though, they represented far more than that; they were her freedom.

Everything screamed at her that this marriage was wrong.

The fabric slipped through her fingers like sand. The outfit she was to wear for her reception was of chiffon satin in the fashionable 'ashes of roses' shade with an overdress of silk and gold net. It was the most beautiful thing she had ever owned and he had cheated her out of wearing it. The only time expense had ever been lavished upon her, and it had gone to waste. She replaced the dress in her trunk and packed away the last of her things, wishing she could load it onto another ship and sail back the way she had come.

There was a tap on the cabin door. Maisie jumped up and clutched the neck of her dress, her heart stuttering. Was this Maitland, come to claim his prize?

'It's the porter, Miss. May I collect your cabin luggage?'

'Yes, of course,' she rasped, and coughed in an attempt to ease the pressure clogging her throat. 'Give me a moment.'

She took a final look around the hot, brown box that had been her home for eight days, and opened the door. She followed the porter out onto the deck, which was piled high with baggage and crates of drink. From the bar, she could hear the *plonk plonk* of an untuned piano and, in the distance, a train whistle. She found that surprising. She hadn't expected a locomotive in Buccaneer Bay.

Maitland hadn't bothered with private transport for his bride. Normally, he told her, he would have walked home, as it was only half a mile over the jetty. She'd had a long day though and might be glad to take the steam-tram. He helped her onto the open carriage and squeezed her onto the last vacant bench, wedged between the window and an elderly man of significant girth. Maitland slumped down in the corner opposite and closed his eyes. The tram shuddered to life and soon they were rattling over its rails across the wooden jetty towards the lighthouse.

Maisie leaned forward and tapped his arm. 'Tell me about your life here,' she said.

He opened his eyes and cracked his knuckles, one by one. 'Nothing to tell.'

'But I'd really like to know what to expect.'

He looked at her once and turned away, his foot banging up and down on the steam-tram's floor.

Theirs was the first stop. He stood up and prodded her shoulder with the stem of his pipe. 'Here we are. This is where we get off.'

The single-storey house was on the edge of town. In contrast to the tall grey townhouse where she had grown up in London, this was low – a squat white rectangle, one of the long sides facing the sea. Beyond that, it was too dark to see.

There were three steps up to the verandah. She put one foot on the bottom step and clutched the handrail. Maitland nudged her up towards the front door. 'Home, sweet home,' he said.

Maisie worked the gloves in her hands, hoping the torque of the twisted fabric would give her strength. 'It's a bit too dark to really appreciate the house, Maitland, and it has been a very long day.' She thought of Mrs Wallace. 'I have a dreadful headache and I'd really just like to go to bed.'

He didn't seem to register her remark. He struck a match and flared a carbide light.

The smell was too strong: an overwhelming reek of garlic mixed with damp. Maisie's nostrils flared at the sting of the smoke.

'Maitland?' She shuffled her feet. It had been hours since she last used the ship's facilities and her bladder was stretched tight, like her nerves.

'What?'

'Might you show me where I can tidy myself?'

A jagged streak of lightning illuminated a wide verandah, which ran the length of the house. He took a half-step towards her, his huge hand extended. She shrank back against the doorjamb, fearful that he might touch her.

'Maitland?' Her voice was small.

Something in her tone reeled him in. 'The bathroom is at the back,' he said. 'I'll show you.'

He didn't understand the euphemism. Hardly more than a rudimentary shack tacked onto the back of the bungalow, the bathroom housed a stained tin bath and shallow basin sunk into the top of a wooden table. A small woodchip water heater sat on the floor beside a large enamel jug. Two taps were connected to the heater – one stretched over the bath and the other was attached to the end of a long metal pipe, running the length of the wall and coming to a halt over the basin. A single shelf over the sink provided the only storage space. It was cluttered with his own things. He had pushed nothing aside to make room for her in his life.

'This is the bathroom, Maitland, but what I need is the lavatory. Might you show me where that is, please?'

The toilet was outside, housed in its own separate cubicle abutting the back fence, fifty yards from the house. A crushed-shell path, lined with upturned glass bottles sunk deep in the soil, led to it from the back door.

Maitland waved a fleshy hand. 'There's your lavatory, Maisie. It's out the back so you won't be disturbed when the shitcan collector comes to empty the dunny in the early hours.'

The obscenity slapped her in the face, like a blow. 'Do you have a lantern I might borrow?'

'No, I don't. I piss off the verandah at night.'

He watched her pick her way down the path.

'Watch out for snakes and spiders,' he called after her. 'Lots of them bite.'

The toilet was housed in a galvanised-iron hut. Squares of paper, threaded on a string, were nailed to the wall. She had no words to describe the smell. She covered her mouth with her handkerchief and hurried back to the house, the hem of her dress trailing through the thick, dark earth.

Maitland hadn't moved from the back door. 'Drink before bed?' He waggled a bottle at her.

Maisie was dry-mouthed, her heart thumping so hard she wondered if he could see it through her dress. *This is it.* Coarse and without appeal, the man repulsed her. She had spent all her life dreaming of Snow White's handsome prince who would kiss her gently awake from her sleepy existence. He would kneel at her feet, hand pressed to his heart, and beg her to be his bride. The reality was that she had married a fat, ugly toad.

Mrs Wallace had not painted a romantic, loving picture of the marriage act. If he was a good man, she said, he would coax her, his frightened bride, with kind words and understanding. Otherwise, among a lot of talk about sheep and animals, things would have to be borne. She sank onto a kitchen chair with shaking knees and picked at the neck of her dress. 'Perhaps I might,' she said.

'You'll have to get up. The drinks are next door.'

She followed him down the passage, their footsteps echoing on the floorboards. A pile of unopened letters lay on a polished wooden table and, somewhere in the house, a clock chimed the hour. He stood in front of a side table, and over his shoulder said, 'What's your poison?'

'Sherry?' she replied, both hands locked on her handbag.

'No can do. Gin, brandy, whisky, champagne or wine.'

'Gin, then.' Her voice was high and thin.

He turned towards her and held out a glass. 'Quick nightcap and then let's get off to bed.'

For the second time that day, Maisie was taken to a room she had no desire to enter. It was a small box room whose walls and ceiling were covered with beige hessian. It was intolerably hot and smelled of damp.

'This is your room. It's adjacent to my own,' Maitland explained, lighting another carbide lamp. 'You'll be all right in here. There's an empty drawer for your things in the dressing table but not much space in the wardrobe. You'll have to manage. The bathroom is down the verandah on the right, if you've lost your sense of direction. I'll be able to hear when you've finished in there.' He stood in the doorway and seemed to hesitate. 'I'll probably be gone in the morning before you're up, so just have a look round and sort yourself out. Good night.' He shut the door behind him.

Alone among his clothes, she sat on the bed, quailing in the near dark. Though her parents had separate rooms, she had imagined a shared bed for her wedding night. Maybe Maitland was preparing to receive her on the other side of the door and his bachelor room would eventually become theirs? An image of him undressing came into her head, but she squeezed her eyes shut to block it out and tried not to panic. After a while she opened her eyes and looked around. Her trunk was not there. She was without friends, possessions or courage. She undressed and folded her clothes neatly into piles on a chair, shoes side by side underneath, through years of habit. The bed was low, covered with a single sheet, tucked in tightly at the corners like a parcel. She peeled back an edge and got in, dressed only in her shift. A few moments later she thought she heard Maitland close a door along the passage. The sound of whispering and then a deep cry. Her heart quickened and sweat trickled down her neck. She strained her ears listening for footsteps and stared at the wooden handle on her door, waiting for it to turn. *This is it*, she thought, *the absolute edge of the cliff*.

She lay on her back, eyes open in the darkness, and stared at the knob for most of the night, scarcely blinking, but it never moved.

CHAPTER 5

THE NEXT MORNING, SHE was startled awake by the smash and splintering of crockery. She lay absolutely still, rigid, her eyes wide, waiting with panic for the door to burst open and Maitland to appear, demanding his husband's dues.

'Knock, knock.' The voice was unfamiliar, certainly not Maitland's.

She was too scared to sit up, and so sank down dragging the sheets to her chin, her pulse jumping in her throat.

A Chinese man with a coffee-coloured face, his teeth shining even whiter than the dazzling singlet he wore below it, peered round her door. His gums looked blue against the shiny white enamel. Maisie twisted the gaping neckline of her nightgown closed between her thumb and forefinger.

Pinned to the bed by his enquiring gaze, she pulled the sheets more tightly around her. 'Who are you?'

A half-smile hovered at his mouth. 'Cook-houseboy, Mem. I everything here.'

'Do you live in this house?' She shrank back against the pillow, her stomach contracting. Maitland hadn't mentioned servants, though she had realised there must be some. 'What's your name?'

'Duc, Mem.'

'What do you want?' She tightened the sheet round her neck.

'Bossman say me bring you cuppa tea.'

She willed herself calm. 'That would be welcome.'

'You okey-dokey, Mem?'

She dipped her chin. 'Is Captain Sinclair here, Duc?'

'Boss? No, he gone working. He come back afternoon or night time. Maybe if.'

She sat up from the pillows and elbowed her way up the headboard. 'Maybe if?'

'Seven o'clock. Maybe if eight.' He seemed to nod and shake his head at the same time, leaving Maisie with no idea what he meant.

'What time is it?'

He gave her a look, which made her feel stupid. ''Bout morning-tea time.'

'Has my trunk arrived from the steamer?'

He put his head on one side and wobbled it again, grinning like a madman. She could see he hadn't understood her question.

'Big black box.' She drew a rectangle in the air with both hands.

Duc pulled his mouth wide. 'Yes. Him arrived. I bring for you?'

'Tea first. Then you can move the black box.'

The mouth widened. 'You get up and go verandah. I bring tea. You want eat?'

She couldn't remember when she'd last eaten. 'Maybe something small?'

'I go see what's what.' He put his hands together and bowed.

She half-expected him to reverse out of the room. For the first time in days, she almost smiled.

Duc carried the tea tray as if he were carrying the crown jewels on a velvet cushion, his arms stretched out and reverent. When he saw her, his face lit up. He dropped the tray on a side table and bent at the waist, paying homage as if she were a minor royal. Clay tea things and a plate of scones rattled together, sloshing sugar and milk onto the tray cloth. Maisie wondered about him, supposing the smashed crockery that had woken her had been his handiwork. She picked up a sugar-crusted cake and took a bite. It was as dry as the Sahara.

'Is there any butter?'

'No. Him butter come in tin. Very oily.' He shook his head to one side.

'Milk?'

'Milk him cow gone.'

Maisie had trouble with this one. Did they have a cow that had gone away? Or died? Or did they have a milk source that had run out? She would have to try harder. 'Jam, then?'

'No, him all used up. Poof.' Duc threw his hands in the air.

Maisie shifted in her seat.

Duc missed nothing. 'You not comfy in boss fella's house? You want I bring more something?'

'I'm fine, thank you. Does the captain have a maid? A girl who comes in to help you?'

'Oh no, Mem. No girls.'

Maisie looked at him. 'No girls?'

'No. Just him and me here, Mem.'

Maisie drank her pot of tea and washed down the rock-hard scones, which were stale enough to endanger teeth. She had only intended to eat one but had allowed herself to become distracted by her new surroundings. In the daylight she could see that the house was built on concrete legs, and from the shady west-facing verandah she looked down onto a stretch of sand alive with activity. The tide was out and it seemed as if an army of tea-coloured locusts was stripping the beached sailing boats of their contents. Coils of rope, baskets and lengths of anchor chain were being lugged up the sand. Sails were taken down from the riggings and dragged up the dunes where they were spread out for inspection across the high ground.

She shifted her gaze towards the lighthouse, which was as clean and bright as tooth powder. Next to it was a collection of iron sheds and warehouses. Two men were separate from the rest, deep in conversation. The shorter of the two was waving his arm at the task force on the beach. The other, she saw, was William Cooper – the tall English diver from the steamer – his dark head framed by the brilliant blue sky. Something tugged within her and she stared, her chest tightening as she took in the tilt of his head, the set of his shoulders. Even from this distance she could see that his skin was glossy with sweat. It glistened on his face like sunlight on water, and she could almost feel his body heat. She watched him twist off his boots and socks, and fold his trousers in neat pleats to the knee. He looked as if he was going to walk down to the water's edge and paddle in the sea.

He patted his trouser pocket and pulled out the makings of a cigarette. The process made her frown. She knew she had seen him do it before but she couldn't remember when.

Duc shuffled into view, his big toes straddling a Y-shaped strap on flat, slappy shoes. 'You all done tea, Mem?'

Maisie tore her gaze from the figure on the foreshore and tried not to stare at Duc's feet. She had never seen footwear like it. 'Yes, thank you, Duc.'

She drained the last drop of lukewarm tea from her cup and rose from the chair. Her dress, the same dress she had worn for her marriage ceremony the day before, clung determinedly to her skin. She pulled at the neckline and flapped it up and down, trying to find some respite from the stifling heat.

'Perhaps you could show me round the house?'

Duc beamed, his eyes sparking with what she thought was happiness.

Maitland's bungalow – he had named it Turbine after a winning racehorse he had once backed – was a large oblong. Elaborate white fretwork surrounded wide latticed verandahs framing the house. The bungalow was set away from the acre-block housing she would learn was the 'English' part of town, and Maisie couldn't help but wonder why he had built his house so far from the centre of things. At the front of the house, Turbine's lush green lawns rolled out to the edge of a blood-red cliff that overlooked the ocean. They had no neighbours.

The bungalow was designed to be airy. Duc explained that the boss fella's house had been built to follow the construction lines of a ship.

'This housie builded by them Jap fellas.'

'I'm sorry?'

'Them Jappy fellas in Asia Place. Before him government say bye-bye to best workers.' Maisie let his remark pass. She had been force-fed a diet of racist extremism since she boarded the steamship to Port Fremantle almost two months ago and was still struggling to digest the bigotry.

'Mem Tuan. You listen?'

'Yes. I'm listening. Tuan?'

'Means boss. Them Jappy fellas build things good and use same wood for lugger boat. So him deck become verandah, inside boat is inside bit of house and sails on boat is big blow shutters.'

Duc was speaking a language she couldn't comprehend, and she found herself mirroring his expression, stretching her mouth wide in a mirthless grin till her jaw ached with effort. She waved at steel cables that crossed over the roof like rigid string, anchored to the ground by fastenings sunk deep into cement.

'Is for big-blow windies, Mem. Keep house on spot.'

She pointed at the metal-capped cement pillars beyond the verandah.

'Hims is for creepy-crawlies and snakes and eaty ants.'

'You eat *ants*?'

Duc rolled his eyes. 'No eaty ants, theys eaty house. We no eat-im.' As they continued the tour of the house she pointed, he explained, and neither comprehended the other. She thought that the house perfectly reflected her husband: flat and stretched sideways rather than up.

The dining room was next to the kitchen at one end of the west verandah. The walls were covered with framed pictures of hunting scenes – slaughtered deer, tigers and elephants immortalised in their final moments. Huntsmen and hounds posing by their bleeding quarry. She imagined she could hear the call of hunting horns, and tried not to look.

At right angles, the verandah widened to accommodate the lounge furniture, which, Duc explained, was made of cane imported from Singapore. At the far end of the same verandah was a long, partitioned space.

'This, Mem,' Duc paused, waving his arms like a policeman, 'is mosquito room. Where you and boss have sleep. Afternoon time.'

Maisie steadied herself on the back of a chair. So, this is when it would happen. The consummation of her marriage would be this afternoon – in the mosquito room – with Duc listening in.

Duc explained that the quasi-dormitory area was enclosed by fine steel mesh to keep out the biting insects. Full-length iron shutters protected the space from the elements.

'And do you have a room in the house, Duc?'

'I's live at back near to boss fella's room.'

Maisie was shown a further small verandah at the back of the bungalow that faced the garden, which Duc told her was his space, or words to that effect. At the back was also a small shuttered area the boss used as a second home-based office, and a large storeroom, which housed an impressive larder of canned food.

'The three of us will be totally self-sufficient if the sky falls in!' She laughed.

Duc looked at her with a broad grin, his eyes wide with hope.

'What you say you teach me cook, Mem, so we okey-dokey when sky falls in?'

CHAPTER 6

THE SEAFARER'S REST HOTEL, built of iron and wood and overlaid with latticework, sat on a rise at the Japanese end of Royal Avenue, its elevated position giving it a good vantage point over the rest of the town. Buccaneer Bay had no high street in the traditional town-planning sense. There was no nucleus to the collection of buildings that had grown up behind the coastal sand dunes. As far as Cooper could tell, its only excuse for existence was that its inhabitants all shared the same unshakeable belief that there was a fortune to be made from pearl shell and another from the occasional treasure within. It was why he, too, was there.

It was 'lay-up' in Buccaneer Bay, a season of unrestrained madness. The lugger crews had lived and worked for nine months of the year in conditions in which even the most placid dog would have savaged its handler – and school was now out. Captain Sinclair had billeted both of his new employees, William Cooper and John Butcher, in the Seafarer's, and the rent would cripple them until they could get out to sea and start hauling the pearl shell. The Englishmen found themselves hunkering down among men of every nationality who were steadfastly working their way through their pay. Drinking or gambling were the preferred nightly pastimes. There was little else to do.

Cooper paused now on the doorstep of the hotel and lowered himself gingerly onto the pale cane seat. His head ached in pulsating waves. The previous evening was a queasy blur. Between sunset and sun-up, he had held centre stage in the bar among Filipino, Koepanger and Malay residents, playing poker and matching their drinking, glass for intoxicating glass. Early in the evening, he had accepted a glass of potato-gin from a middle-aged Filipino man everybody called Slippery Sid.

Taking an eye-watering sip of the noxious liquor, Cooper leaned forward. 'How many luggers are in this place, Sid?'

'Mebbe more than three hundred.'

'Does each one have a different owner?'

'Nope. Some mebbe two, mebbe three. Big Tuan boss Mayor, he has lots, mebbe twenty.'

'Captain Sinclair has how many?'

Sid took a swig of gin and held up three fingers.

'How many men on each lugger?'

Sid explained that each lugger held two divers: a number-one diver – usually Japanese – and a trial diver, who was less experienced than the principal. They dived in turns. The diver had a man on board who tended his equipment, which made a total of three diving-related people. A common crew comprised the cook, four men to man the air pumps in shifts throughout the day, and the shell-opener, swelling the number to nine. Sometimes the owner-captain worked on board too. So, as far as Cooper could make out, there were generally nine or ten people on a lugger.

'Does Captain Sinclair go out to sea?'

'Him's no sea legs.'

Cooper chopped at his windpipe and contorted his face. 'Is the diving dangerous?'

Sid laughed. 'You's a scaredy-cat?'

Cooper shook his head. 'No. The diving I'm used to is much more dangerous than here.'

'Japanese dive best.'

'Why?'

'Have lotsa guts.'

'And the best crews?'

'All mix-up. Then no fighting.'

'And do the Aborigines work on the boats?'

'He no work on boats. White man don't like blackfella.'

'Why not?' Cooper knew that imported labour was an issue in Buccaneer Bay, but not to use the abundant local workforce seemed like lunacy.

'Blackfella scared of diving gear.'

'So, the crews do not originate from here.'

'All crew come work for three years then go home again. All very snug.'

Somewhere close to midnight, Cooper fell asleep over a glass of rum. Someone shook his shoulder and hefted him up the stairs to his balconied second-floor room, and he had woken the next morning at nine o'clock, slumped across the edge of the mattress, one leg tucked underneath him, still drunk.

He squinted at his watch. Captain Sinclair wanted him at his office before ten. The initial meeting with the captain on the steamship had made him jumpy. He'd been expecting a big welcome party, along the lines of the fanfare at Port Fremantle, but the captain had barely acknowledged him and had completely blanked John Butcher. Cooper had accepted the four-page contract from his poker-faced employer but had refused to sign it unread. The captain's pale grey eyes had not been friendly. Perhaps Cooper was misreading it. After all, the man could not have known of Cooper's attraction to the woman he'd watched the captain wed or that his bride looked like she'd made a dreadful mistake.

Cooper leaned back in the wicker chair and began to roll a cigarette, booze-shaky fingers making heavy work of the task. He licked the sticky edge of the cigarette paper and placed one end of the slim tube, pointed like the sharpened lead of a pencil, between his lips and lit up. He shook out the match, inhaled deeply and crossed his legs, shutting his eyes against the glare of the morning sun.

'The view isn't up to much, is it?' a young-sounding female voice said.

Cooper cranked open his eyes, his roll-your-own smoke dangling from his lip.

'Black mud and luggers. That's all you can see during the lay-up.'

'I wasn't really looking at the view.' He struggled to his feet.

'I'm Dorothea Montague.' She held out a gloved hand.

Cooper looked into the girl's face. Dark hair piled up under a hat, round blue eyes, her mouth wide and soft. 'William Cooper.'

'I know who you are. My father is the mayor. We've been anticipating your arrival with great enthusiasm.'

'We are all excited to be here,' he batted back. 'And keen to get started lifting shell off the ocean floor.'

'A bit of a wait then for you, I'm afraid. Until the Wet's over.'

'Wet?'

'Gosh, I always forget that Britishers from England don't know what that means.' She giggled. 'It's the time from November to March when the threat of cyclones keeps the fleets and crews onshore. Everyone gets drunk all the time and we have lots of parties. It's great fun. And the repairs are done to the luggers. I expect you will be given some jobs to do. The paid workers are expected to muck in.'

'Are not all Britishers from Britain?' he queried.

'No, silly boy. We are all Britishers in Buccaneer Bay. White people. Don't you see?'

'Yes, I do see. Thank you.' Although he didn't. He stole a glance at his watch. 'Please don't think me rude but I have to be at Captain Sinclair's office before ten o'clock.'

'Oh goodness. That's right at the other end of town. Would you like me to give you a ride in my buggy?'

'Would your father be happy for you to ride with a stranger?'

'Of course. White people have to stick together, and we don't go in for that chaperone Victorian nonsense that goes on in England. There aren't enough women, silly boy. It's no trouble, and I could call on the new Mrs Sinclair. She arrived last night and I heard her to be about my age.'

'Yes, she is.'

The blue eyes expanded. 'You know her?'

'I've seen her. We travelled on the same ship from England.' Cooper thought of the slight, blonde-haired girl with her pearl-white skin, and wiped a handkerchief over his forehead. Oh yes! He'd seen her walking on deck with an older woman he'd assumed was her mother. Last night she had married Captain Sinclair in the most bizarre wedding ceremony he'd ever witnessed. *She is now his*, he told himself, but the realisation gave him no joy.

Miss Montague twirled her parasol, shading pale skin. 'You should buy a hat. Your skin will really darken with the sun, and you don't want people mistaking you for a coloured. That would be suicide, socially. Our people won't invite you to anything if you're all brown.' She pointed at a horse trap tethered to a rail under the hotel's awning. 'Shall we go? The sulky is just there.'

He was sweltering and nauseous with a hangover beating a call to temperance in his skull. Without altogether thinking it through, Cooper accepted the offer and followed her out. He regretted it seconds later.

Miss Montague, he learned, had no mother. Of course, she corrected herself, she did have a mother once but she died of neglect. Or incompetence. No-one really knew the truth of the matter. Her Mama had developed an infection from a cut and went to see the white doctor, at the government hospital. Everybody said she should have gone to the Japanese doctor but her Dada wouldn't hear of it. Dada said that Asian people were inferior to white people and he wouldn't fall so low as to allow his wife to be treated by an immigrant. But the white doctor was busy with the divers who needed to be passed fit to work – even though some of them weren't – and there was lots of paperwork to fill in. So, he forgot about her Mama, and the infection spread and Mama died. Now Miss Montague was alone with darling Dada, who still hated the Asians, the mixed-race people, the poor whites and the Aborigines. Dada was thrilled that the white divers had arrived to swell their number. He had said so at breakfast.

They clattered down the backstreets past a maze of whitewashed iron-and-timber constructions and houses so jammed together that a stray lit match would have torched the lot. Rows of shops with fronts opening straight onto the road were cluttered with cheap merchandise, and everything for sale was being peddled by bawling tradesmen. It reeked of spicy food, fish, frying onions and the sickening odour of insanitation. Cooper tried to breathe through his mouth as they slowed for a corner, his ears ringing with horses' hooves and the echo of underprivilege.

He craned his neck. 'What's going on over there, Miss Montague?'

A line of Aboriginal men was approaching, each one barefoot, the whole pageant trudging one behind the other in a dejected convoy. At the head of the column a white policeman in a heavy twill uniform shouldered a rifle, whistling idly, keeping himself company. The black men behind him, each wearing nothing but a loincloth, were skeletally thin, their ribs sticking out like toast racks. They were tethered together by steel neck chains.

Miss Montague halted the horse and turned to her companion. 'Those are the Abos who spread the white shell-grit on the roads. You should see them later on when they've finished for the day. They get covered in white dust and gleam in the dark like ghosts. It's terribly spooky!'

'Why are they chained up?'

'There's only one warder for all the prisoners. How else is he going to control them?'

Cooper didn't understand. 'But why are there so many of them?'

'I think someone once calculated that you need fifty men to build a road, so they try to keep the numbers up.'

'What did they do?'

She shook up the reins. 'Killing cattle, mainly. The Abos are quite docile really, until they're hungry or full of drink. Then it's a different story. But I think they have quite a nice life as prisoners.

Dada says some of them get themselves caught on purpose. They are fed three times a day and the gaoler's wife cooks them treats from time to time. They get two hours off at lunchtime and then a swim in the creek after work to get the dust off.'

'Are neck chains used for European prisoners?'

'Of course not. White people don't work on chain gangs. It wouldn't be civilised, would it?'

Cooper stared at her for an instant as she in turn looked at him, expectant. Rather than searching for words he couldn't summon, he changed the subject. 'And how do you fill your time, Miss Montague? Is there much to keep you occupied?'

She lifted her chin, her voice rather high. 'Me? Goodness, there's so much to do! Bridge parties, croquet and the tennis club . . . then we have picnics and lots of balls and concerts and fundraisers at the Catholic school. There isn't a single minute to get bored.'

Miss Montague pulled hard on the reins and smiled a little too brightly, Cooper thought. 'Here you are, Mr Cooper,' she said, nodding across the street at a cluster of whitewashed shacks. 'Delivered safe and sound. Captain Sinclair's office is in the packing shed over there.'

She pointed the tip of her parasol at a sandy path that snaked down to the beach. The tide was out. A flat expanse of black mud was littered with luggers, some on their sides but the majority dug deep into trenches and sandbagged upright, temporarily beached by the receding tide.

'And don't forget about the hat. I declare you're two shades darker now than when I picked you up!'

Cooper took a deep breath of air and wished he hadn't. It reeked of putrefying fish.

'Thank you for the ride, Miss Montague. I am most obliged.'

Her lashes flickered. She reached out and with a small, gloved hand touched a lock of his hair. 'It's what we do out here,' she said. 'Look after one another.'

As the sulky pulled away, Cooper shaded his eyes with the flat of his hand and squinted at the iron shed. The sun was a bastard. He patted his jacket and reassured himself that his contract was still safe inside. He was anxious to discuss it before finally signing on the dotted line. Funds were running low and he wanted to know when he could get out to sea. Reaching into his pocket, he brought out the items he needed to roll a fresh cigarette and turned towards the foreshore. For as far as he could see, luggers lined the beach. Sid was right. There must have been several hundred hauled up onto the sand, their masts stripped of rigging like dead trees. He had expected the boats to be bigger. Loaded up with diving equipment and supplies, there would be scant room for all nine members of the crew. He shook his head. Sid had probably made the numbers up, and anyway, what was a little discomfort when a fortune was out there to be made?

The beach was teeming with sturdy, short-legged men, trousers rolled up, crawling over the boats. Repairs and maintenance of the fleet was in full swing and Miss Montague expected him to keep out of the sun? All of them, from their heads to their calf muscles, were burned brown. He took a last drag on his cigarette, crushed the butt beneath his heel and set off down the path.

Captain Sinclair spoke like a machine gun in brittle, strident bursts. A one-man firing squad.

'So, Cooper. Good news. I've just had a cable from New York. Our last shipment of shell sold for three hundred pounds per ton. A record price. Where's John Butcher?'

'He may be a little late.'

'Tarts?'

Cooper shook his head and winced with the movement.

The captain clenched his pipe in his stained teeth. 'Is he reliable?'

'JB? He's the best tender I could hope for,' Cooper affirmed. 'I won't dive without him.'

'What diving experience do you have?'

'My years in the Navy. I trained at the gunnery school in Portsmouth.'

He banged the pipe bowl on the desk. 'We need to discuss your contract. I am supposed to pay you thirteen pounds per month and your tender six pounds.'

Cooper dipped his head in agreement. 'That was what we were offered to leave England.'

'Thing is, Mr Cooper, for a month I can get a Jap diver for three pounds, a Malay for two pounds, and a tender comes at about one pound. I've already paid twenty-four pounds for you and your John Butcher just to get here from England and I have no idea if you can find shell. What guarantee can you give me of return on my investment?' Captain Sinclair's face was unfriendly.

'I don't see how we can fail, sir. The Navy's finest has trained us. If the Asiatic can come here and make a success of it you have my assurance, Captain Sinclair, that a Navy man can do better.'

Maitland threw back his head with such force he almost toppled over backwards in his chair. 'You pompous arse! You're not in a position to assure me of anything! Do you know what shell looks like, Cooper?'

Cooper had assumed it would be obvious to spot. He hadn't considered it an issue.

'Come with me.' Sinclair led him to the adjacent packing shed and plucked a half-shell from a sorting bin. The mother-of-pearl glinted in the sunlight.

'This is what you are diving for.' He tapped the shell. 'But this is not what you will see. It's a different thing when it is lying on a tidal bank at twenty fathoms down. It's the colour of the sea bottom. It takes a top Jap diver a number of years to become proficient at spotting the stuff by himself, and you are a novice on contract for twelve months.'

'I thought we were to dive in pairs to begin with. To learn the ropes.'

'I'm not sure that you quite understand the situation, Cooper. To take you on, I shall have to lay off one of my experienced Japanese divers. The Japs are getting demanding. They can afford to be. They know they are the best and won't sign on for the season unless they have an advance on their earnings. That way, if they croak – and lots do die – they have something to send home. I have paid out money to someone who is not going to earn his keep. That, Mr Cooper, is not good business.'

Cooper stared at his employer. 'Then why exactly am I here, Captain Sinclair? Your representatives in England insisted that all the master pearlers in Buccaneer Bay were on board with the idea that white-manned luggers would be a more efficient and profitable option than the foreign-crewed boats you normally operate. We were told that the Australian government is committed to this belief. All of us have come out here to prove the point. If the sums don't add up, why have you brought out a boatload of white divers to work for you on the pearl beds?'

The captain folded his arms across his chest and blew out his cheeks. 'I'm sorry, Cooper, if I sound a little unfriendly. You must understand that from now, until the fleet goes to sea, we are swamped with work. The costs of buying, equipping and running a lugger are crippling. It's a business of continual risk, and many things can go wrong. It makes us all jumpy. But it is not your fault and not your concern, and I apologise if I have given you the impression that you are unwelcome. I have high hopes that you English blokes will be great and make us all a pile of cash. Then we will be able to send the foreign crews back to where they came from. You mentioned just now the possibility of learning the ropes before you put out to sea properly after the Wet. How would it be if you spend the next few days working with Squinty?'

Cooper wondered at the sudden change in attitude, but money was money and he was running short. 'Sounds good if you're going to pay me. I don't work for free.'

'How about ten bob a week?'

Cooper looked at his boots. 'Rent's thirty bob a week at the Seafarer's.'

The captain shook his head. 'I must be out of my flaming mind. Thirty bob, then, till the Wet's over.'

When Cooper nodded, the captain added, jutting out his chin, 'Go outside. I'll send Squinty to you.'

'How will I know him?'

The captain looked Cooper in the eye. 'Take a wild guess, mate.'

*

Cooper left the packing shed with a sigh. It was marginally cooler outside but his ears still seared. He shaded his face with his fingers. It was now mid-morning and the sun was hot enough to blister paint. There was also a slimy heaviness in the air that made breathing a chore, and fat black flies were queuing up to suck the salty moisture from his eyes and mouth. He flapped them away irritably.

He could see the tide was on the turn.

A young Malay – who could not have been more than twenty – picked his way across the hot sand, barefoot and saronged. He wore a chain round his neck on which hung a studded leather pouch, which swung from side to side as he walked. 'You Cooper?'

'Everyone calls me Coop. You Squinty?'

The Malay nodded, his eyes rolling in different directions. 'You working with me today. We's chasing the vermin off luggers. But we need be quick.'

'Tell me what to do.'

'Okay. We join up others.' His eyes did another circuit. 'We get stuff off luggers and undo stopcock. Then we wait. For him seaboss tide fella. You got it?'

Seaboss? 'Yes, I got it,' he bluffed.

Squinty slapped him on the shoulder. 'Come. No time for dilly-dally.' It was too far to go back to the hotel, so Coop took off his boots and yellow socks and rolled up his trousers, in the style of the labouring crew. He unbuttoned his jacket, removed his cigarette papers and tobacco from the right-hand pocket and shrugged the jacket off his shoulders. Wondering if Miss Montague had a point about a hat, he brushed his hair back from his forehead and tied a cotton handkerchief around his head.

Squinty relieved him of his excess garments, rolled them into a sausage-shaped bolster and trotted up the path to the shed.

'You start remove stuff. Quick smart. Seaboss come soon.'

'Seaboss tide fella?'

'Yes, yes, he come cover boats.'

'Where shall I put the stuff?'

The Malay gestured with his hand towards the red sand dunes, already piled high with baskets and ropes.

Coop rolled a cigarette, and got started. It was backbreaking work. With weeks at sea and only an occasional game of deck quoits for exercise, his muscles were weak and flabby, but he was not a quitter. Back and forth, he squelched through the black mud, dragging the endless contents of the captain's luggers on heavy-laden pallets through the burning sand, until he could barely see through the veil of sweat dripping before his eyes.

Sucking noisily on a foul-smelling cheroot, Squinty scampered up the dunes. The tide was almost upon them.

'We stop now. Big seaboss coming.'

Coop trudged up the sand and sank down alongside the assembled seamen to wait for the tide. He framed his face with his hands, giving his eyes temporary relief from the glare. The flies were having a field day.

The tide surged towards them, angry white-topped waves smacking the wooden boats on the stern and surging over the decks. Coop steadied his head in his hands. As the water flooded the holds, thousands of cockroaches clawed and scrabbled over each other, their hidey-holes flushed out. Swirling higher and higher, the tide swept the insects away; Coop retched and swallowed down the bile.

Squinty leaped up and down, his arms pumping, and his enthusiasm ripped through the workforce like a tsunami.

'Him seaboss strong today. Good fun coming. You need stick.'

'I'm feeling rough, Squinty. I'll sit and watch.'

'Tuan say white man weedy.'

'He says I'm weedy? Or that all white diver men are weedy?' Coop pushed himself up off the sand.

Squinty missed the subtlety. 'He say new divermen weedy. My job make you tired out a lot. So you no think straight.'

Coop sensed trouble. 'What's your job on the lugger, Squinty?'

'I have lot jobs. Maybe sometime I cook little bit. Maybe I clean shell little bit. Sometime I do air hose little bit. I do what Tuan says me.'

Squinty's eyes were on the circular track. Round and round. Out to sea. Up to the sky and impossible to read.

'Look, see rats coming up,' he screeched. 'You need stick so you can bash him!'

Thrashing in the salty water, desperate to gain dry land, hundreds of terrified rats, blind in the unfamiliar sunlight, made a dash for the shore. Overhead, birds shrieked. In the water, doomed rats squealed for salvation. On shore, the yelling was intense. Someone had laid a bet on who would kill the most and money was exchanging hands.

The sun beat down. The racket on the dunes was too much. Coop clutched his head and tried to cool the scorching thoughts in his brain. What on earth had he signed himself up for?

CHAPTER 7

MARCH ROLLED IN WITH a fresh wave of homesickness.

Maisie sank back in her chair and shut her eyes, trying to recall the detail of the park opposite her parents' house, with its railings painted midnight black, its bright yellow daffodils and neatly trimmed hedges. In the ten days she had been in the Bay, England would have started to turn green, and the soft spring grass would soon appear in bright juicy tufts. She hated the suffocating humidity, the heat and the pervasive red dust and the endless hours she spent cooped up in the house on her own. She had set out to be a good wife and offer Maitland affection and companionship, but what sort of existence was he offering her when he was out of the house all day and slept alone in his own room at night? She found it both puzzling and worrying that he didn't seem to desire a wife in the physical sense of the word; he wanted a well-connected facilitator who did what he said and didn't answer back.

The first time Maisie had entertained Maitland's friends, four or five days after she arrived in the Bay, Duc threatened to leave.

'White bossman bad. I tell boss fella. No can work here no more. Knife and fork sit on table. Why's important who they next to?'

Maitland had insisted he set the table with a white tablecloth and use the new dinner service Maisie had brought from England.

'I no know who sit next to who. Boss he go shouty mad and smash booze bottle.'

Maisie managed to calm him down and explained that cutlery was put on the table in the order that the food would appear, from outside to in. The soup spoon, dinner knife, dessert spoon, cheese knife on the right, and the side plate, large fork, dessert fork on the left.

In upsetting the domestic applecart, though, Maitland had badly misjudged his wife. He hadn't in the least expected her to go into bat for their staff.

'I call the tune on domestic arrangements, Maitland, and let's be quite clear: you do not raise your hand to nor do you bully Duc. Ever. He is loyal to us both and you are to treat him with respect.'

Maitland looked taken aback. 'My castle, my rules.'

'No, Maitland. Duc lives on our property and we are responsible for his welfare as his employers. Anyone with domestic staff has a duty of care whether they live in an English stately home or a bungalow in Buccaneer Bay.'

Maitland was what her father would have called a ruthless social climber. He had backed down in the face of ruffled social propriety.

Propriety . . . After an early meeting at the church this morning, Maisie had endured an hour at the knitting circle and was now drooping on the verandah, her clothes clinging damply to her skin, her feet puffed up and sticky inside her shoes. She stared listlessly across at the discarded knitting dolly the bishop's wife had given her and bit her bottom lip.

Winding a strand of hot scratchy wool round and round four pegs held scant appeal. The wool made her hands sweat, and she couldn't see the point of creating yards of useless rope. She didn't want to make a teapot cover or egg cosy or, frankly, anything whose purpose was to keep the heat in. She closed her eyes and tried to think of things that would make her feel cold: snow, frost, ice, her mother's freezing study.

Mrs Wallace had been very clear in her advice at Port Fremantle and had reiterated it since in her letter. *I do sense your resentment and frustration, but what you mustn't do, Maisie dear, is mourn your life at home or chafe against small-town isolation. You must fit in and adapt or you will find yourself a very lonely young lady. And don't attempt to change your husband or refuse his advances. It won't work and he will make you miserable and likely plant his affections elsewhere. The best thing you can do for the health of your marriage is have a baby and develop an interest of your own.*

Maisie was making a great effort to fit in, but having a baby was another matter. Mrs Wallace had said that most men had insatiable bedroom urges. Maitland hadn't had one.

Maisie had been in the house a few days before she broached the subject of domestic staff.

'This is a large bungalow, Maitland. Don't you think we need someone to help Duc? He can't be expected to do all the household chores and cook as well. It is too much work for one person.'

'He's managed till now.'

She ran a finger over the arm of her chair. 'The house is dirty, and I'm sure he would appreciate some help.'

'Duc doesn't give a toss about cleaning, but get a houseboy if you want.'

'I'd really prefer not to have a boy. Aren't there black girls who can be taught?'

'I'm not having a black gin with the morals of a dog in my house. Lubras can't be tolerated in a decent home. They're all lazy and dishonest. Disease and dissipation is what you'll bring into this house. Pound to a penny, she'd steal my whisky or creep into my bed at night.'

'Maitland! I know I've only just arrived and understand very little of what goes on here but I'm sure you must be exaggerating. I can't believe that every Aboriginal woman in Buccaneer Bay has flawed morals or a propensity towards theft.'

'You have no idea what you're talking about.'

Maisie was stung by his tone. 'Why did you bring me out to Australia, Maitland? You do nothing but snipe at me. I'm sure I would annoy you less if you were to spend a bit of time at home and give me some guidance.'

He took a cigarette from the box on the table and lit it. Blowing smoke towards the ceiling, he shook out the match. 'I see the little mouse is growing fangs.'

She said nothing. Just sat. *That would make me a rat, wouldn't it, Maitland, and there's no room for two in this house.*

The disagreement had persisted all evening but Maisie would not give in. Just before midnight, Maitland drained his umpteenth glass of whisky and pressed his flabby hands against his ears.

'No more, Maisie. I'm going to bed.'

Maitland had not referred to their domestic arrangements again, and two days after their argument, Marjorie had appeared on their doorstep.

'I want to speak with the new Missus,' she said. 'I come allonga work in house.'

'I'm Mrs Sinclair.'

'I'm Black Marjorie.'

'Is that both your names?' Maisie knew that the French always gave their surname before their first name. Maybe it was the same here.

'No. Is how you refer to me. I bin Marjorie. My colour is black.'

'Marjorie, I can't refer to you as black. It's very offensive. It would be like you calling me White Mrs Sinclair. Or calling our cook Brown Duc.'

'It's okay.'

'I'm sorry, Marjorie. It is not okay to me. I shall not call you Black.'

'Okay, Missus. You might like know anyhow we call white people Paleface. So, you would be Paleface Missus. Just so's you know.'

Maisie was deeply affected by colour: the tomato-red earth, the brilliant red heads on the poinciana blossoms and the cool lime-green bird-of-paradise hedge with its orange pea-flower plumes that bordered her garden. By day, the Bay was bathed in painful white sunlight, which sparkled on the multi-hued ocean; at night, the dark navy sky was studded with dripping silver stars. She loved the vibrancy of the artist's palette, but she would never refer to people by their colour.

Marjorie was an amply proportioned native woman about thirty years old and told Maisie she had been trained in domestic duties by the nuns at the Catholic Mission. She was as bright as sunlight and right from the start, as a small child, had wanted to learn. To get to school she had to walk nearly four miles a day each way. In the Wet, walking in the heat and then slushing through the cloying mud was the stumbling block – because Marjorie did not own shoes. The soles of her feet blistered in the hot sand or became infected in the cruddy monsoon sludge. At first, she'd tried to jump from grass patch to grass patch waiting for her feet to cool or dry off. Once she'd proposed a shoe-sharing scheme with a friend who had a pair of second-hand boots. The friend would wear the left and she the right – but they'd both regretted the blisters. Another time she'd tried to hop on alternate legs but the effort had been too much. She'd given up with school after that.

Maisie liked Marjorie very much.

A bird flew out of a tree and vented a long plangent cry. The sound shook Maisie out of her torpor. She raised herself up out of the cane recliner and looked beyond the fly-netted verandah, trying to identify what had made the noise. She frowned. Duc and Marjorie were out on errands, and there was a *man* in the garden sitting with his legs splayed wide and his back to a large poinciana tree.

He was not the first native man she had seen. He was about twenty years old, she guessed, and she could see that he had patches of raw skin on his face. He had a large head with a rounded forehead and his eyelids were half-closed. She wondered at first if he was asleep, but from time to time he lifted his hand and wafted it to shoo the flies from his eyes. His nose was large and shaped like a bottle, and hung over full lips and a wide mouth. His hair held her attention. It was as black as tar, girlishly curly and fell to his shoulders like a fur cape. After a while, he stood and stretched his hands behind his back, pulling his shoulders square. She could see that he was tall, straight-backed and very thin. His ribcage projected through the thin fabric of his shirt. She could almost count the bones.

He looked towards the house and called to her. 'Missus. I needa water the grass but mule's gone allonga walkabout.'

'I'm sorry.' Maisie took a step backwards. 'I don't know who you are.'

'I bin look after garden. I Charlie.'

'Charlie.' She lingered over his name, wondering what to say next. 'Why do you need the mule to water the garden?'

'To fetch water from soak.'

'Oh. I see.' She didn't see at all. 'Where's the soak?'

He tapped his nose with his fingertip. 'Only mob know.'

'Mob?'

'Family. All the aunties and uncles.'

'So, a secret location then?'

He lifted up his head and squinted at her.

'Why do you need to water the grass? It rains nearly every day.'

'I's bin water Tuesday. I gonna water or boss man go crazy.'

There were tanks at each of the four corners of the house, which collected the rainwater they used in the house and for drinking.

'Why don't you use the tank water?'

'Taps bin locked, Missus. We don't use that water for grass.'

'Well then, use the artesian water.' She threw her arm at the large square tank partially screened behind a hedge that held groundwater from the well.

She wanted the job done and the man out of her garden.

Charlie looked doubtful. 'I dunno.' He dipped his head downwards like a dejected animal.

'Use the artesian water, Charlie. We use it for the laundry. It will be fine for once.'

He stared at her, his round face vacant.

'It will be fine,' she repeated. 'You need to get on with your work.'

He rolled his dark eyes and set off towards the high tank stand. His boots had no laces and plip-plopped on the hard earth.

At five o'clock Maitland slammed into the house, rattling the storm shutters on their cabled moorings. Maisie looked up from her desk, her pen a mid-air question mark.

Her husband poured himself a measure of scotch and planted himself before her. He eyed the notepad on her desk. 'What's that for?'

She covered her letter to Mrs Wallace with her hand. 'I'm making notes.'

'About what?'

'The benefits of being married to you,' she said, a flash of sarcasm in her voice.

He flung out a fat hand and swiped her writing paper to the floor. An ugly look twisted his face. 'I don't intend to take any lip from you.'

You wouldn't have to if you were ever civil to me, she thought.

'The bloody Abo has burned the grass. Wait till I get hold of him, he'll be sorry for this. I'll bloody skin him alive.'

'What's happened?'

'There's brown marks all over the lawn is what's damn well happened. He's bloody wrecked my bowling green. That nigger needs a lesson he won't forget in a hurry.'

'Charlie said the mule wasn't here so he couldn't get to the soak.' Maisie fiddled with the neck of her blouse.

'Charlie? When have you been on sodding first-name terms with the bloody blacks?'

'Do you want me to call him Mr Charlie, Maitland?'

He leaned his hands against the mosquito netting and stared out through the lattice. 'He's got legs, hasn't he? He could have walked. These Abos are not worth a fart in a whirlwind. They go walkabout for weeks at a time but walk to a well? Might as well ask them to walk to the moon.'

'I'm sure it was a misunderstanding, Maitland. He doesn't have your education or your brains.' She hoped the flattery might calm him down. 'Anyway, *I* told him to use the artesian water because the taps were locked. If it's anyone's fault, it's mine.'

'Don't think about defending him, Maisie. Even a half-wit would know not to use that water. You make yourself look ridiculous – and talking of being bloody idle, what the dickens have you done all day? I'm sick of you loafing about writing non-stop letters to England and that sheep farmer's wife you met on the ship. If you want to wield your pen so much you can take over running the slop chest off the schooner.'

Maisie opened and closed the lid on the silver inkwell. 'What would I have to do?'

Maitland stepped back from the lattice and drained his glass.

'If you want me to help you with the slop chest, Maitland, you are going to have to fill me in. I am not prepared to commit to do a job if I don't know what it entails.'

‘I’m not asking you to sail the bloody schooner single-handed, Maisie.’

‘Then tell me what the schooner’s for. What is the difference between the lugger and the schooner, for example?’

He turned his empty glass upside down and began to move it across the desk. ‘The lugger is the working boat. Got that? The divers bring up the shell we sell and store it on the boat but–’ He held up two fingers. ‘Two things. The luggers are small, and the pearling beds are way out from port. The schooner is the boat that carries the supplies and goes out to the fleet to take off the shell and leave fresh rations for the men. That way, the luggers and crew can stay out and dive non-stop, which is what we pay them to do.’

‘For six days a week, dawn to dusk through nine months of the year.’

‘Who told you that?’

‘I have ears, Maitland. What do I have to do on the supply ship?’

‘First thing to understand is we run the schooner to make a profit. You count the shell, double-check it against the diver’s tally book and record it in the shell ledger. Shell is sold by the ton, and fifteen hundred pairs of shell equal a ton, give or take. You need to keep your wits about you because some of these Jap bastards will try to get you to falsify their shell weights in the shell books.’

‘Why would they do that?’

‘To make them seem better than they are. If they get a reputation as a crack diver they can negotiate better advances on their pay for the following year. They’re all thieving bastards.’

‘I am sure there is the odd honest diver about, Maitland. What else would I have to do?’

'The lugger crew's mail comes to the packing office and you take it out to them. It's tied up in red tape and they have to sign for it. They row over to you, first with the shell – which comes on board in baskets. They take the mail and then they row back again when the slop chest opens.'

'Which is what?'

'Our floating emporium. We carry anything that a bloke might be missing after a few weeks at sea. Tea, coffee, tobacco, fruitcake, tins of fruit and veg, tons of other man stuff, and gallons of grog. We record it as a cash advance against their wages in one ledger and the actual items we've sold in another.'

'Why the double entry?'

Maitland didn't reply. He picked up the letter knife and began to ply it back and forth between his knuckles.

'I'm not doing the paperwork if you don't explain why, Maitland.'

'We get fleeced enough for export duty on the shell we sell at four pounds per ton. This is a way of ensuring that we avoid customs duty levied on the goods we sell the men.'

'So, the customs duty officer sees nothing amiss in the accounts books and you keep track on the stock to replace in another. Do you give it a hefty mark-up as well?'

Maitland ignored the question. 'Think you'll manage the job?'

'I'll muddle along,' she said.

He pulled back towards the door and smacked his leg hard against the corner of her desk. 'And move this bloody furniture back to where it was.' He snatched up a stockwhip from one of the cane chairs. 'I didn't say you could rearrange the whole sodding house.'

It was on her lips to say that it was Duc who had moved it out of position, but the words died, unformed. 'What's that for?' She glanced at the whip.

'I use it to school the horses.' He gave her a hard look, as if daring her to argue.

It was late afternoon, the red pindan stained gold by the sinking sun, when Maitland caught up with his gardener. In his right hand, the stockwhip handle felt smooth and familiar – an old friend returned home after a long absence. The whip had cost him a small fortune. Made of tanned kangaroo hide and crafted for him in Queensland, it was loaded and balanced to suit the particular usage he'd specified.

This wasn't the first time he would belt the guts out of a black.

Action. Reaction. There was no guilt involved. Maitland had no fear that retribution might be wrong. Driven hard into his belief, like crucifixion nails into human flesh, pain was linked to sin. The bastard black had burned his lawn and he was going to pay.

The Abo hadn't been hard to follow. He'd almost invited it. The stupid bastard had shuffled through the bush, kicking up a dust plume as high as a fucking flare. He'd heard the police force were thinking of using the Abos as trackers. That had to be a bloody joke. The sodding bastard was on his back in the scrub, slumped on the ground like a drunk. Head in the shade, jammed hard against a gum tree, his legs were splayed wide, at ease in the sunshine. He was fast asleep, the corners of his mouth slack.

Maitland took off his jacket, folded it carefully lining side out and hung it on the tree.

He woke the Abo with a boot to his crotch.

'Wake up, you fucking bastard. You burn my fucking lawn because you're too idle to get off your skinny arse and think I won't care?'

Charlie rolled over, shielding his genitalia with his arms.

Maitland squeezed the handle of his whip and, nodding to himself, laid a stripe across the young man's cheek. He watched the blood bead up from the broken flesh. He thought first of pearls – dozens of tiny pearls lined up in a neat row – but he changed his mind. The beads were dark red. More like garnets, he decided.

Charlie pulled his face down towards his shoulder.

Maitland's boot to his bum flipped him on his face. He swung the whip again and again, the plaited thong landing anywhere it could find. He enjoyed the sound, the snap and crack of leather against skin.

'Learned your lesson yet, you black fucker?'

Charlie tried to make himself smaller.

Maitland was affronted by his silence, the silent acceptance of his lot. There should have been something. A scream. An apology. A pitiful begging for him to stop. A sob at the very least.

Maitland pulled his legs straight and yanked down his trousers. He unbuttoned his own fly and doled out something extra, just to be sure he'd really got the message.

Funny how you notice things. The Abo had ruined boots. The leather scraped clean off the toes, no laces. Not even metal eyelets where the laces should have been. *Who the fuck wears boots with no laces?*

Maitland took his jacket off the tree and flung it over his shoulder. He felt a little too warm to put it on straightaway.

On the way back to his bungalow, Maitland took a final glimpse over his shoulder and began to whistle. He'd always had a good ear for a tune and he liked the hymn. 'Comfort, comfort ye my people'.

It seemed fitting somehow.

When Maisie woke the next morning, the sun was already well up. Maitland had made it clear from day one that he didn't want to see her at breakfast, so a tray was brought to her room. She found his temperament difficult to fathom and even harder to manage, but she was learning to recognise the signs. It hadn't taken her long to work out how the land lay. She kept out of his way before he left for the packing shed. He was never in the best of moods first thing in the morning, and she couldn't fake much sympathy for his self-inflicted hangovers. She listened for sounds of him, then relaxed against her pillows.

There was a persistent tapping at the back of the house, a scramble of sound she couldn't unravel. Maisie kicked the bedclothes off her feet, reaching for her floral cotton wrapper. It was too hot to wear it, but Mrs Wallace had been insistent. Propriety must be observed if she was not alone and the house unlocked.

'Marjorie,' she called. 'There's someone at the back.'

Tap, tap, tap.

'Marjorie!'

Tightening the belt around her waist and holding the wrapper closed across her chest, Maisie pushed her feet into slippers and followed the noise along the verandah, patting her overnight hair into place with her free hand. She could see Marjorie in the garden, hanging out bedsheets on two long wire lines. She was wearing a white cap and apron over a brown frock and had bunged her ears with wine-bottle corks. Duc was singing in the kitchen and his voice was a shocker. No wonder she'd not heard the tapping.

'Hello?'

A tea-coloured face peered in through the netted lattice.

'Mem. Doctor Shin says can you come?'

'Who is Doctor Shin?'

'Japanese doctor at hospital.'

'Now?'

'Very urgent. I have letter.' The young Malay held up an envelope so she could see it through the flyscreen. She read her name, written in loopy black ink.

She opened the door and stretched out her hand. The edges of the envelope had been stuck down tight against prying eyes. She went to fetch her letter-opener, instructing the boy to stay where he was. She worked the tip under an edge and slit through the paper casing with the sharp blade. It contained a single sheet of flimsy paper. The message made her stomach churn. She folded it, stowed it in her pocket then went back to the boy.

'Tell Doctor Shin that I am coming straightaway. I will get dressed and then I will come. Do you understand?'

'Yes, Mem. I tell Doctor Shin you come soon.'

Maisie took the bicycle from the side of the house and decided to pedal along Royal Avenue to the Japanese hospital – it would be quicker than asking for the sulky. She tucked her skirt up to clear the chain. In London, she had bicycled a lot and had a skirt with full flat pleats that gave her plenty of room to pedal. She'd left it in England, though, not thinking for a moment she would need it here.

It was hot enough to fry an egg on the handlebars, and for once she was glad to wear gloves and insulate her hands from the sticky rubber grips. Thick coastal bush grew either side of the road but there was no shade to speak of. She squinted as the glare from the white shell road knifed at her eyes.

Buccaneer Bay was set out on a grid system, the township stretching two miles from the lighthouse to the Japanese hospital. At the fourth block, she passed the government hospital, which was little more than a large house under attack from white ants. The peeling paintwork testified to its neglect.

As Maisie pedalled past the blistered front entrance, she went over Miss Locke's whispered words at the knitting circle the previous week. She had wanted to know if there was a good doctor in the town, one who might help her find a way to conquer The Visitor without knocking herself out every month.

'The British doctor is not in good health. He's ex-Indian Army. You may have seen him at parties. He reeks of stale brandy and cheap tobacco. I probably shouldn't say this but his patients look healthier than he does. He is pale and mottled and his hands tremble. I have heard, too, that he is not well qualified, but that might be nasty gossip. What I can tell you, though, is that at the hospital there is no provision for ladies. With those things we must endure. I am sure when the time comes, you will want to go home to have your babies. Or travel to Perth.'

Maisie flushed and fanned her face with a knitting pattern. She scrabbled around for a change of subject.

'What happens to people who are really poorly?'

'Any infectious disease is dealt with by putting the sufferer in a bungalow in the grounds. There was a Japanese sailor who came here a couple of years ago who had the small pox. The doctor installed him in a tent on the beach. The Jap died, but the disease didn't spread. So, that was a good thing. They never put him in the hospital.'

'Is there no alternative? Another physician?' Maisie had asked. 'Or must we sail back to Port Fremantle?'

Miss Locke swept the room with her eyes. 'Can I trust you, Mrs Sinclair?'

Maisie nodded.

'A few of us – what you might call the more broad-minded among the Britishers – consult the doctor at the Japanese hospital. He speaks excellent English and treats the usual range of medical problems you might expect out here. Broken bones, runny noses and prickly heat. He's very discreet.'

'I'm surprised that a Japanese hospital has been allowed to exist. It seems improbable that the town would permit it to happen.'

Miss Locke coughed and lowered her voice. 'You are quite right, Mrs Sinclair. At the start, when it was first discussed, the existence of the Japanese hospital and a Japanese doctor in Buccaneer Bay was not at all popular. The mayor told everyone the very idea was an example of non-white races challenging the authority of the white man. He had the support of his business colleagues here, but there was an entire workforce of Japanese in town holding down myriad types of job, from gardener to deep-sea diver – and they wanted their own Japanese-speaking doctor. During the lay-up, there are about two thousand Japanese men in Buccaneer Bay.'

Miss Locke glanced round the room, inched forward in her seat and clicked her needles loudly.

'I think the problem was that all the plans regarding the building of the hospital and appointing a doctor were made in secret. By the time the mayor realised what was afoot, the Japanese had sought the assistance of the consul general in Sydney and he had expedited the whole process. The new doctor and his wife arrived soon after and the hospital was built almost overnight, funded by donations from the Asian community.'

Maisie tried to concentrate on what she was being told. 'But, Miss Locke, you said the government hospital offered very little in terms of medical care, so surely this was a good thing?'

'Yes and no. It's a good thing to finally have a medical facility that could actually care for the sick, but everyone here was scared that the Asians might think themselves equal to the European. That is what everyone fears. Every day the government preaches its White Australia policy and wants the coloured workforce banished from its shores, but . . .' Miss Locke cast another anxious eye at the fellow knitters. 'The Japanese venture is a success. No-one can deny that. The doctor now has more patients than he could possibly have imagined, and a lot of them are white. We just try not to talk about it too much.'

At the Japanese hospital, Maisie leaned her bicycle against a broad-leafed mulga tree. The humidity was drenching. She peeled off her gloves and fished in her skirt pocket for a handkerchief, mopped her throat and forehead, and pushed open the front door.

Doctor Shin sat on a stool in his office, a cigarette hanging from his lips. Wearing a white doctor's coat to protect his clothes, he was small and neat, his fingers stained yellow, his mouth full of gold teeth. He stubbed his cigarette, stood, bowed and seemed relieved. 'Mrs Sinclair. I am most indebted to you. Thank you for coming.'

Maisie put her hands together and bowed back. It seemed natural.

'Please come with me, dear madam. I am at a loss with the magnitude of what has occurred.'

The doctor led her down a long stretch of corridor. She saw that many of the side wards were occupied.

'Is there much sickness in Buccaneer Bay at the moment, Doctor Shin? I haven't heard that we have an epidemic.' She pressed the edges of her blouse round her throat.

'No, dear lady. These patients have the divers' paralysis.'

'These are all divers who can't move?'

'Some can, a little. Some are more affected.'

'In what way?'

'I'm not sure, but I am attempting to make a study. These men are hard-hat divers who spend their days on the seabed – most often at great depths – collecting shell. I have read many reports from the *British Medical Journal* and I believe that, under pressure, the human body becomes saturated with nitrogen. While the diver remains at the same depth the pressure is constant and he is in no discomfort. Think of the diver as a bottle of champagne. When he comes up gently from the seabed, the nitrogen releases into his bloodstream with a little fizz. But if he comes up too quickly it is like shaking up the bottle. At the surface, the bubbles explode into his body exactly like the moment when the champagne cork pops out. It affects their joints the most, and is painful almost beyond bearing.'

'Surely it would make sense to come up slowly and avoid the pain.'

'Some divers do come up in stages and still suffer the paralysis. Other divers sink to the depths day after day and are not affected. This is why I am trying to make a study to try to find out why this happens, scientifically. Everyone has his theory. Some think that thin men with long necks do not suffer, while barrel-chested men with short necks will be dead after a few weeks. White men, the crews say, are particularly at risk.'

'But that's incredibly worrying. All the new divers are white, Doctor Shin. Are they not committing suicide by diving for shell?'

'Time will tell. They have come from England boasting the latest equipment and diving charts to regulate their ascent from the bottom of the ocean. Let us hope it will be enough to keep them safe. But let me show you why I asked you to come to the hospital today.' He pushed open a door at the end of the corridor and stood back to let her through.

It occurred to Maisie that this was the first time a man had shared his thoughts with her without patronising simplification – as if she were an equal, capable of understanding.

The treatment room was stuffy and it seemed to her that evil had been trapped in the airless room. Charlie lay on his front, arms by his sides, fingers splayed. Blood-soaked sheets were pulled down off his body in a twist of hospital cotton, and the acrid odour of the young man's sweat nearly overwhelmed her. She took a step back, thinking she might faint, and clasped her hands tight.

'I found him on the steps this morning,' Doctor Shin said.

'How did he get there?'

'The night-pan collector brought him on his cart.'

She stared at the young man on the trolley, her face white with shock. 'Why didn't you treat his injuries straightaway?'

'I need an assistant. You will understand, Mrs Sinclair, in a moment.'

Charlie had told Doctor Shin – in rambling fragments – that he'd waited a long time in the garden for Captain Sinclair so he could explain that the woman in the house had told him to water the grass with the artesian water. When it was knocking-off time, he'd set off into the bush. He didn't think the boss would track him down and whip him.

'But why have you asked for *my* help, Doctor Shin? You must have qualified staff to assist you?'

He waggled his fingers towards the patient. 'Would you not prefer it this way? Would you like it to be public knowledge that your husband was capable of this?'

Maisie stood up straight but couldn't look him in the eye. She understood the value of what she had been offered, and knew she was now bound in some inexplicable way to the Japanese doctor.

'The responsibility for this must be laid at my door, Doctor Shin,' she said finally. 'Charlie told me that he was not supposed to use the artesian water on the grass but I wouldn't listen because I wanted him out of the garden.' She stabbed at her chest. 'I am the cause of this – every bit as much as Maitland.'

Doctor Shin positioned himself at Charlie's head. 'You cannot share the blame in this, Mrs Sinclair. Look closely at what your husband has done. Some of the cuts are an inch wide and twelve inches long. You can see that there are bits of fabric cut into his flesh – half-an-inch deep in some places. This is not a mere whipping. It is a murderous assault. A man would not beat a dog so severely. We must wash his back and his arms and shoulders and everywhere that terrible thing has cut him. Do you think you could assist me?'

Maisie first shook her head, then nodded. She always nodded. It was less painful to agree even if sentiment told her not to. The doctor watched her scrub her hands in the sink then select a pair of forceps from a kidney dish. She began to pick strands of cloth from the weals.

'Do you have medical training, Mrs Sinclair?'

For a second, Maisie's face froze. She had wanted to be a nurse like Florence Nightingale and had tried hard to persuade her mother. *Don't be ridiculous, Maisie. You haven't the mental tenacity for study.*

She swallowed hard. 'No. I did some voluntary work in a hospital in England but that's all forgotten now.'

'There are no trained nurses in Buccaneer Bay. I had a nurse coming to join me from Perth, but she changed her mind when she stepped off the steamer, and went straight back. The nuns at the Mission have been helping to nurse my patients.'

'Does that work?'

'Sister O'Reagan came at the start and has taken charge of the hospital. But she is not a trained nurse. She is very kind, but not a professional.'

'Is Charlie in great danger?'

'Is there any other kind?' he said in a tone that offered little hope. 'I am very worried, Mrs Sinclair. His clothes weren't clean, and dirt is the unseen enemy of torn flesh.'

'I know that, Doctor. Miss Nightingale founded the nursing school where I volunteered. She preaches the importance of hygiene.'

'I'm going to try a dry antiseptic in these cuts. Ointment is no good in this humidity, as wounds fester. Can you help me puff this white powder onto the welts?'

Maisie nodded and did the best she could.

The light was fading by the time they finished. They were packing up, washing hands, preparing to leave when she noticed an object on a small table next to the treatment couch.

'What is that?' She motioned with her chin.

'It's Charlie's dilly-bag.'

She scratched her cheek, puzzled.

'It is made of kangaroo hide, which the natives soften with grease. The strap is made of plaited human hair. His own, probably.'

She stroked the soft pouch, her fingers tracing the outline of its contents. 'What would he keep inside, do you think?'

'Take a look.'

'Oh no, I couldn't. It would be like looking inside someone's handbag, or reading his private journal.'

'Consider it in the interests of anthropological understanding.'

Maisie hesitated. It felt wrong.

'Go on,' the doctor encouraged.

She slid her hand into the dilly-bag and drew out four stones, the beak of a small bird, a pointed length of bone and a plug of chewing tobacco. She separated them with her finger.

'Charlie's a medicine man,' he said.

'How do you know?'

'Miss Locke is conducting a study of Aborigines. Have you met her?'

'Yes, a few times.'

'If you work in a mixed-race community, Mrs Sinclair, it is one's duty – particularly as a physician – to try to understand the customs and beliefs of the patients in one's care. It would be most disagreeable to offend. Miss Locke advised me that the stones are for healing and the bird's beak is a charm.'

'And the piece of bone? It looks like a long needle.'

'His killing bone. For curses.'

She blinked. 'Go on.'

'I would guess he is a Kurdaitcha man. What you might call a ritual executioner.'

Maisie carefully replaced his belongings in the kangaroo pouch. 'The raw patches on his face. I saw them there before this beating. They are not new.' She pushed a strand of hair off Charlie's cheek and ran the back of her hand over his skin, his bones sharp against her fingers. The doctor watched her face.

'Did you expect black skin to feel different?'

'Um. I . . .' Heat stained her cheeks.

'He also has two badly blackened eyes and bruises on his face. Not so obvious on darker skin. But they're there all the same.'

'Do you think that my husband–'

The doctor cut her short. 'I'll ask Sister O'Reagan to sit with him overnight. She will need to re-apply the powder at intervals. It might numb the pain, though I doubt it will help a great deal.'

A tear leaked out of the corner of the Aboriginal man's eye and trickled down his cheek. Maisie pulled her handkerchief from her pocket and gently dabbed his face.

'We know who did this to Charlie and maybe the other, older injuries too.'

She swallowed hard. Her mouth had gone dry and she tried to moisten her lips with her tongue. She watched his thin back lift and fall and wished with all she held dear she could give him some relief. She looked up at the doctor and something in his expression – acceptance, understanding or sorrow – made her heart quicken. 'Are you going to report my husband to the authorities?'

'What would be the point, Mrs Sinclair? The white man rules this town. Your husband is in cahoots with the mayor. He is an important white fish, as you say. We have police constables and a resident magistrate, but laws that are passed in cities thousands of miles away are not enforced here in Buccaneer Bay, certainly not when it is a case of native versus a white man. Government officials seldom visit this little town. If a law is inconvenient, it is ignored. The financial and physical abuse of the indentured workforce will continue and the Aborigines will forever be viewed as malingerers out to cheat the white man. No-one will be called to account, and I can't see that this will change any time soon. So, I will continue to repair the physical damage that comes with diving too deep, poor nutrition, or working for a violent boss. It is what I trained to do as a doctor. But, Mrs Sinclair, if this is your husband's handiwork . . .' He nodded at the patient on the treatment couch. 'It is *you*, dear madam, who must take the utmost care.'

CHAPTER 8

MAISIE WAS IN A flap. Her one formal dress, not counting her unworn wedding gown, was covered in black mould. There was no point in regretting Mrs Wallace's advice about stocking up on dinner wear; she hadn't believed she would need it. She fought to keep the panic out of her voice. 'Marjorie. Could you come and help me, please?'

Marjorie was mopping the wide jarrah floorboards on the verandah. The wine-bottle corks were now plugged in her nostrils. The greasy floor polish was a potent cocktail of tobacco, wax and kerosene, and she was not impressed with the smell.

'Missus. Why's your face look like a bruised banana?' She removed the corks from her nose and put them in her apron pocket.

'Look.' Maisie pointed at her dress.

'It's the mouldy. Should've sewn it into one of them calico bags.'

'Well, I didn't, as you can see. I didn't realise I needed to insulate my clothes against this hideous climate. I've barely been here a few weeks. I have the party tonight and now I have nothing to wear. I'll not be able to go.'

'You told me you're top guest. You have to go, or the ladies will talk and boss fella go crazy mad. So's unless you's stone-cold dead in a coffin box, you's goin' to dat party.'

'Can you do anything?'

'Can't wash it, Missus. Could mebbe try sponge with baking soda.'

'Will that work?'

'Mebbe. We sponge and put in the sunshine. Maybe mister sun will bleach the black spots.'

'All right. Shall I help you?'

'No.'

'Shall I finish the polishing?'

Marjorie stared at her. 'I told you before you ain't to go cleaning.'

'I want to help you, Marjorie. I can't just sit here when I see you working and I have nothing to do all day.'

'Okay. You go ask Duc for the baking soda and put him in a cup. Use the inside water and stir it 'bout. Don't use bore water. Him'll go brown. Then we do spongin' and prayin'.'

'Praying?'

'I was raised a good Catholic by the nuns. Of course I do prayin'.'

Maisie studied the serious face and laughed out loud. 'And I, Marjorie, thank the Lord every day for sending you to me.'

Marjorie was unmoved. 'Mebbe we should look at your gloves and shoes in case mouldy have attacked him too.'

Maisie was relieved. Maitland was in a good mood. Tonight was easy. He had taken his whisky into his dressing room and had been ages getting ready. She knew he liked parties. He loved the attention, the banter with his friends and the endless drinking. She, though, was not so comfortable. Marjorie had rescued her dress – if one didn't look too closely – but she was dreading the event. She patted her disobedient hair, which had become as dry as old paper in the heat, and wished, not for the first time that day, that she could stay at home and soak for a very long time in a cool bath.

Dressed with time to spare, Maisie now sat on the verandah, sipping a glass of lemonade. Maitland was at the drinks table, an elaborate floral arrangement in his buttonhole, mixing things with a stick. He put down his glass and manoeuvred his leather purse into a tight trouser pocket then patted the bulge. He laughed and sloshed another fingerful of whisky into his tumbler. She supposed he was anticipating some gaming later on and was feeling lucky. It didn't bother her one jot as long as it sustained his mood.

The Sinclairs jog-trotted in the sulky to the mayoral party, Maitland flapping the reins irritably at the long-suffering horse. They left the elderly grey-muzzled beast tied up outside the hall with a skinny Aboriginal child who was paid a penny to watch it. From time to time its sweaty flanks quivered while the little boy swatted listlessly at the cloud of mosquitos.

William Cooper had no desire to go to the party, but John Butcher wasn't going to let him turn down a free meal. Coop wore his only suit, the same double-breasted wool two-piece that had parboiled him in Port Fremantle. It smelled of tobacco and stale sweat. Set off by a fancy white waistcoat, with ritzy socks peeking out above his patent-leather shoes, it was the best he could manage towards evening dress. He was uncomfortable in every respect. The event would showcase the haves and have-nots and deliberately emphasise the difference between them. He was not at ease in Buccaneer Bay, and longed to get on with the job he had come to do. The people here were unlike any he'd known in England, a hybrid population of different races, all vying for social position. He respected few, liked even fewer, but there was one who quickened his pulse. The second time he'd seen her on the steamer he'd been playing cards on deck and stared at her until his eyes burned. He'd longed to kiss her full lips. He shut his eyes and tried to block the memory; she had married his boss right in front of him, and Maisie Sinclair could never be anything to him but a beautiful dream. He would tell no-one. He was well used to keeping his feelings to himself. A born oyster, his father called him. If that were the case, then Maisie Sinclair was his pearl. The beautiful, lustrous secret that he would forever keep to himself.

He did not appreciate the white chalk line across the dance floor to mark off the dinner-suited colonists from the hoi polloi. It was a crude reminder to keep the masses away from their betters, and did nothing to improve his opinion of the upper stratum of white Buccaneer Bay society, such as the mayor and his cronies.

He had been watching Mrs Sinclair. Standing next to the stocky, bald captain with his brick-red complexion, she was wearing a pale pink dress and long white gloves, her fair hair caught up at the nape of her neck. He saw the faint colour in her ivory cheeks and guessed she was nervous. She had turned her head towards him and he thought the pickings of a smile lifted the corners of her mouth.

The insistent drill of his pulse reminded him that she could never know that he wanted more. He dipped his head in acknowledgement and then turned his back. He was a tradesman's son and she was class, but nature cared nothing for prejudice or social divide. He joined JB at the bar and set about getting comprehensively drunk.

With the exception of Maisie and the recent white imports, none of the party guests had set foot in England. It was all the more laughable, therefore, that this tiny white population, outnumbered ten to one by its coloured workforce, was trying to replicate something it could only imagine.

Dorothea Montague had copied the décor for the mayoral function from the society pages of an out-of-date English newspaper. It was exquisite in its cringing inappropriateness.

The long supper tables were covered in heavy gold cloth, bedecked with all manner of crystal and elaborate chafing dishes, laden with food more suited to a winter's evening in a chilly English dining room than a suffocating community building where the temperature rarely dropped below a hundred degrees. The serving staff were costumed in baggy white pantaloons, their brown, working hands covered with clumsy white gloves. The silver cutlery twinkled maliciously in the glare.

The evening ground on and Maisie longed for release. She was horrified to discover that Dorothea Montague was wearing a spotless version of Maisie's own dress, in a far more attractive shade. Maisie had only worn it once before in Buccaneer Bay, and the thought that her dress had been so carefully observed and copied did not trouble her as much as who had managed to do so.

The dark-haired English diver, she saw, was drinking at the bar. Had he noticed her? She smoothed the skirt of her dress and tucked up a wisp of hair. He made her feel self-conscious in a way she couldn't explain. She looked away and found herself abandoned in a large room where she hardly knew a soul.

Maitland had disappeared.

A waiter dressed in a ridiculous pantaloon suit like a character from the *Arabian Nights* walked past with an empty tray.

'Could I have a gin martini?' she said brightly. 'With ice.'

'What brand, madam?'

'Square Face.' It was her first rebellious step towards her new life, or a step away from her old. She didn't much care which.

When she'd received her drink, she slipped out onto the verandah and took a large gulp. 'Delicious!' she said to no-one in particular. The cold liquid was bitter perfection, and she began to relax a notch.

Someone else was on the verandah, further down, on the 'wrong' side of the chalk line. He had his back to her, but she saw the tip of a cigarette glowing in the dark and could smell tobacco. She pushed back into the shadows and watched the light, a spectator at a show.

He stood on the gas-lit verandah and wiped the sweat from his forehead with his shirt cuff. He was chain-smoking, flicking the tiny butt-ends towards the sea and drinking something with ice. She could hear the *ting ting* of crystals against the glass.

There were heels approaching, a purposeful tread clicking on the wooden floorboards. Maisie took another swig of gin, tucked herself behind a wooden post and sucked on the crunchy shards of ice. Miss Montague marched past her, face set, a huntress with her sights on her prey.

'Good evening, Mr Cooper. I hope you are enjoying the party.'

He spun round, an odd look on his face, Maisie thought. As if she was the last person he was expecting to see.

'Do you like my dress, Mr Cooper? I had it made here in town. It is copied from the very latest London design.'

'It's a pretty dress,' he acknowledged.

'I was wondering, Mr Cooper, if you would do me the very great honour of dancing with me? They are about to play the twelve-step and I adore taking a spin across the lovely polished floor. It is such fun. Would you, please?'

He took a step backwards. 'I'm not sure that it is fitting for you to be seen with me, Miss Montague. I am only permitted to stay on my side of the chalk line. I think it might restrict your enjoyment.'

The sarcasm was lost on Miss Montague. With the persistent audacity of naïve youth, she chattered on. 'Oh no! It would be completely acceptable if you were dancing with me. No-one would dare to say anything. My father's the mayor, you know.'

'Then I dare not refuse, do I?' he said, with determined pleasantness.

Maisie watched the pair head towards the spacious supper room, her thoughts swimming. Had Mrs Wallace not said that William Cooper was an inveterate ladies' man? And yet he had just tried gently to turn Miss Montague down. Dorothea clip-clipped along the floorboards and kept touching Cooper's arm as if to reassure herself he was still there. Moonlight bathed her profile and Maisie saw she was giggling to herself as if enjoying some enormous private joke.

I am becoming a slave to the King of Gin, Maisie thought as she drained the last of her drink, *and I don't care*. She pushed away from her hiding place, intent on fetching another – and found herself face to face with William Cooper.

He stepped to the side to allow her past. He had slackened off his collar, and a button had come loose on his waistcoat where it was hanging by a thread. *I could sew that on tight*, she thought. *If you asked me.*

'May I congratulate you on your recent marriage, Mrs Sinclair. I'm William Cooper, your husband's new diver.'

'Yes, I heard you speak on the steamship at Port Fremantle, and then you came to my assistance on deck when I knocked over my handbag.'

'I do remember that,' he said. 'Is there anything I can help you with just now?'

Maisie glanced towards the bar. 'Thank you, Mr Cooper. I was about to hunt out a drink.'

He smiled. 'It's stifling inside the supper room. I have been dancing with the delightful Miss Montague and came out to cool my heels. Perhaps I could fetch the drink for you?'

'That would be kind. I'm not sure where my husband has gone, but then I ought to be used to that by now.' The alcohol was loosening her tongue.

'It seems that some of the gentlemen are difficult to track down this evening. Miss Montague has mislaid her father too.' Cooper offered a wry dip of his eyebrows. *Mocking, but is he mocking me?*

She waited but he did not move. 'A gin martini, perhaps?'

'Yes,' he said. 'Allow me a few minutes to the bar and back.'

Maisie laughed lightly. 'Take your time. There's absolutely no rush.'

Blair Montague stretched back on his wicker chair in the room reserved for Masonic meetings and rolled his cigar between his palms. 'You heard anything from the Pearlers' Association, Mait?'

Seated next to him, Maitland Sinclair picked his nose. 'No. Have you?'

'Nothing yet, but they know I'm only standing in as president and I've talked you up as much as I can. Things take time. The wheels grind slowly, but no news is good news.'

'What do you reckon my chances are?'

'You're doing all the right things, but you need to quash the rumours. Exercise a little self-restraint.'

'Doing all of the above, Blair.'

Blair stopped to light his cigar. 'Good. Tongues wag, Mait, and we need to keep things tight. You need to inject some respectability into your life – or at least the semblance of it. I told you before. Now you've got the English wife, hump her and get her pregnant. Play the devoted family man, like I am. When the time comes, take your son swimming and fishing. Just divert the beam of suspicion from your door. Otherwise you are wasting your time. The Bay will never accept you properly and never vote you in.'

'They accepted *you*.' He flicked the contents of his nose into the air.

Blair's nostrils flared. 'I played by their rules. They saw what they wanted to see: devoted family man with wife and child.'

'Maisie isn't pregnant.'

'Jesus, Mait. Use some imagination. What about Mason? He's a horny bugger and is always round your place when he's not out with his fleet. If you can't manage it yourself, then get him on the job. Invite him over, get him to spend the night. He'll get himself inside your wife's knickers in no time.' Blair rubbed his eye with one finger, and let out a low, defeated sigh. 'The Wet won't last forever. We'll need to get the English boys out on the luggers. Show willing.'

'I've been thinking about that.'

The mayor extracted his handkerchief from his pocket and dabbed the corner of his eye. 'Oh yes?'

'I'm going to send Cooper out on the *Sharky* when the time is right. Training run, you could say.'

'That lugger's barely seaworthy, Mait.'

'That's the whole sodding point. It hasn't had a refit and the sails are full of rot. If there's a sudden blow it'll sort out the problem.'

'You can't make it too obvious.'

'I'm not a total tosspot. I'm keeping my eye on the barometer. As soon as we get a dip and an easterly wind I'll send the lugger out for two, maybe three, days with a skeleton crew. Cook, Squinty, Cooper and his tender, and one of the bolshy Jap divers to teach him what to do. They don't need a shell-opener. We can sort that out if they get back in. Might have to sacrifice the boat and crew, but it should be enough to make it look legit.'

'You got insurance on that old crate?'

'You insure any of yours?'

Blair rolled the tip of his cigar round the ashtray. 'Fair point, but I can afford to write off a lugger or two.'

'I'm not on my uppers, you know. I've got fingers in other pies. And let's face it: given the current climate, who's going to regret a brown face or two?'

Blair nodded. 'There's still a lot of men in town looking for work. I can always help you out if you're short.'

The annual intake of indentured workers took place in February, and the numbers were supposed to be strictly controlled according to the number of work permits held by each of the pearlers. At the end of a three-year contract – if the immigrant worker lived that long – the government decreed that the coloured alien must return to his country of origin. The vast majority did not, even though the official paperwork suggested that they had.

Blair Montague had far more permits than he was entitled to and had the sub-collector of customs on his payroll. He hired out his surplus labour, indentured or otherwise, in the manner of a recruitment agency. The workers did as they were told; the threat of deportation was a powerful rod.

'Cooper has that new motor air compressor with him. You prepared to lose that too if the lugger goes down?'

'Same thing, Blair: not my worry. The Japs won't use them. Bottom of the sea's the best place for it, if you ask me.'

'Okay. So, supposing there's no blow?'

'They come back, we offload the shell and send them out again with the rest of the fleet at the back end of the month. What we normally do. Totally above board.'

Blair leaned across the table for the ashtray and parked his cigar. 'Then what? Have you got anything else in place if that doesn't work?'

Maitland took a gulp of brandy and rolled it round his teeth. 'We keep all the English boys apart. We'll get them diving on the beds where the shell is gone, already worked out. Send them away from the rest of the fleet. I'm getting the *Hornet* ready and putting Maisie on board. She'll run it out to them so they can't get back into town to compare notes. You'll have to make sure that Espinell, Hanson and Mason, anyone else who's got white divers, are in on the plan.'

Blair pulled a sheet of paper from his pocket and scanned his notes. 'Yes, those are the blokes with the white boys. We'll get them together and put our cards on the table. And your wife – you got her trained already? Knows to keep her mouth shut?'

'No worries there.'

Blair cracked his neck from side to side. 'Any word from the girl's parents?'

Maitland shook his head.

'It's the mother's family with the money, isn't it?' Blair persisted.

'Yes. I told you they cut her off, remember.'

Blair held up his palms. 'Help me out, Mait, because I'm not following. Are we talking Maisie or her mother?'

'Jesus, Blair, try to keep up. Maisie's mother.'

'Why'd they cut her off?'

'I don't know. Maybe they didn't like her husband.'

Blair scratched an itch under his nose. 'Families, eh? Always bloody trouble.'

Maitland nodded, his face blank.

Blair looked at his watch. 'Better get back to the dance floor and give the girls a trot round. I'll do the presentation after supper. The collection is quite decent. We've got about a hundred quid. What about some gaming with the English blokes later on to win it all back?'

Maitland forced a smile but there was no joy in it. He clamped his pipe between his teeth and heaved himself up from his chair. Blair was a cunning snake, but Maitland was a slither or two ahead.

Maisie leaned back against the verandah rail and closed her eyes. She was more than halfway down a second martini and her head felt swimmy.

William Cooper was standing next to her and she could sense his eyes on her face. The concentration of his gaze made her nervous, and at least with her eyes shut she couldn't see him stare.

Wordless, she couldn't think how to cover the silence. In the distance they heard the hoot of a steamship.

Maisie blinked open her eyes and hoped that he would not read in them her relief. 'I will never be able to hear that sound without thinking of weeks on board. How was your journey out, Mr Cooper?'

'Necessary,' he said. 'How about your own?'

Compulsory, she wanted to shout. *Because my future was decided behind my back, written down on a piece of paper by your boss. Not my choice and not what I wanted by any leap of the imagination.*

'As tedious as your own,' she said. 'But we both had our particular reasons for travelling such a long way, did we not?'

William Cooper moved the ice round his glass with a finger.

She sailed on, navigating the awkwardness between them. 'Which is why we both find ourselves here tonight, celebrating your arrival in the Bay and the recent fact of my marriage.'

He gave his drink another stir and waved a dripping finger at the Masonic Room. 'I see the two missing gentlemen have been located.'

Liquid fell from his finger and raised little puffs of dry dust from the floorboards. Maisie turned to look at him and attributed the fluttering in her chest to the gin.

'Thank you for the drink, Mr Cooper.' She handed him her glass. 'If you will excuse me, however, I had better rejoin my party.'

CHAPTER 9

Maisie was tired, her head pounded and she longed for their guests to be gone. Every evening, for the handful of weeks she had been living in the Bay, Maitland had surrounded himself with people. He stacked them up like a wall. She'd dined with the bank manager, who spoke to her as if she had learning difficulties; the English doctor, who, Miss Locke had said, was a closet drunk; the bespectacled bishop with his tartan-clad wife; and, over and over, the hardcore drinking cronies who clinked glasses till the small hours. Maitland slipped in late and did everything he could to ensure they were never alone. By the time they had eaten supper, he was either so sleepy or so drunk that he went straight to his bed.

She knew all about avoidance – keeping out of the way, suppressing her thoughts, clamping her mouth shut and dodging blows. She had played the role of someone else so often it was second nature. It never turned off the inner monologue though.

The memory of their wedding night still gave her pause. She wished she had Mrs Wallace to talk to, with her trunkful of worldly wisdom, to unburden herself about that area of her married life she could never mention to anyone in the Bay. Good as her word, Mrs Wallace had sent the marriage-guidance book but it had given her no clues. Maitland still had made no attempt to claim his conjugal rights. Maybe he was being a gentleman and giving her time to adjust? She shook her head. No. That wasn't like Maitland at all. But this was not the normal way of married life, surely, if babies were to be made? There was also something else niggling at her about that frightful first night, but she couldn't bring it to the surface.

She'd once asked Maitland why he'd brought her to the Bay, but he'd never bothered to say. In fact, she hardly saw him. By breakfast each day, he was gone. By early afternoon, it was siesta time. Maitland did not reappear for lunch but returned before that same draining time of the day when nothing with legs moved in Buccaneer Bay. Only Duc's ancient goat – possibly the town's only resident with fewer brains than Dorothea Montague – was upright at that hour; even the angry blowflies sought the shade.

The supper guests were predominantly male. Maisie knew that networking with business colleagues was important. Her father brought his colleagues home on occasion and she had sat with her mother, silent spectators at the dinner table until it was time to retire, leaving cigars and port to the men. The women sipped their scalding coffee in her mother's icy parlour. Hot and cold: it was the way her mother blew.

Maisie shielded her mouth with her hand, disguising a yawn that almost cracked her jaw. Tonight, for the umpteenth time, it was the Montagues, a father-and-daughter combination she found particularly tedious.

The mayor, she thought, looked like a medieval page and larded his dinner conversation with fragments of schoolboy French.

She had seen pictures of his relatives in her history books. A lute, doublet and hose, and he would have been all set for life in fifteenth-century England. The black-haired Blondel (as she thought of him) was an oily *parvenu*. Dorothea, as shallow as a bedpan, was all curls and froth and personified the ridiculous idea of Englishness in their tiny settlement. Maisie knew it was mean-spirited of her and that she should have tried harder to make a friend of the mayor's daughter, but the reality was they had no common glue to bind them.

The residents she had met seemed to be trying to copy an ancient British class system they thought they could emulate but had no rulebook to follow. It seemed to Maisie the new-wave impostors were pouring all their financial resources into the appearance of possessing class without having the first idea what that meant.

Blair Montague bent towards her, an elbow glancing off the edge of the table. He repositioned his arm, stabilised it with his left hand and cupped his chin in his right palm.

'*Eh bien*, Mrs Sinclair. Do you hear often from your parents?'

Maitland's teeth chattered on his pipe stem.

Maisie held back another yawn. 'No, Mr Montague. I haven't heard from my parents. I suspect it has to do with the vagaries of the postal service.'

'But you write to them, *non*?'

'Religiously. I write to Mrs Wallace and she writes back every week using the postal steamer. Perhaps it's because England is so much further away that more things are apt to go wrong.'

Dorothea frowned and tapped her glass. 'It's very circumstantial that all your letters to England are unanswered. One might suspect a little sabotage, do you not think?'

'I think that's highly unlikely, *mon trésor*.' Blair put his hand on his daughter's wrist, and leaned forward to Maisie. 'And in the letters that Dorothea fears may have been spirited away by a malfeasant, what does Madame Sinclair tell her parents about her new life in Buccaneer Bay?'

Maisie tilted her head to one side and considered the question. In the lamplight, Maitland had taken on the appearance of a laboratory exhibit. His eyes glittered and the hot, cloying air had left a sweaty sheen on his pitted face. She shuddered. *My life as his wife?* She longed to tell someone how it really was: that he showed no interest in her; that he was a narrow-minded bigot; that his manners were studied and his behaviour was gross; that he must have a mistress – how else to explain his long absences from home and his lack of physical interest in her? Not to mention his cruelty; that he had almost murdered their gardener.

Maisie produced the lie. 'I say that I am settling in well, adjusting to married life in this trying climate and have made new friends.'

'And is Maitland keeping you busy?'

'In what respect?'

Blair Montague gave a nasty laugh. 'Running his beautiful home, looking after the staff and seeing to his needs.'

'And more besides, Mr Montague. I am not sure that looking after one's husband's needs is necessarily a cause for ridicule, however. Inside or outside the home, I am busy. Indeed, I am to run the *Hornet* supply schooner as soon as the Wet is over, and I am cultivating other interests.'

If Dorothea had noticed that Maisie had taken a stand against her boorish father, she made no show of it. 'Oh gosh, Mrs Sinclair. How thrilling. I'd love to sail away to distant lands on a schooner.

Dada and I sometimes have picnics on board our schooner but we don't put out to sea. Dada gets terribly seasick and he likes to be here to oversee everything from his offices. He has one office at the packing shed and one in our house, and he's always doing business, even after I have gone to bed. No wonder he gets tired and grumpy! I heard someone calling him a "verandah pearler" once.' She turned to her father, her eyes moist, like a puppy. 'I thought it summed you up perfectly, Popsie.'

The mayor's expression closed. Maisie had heard the term 'verandah pearler' too; Miss Locke had explained it behind a gloved hand. It wasn't complimentary. It referred to someone who conducted his pearling business from the safety of the shore, while his workforce risked all on the ocean floor to make him rich.

Maitland lurched for the port. 'Yes, Blair likes to run his business from his verandah with a whisky-and-soda in his hand.'

A look of slight enlightenment flickered across Dorothea's face. 'Mrs Sinclair, I have the perfect solution for you with your letter-writing conundrum. Why not send a cable! We have the cable-station office now, which connects us to the rest of the world via the colony of Java.'

This fact, casually introduced by Dorothea, threw all three of them into a spin. Maitland and Blair simultaneously reached for the grog. Maisie swallowed too quickly and gave herself hiccoughs.

'Yes. I think a cable would be the perfect answer.' Dorothea seemed determined to steer the conversation back to where she felt secure. 'What you should do is go along to Cable House and ask for Wayne Ramsey. He's a clerk there. I know him a little bit.' She looked quickly at her father. 'Not socially, of course, because he isn't one of *us*. But he's a really sweet boy and rather good at croquet. I met him last year at one of Mrs McMahon's afternoons because he is a friend of Miss Locke's, and he was terribly proficient with his mallet.' Dorothea babbled on. 'I think that Wayne could tell you what you would need to do to send a cable. Uncle Maitland sent a cable when he decided that marrying you would be the icing on the cake. I heard him tell Dada.'

Blair Montague tightened his grip on his daughter's wrist. 'I'm not quite sure you understood what Uncle Maitland meant, *chérie*.'

'Oh I did, Dada. I distinctly heard Uncle say it.'

'I believe I wrote to Maisie's parents, asking for their permission,' Maitland said. 'I send a lot of cables, Dorothea, for work. That's probably what you overheard.'

Dorothea pouted and looked across at Maisie. 'You must be so anxious to know if your parents are in good health and have received your letters. And I am sure they must be concerned about you and long to tell you their news. Should I call for you tomorrow and take you to the cable office in my sulky?'

Maisie held back a small sigh. Her mother had not received a cable from Maitland. There had been a letter. She had sat in the chilly presence as the contents had been read out. The girl was a nitwit.

Blair Montague, marginally less drunk than Maitland, sniffed and patted a glistening nostril with his handkerchief. It was so stiff with starch it almost refused to bend to do its duty.

'What would be more gallant of me and less fatiguing for you, *chère madame*, would be for you to allow me to do the running around for you. If you would care to pen a message, I could pass it along on your behalf. Junior clerks may be very obliging in one sense.' He looked pointedly at his daughter. 'But they might not be the very best person to get the job done. As mayor of

Buccaneer Bay, you could rest assured that your communications with England would be put in the right hands.'

Marjorie knocked on the doorjamb, her face scrunched in annoyance. ''Scuse me, Missus. There's gentlemen here for Captain Sinclair, though nobody told me they was comin'. I put 'em on the west verandah with the coffee pot. Hope dat's good.'

'Yes, thank you, Marjorie. That's very good.' Maisie stared at her husband. He hadn't told her to expect more guests.

The mayor consulted his watch and clutched the edge of the table unsteadily. 'I must pluck my little girl away, *mes chers amis*, and take her home to her bed. I hadn't realised it was so late. Thank you so much for a delicious supper, *madame*, and don't forget about your cable. I shall send someone round to collect it in the morning.'

Maitland swayed to his feet. 'You may as well go off to bed, Maisie. I've business to see to. Blair,' he turned to his friend, 'I'll walk you both out.'

Maitland handed Dorothea into the carriage and turned his back so that she might not hear. He spread his feet to secure his balance. 'Heard anything from the Association?' He tried to capture the right note of casual indifference for the question.

'No, not yet, Mait. These things take time.'

'Anyone else you can think of who could be useful?'

Blair tipped his head back and studied the sky. 'Would it be so bad if you weren't elected in?'

'For God's sake, Blair, how can you be so flipping indifferent? You know it's what I want. I've done everything you suggested. Even got a crappy wife and the right china.'

'She's doing a good job, Mait. She'll ingratiate you with the membership.'

'What can be taking so long?'

'Most people are still down south for the Wet.'

'It's been six years, Blair, not six bloody months.'

'There's a new bloke in town. Pierre Fornallaz, the pearl doctor. He's Swiss or French or something and is supposed to be a regular hot shot with a reputation as long as your arm. Get Maisie to have him and his wife to supper. I expect your wife can speak some French – she seems to be able to do everything else. Can't hurt. Now get away from the sulky. It's time to get Dorothea home.'

Maitland paused on the bottom step and took a steadying breath. The night air was sharp with the briny tang of the sea and it felt good to fill his lungs. The three men he'd invited were lounging on the verandah. They had helped themselves to his box of cigars and were well down the contents of a bottle of brandy. A pot of coffee sat cooling on the sideboard.

Captain Hanson looked as if he had stepped off the pages of a seafaring magazine. A drooping moustache and long side-whiskers framed his large, weather-beaten face. His hands were callused, spatulate and scarred; the tip of his left forefinger was missing, severed by a mistimed blow with a tomahawk. He revelled in the freedom of the sea and sailed with his fleet for weeks at a time, enduring the sub-human, cramped, cockroach-infested conditions alongside his Japanese and Malay crew. He rolled up his sleeves and was prepared to do any job he set his workers. Straight-talking and fair, the men respected him.

Captain Espinell was his opposite – tall, lean and leathery, all fingertips smooth and intact. He was clean-shaven, and his eyes darted in his weary face, anxiety etching worry in his flesh. He ran a sole lugger and was currently down on his luck, living on the foreshore in a ramshackle collection of cast-iron huts. But a master pearler down on his luck was still a big white fish in a muddy pond; the colour of one's skin was good currency in the Bay, and he was surviving, financially, just about.

Captain 'Shorty' Mason was a shaggy giant of a man, heavy-jowled with ice-blue eyes. Like Hanson, he was a man's man and was in his element in the male-dominated Bay. Women had to be amusing, pretty or flirtatious to warrant his attention; he could take them or leave them. He stretched out his long legs and took an appreciative drag on his cigar.

As Maitland entered the room, he heard Mason say, '. . . I thought this afternoon had a ring of panic about it.'

Maitland flopped down in a complaining verandah chair and reached for the brandy bottle. 'What had a ring of panic about it, Shorty?'

'Your summons this evening. Sounded a tad desperate.'

'Not desperate but important. I'm not going to pussyfoot about, boys. Our livelihood is at stake. Blair wants me talk to you about these English boys we've had thrust on us.'

Espinell fiddled with the cigar box. 'Are we at risk? What did Blair say?'

'We could be if we don't stick together. Blair's sorry he can't be here but he had to escort Dorothea home. He says we must agree on how we're going to handle the situation.'

Shorty Mason snapped his head from side to side, the vertebrae in the top of his neck crunching appreciatively. 'What do you have in mind?'

Maitland bent forward, his fingers steepled together. He pressed the index finger of his right hand to his lips, elbows balanced on his knees. Shorty dragged his chair closer. The other two narrowed the circle as Maitland primed the gun the mayor wanted them all to fire.

Although their voices were raised, Maisie couldn't make out what they were saying. She crept along the verandah and flushed out Marjorie, who was stacking dishes in the kitchen.

'I want you to take them in some coffee.'

'Boss fella had coffee, Missus. Remember? You want him up all night? Wanderin' 'bout the house? Coming into your room all drunk?' She tiptoed her fingers through the air like Wee Willy Winkie.

'I know, Marjorie. But we can give the other men coffee.'

'I already gave them coffee, too.'

'Oh! Did they drink it?'

'I dunno. Mebbe.'

'So, go back in and see and dawdle about. Spill the coffee and take your time mopping it up. I need you to tell me what they are talking about.'

'I'm spying on him's conversation?'

'*Listening* to their conversation. It won't occur to them to shut up if you are in there. They won't talk if I go in.'

Marjorie nodded, knowingly. 'Captain Sinclair gonna slap me if I spill it.'

She had a point. 'We don't want that. Maybe just try to be really slow putting the cups out. Then go back for the sugar. Or something.'

'All right. How longa you want me beum there?'

'I don't know. Try to work out what they are talking about, then come back to the kitchen and tell me.'

Marjorie scratched her head. 'Okay. I go find Duc and tell him make more coffee. He's gonna screech big. Then I go down the verandah and pretend I forgot the captain's already drunk his.'

'Where is Duc anyway, Marjorie?'

'Being after work time, in my house most like.'

Maitland worked a hand into a straining trouser pocket and pulled out his bulging purse. It was a tight squeeze and he swore into his moustache as the starched cotton cloth grazed the skin on his knuckles. The meeting was not going as well as he had hoped. The lubra maid was hovering about, fussing with coffee; he'd already drunk some that evening – could still taste it in his mouth – but he was too distracted to scold her for bringing it twice.

'So, Maitland.' Espinell summed up their conversation. 'We're going to send our divers off in completely different directions for two to three months at a time as soon as the Wet is over, to pearl beds that have been over-harvested. The pickings will be slim or non-existent. It will appear that our English colleagues are unable to see shell on the ocean floor. But they will never meet up and compare hard-luck stories. Meanwhile, our Jap divers will dive new fertile beds and demonstrate that they are more efficient at bringing up shell and should not be deported to where they came from. Is that about it?'

'In a nutshell.'

'How is that going to help me meet my financial targets, Maitland?' Espinell countered. 'I'm almost on my uppers as it is.'

'It won't. That's the ruddy sticking point. We're all going to be out of pocket in the short term. That's why we've got to pull together. But we have to make sure that this White Policy experiment the government has dreamed up fails. The English divers and their tenders are too bloody expensive for the fleet. We're even paying them a bigger percentage on any shell they do manage to haul up. The English divers on average will cost eight times more than the Jap fellers. We'll all go bust if we allow this madness.'

'But what if they do happen to be good at the job? That will work for me. As long as they harvest the shell,' Espinell whined.

'It doesn't matter whether they're any good or not. We can't afford to pay the sort of money the government has told them to expect. Not if we want to stay in business. We have to make sure they fail. Doesn't matter how you do it. Get someone on board to engineer a little accident – with the air hose, for example, or tamper with those nutcase Admiralty tables they brought with them. A small miscalculation with the stop times should do the trick.'

The master pearlers did not understand the Navy Admiralty tables and were certain that their indentured crews wouldn't either. If a diver followed the recommendations in the tables, Maitland argued, he would spend most of his working day suspended underwater on a rope somewhere between the surface and the ocean floor rather than harvesting shell from the sea bed. The charts were based on mathematics. If a diver worked at fifteen fathoms, and remained there for one hour, he should come up to the surface slowly in separate, predetermined stages. It would take him thirty minutes to reach the top. If he went deeper, it would take him longer to come up. The master pearlers knew it would be impossible to keep a diver down, doing his job. The longer the divers remained on the ocean floor, the more chance they had of picking up shell. But a long dive would necessitate a much longer resurfacing time. There was also a recommendation that a diver should spend a minimum rest time between dives of three hours – not the fifteen minutes the Japs took for a smoke and a cup of coffee – and if the dive was deeper than fifteen fathoms, there should be no second dive that day.

Shorty turned to Hanson. 'We seem to have a split deck here. How about a wager to settle the vote?'

Hanson ran a hand down his side-whiskers. 'I'm up for that. What's the game to be?'

Espinell shook his head. 'I'm going to pass.'

Shorty swallowed some brandy. 'I'm not in the mood for cards or high stakes, either. Let's play Two-Up. You got any pennies in that fat purse of yours, Mait? We can take it in turns to be spinner and count up when we've all had a go.'

Maitland liked the odds of the coin-tossing game. Gambling on whether the wobbling coins would fall with two heads up, two tails up or one of each was less taxing after a few drinks too many than trying to remember the cards. He tossed his two pennies in the air and the three captains placed their bets. Between each toss of the coins, Maitland swigged down another tot of neat spirit. What could be more perfect? His two favourite pastimes in the comfort of his own home.

Except for his bloody wife next door.

*

Maisie was lurking in the kitchen when Marjorie returned with the empty glasses.

'So, what did they say?'

'They's plottin'.'

'About what?'

Marjorie pretended to stir a bowl with a spoon. 'Them boss fellas is cookin' up mischief.'

'What do you mean?'

'They's bin gamblin' with them coins.'

Maisie wanted to shake her. 'I don't understand what you're telling me.'

Marjorie ran her hand impatiently through her woolly hair. 'I just telled you. The boss fellas was tossing up coins and making bets. And laughin'.'

'What were they betting on?'

'Don't knows about dat bit.'

'Have the captains gone home?'

'Yes. Hims left when boss fella went all funny. His eyes gone all turned up and I couldn't see no colour there, only the whitey-ball bits. Then he fell over and crashed his head on da table. Bang!' She thumped the kitchen table.

'Shush! Keep your voice down, Marjorie. Is he still there?'

'Didn't touch him, Missus. Promise. Didn't want him go slap me.'

Maisie scrutinised the maid's frightened face. She took hold of her hand and gave it a squeeze. 'I'm sure you didn't, but we should go and make sure that he is all right – particularly as he hit his head. Then we can decide what we're going to do with him.'

On the verandah, Maitland was snoring. It was worse than usual. The noise seemed to be coming from both his nostrils and his throat. To add to the background percussion, he broke wind loudly.

Marjorie pinched her nostrils. 'You going to wake him up, Missus?'

'No. I think we'll leave him here. We couldn't move him anyway. He's much too heavy.'

'You want cover him up or mebbe take off his shoes?'

'No. But I will put something under his head. It might dull the noise he's making.'

Marjorie nodded. 'I take stuff to da kitchen and then I'll go climb in my bed. Dat okay?'

'Thank you. And Marjorie?' Maisie was still wondering about the whereabouts of Duc.

'Yes, Missus?'

'. . . Never mind. It'll keep.'

Maisie surveyed the fleshy mountain precariously slumped sideways on the table. Another hefty snore, with fortissimo bass accompaniment, launched his frame sideways to the floor. He scarcely flinched. On the table, where his arm had rested, was his purse. Mrs Wallace's voice echoed in her head: *Never trust a man who has a purse, Maisie. He is bound to be mean in every respect of the word.*

Maisie had a chat with her conscience. Mrs Wallace was bang on the money. Maitland had meanness tattooed on his soul. She scooped up the bulgy leather bag, twisted the shiny clasp and tipped the contents into her left hand. The weight of the coins felt wonderful in her palm, like retribution. She dropped the empty purse on the table and pushed it away.

If Maitland is this drunk, he won't remember where his money has gone.

Maitland gave Duc money when he sent him to the shops, but she was expected to sign for everything she bought by chit. She had no actual cash of her own. Maitland knew exactly how much she spent and what she spent it on. This was the first opportunity she'd had to be independent in her life. She waggled her head from side to side.

I am his wife, so technically what is his is also mine. Yes. That's right. She nodded resolutely as she dropped the coins into her pocket. *Now, where to hide the stash?* The large screw-top jar where Marjorie had advised her to keep her silk underwear safe from the champing jaws of moths and silverfish seemed a very good place.

In her bedroom, she began to undress, shedding layers of clothing like dead skin. As her underwear lay on the floor, a tangle of fragile silk, she knew that a different person was emerging from its childish cocoon. She wrapped herself in a cool cotton kimono and pulled the belt tight around her resolve. She would lay a bet of her own that four of the Bay's most influential pearling captains were up to something fishy.

'I'm going to find out what,' she said aloud.

A lizard ran across the wall and disappeared into a crack.

CHAPTER 10

'COOEE? MRS SINCLAIR?'

Maisie and Marjorie both heard the screen door creak, and the high-pitched voice made them cringe. Marjorie was waging war on the bougainvillea petals that blew daily onto the verandah while Maisie sat at her desk, aimlessly doodling on the blotter with her pen. She had just read her weekly missive from Mrs Wallace and was feeling markedly downcast. *You are starting to sound peevish, Maisie, as if you have given up before you have been in Australia five minutes. I never would have suspected this from a girl who took her corset off when she thought my back was turned! I'm sending you some packets of seeds. Plant them in the garden and watch them thrive. It will be a good lesson for you and give you an interest.*

Marjorie picked up the pace of her sweeping with an uncustomary energy and bent to gather up the skittering purple confetti. 'You in, Missus?' she said over her shoulder.

Maisie rolled her eyes. 'Give me a minute.'

Marjorie straightened up, leaned on her broom and called through the screen, 'Missus bit busy, Miz Montague. But she know you come allonga.'

Dorothea appeared in the doorway and gave the Aboriginal maid a long-lashed stare.

The maid blocked the entrance, her feet firmly planted on the ground, hands on well-upholstered hips, and gave no quarter. They stared at each other, two predators assessing their quarry. 'So, you young missus. You come in dat sulky o' yours?'

Dorothea flicked the top of the verandah rail with her white-gloved hand and inspected the fingertips. Her displeasure showed in her risen shoulders. 'Why you wantum know?'

The Bay's white Europeans spoke to the domestic help in pidgin English. Whatever their rationale, Maisie found it ill-mannered. The language of the majority of residents was not English; expecting everyone to speak it was yet another example of the white minority suppressing the coloured majority. She squirmed at her own hypocrisy. She was no better than the people she so despised, having made no effort at all to embrace any language but her own.

Marjorie scratched the ample padding over her stomach. 'Him horse might like go allonga our horse.' She picked up her broom and continued to sweep, head bent, looking for more floral treasure.

Dorothea blinked twice and twisted her mouth to the side. 'Why him wantum?'

'Bit of visitin', only dey don't have them white cards wot you has.'

Maisie got up from her desk and edged along the wall. Dorothea was wavering by the doorframe, and Marjorie's mouth had dropped open like a sharp-toothed whale. The prey was corralled and she was ready, jaw hinged, to swallow her whole.

'Marjorie!' Maisie said. 'I think you could let our visitor in the house.'

'Thought you gonna bin hours,' Marjorie whispered, and pottered off, muttering darkly to herself.

Maisie smiled at Dorothea and walked towards the front door. 'Dorothea. I'm so sorry to keep you waiting. I must have forgotten you were coming.'

Dorothea did not seem to think that calling cards were meant for her. Certainly, Maisie had never seen her with a supply. She had a habit of turning up at any time, unannounced, on an impulsive girlish whim.

'Oh, Mrs Sinclair. It's an impromptu visit. Dada doesn't know I'm here. He's at a mayoral meeting. I know he said he would send your cable for you and I know it was a few days ago but I hope you haven't sent it already. Probably, you haven't had time and Dada most likely forgot. He doesn't always remember what he said, like Uncle Maitland. I did look up in my journal about the cables, by the way, and I was almost right. I think he wrote a letter to your mother and didn't send a cable, which was my mistake because I didn't remember properly, but he definitely said that getting you to the Bay would be the final piece in his overall financial plan. That's almost the same as the icing on the cake, isn't it?'

Maisie looked at Dorothea's face, watched her lips move, not believing what she had just been told. Her parents had never once mentioned any kind of financial settlement. She waved at a chair, feeling that she was falling from a very high platform with no safe place to land. She heard herself speak, the words coming from a long way off.

'Do please sit down, Dorothea, and make yourself comfortable.'

Dorothea flopped into a high-backed chair and filled her lungs with air. 'Anyway, Mrs Sinclair, I was thinking you could be a little bit naughty and send two cables. I like Wayne quite a lot and it would be really nice just to see him with a proper business reason, otherwise people might talk if I just popped in. It's quite hard to invent excuses to see someone here, don't you find? So, could you do that tiny thing for me, do you think? Not tell Dada you've already sent the cable, so that I might see Wayne?'

Maisie tried to look interested in her bright chatter, but shock was barely disguised behind her forced smile. She suggested tea.

Dorothea shook her head like a dog ridding itself of water.

'Frankly, Mrs Sinclair, I hate tea – the milk nearly always tastes curdled – and the cable was a bit of an excuse, although we must go to the cable office before Dada comes out of his meeting. I need to let Wayne down gently and tell him in person that he must abandon all hope of us ever being together. The real reason I've come to see you is because I'm bursting to tell someone! I can't tell Dada, obviously, or Uncle Maitland – because he knows the person – I just need to tell someone who will understand!'

'About what, Dorothea?'

She leaned forward, elbows on knees. 'I'm in love!'

Maisie fell back in her seat. *Lucky you*, she thought. 'With whom?'

Dorothea sat up and, like a nervous witness, glanced at Maisie to assess the effect as her words landed. 'Mr Cooper, Uncle Maitland's diver. He is *so* handsome. I gave him a ride in my buggy the day after he arrived and, I can tell you confidentially,' she clasped Maisie's arm, 'he is really handsome. Divine, actually, when one is close up. And such a gentleman. He tried to give the impression that he was uninterested in me, but I know he feels the same way and is simply bursting with desire.'

Maisie strengthened her grip on the chair arm. Her heart was beating too fast, tumbling over itself as if it were rolling downhill, and little black flecks swam in front of her eyes. She hoped she was not going to faint. She was, in equal measures, horrified and desperate, and in a tight voice she managed to say, 'I wasn't aware that you knew him socially.'

'You are right, I don't. Not officially. That's why it's a huge secret. As I said, I met him on the first day all the white divers arrived. The day after you were married on the steamship. It was such a shame I was unable to attend the ceremony, but Dada thought the crush and the heat and all those rough men might be horrid for me. But there are so few men here that I absolutely had to see for myself if they were really dangerous and ugly. So, while Dada was out at your wedding party, I went to look at the Seafarer's Rest Hotel – I'd overheard Dada and Uncle Maitland say some of the divers were staying there because Uncle Maitland owns a bit of the hotel.' Dorothea raised her voice at the end of every sentence, as if asking a question, and Maisie found the habit intensely irritating.

'We didn't have a wedding party,' Maisie countered. 'Wherever your father may have said he was that night, he was certainly not celebrating our nuptials.'

Dorothea shook her head. 'No, I'm sorry but you are wrong. He definitely said that was where he was. I wrote it in my journal. I asked him about it and he told me the party had gone on all night and then continued into the next day.'

So, the mayor is a liar like Maitland, Maisie thought. She could not resist asking, 'And the English diver?'

'Yes! Mr Cooper. While Dada was still at your party on the ship, I slipped out and found him there at the Seafarer's.

He was sitting on his chair on the verandah, all alone and smoking a cigarette as if he was waiting just for me. It was obviously fate that we would be thrown together in such a romantic way, and I was so pleased that I had been brave and gone there alone – otherwise it would never have happened. I gave him a ride in my sulky and we chatted as if we had known each other forever.'

Dorothea misread Maisie's silence for encouragement. 'He is so adorable. And,' she paused before delivering the next little pearl, 'we kissed at the Welcome Dance.'

Needles of sun pierced Maisie's eyes through the lattice. 'Were you seen?' Maisie asked.

Dorothea looked startled, as if this had only just occurred to her. 'I don't think anybody saw the kiss. Our encounter was very public, on the dance floor. We were flying across the floorboards – he is such an accomplished dancer – and we got to the end of the reel and I wanted to throw my arms about him and embrace him there and then, but I remember thinking that I should not kiss him in front of the ladies from the knitting circle or there would be a great deal of fuss. No. The kiss came later on, when he was fetching drinks at the bar. I followed him and – you're going to think me very forward, Mrs Sinclair – I bumped into him on purpose and kissed him passionately on the lips. It was absolutely glorious. So, now we have embraced, we are engaged in secret. And you must promise not to tell a soul.' She sat like a Siamese cat on a cushion: a cat who had licked the cream and very much liked the taste.

'Did he propose marriage?'

'Not in so many words. But he did say that I was charming and light on my feet and that he had enjoyed our dance together. And when he goes out to sea, which will be very soon, Dada says,

William said we would rarely meet, as he will be working so hard. And that he was sad that our acquaintance had been sweet but too brief. So, I was wondering, dear Mrs Sinclair, as you are to provision Uncle Maitland's fleets on his supply schooner, if I may not accompany you from time to time so that I might see my darling William? He means everything in the world to me, and how else will we make plans for our wedding?'

Maisie felt sick. 'I'm not certain that would work, Dorothea. Space is very cramped on board the schooner and I believe that single white women are not permitted to stay aboard a floating vessel. I'm really not certain that my husband would consent to subjecting you to such discomfort or to the possibility of scandal. Perhaps you could write to him? I would be happy to deliver your letters with the general mail packages for the crew. And your father would never find out that you even knew Mr Cooper.'

Dorothea's eyes filled. She produced a handkerchief from her pocket and mopped her tear-swollen face.

Maisie had been brought up to consider tears an unthinkable indulgence. *Tears are not a requirement, Maisie, like congratulations after a job well done. Female wiles are cheap.* Her mother's words rang in her mind.

'I hadn't realised that love could be quite so painful, Mrs Sinclair,' the girl wailed. 'I am barely sleeping, such are my dreams filled with him. If I may not see him for weeks, at least I can be sure he will be aware of my feelings if I write them down for him. And you are quite right. I will have to convince Dada that William is the only person in the world for me and I shall die of grief if I may not have him. He will soon notice my suffering at being parted from the only man in the world who can make me happy and will want to know what ails me. He can never deny me anything when I am upset.'

Maisie was still, her face a mask. 'Dorothea, I think you need to prepare yourself for a little disappointment. I am certain your father will not allow you to marry a diver, an employee of one of his closest friends. Should you not be seeing other, more suitable types? Perhaps one of the unmarried men at the bank? It would be dreadful for you to become very attached to someone and have your hopes dashed.'

'Oh, it wouldn't be right for me to encourage others now that I am engaged. What would William think?'

Maisie hoped that William Cooper would be appalled to discover that Dorothea Montague, the most skittish, witless girl in the town, considered them engaged. Surely he now regretted every second of that sweaty gallop over the dance floor? She said he had kissed her. That was a much bigger something else to think about. If she had initiated it, had he returned the kiss when he hadn't seemed keen to dance with her at all? Perhaps Mrs Wallace was right all along. William Cooper was nothing but a predatory flirt.

I am not jealous, she told herself, but her heart caught her out in the deception.

She nodded and patted the silly girl's arm but couldn't process her own disturbed feelings. She watched the second hand move on the wall-mounted clock, ticking off the minutes in loud, hollow clicks. *Tick, tock, tick, tock*, like the beat of her heart. She was joined to a man with whom she had nothing in common, save a shared great-grandparent and a marriage certificate. She lived with a man she did not love and who certainly did not love her and had shown no physical interest in her. She'd been sacrificed to him by parents who had sent her away and now, according to

Dorothea, had happily paid to do so. It appeared that she meant nothing more to Maitland than a profitable acquisition to round off his financial portfolio. She was starved of affection, and yet, when she thought of William Cooper, deep inside she felt a burgeoning tumult of excitement that she did not understand. She barely knew him and hadn't expected the surge of longing that now engulfed her, or the sour green sea of envy that threatened to drown her.

Tears out of the way, Dorothea brightened up. 'So, shall we go off and send your cable, Mrs Sinclair, now that we are sharing secrets?'

The two young women trotted north in Dorothea's sulky towards the cable station. The air was shrill with cicadas, but even they could not compete with the high-pitched insistence of Miss Montague's chatter. They steered away from the main avenue and took a rough track consisting of two parallel ruts ploughed deep in the blood-red earth. It was sticky from a recent downpour and the horse laboured through the slippery mud, blowing hard through its nostrils, its withers slick with sweat.

The cable building was set in its own plush grounds. Auxiliary buildings and bungalows supporting the needs of the staff were sited on the same plot, shaded by spreading tamarind trees.

Dorothea tethered her sweating animal to a low-slung branch and said, 'Follow me, Mrs Sinclair. The cable office is the rectangular one over there with the steeply pitched roof. That's where we will be able to send your message.'

Wayne Ramsey stood behind the counter, his shirtsleeves rolled up and clamped in place by two expanding spirals of shimmering metal that looked like flexible toast racks. He was a handsome man with a thick blond moustache, which lay across his top lip like a rigid stick of chalk.

'Morning, Miss Dorothea Montague.' He intoned his greeting like a congregational response at Evensong.

'Mr Wayne Ramsey.' Dorothea was clearly trying to flirt. 'Mrs Sinclair has a cable to send to England. Would you be able to help her? It's a clandestine affair and not a word must be uttered to my father.'

Wayne winked at her, then turned towards Maisie and said importantly, 'No worries, Mrs Sinclair. It'll only take a jiffy.'

He stepped away from the counter and from a tray plucked a printed form, which he slid under the glass window together with a sharpened blue pencil. 'Just write down the message and who you want to send it to. I'll do the rest.'

Maisie filled in her parents' names and address at the top of the message section, then wrote the three words she had decided upon. She had chosen them even before she had learned that they had settled money on her marriage, and now she felt even more resolute that they were well aimed. *Ne cede malis.*

Her parents would understand the Latin poet Virgil's words, 'Yield not to misfortunes.' She had done what they wanted. She had come to Australia and married Maitland, and although it was not what she had dreamed of, she was digging in and making the best of it. Her message should be clear to them. And, what? Perhaps she would finally gain their approval?

Even in the morning semi-darkness Maisie could see that the water drained in a different direction to the bathroom sink in England. Had her father been next door – her wise, dependable encyclopaedia – she would have consulted him. It was said to be something to do with the earth's rotation, but at the back of her mind she could hear him saying it was more to do with the design of the sink. She bent over for a closer look.

'Missus?'

The sound made her start. 'What is it, Marjorie?'

The maid stood in the bathroom doorway, her large frame blocking the light. 'Could you gimme some of those quids you got in your skimpies jar?'

Maisie stood up too fast and almost gouged her head on the bathroom shelf. 'How do you know about the money?' she said, fingering her scalp.

'I does the washing and the putting away. I seed them there.'

'Why do you need money? Doesn't Captain Sinclair pay you?'

'Not in quids money. Me and Duc get cooking stuff and baccy. Mebbe Duc gettum some coin quids for other stuff. Don't know 'bout dat, dough.'

Maisie knew Maitland didn't pay the garden boy. Doctor Shin had told her that no-one in the Bay paid outside help, but she hadn't known that her indoor staff were not paid properly for the work they did either. 'Can you tell me what you need it for?'

Marjorie beat a tattoo on the sides of her face. 'Firstum. I need pay some peepy gogglers.'

'Peepy gogglers?'

'Yes, Missus. Gettin' desperate. I can't see no good when Duc comes allonga my house.'

Maisie tried not to blush but a disobedient flush crept up her neck. Thoughts she would rather not entertain chased round her head like greyhounds after a lure. Wouldn't people take their spectacles off in the bedroom? Everything would be slightly out of focus, but wouldn't that be a good thing? She fanned her embarrassment with her hands.

'What you thinkin', Missus – dat something going on with Duc, skinny brown fella and me? Dem peepy gogglers be for reading. I bin teaching Duc to read. He's taked a fancy to dat cooking book you got but can't read wot the stuff says. I ain't one of those bad girls dat goes allonga the sailors and catches diseases. I got standards. What you think of me?'

Maisie's mouth dropped open. 'I'm so sorry. I've heard you both chattering together after dark and I just thought . . .'

'You bin hurt my feelings, Missus. Thought you knows Duc don't like girls. Might be now you give me some spending quids so I's feel allota better.'

Maisie considered for a moment then gave a brief nod. 'All right, Marjorie, but you will still need to get your eyes tested properly. You'll have to make an appointment.'

Marjorie waved the suggestion away with her hand. 'You heard of chiffa, Missus?'

Maisie shook her head.

'Dat's thingum two I wanted tell you 'bout. Why we mosta need quids. We get cuppa tea with Duc and him'll tell you 'bout it. I think it good for you, you being brainy and all.'

Duc was knocking back and reworking the bread dough he had set the night before. He leaned forward, panting with the effort. His breath smelled yeasty, as if he had worked the mixture with his teeth. Maisie wondered if he brewed his own beer, or if he had been drinking. She banged her forehead with her fist as if to push the thought back in.

'You want me do something, Mem?' He stared at her, waiting for orders.

Maisie lifted out a chair from under the kitchen table, careful not to scrape its legs on the polished floor, and stood with her hands resting on the rounded wooden back. Apart from a daily glance at his spotless domain and a brief discussion about menus, she rarely set foot in the kitchen.

'A cup of tea would be nice, Duc, and perhaps a biscuit? And then you can tell me about chiffa.'

She looked at Marjorie to check her pronunciation. The maid nodded, pulled out a second chair, its back legs scoring parallel lines through the damp polish, and lowered her frame onto the gleaming seat.

'I's been telling Missus 'bout our plan.'

Duc brushed up some crumbs from the floor and threw them into the dustbin, banging the residue from his hands against the sides. He was quick and competent, and an obsessive mopper. He dedicated hours each day to washing the floor and now stood behind Maisie, mop in hand, ready to scrub her visit from his floorboards. 'You plannin' on make mess with them biscuits, Mem? Loadsa work. No good for floor. More better you stay out.'

'You one rude fella, Duc,' Marjorie said.

He grinned at her and turned his attention to swirling the contents of a pot on the stove like a sorcerer concocting a potion. 'Most popular card game is fan-tan, Mem. Very ancient. Go back mebbe two thousand years. Next more popular is chiffa.'

Chiffa, Duc explained, was a type of Chinese lottery run in the Bay by Mr Kyougoku, who also owned the town's department store. It was drawn twice a day: at noon and again in the evening. Bets were placed on solving riddles. The clues were given after each draw had been made, to give the participants plenty of time to consider their answers before the next one. During lay-up season, with so many people in town, more bets were laid, so the pot was correspondingly larger. The twice-daily draw was a big occasion. Anyone could go to witness it. Anyone could place a one-shilling bet. Anyone, that was, unless you were white.

'Really?' Maisie sat down and took a sip of tea.

Marjorie nodded. 'Many us mobs need gaming house in Asia Place for food. We wins bit, we eats bit. Whites no needa money like dat.'

She explained that the police turned a blind eye to gambling in the Bay, as long as an Asian ran the game and there were no fights. The Aborigines were permitted to bet, but they couldn't run their own games in public. Of course games were run in some 'known' houses, though, and were the sole source of income for a lot of families.

Rations were only available outside the Native Affairs office one day a week. There was nowhere else for desperate non-white people to turn other than the chiffa draw. Desperate whites remained desperate, or sponged off their white neighbours.

Marjorie drained her cup with a noisy slurp, as if she were siphoning mud up a straw. Maisie cringed and pulled a face, but the maid took no notice.

'Is logic, Missus. You gamble, you mebbe win. You lose so, you don't eat anyways.' Marjorie threw her hands up towards the ceiling. 'You no take part, might as well stay in bed till gubberment office opens.'

'So, you want me to gamble. Is that what you're saying?'

'No, Missus, you no listen. You give us betting quids and work out them riddles, then we go gamblin'. White folk ain't allowed.'

'And if we win?'

'Then we divides up pot. There's big pots in the Wet with all them crew fellas in town. You makes your money work for a livin'. More better than leavin' it festerin' with them ridiclus things you try wear in this heat.'

Maisie scratched her head. These two were priceless. They had discovered her stash, cooked up a scheme that would involve no risk or money on their part, and would take two-thirds of the winnings if they were successful. Duc spread his face wide, anticipation bright in his eyes.

'All right.' She nodded. 'I'll provide the stake money but I'm going to make some rules. I keep half and you both may take a quarter. It's my money, I'm taking the risk, so it's only fair I take more profit. But I want to know why suddenly you two are in need of ready cash. Are you planning to run away?'

Duc shook his head. 'Me big plan comin'. Jap yeller fella him dummyin'. But we needs quids and white person as part of plan.'

Maisie turned to Marjorie. 'What's dummying?'

Marjorie explained that only white men were allowed to own pearling boats, but some of the master pearlers were selling on their old-fashioned or near-defunct boats – they called them 'cockroaches' – to indentured divers, or anyone mad enough to take them on. The stumbling block was the pearling licence, which had to be held by the original white owner.

'We'll talk about that another time. Find out the next riddle when you see about your eye appointment. Riddles are not obvious. That's the point. The obvious is too obvious and people could fall into that trap.' She pushed back her chair and stood up. 'I also have a little money-making idea of my own. Where do you get our fruit and vegetables from, Duc?'

Duc looked put out. 'Why you want know? You no like my food all of sudden?'

'Quite the opposite. I'm thinking of selling fruit and vegetables to the divers when I see them once a week, but I don't know where to buy them in the Bay.'

Marjorie shook her head. 'Dat not gonna work.'

'Why not? The divers don't have fresh food. Everything they eat comes out of a tin.'

Marjorie planted her elbows on the table. 'How you keep stuff good? You buy vegetables, you go out on dat boat fella and find divers. Dat take three days my reckonin'. Them divers can't keep fresh tucker on lugger boats. No, Missus. Don't reckon dat would work. Dummyin' much better idea.'

Maisie stared into her teacup. 'I'm going to give it a try. If it doesn't work, then I'll think of something else. So, tell me please where to buy the fresh vegetables.'

Marjorie reached for a biscuit. 'Chinky garden fella. He's a big garden near church.'

'Which church? Anglican or Catholic?'

Duc looked suspiciously at the contents of his saucepan and gave the pot another stir. 'Half far church as Japanese hospital.'

So, the Anglican church, Maisie nodded. 'What are you cooking up in that saucepan, Duc?' she asked.

His laugh was deep and infectious, inviting complicity. 'Bit of a storm, Mem. That okey-dokey?'

*

Maitland tapped the barometer on the packing-shed wall. It had dropped to 28.85 inches, a sure sign that a blow was on its way. The willy-willy, nor'wester, or cyclone – as it was variously called – was the deadliest of natural phenomena in the north-west. A freak of geography had turned Buccaneer Bay into a virulent storm-breeding ground with a vast expanse of warm shallow sea and hot sun.

Pearling bosses would confine their luggers to the bay, but Maitland rubbed his hands together, a secret smile on his lips. It was what he had been waiting for.

Holding the bowl in his left hand, he puffed on his pipe and yelled, 'The English diver wants a training run with his tender. I'm putting you out to sea for a few days on the *Sharky*.'

A shout rang out from the shed and Squinty appeared in the doorway. 'That lugger no refit, Tuan. Still in Mangrove Creek. Him no good even in good weather. Weather look bad now.'

'You don't want to go, Squinty? Shall I get someone else?' Maitland knew the Malay needed the money and didn't have the choice.

Squinty's eyes did a circuit. 'No, Tuan, is good. I just say. In case you no know 'bout boat.'

'Of course I know. D'you think I'm a total twerp? Here's what you're going to do: get down to the foreshore camp and make sure the other luggers are pulled up high and staked down.'

Squinty wedged himself against the doorjamb.

'I normally wouldn't put a boat out to sea if it wasn't fit, but the Chinese chandlers have been laying odds on when they'll get their refit money, and . . .' Maitland rapped his pipe on the desk and fractured the stem. He swore loudly. 'Get over to Asia

Place and rout out Daike. He'll be number-one diver. You go tomorrow with the tide.'

Squinty slid his foot back and forth in an arc on the floor. Having Daike on board would calm him down, Maitland thought. Daike was indisputably the best, and the Japanese diver wouldn't share local knowledge with the new recruit. The tally of shell brought up by individual divers was of keen interest both to the diving community and to the master pearlers. The top diver for the season would attract celebrity attention. But Daike was an opinionated, argumentative, arrogant know-it-all. He was not popular with the crews and, frankly, Maitland was tired of dealing with the flak. Fear was not in the diver's vocabulary and he despised it in others. Maitland knew he would push his team to the limits of their endurance, no matter what the weather was doing. He was counting on it.

Squinty looked less wary. 'Okay, Tuan, so I get Daike. Then who more?'

'Small crew, Squints. Cook, two deckies. That's enough.'

'Opener?'

'No. If the boys bring up shell, you bring it back here. Only three days. Okay?'

Squinty frowned. 'You want tell me what happening, Tuan?'

Maitland smacked his right hand on the desk. 'What is happening is that you will have no job soon, Squinty, if you don't bloody move quick smart. The *Sharky* goes out tomorrow morning from the Mangrove camp. You got that?'

Squinty took a step back.

'Those English boys are going too, but I'll deal with them. Can't risk a cock-up. Just round up the others. Now move it!'

The Malay shot off like a bullet.

*

The captain slid the box of cigarettes across the desk. 'Smoke?'

Coop helped himself. He'd have liked a handful. Money was perilously tight and he couldn't stretch to ready-mades.

'Squinty's getting a crew together, Cooper. The weather doesn't look too bad for the next few days, so I'm sending you out with that tender of yours on the training run we talked about. Don't brag about it, though. The other English blokes aren't going to have the same opportunity. They'll be expected to jump right in and spot shell from the word go.'

Coop forced himself not to grin. At last, they were getting on with the job they'd come out to do. And he'd landed a decent pearler who wanted to give him a chance. He nodded. 'Who's going to be number-one diver?'

'Daike. He's my top Jap diver. Very experienced. He knows the crews, the shell beds and all about responsible diving. You'll be in safe hands.'

'It's not the diving that concerns me, Captain Sinclair. It's finding the shell. Is he happy to help me with that if it's going to affect his own shell tally in the long run?'

Maitland studied the Englishman. 'He's a show-off, Cooper. It's a certainty Daike will take you to a prolific shell bed and show you how he can spot the shell and haul up a fortune. Don't let him piss you off. Just watch him and learn. You'll pick it up in no time.'

Coop nodded.

Maitland pulled a fat white ledger from a desk drawer. 'And, Cooper, I take the well-being of my crews very seriously. I undertake personally to make sure you are insured and there are adequate safety measures in place while you are working for me. I must ask you to sign your contract.' Maitland unscrewed the top of a bottle of ink and reached into an inner jacket pocket. He unclipped a gold fountain pen and dipped the nib in the black fluid. 'I've marked with a cross the place for you to sign.'

Cooper had travelled thousands of miles to prove that he was an accomplished diver, that he was better than the best. Fame and fortune were now within a few days' grasp. He looked up, smiled and took the pen. He signed his name against the pencil cross without letting on that, at age twenty-two, he still couldn't read the small print.

Captain Sinclair screwed the top back on his pen, staring intently at the paperwork. He didn't look up to meet Coop's eyes. 'Excellent, Cooper. You are now good to go. Fully signed up and ready to dive. You will sail out on the tide from Mangrove Creek, tomorrow I hope.'

Cooper sprang up from his seat and grabbed his hat off the desk.

'One more thing, Cooper. Could you trot up to the bungalow and tell my wife she's needed in the shed?'

With a surge of excitement he was finding difficult to conceal, Coop gave a slight shrug and swung towards the door.

CHAPTER 11

MAISIE WAS BACK IN her bed, watching the sun play hide-and-seek with the lattice. *Now you see me, now you* – She winced as a bullet of pain shot through her abdomen. *I measure my life in blocks of four weeks*, she thought. Mrs Wallace had said it would be easy to lose track of time, left to her own devices with long days rolling into one another and not enough to keep her occupied. For once, Maisie disagreed. *This monthly thing will never let me forget.* She swung her legs over the side of the mattress and stumbled along the verandah corridor to the bathroom. The rust drips under the taps made her cringe. She crossed her arms over her chest and caught the fine cotton of her nightdress in her fingers, raised her arms like a ballerina, and pulled it over her head.

Standing on a towel, she rummaged in her trunk. Duc had dragged it into the bathroom where she now stored her personal items. The maximum dose of Mrs Barker's Soothing Syrup was, she read, two spoons. *Bother that!* She gulped down half the bottle.

A pounding on the front door made her start. 'Is anyone there?'

She shrank back against the wall and flung on her nightdress.

'Duc!' She leaned towards the back of the house. 'There's someone outside. Can you go and see who it is?'

'I go, Mem. Chop, chop. No worries.'

She wobbled back to her bedroom, feeling decidedly unstable.

Duc appeared in the doorway. 'Is mister diver white fella. He needs speak you.'

Maisie tensed, but she couldn't say why. 'Can you tell him I'm not here?'

'Oh, too late. I told him you come out soon.'

'Did he say what he wants?'

Duc stood on one leg, the inside of one foot pressed against the other ankle, like a yogi. 'I no know.'

'Did you ask him?'

Duc shook his head, then brightened. 'But I have made cake you learn me. Just in case.'

Maisie rubbed her forehead and tried to keep her voice level. 'Thank you. That was thoughtful. Could you make some tea and put him on the east verandah while I get dressed?'

'Yes, yes. I do now.'

She felt light-headed, nervous. *Excited?*

Throwing her loosest-fitting housedress over her head, she twisted her heavy hair into a pale roll and secured it at the back of her head in a spiral. Already it was escaping and stuck to her neck in limp whorls as she went out to meet him. It was the first time she had entertained a man on her own and her heart thrummed so aggressively that she thought it might rise up into her throat. *Must be the syrup*, she thought. *Giving me the jitters.*

He was standing, hands thrust deep into his pockets, hat tipped jauntily off his forehead. He scratched under the rim and stretched out his hand. She took a step towards him but caught her shoe heel on the rug. Flinging a hand out behind her, she flopped down on an upholstered seat, windmilling her arms at the chair opposite. Her face seared with embarrassment. She pulled the cushion out from behind her back and pressed it to her stomach. The pain seemed to be easing, but her tongue felt lazy. She waggled it against her lips but couldn't seem to wake it up. She took a deep breath and spread out her arms, the words locked inside.

They sat for several seconds, isolated from each other but curiously connected by their mutual unease. Coop inspected the weave in the upholstery and Maisie did not trust herself to speak. She could feel her chest moving with each breath, too fast in and out. She hadn't seen him since the Welcome Dance, and he seemed thinner, sunburned and sitting far too close. She leaned sideways to gain some distance from him and almost unseated herself.

'Mrs Sinclair. I hope you are in good health.'

Her head lolled back and smacked the headrest. Mrs Barker's Syrup had also affected her eyesight. The Englishman seemed out of focus, dancing in front of her eyes like a heat haze. She blinked a few times, narrowed her eyes and straightened her neck.

He was concentrating on his fingers, pushing at the cuticles, his dark eyebrows slightly raised, and then he looked up. When their eyes met, she saw a glimmer of puzzlement cross his face. She sucked her cheeks in and out a couple of times and tapped her face with her fingers. 'Some form of refreshment, Mr Cooper?' she tried. 'I'm having tea.'

'Tea is fine. I prefer to wait till the end of the day for the hard liquor. A little tipple could easily escalate in a town where alcohol is safer than the water to drink. Do you not think?'

'Yes. Me too. Drinking is not one of my particular vices. Though . . .' She tried to angle her head and managed to lurch towards him instead. 'I have taken up smoking Egyptian cigarettes. I steal them from Maitland when he's not looking. He never notices me.' She slapped her hand over her mouth but the words had become slippery and escaped from the corners.

Duc appeared with the morning-tea tray. He had aligned biscuits in a neat row, like soldiers on parade. Again he stood on one leg and scratched at the other with the toe of his slappy shoe.

'Were you not bringing cake?' she said.

'No, Mem. I no bring cake. Is all splat-splat on floor.'

'Oh dear, never mind. The biscuits look very . . . straight. You can go now and . . .' She raised her teacup as if proposing a toast. But even though her tongue had loosened up, her brain couldn't remember what to say.

Coop spoke for her. 'Would you like me to pour?'

'Too kind. My hand is a bit shaky.' She waggled the teacup to demonstrate, set the cup on the tray and collapsed back again, two patches of pink colouring her cheekbones. The room was like a furnace.

'Do you need a doctor, Mrs Sinclair?'

This caught her off guard, and she felt herself spinning, unable to produce an appropriate response. 'Did you tell me the purpose of your visit?'

He took a sip of tea, watching her over the rim of his china cup, then tilted his head towards the sea. 'Captain Sinclair sent me to fetch you. He says he needs you in the packing shed.'

'Can't get up.' She threw her hands in the air and let them flop down in her lap, and then she slowly slid off her seat until she lay flat on the floorboards. She closed her eyes.

There was silence for a while but it felt a lot cooler, stretched out on the hard naked wood. *Hot air rises, Maisie. Any fool knows that.*

'Go away,' she muttered. She wanted to be free of her mother.

A warm hand shook her arm. 'Excuse me, Mrs Sinclair. I didn't hear what you said. What should I tell Captain Sinclair?'

She opened her eyes and stared into his, her voice low and firm. 'Tell him I'm busy.'

The day was pale grey at the start, already an oven and buzzing with insects. It was business as usual in Buccaneer Bay.

When Maisie told Marjorie to be ready to go into town after siesta time, the Aboriginal maid was not happy. Scrunching up her face, she thrust one hand into her apron pocket and rummaged her uncombed hair with the other. She inspected the cull of her scalp under her fingernails. 'Why's we doing that, Missus?'

'You said you need spectacles, so I am taking you to an eye specialist.'

'Wot? You and me?'

'Yes.' Maisie was confused. 'You said you need "peepy gogglers". You meant spectacles, I'm sure.'

'That not gonna work.'

'Why ever not? You need to see an oculist, so I'm taking you.'

'No, Missus. Don't work dat way. You not pickin' up wot I's puttin' down.'

Maisie considered she was picking up far too well how things worked, or in some cases how they didn't. She steepled her fingers together in a silent prayer for patience. 'In what way, particularly with the spectacles, do I not understand?'

'No. See, I can't go in for the fiddly-doo-dah test thing-um in white man's shop. I ain't allowed.'

Maisie hitched up an expectant eyebrow. Marjorie knew the drill and waited for her prompt.

'Yes, Marjorie?'

'So, you do test thing-um for me.'

'Marjorie, how can I possibly do that? Your eyes are yours, not mine! I don't suffer from poor eyesight.'

'Missus, sometimes in life you got to do fakin', knows what I bin saying?' She tapped her nose.

Maisie sighed. 'All right. Let's draw some letters on a page in different sizes. You have to tell me when you can't see them clearly and I will try to convince the oculist.'

Marjorie tapped her fingertips together. 'You startin' to be a Buccaneer Bay woman, Missus. I's a proud Black Marjorie!'

Maisie fanned out the calling cards on her desk with the dexterity of a croupier. *Someone* had to have an at-home on a Thursday afternoon. She needed advice on obtaining spectacles and didn't know where to start. She pointed at a name and sucked her finger when she saw whom she would be visiting. There was nothing else for it. Desperate measures and all that.

An hour later, she was sitting on the verandah of Bishop McMahon and his wife, sipping tea in hundred-degree heat.

'These are delicious sandwiches, Mrs McMahon,' Maisie said, scanning the room. The hostess was wearing an unfortunate dress in mustard-coloured tartan, which did nothing to flatter her sallow complexion. The voice in Maisie's head would not be still, her mother's opinions still coming to mind before her own. *Jumble-sale clothing. If you marry a vicar, Maisie, that is what you will have to look forward to: picking through the worst of society's rejects.*

The usual cluster of old biddies endorsed these at-home visits for ladies. With their rickety legs crossed tight at the ankle, they nodded in approval of Maisie's presence and passed the time on a loop of recycled small talk. Others wiped crumbs from bristly chins. Tantalisingly, a box of cigarettes lay open on the table where the maid had deposited the afternoon-tea tray. Maisie's hand itched to pick one up and fill her lungs with delicious, liberating smoke in plain view of this tongue-clicking set. *Only loose women smoke, Maisie.* It made her smile at how quickly she had become one, or perhaps that woman had always been lurking beneath the surface, desperate to break out. Still, she sat on her hand and put the devil behind her.

'You are so sweet, Mrs Sinclair. Miss Locke, my companion, makes the most dainty cucumber sandwiches. She cuts the bread very thin. That's the secret. Of course, our cook-boy sets and bakes the bread – under supervision, naturally – but he has got the hang of it at last. And we grow the cucumbers in the yard here. Our Aboriginal garden boy sees to that. Oh, that reminds me! How is your boy managing your husband's magnificent croquet lawn?'

Maisie felt as though her stomach had been squeezed. Her lip trembled over her teeth. 'Charlie – the garden boy – had an accident a few weeks ago. I think Maitland has organised a replacement or a stand-in until he's better.' She was waiting for a thunderbolt to smite her from on high and roast her for the lie. 'Duc, our cook, is very competent. I rather leave him to the cooking. To both him and Marjorie, as a matter of fact.'

'Do I know such a person in your household?'

'I am sure you do. Marjorie is my maid.' Maisie pushed back her shoulders and elongated her spine. *Sit up straight, Maisie. A lady never slouches.*

'Oh, you mean Black Marjorie? Your lubra? I see! But you don't mean to say that you let her work in the kitchen and touch your food?'

Maisie looked away. All the whites had ethnic cooks, but Aboriginal people were prohibited from any employment in the town involving the handling of food. She hadn't planned to jump right in with the purpose of her visit, but she had no intention of devaluing her maid in public. 'Mrs McMahon, I wonder if you know where I might have my eyes tested? I'm concerned that I am not able to read my patterns at the knitting circle, and the words in my hymn book at the Sunday service seem to shiver on the page like a mirage.'

Mrs McMahon's personal bible of beliefs didn't seem to include twenty-twenty vision as a Godly attribute, it transpired. 'We don't have an oculist, as such, resident in the Bay, Mrs Sinclair. A visiting specialist offers appointments every now and then, but I am not aware that we are expecting Mr Barnes from Perth anytime soon. Certainly not until the cyclone season is over. He won't want to risk the steamer from Port Fremantle in a storm. I believe that there are Chinese men who claim expertise in Asia Place, but really, would you want to entrust your vision to an Oriental? The Chinese have appalling eyesight. They are renowned for it. I think you are going to have to dig deep, be patient and squint a little, like the rest of us.'

Maisie put down her teacup and patted her mouth with a napkin. She hadn't planned, either, to be scolded like a schoolgirl by the bishop's wife.

'You are quite right, Mrs McMahon. How silly of me to bother about my own little problems when we have a town far needier than any of us here in this lovely room – like Aborigines with venereal disease and leprosy, and Japanese divers in the hospital maimed by the diving sickness. You are quite right. I should hang my head in shame, worrying about my eyesight. What must I be thinking?'

Mrs McMahon was temporarily lost for words, caught on her own barb. 'Anyone for more tea?' she boomed. 'And, Augusta, I need to speak to you about the church flowers, they were a disgrace last week.'

Miss Locke, who had watched this exchange with an amused expression, seized her moment while her companion was ticking off the church's senior workforce. Voice low, she cast the conversation in an alternative direction. 'Do you remember our talk at the knitting circle? About European medical preferences?'

Maisie said that she did.

'Maybe that would be a more profitable avenue to explore. Perhaps. For you?' She looked down and stirred her tea. 'With your eyesight problem.'

Maisie lifted the corners of her mouth and produced a grateful smile. She sat back in her chair and looked into the intelligent grey eyes in Miss Locke's forty-something face. 'Thank you, Miss Locke. That would seem to be a very sensible avenue to pursue. I wonder, if ever Mrs McMahon could spare you from your duties, might you care to join me for afternoon tea one day soon?'

The route Maisie took to the Japanese hospital from the bishop's residence was not the most direct. She had time on her hands and wouldn't be missed at home. Maitland had no interest in what she did and lacked every conceivable social grace she had been brought up to embrace. Her journey led her through the hinterland of backstreets, a wilderness wound together by narrow lanes wedged between the wide main streets. It took her past long stretches of grimy housing, the sour stench of cat wee burning the air. Duc had told her there was a prolific population of feral cats in Buccaneer Bay. It kept the rats down, he said. *Hurrah for the cats.*

She wedged her forefinger under her nostrils – blocking things out had now become a reflex – and picked up her feet; the ground underfoot was too hot to dawdle.

The Chinese, who doubled as cooks, gardeners and tailors, ran many of the businesses she passed on little alleyways and wider lanes until she came to the Seafarer's Rest Hotel. She knew that William Cooper resided there, and her subconscious poked at her with a sharpened stick. *Is this why you have walked through here and not taken the more direct route? Are you hoping to run into him? He has no interest in you. You made a complete fool of yourself the last time you saw him. He is engaged to be married to the vacuous Miss Montague, who will never make him happy. And you are married, Maisie. Or had you forgotten?*

She passed a man she recognised from one of the endless parties she'd hosted. Maitland wanted to be seen in certain circles – that much she had worked out – but his reasons for schmoozing the second-tier whites eluded her. This man was a local accountant with a taste for profit. A 'money squeezer', her father would have called him. He was wearing spotless white – all the men wore white – and a sun helmet.

It's downpour season, she thought. *What a nonsensical affectation.*

The money squeezer was intent on a spot in front of him, and did not look up. He probably hadn't even seen her.

I wonder if he knows what a valuable asset I am on Maitland's balance sheet?

She knew her husband had plenty of money – they all did, these affluent bungalow dwellers. Money made with little regard for anyone else, by financing and trading with the pearling industry from the snug safety of shore.

Maisie stopped dead. She was now, she realised, one of the white-faced of Buccaneer Bay, a community that seemed to her to be struggling with its own identity. Within the white population, from Blair the mayor to Mister Gregory, who emptied the night pans and collected the rubbish, there was a sliding scale of respectability. That wasn't so different from England. What she could not abide was the deeply assumed superiority by all the white people who thought they were kings – in a country that had no royalty.

The smell in Asia Place pulled her out of her thoughts. It came from everywhere – the reek of mildew, tropical rot and desperation. Large iron buildings stood alongside tiny shops selling everything from diver's boots to Oriental clothing. There were no windows, only open slits under eaves ribbed with rusting bars. She saw that some of the shopkeepers were shuttering up their premises although it was barely mid-afternoon.

The air was oppressive, worse than normal, and the humidity hotly suffocating. Strands of hair, escapees from her neatly pinned chignon, clung to her neck. The doctor was on the hospital verandah, leaning over the lattice, a cigarette between two nicotine-stained fingers.

'Doctor Shin,' she said, as she climbed the steps and held out a grubby hand. She had left her gloves behind at tea. 'Please forgive me.'

He lifted a neatly trimmed eyebrow. 'For what offence?'

'For not making an appointment to see you. For not coming back when I promised I would. For not taking an interest in your hospital. You must think me shallow and indifferent and a complete mess.'

The doctor laughed. 'I think nothing of the sort, Mrs Sinclair. Indeed, I rarely have the luxury of time for idle thought. However, I can assure you that my musings would never reach such a conclusion and I am not sure that you did pledge to return, so cannot be judged negligent.'

Maisie placed her finger on the lattice and absently followed the wooden outline. 'Then I am more guilty than I feared. I have plenty of moments for action, and too much time for thoughts that I do not act upon.'

Doctor Shin took a pull on his cigarette and exhaled the smoke in a prolonged sigh. He rubbed his forehead. The rain was blowing through the lattice, leaving greasy puddles on the decking.

She thought about Charlie, took a deep breath and cast about for something else to ask first. 'I don't really understand why the Asiatics crew the luggers, Doctor Shin. A good number of the whites in the Bay do manual work, so why not on the boats? It's just that everyone seems so concerned about keeping the races separate here. This exception strikes me as out of place.'

Doctor Shin finished his cigarette and ground out the stub under his heel. The wind gathered up the smoke and spiralled it towards the sky. 'They are here because they are willing to work. Because the alternative is a life of grinding poverty in the countries they have left behind. Lugger-work is unpleasant, and they are cheap to employ, Mrs Sinclair. But nature has favoured the Japanese diver. He seems, from my observations, to be almost immune to inflammation of the ears, and to bleeding from the nose and ears when diving. There are more Japanese diving here than any other race. They are just as susceptible to paralysis as other races, though.'

'Is paralysis the only danger the Japanese divers face?'

'Sadly, no. The Japanese divers frequently suffer from the beri-beri disease.'

Maisie shook her head. 'I am afraid I have no idea what that is. Is it contagious?'

The doctor sighed. 'No. Not in my view. Divers suffer an unvaried diet of tinned and salted food for nine months of the year, and eat a good deal of white, polished rice with few vegetables and little fruit. The disease can be as deadly as the diver's paralysis, and many of the symptoms are similar to it – fluid-filled limbs, inability to walk and breathing difficulties. If not treated, beri-beri will certainly lead to loss of life.'

'Is there not a cure?'

Doctor Shin produced a packet of cigarettes from his coat pocket. He tapped one out and lit up. 'Yes. Fresh fruit and vegetables, dried peas and beans, or unpolished rice, and a squeeze of lemon or lime juice in a cup of tea.'

'And shall the white divers be at risk of this?'

'Almost certainly. Until just now, the only white man aboard the luggers will have been an occasional shell-opener or a hands-on master pearler fearful that his crew might steal from him.'

Maisie brightened. 'I'm thinking of taking out fresh fruit and vegetables to the men on my husband's supply schooner. That's bound to help them stay well.'

Doctor Shin shook his head. 'While that is a laudable idea, there is no way for the men to keep fresh produce from spoiling.'

'Yes, my maid said that.'

'But if you were very determined to try, lemons and limes can last for a few weeks if stored out of the direct sun. You could tell the divers that.'

Maisie looked at him and smiled. 'I will certainly do that and tell them that it was your suggestion to keep them in good health.'

They stood for a moment in silence.

Doctor Shin took a long pull on his cigarette. 'Was there something else?'

Maisie bit her lip and swerved round the question she longed to ask. 'And how is our gardener, Charlie?'

The black eyes clouded. 'He has gone now.'

All the blood seemed to rush from her face. 'He died?'

'No. Charlie has gone back to his mob. He was very sick for a while, but he was able to leave, eventually.'

'It is a relief to know that he is better.'

'If that is all, Mrs Sinclair, I have much work to do.'

'Just a quick question before you go, Doctor Shin.'

Doctor Shin pasted on his best listening face. 'Mrs Sinclair?'

'How do I go about having my maid's eyes tested? She needs spectacles and insists that no-one will be prepared to help her in Buccaneer Bay by dint of her colour, and . . .'

The doctor smiled. 'Make an appointment for her on your way out, Mrs Sinclair. In the great scheme of things, eyes are easy to fix.'

Maisie felt her heart pumping in her chest. She could see the doctor was anxious to get back to his work. *I can't ask him, and yet . . .*

Doctor Shin pointed to a chair. His voice was very quiet. 'Do sit down, Mrs Sinclair. I believe we are playing cat-and-mouse with the real reason for your visit.'

She sat down and pulled at the neck of her blouse. Without looking up she said, 'Is it normal for a man to avoid all physical contact with his new wife? To have never once come near her, even on her wedding night?'

CHAPTER 12

THE NIGHT BEFORE THEY set sail, three days after they were supposed to have left, Coop couldn't sleep. The intense heat had not abated and he had again dragged his bedding outside. Backwards and forwards, he played a never-ending game with the elements. When he tried to sleep in his room, the air hung hot and oppressive like a suffocating blanket. On the balcony, where it was marginally cooler, insects swarmed out of the darkness; he squashed mosquitos one after another until the fabric of his shirt was blotched crimson with his own blood. He could feel the burn of the sun in his skin and prayed it would be cooler at sea. The Japanese diver accompanying them had taken a lot of convincing to dive before the end of the cyclone season, and the wait had almost driven him mad.

Coop sank back on the pillow and closed his eyes, but sleep would not come. His mind swirled in uncharted seas, keeping rest from him. Even when he did sleep, a face wandered across his dreams: Maisie Sinclair. His heart bumped uncomfortably against his ribs at the thought of her and a shiver of desire edged its way down his spine. He rubbed a hand over his chin and wished that he'd shaved more carefully before his visit. He'd got sloppy since arriving in the Bay; she would have seen the dark stubble and thought poorly of him.

Had she known, he wondered for the umpteenth time, that he could barely keep his eyes off her the whole time he'd been there? That he'd stared, wretched with envy, at the delicate oval of her face as she lay on the floor like an alabaster sculpture? That he'd been almost overcome by the urge to pick her up, to keep her safe within his arms? And yet why had she been drunk at barely ten in the morning? Was there some deep unhappiness in her marriage that had turned her to the bottle? Despite his torment, he smiled in the dark, clutching at her words like hope: *Tell him I'm busy*. She hadn't stirred herself for her husband, but had made time for him.

A loud snort derailed Coop's train of thought. On the balcony next door, JB was puttering through his nose and lips. His friend was curled on his side, his head resting on his hands like a pet in its basket. Coop envied him – after years as a tender, he could sleep anywhere.

Even from his hotel, a mile from the beach, Coop could hear waves thrashing in the bay. Thunderclaps cracked like whips overhead, the sky an electrical show of flashing white lightning slashing through the stars, keeping sleep a dream. Inch by inch, he stretched out his limbs to the cool corners of his bed, relishing the relief until he was again stewing with heat.

At six the next morning, Coop pushed his half-eaten breakfast plate away. He had no appetite for the greasy chops, and was too nervous to work his jaws on the stringy meat. He heaped sugar into a mug of tea and replayed the meeting with Captain Sinclair in his head again, wondering if he'd missed something key. What *had* prompted the great change in the captain's opinion of his ability to 'see' shell? A few weeks ago, the boss had been pretty scathing of his chances.

By six-thirty, dawn was breaking in the east. The Seafarer's Rest Hotel was quiet as Coop and JB set off along the beach. The rain had eased but the wind was wildly insistent, whipping the waves white and sending them thundering against the rocks. The two men bent over, turned their shoulders into the force of the gale and forced their way towards the lay-up camp. The sand, no longer benign, blasted sharp-edged shrapnel against their skin.

JB used his sleeve to wipe the gritty residue from his face. 'You all set, Coop? Nervous?'

Coop breathed in a lungful of salty air. 'Always am before a dive. You know that. Not sure about this weather, though. It's really blowing up. Visibility will be nil.'

'You've dived in wild weather, Coop. Think about that job we did last year off the north coast of Scotland.'

'That was different. It was freezing and the middle of winter but it wasn't a storm-force blast. No-one with a grain of sense would go out to sea in weather like this.'

'Then why are we?' JB said.

Coop punched him lightly on the arm. 'Good question, JB. I asked for this dry run, so we have to go. It's the first decent thing Captain Sinclair's done for us, so we're not going to back out because the sea's a bit rough. Anyway, he said the forecast was good.'

'And that's a load of bollocks,' JB muttered.

They trudged on, battling through the loose sand, their canvas kit bags stuffed with diving gear. At the end of the beach, they turned inland. With the wind gusting relentlessly against their backs, they almost ran along a snaking path to the creek where Maitland had his boats laid up during the Wet. JB braced his shoulders and leaned backwards into the wind, trying to slow himself down.

'Can you pick up the pace a bit, JB?'

'I don't have a good feeling about this, Coop.'

'It's what we came for.'

JB straightened up. 'I know, but it feels – I dunno – like we're being set up. Those are storm clouds on the horizon, and you know it as well as I do.'

A pale cream blob of light winked at him from the lighthouse and stretched out its arc across the bay. 'It'll be fine, JB. Sooner we get there, sooner we can show them what we Brits are made of, eh?'

At the lay-up camp, Coop exchanged his shoes for heavy caulked sea boots, tucked his dive helmet up under his arm and squelched across the mud to the small snub-nosed craft floating in the creek, its Christmas-green paint blistered and scratched like an old door. JB removed his shoes, hitched his duffle bag onto his shoulder and followed barefoot, furrowing lines of misgiving on his face.

They knew Captain Sinclair had a policy of mixing his crews. His multinational workforce barely tolerated each other, which some said suited him down to the ground. The Japanese considered themselves superior, and treated the Malays and Filipinos with contempt. The Keopangers were bottom of the pile.

Daike, the number-one diver, was already on board, sitting amid a clutter of ropes and supplies. He was watching the light change over the water, the clouds race overhead and the hawks chase down their prey, claws stretched out beneath them in the strange watery dawn. As Coop approached, the Japanese diver fingered the rice-paper charm he wore under his vest and took a spoonful of his breakfast rice. A flick of his wrist tossed it over the side.

'Fish's favourite food?' Coop said.

'You take from sea, white boy, you give back to sea.'

Coop's mouth twisted. Tension tapped at his temples, his eyes gritty from lack of sleep. He was not in the mood for a duel.

'Is that a Japanese custom?'

Daike didn't reply.

'Okay.' He pointed at a mangrove branch attached to the mast. 'And that?'

'He for safe return.' He pointed at Coop's feet. 'And you no wear boots on lugger.'

'Why not?' Coop said.

'More better.'

'Why?'

'Feet better for . . .' He searched for the English word. 'Upright.'

Coop opened his mouth but Daike held up a hand and silenced him. 'You talk too much, white boy. To see shell you need be quiet. We go now. Before rain come.'

Within half an hour they cast off. The crewman at the tiller steered the rolling lugger down the twisting creek and out into the bay. Wave after wave crashed against the hull, flushing the deck with foam, the sea boiling and angry. The wooden joints in the masts groaned loudly as they negotiated the reef-strewn channel. They finally dropped anchor before the treacherous Neptune's Dairy, a narrow strip of water surrounded by rocky outcrops.

'We stop here,' Daike said. 'Start work.' He refused to go further until he'd seen Cooper in the water.

'Where's my compressor, Daike?' Coop asked, not seeing it on deck.

'No bring.'

'No bring? Why not?'

'No like. Better Malay boys turn handle.'

'Have you ever used an engine air compressor?'

The Japanese diver said nothing.

'Are you scared, Daike, that the engine will bring bad luck?'

'I not scared.'

'That's good, because if we dive together again I'm bringing the engine-driven pump with me. You can dive much deeper, and it's safer if you stick to the tables.'

'We no dive together second time. One time only. Is big favour.'

JB stood on deck, waving the Admiralty tables in one hand and a stopwatch in the other. The waves rocking the lugger were making him work to keep his balance.

Daike announced that they would dive together to fifteen fathoms. 'Is not normal. Normal is I go then you go. That way, we keep man on bottom all day. Today I show you shell.'

'What about decompression times?'

Daike looked contemptuous. 'You want rest like girl? Okay. I go down, I come up. Have cuppa tea and smoko then I go down some more.'

'Are you not afraid of decompression sickness?'

Daike clomped off muttering, 'I not afraid of anything.'

JB put down the Admiralty tables and stopwatch, and wedged himself against the edge of the boat. A major part of his job was to assist Coop dress in his diving outfit, and the pitching lugger was not helping. It was a task with a start and an end, and it could not be rushed. Coop hauled long scratchy woollen stockings over his feet and up his thighs. Then came two woollen vests, a pair of red tweed trousers and two heavy sweaters, crowned with a woolly cap to insulate his head.

On deck, despite the wind, Coop was beginning to sweat. He knew the initial dive water would be soothingly warm, but as he sank like a stone to the depths the chill would envelop him, and he would be glad to be wearing layers of wool.

The big, one-size-fits-all rubberised diving suit was before him. There was no way he could negotiate it by himself.

JB soaped Coop's wrists and stretched the head opening wide, standing back as Coop squirmed himself inside. He then sat on the one piece of furniture on board – the stool – for the heavy work to begin.

Daike was already hanging over the side on a rope ladder, his shell bag draped round his neck, brownish-black water foaming around his waist. The expression on his face through the glass plate was impossible to read.

Coop lunged his feet into his weighted boots – fourteen pounds of lead on the ends of his legs that helped keep him planted on the ocean floor. JB placed lead weighting plates on his chest and back, and a copper corselet over his shoulders.

He moved to the second of the coir-rope ladders for the final fitting of his diving helmet. Perching over the side of the lugger, hanging onto the edge of the boat, he waited while JB dropped the green-tinged copper helmet onto its fastenings around his neck. He dunked the faceplate in the seawater to prevent it fogging with condensation, and twisted a short stub of wood across the screws to tighten the seals. The rubber air hose was fitted into the helmet, the rope lifeline was secured around his chest, and finally Coop was set to go. A deckhand was already busy turning the wheel to keep the number-one diver supplied with oxygen. It was unusual to have two pumps on board – there was scarcely room for one.

A heaving wave hit the hull like a hammer and tipped the *Sharky* sideways. Coop clung to the ladder until the ancient lugger righted itself as it lurched and shuddered in the raging water, then lowered himself feet-first into the sea and sank from view into the murky gloom.

On board, JB waited with his back braced against the cabin and played out Coop's lifeline. It was strange to watch the deckhand responsible for his diver's air supply and he waited, anxious for the shake on the lifeline to signal that Coop was on the bottom. When it came, he started his stopwatch. He kept the divers at fifteen fathoms for sixty minutes, and then brought them to the surface when their time was up. It was a long, slow process.

The first drift over the seabed produced nothing. Back on deck, the two divers drank tea and lit cigarettes.

'What's wiped out all the shell, Daike?' Coop said.

'We spend too much time come up. Not enough time look on bottom. Shell is there. We go back and look some more. We no dangle on rope.'

JB glanced at the black clouds gathering on the horizon. He looked at Coop and shook his head.

'You need rest time, Daike. Have another cup of tea and then we can go again in an hour or so,' Coop tried.

'I no wait. I have cuppa then I go down. I see shell here at start of Wet,' Daike said. 'I go down and pick up plenty. Today I show you how dive here. Tomorrow we sail little bit and you on own. Want help spot shell, you go now.'

Coop quizzed JB with a look.

JB hunched his shoulders. 'Your funeral, Coop. You should be up for three hours. You've barely had twenty minutes. Can't force you, though, if you want to play silly buggers.'

They went down again, over and over. As the day wore on, JB became more vocally concerned. Coop had told him about the poor visibility, and Daike was reporting alternate hot and cold currents, which bothered him. The huge black clouds, shot through with flickering lightning, seemed more menacing than any he had seen in his life. The wind had blown itself into a fury. They still hadn't found any shell.

'Coop,' JB said quietly, 'I think we should hoist sail and head back to the creek.' It was three o'clock in the afternoon, and the sails hung limp like wet washing on the rigging.

Coop agreed, but Daike wouldn't hear of it. 'You want run for cover like sissy boy? Who frightened now?'

'I'm not frightened. Just trying to be sensible.'

'You frightened. I tell boss man you sissy boy.'

'And you are a bloody madman. Do you want to get us all killed?'

JB had heard enough, and put his hand up like a referee at a football match. 'The wind's dropped. Just look at the sky.'

The entire sky had gone black, as if night had come early.

Jane Locke looked up from her paper and smiled. 'You found it!'

Maisie dumped a brown paper package on the tabletop. Her face was burning and she felt rather damp. 'Thank you so much for suggesting this, Miss Locke, and please accept my apologies for keeping you waiting. There were one or two things I needed to do in town and I momentarily lost my way.'

Jane nodded. 'The backstreets can be tricky. I've had my fair share of encounters with dead ends and feral cats.'

Maisie peeled off her gloves and patted the palms of her hands against her cheeks; the heat seemed to be receding. 'I didn't even know this place existed. I haven't really eaten anywhere other than in our bungalow or with our friends at their homes.'

'Do please sit down and let me pour you a glass of water, Mrs Sinclair. The Long Soup and Satay Shop is one of my favourite places to come when I want to get away from the residency, but I appreciate it is quite a stretch of the legs from your bungalow. It's much closer for me, so I try to come most weeks for Mr Truong's long soup.' She pointed to the kitchen at the end of the corrugated-iron shed, where an old, long-haired Chinese man was draping strands of limp noodle dough over a fat wooden pole.

Maisie picked up her glass and took a small sip. 'I am embarrassed to confess I don't know what long soup is, Miss Locke, let alone a satay. It's shameful, really, how little effort I have made to integrate myself in the Bay. My friend Mrs Wallace is constantly chiding me for wallowing in bouts of homesickness.'

'Well,' Jane replied, 'it's early days, and a happy marriage will soon cure you of that.'

Maisie kept her eyes on the checked tablecloth. She was only just getting over her embarrassing conversation with Doctor Shin on the subject of her continuing virginity. 'So, satay and long soup are what, exactly?'

'A popular myth is that Mr Truong's satay – chunks of meat, skewered on metal rods and cooked in a fire pit – is made from the flesh of stray cats. I denounce this myth on the basis that the feline population is far too thin.'

Maisie was not sure how to respond to this, so said nothing.

Mr Truong shuffled over and slapped two menus, spoons and napkins on the table. Maisie stared at hand-drawn pictures of the dishes he served. 'Are there no written descriptions?'

Jane smiled. 'This is easier when there is a large mixed-race community who speak different tongues. What language would you use? Mr Truong came over with the first great influx of Chinese immigrants in the mid-1800s during the gold rush over east. Many of the labourers who came at that time were employed as cooks, and Mr Truong gradually found his way here and quite literally set up shop.'

'Did he tell you that?'

'Yes, when I asked him. Who is Mrs Wallace?'

Maisie ran her hand over the menu. 'I can see from the pictures that long soup is a liquid thick with smooth flat noodles, meat and vegetables.'

Jane nodded. 'What you can't tell, though, is that the liquid is fragrant and spicy, and the vegetables crunchy. I generally skip the meat and dive straight into the vegetables, which at the residence are invariably overcooked and in poor supply.'

Maisie twisted her napkin round her finger and mumbled something vague about vegetables being a universal problem in the Bay.

'Who is Mrs Wallace?' Jane asked again.

Maisie's voice was gone, her whisper faint. 'A very dear lady I travelled with to Australia. I miss her more than I ever thought possible.'

Jane clasped Maisie's hand and pressed it in her own. 'It's very difficult at the beginning, leaving behind the familiar and finding one's feet in a new environment,' she said. 'Friends are too few, and we must take care to nurture the ones we have. Do you think we might move on to using first names?'

Maisie stared at Jane's hand, which still had a tight hold of her own. 'I'd like that very much.' She wondered how she could extricate her fingers without seeming rude. 'First names would be lovely, so please call me Maisie.'

Jane withdrew her hand and reached for the water jug. 'And I am the plain Jane, who senses that you are struggling in your new home.'

Maisie looked properly at the woman seated opposite. A tall, statuesque woman with straight red hair slightly greying at the roots and cut short to her chin, a square face, and an impressive bosom dwarfing her slender hips. She looked cool, comfortable with herself in her drop-waist cotton day dress – the polar opposite of her employer. The bishop's wife was brusque, fat and prone to excessive perspiration.

'I think you do yourself an injustice, particularly on an intellectual level. I heard from Doctor Shin – and thank you for that recommendation – that you are conducting a study into the Aborigines and their culture.'

Jane looked pleased. Maisie imagined there were few people she had met in the Bay who were able to look beyond the lines on her face or the wisps of hair on her upper lip to see the nimble-minded person who lived inside.

'I am, and I would very much enjoy talking to your maid Marjorie at some point as part of my research. But that is not why I have asked you here today.' She looked around the restaurant. 'Do you recognise anyone who might give us away?'

Maisie glanced around and shook her head. A young boy darted in from outside, his sodden shirt clinging to his ribcage, his hair blown wild by the wind. She hardly knew a soul in the Bay, and anyone who might consider themselves an acquaintance had probably thought better of the weather and remained indoors.

Jane lifted a menu off the table and flipped it on its back. 'Please tell me if it is none of my business, but true friends and honesty are in short supply in the Bay. Let me be frank. Are you happy here? Because I worry very much that you are not.'

'I'm not really sure what happiness is, but this,' she waved her hand in circles beside her ear, 'is what my life has become. I was sent here to marry a man I did not know. It wasn't at all my choice.'

'Were you not close to your parents?'

'Why would you ask that?'

Jane gave her an appraising look. 'Oh, I don't know. You never speak of them, and they weren't present at your marriage ceremony. Most fathers give their daughters away. Handing the care of his daughter to someone else is a big moment in a man's life, and a mother would want to reassure herself that her child was cared for and happy. I am surprised neither one of them accompanied you out here.'

Maisie gave a disappointed sigh. 'My parents are not demonstrative in that way, but I am sure they had my welfare at heart when they entrusted my care to Mrs Wallace.'

'But coming to the Bay was not what you had dreamed of?'

'No.'

Jane looked at her. 'Nor me. I have dreamed of many things in my life, but living in the Bay was never part of them. Life is what happens when one's guard is down. Technically speaking, I am not a Miss, although I keep the title. It avoids questions.'

'I don't understand.'

'I have been married. My husband is no longer with me, but I have known real happiness and what it feels like.'

Maisie felt the heat returning to her face. To be looked at so closely was unsettling and made her feel very young. She glanced at Jane and pressed her lips together, willing herself not to cry. Jane Locke understood the utter pain of abandonment, one of the most bruising of human emotions. Tears of self-pity stung Maisie's eyes and ran, for once unchecked, down her cheeks.

'Did your husband catch a fever and die?'

'No. He is a bigamist.'

Mr Truong's voice clarioned from the kitchen. 'You wanna order food, Mems?'

'Just a moment, thank you,' Jane called back.

Maisie stared at her companion, her tears halted and her mouth hanging open. She blew her nose. 'You said he died!'

'No, I said he has gone from my life. Not at all the same thing. I discovered that he had quite the matrimonial career. I was wife number four. It is easy to commit bigamy given the paucity of centralised marriage records in Australia, I have learned. Frank moved around a lot and told lies on the certificate of marriage. He changed his name, his age and his occupation several times. He ought to have become a writer and told lies for a living. He'd have made a fortune.'

'How did you find out?'

'Wife number two tracked him down when we were living in Perth. We'd been "married" for two years. I have no idea about number one and number three.'

Maisie straightened the cuffs of her blouse. 'How then do you find yourself in the Bay?'

Jane reached for the menu. 'Let's order our food and have lunch. That's a very long story for another day.'

Lightning danced in the sky, and clouds were advancing like a mini armada, sailing in shifting formations before battle began. The rain, which had been threatening for hours, began to cascade, hard and fast. Even so, the residents of the Bay were lucky with the typhoon's water surge. The reef, which could exfoliate luggers like dead skin, shielded the town from the worst of the storm. Nonetheless, it smashed its way along the foreshore, wrenching sheltering boats from their moorings, hurtling them into the air and smashing the less robust ones to splinters.

On the cliff edge, next to the lighthouse, an empty oil drum crashed against the side of the bungalow. It was pitch black outside, although barely past five o'clock.

Maisie was not long returned from lunch with Jane and could hear Maitland shouting to Duc at the back of the house. She stood by the bottom verandah step, smoking a cigarette very fast and gripping the rail tight. It felt rough under her hand, like a callus. She blew the smelly evidence away in quick, angry puffs. She knew she needn't have bothered with the deception, but the defiance felt like joy.

'Get a bloody wriggle on, Duc. If we don't get the shutters down, the wind will blow the roof off and you will have nowhere to park your skinny Chinese arse.'

Captain Mason had already appeared for the nightly sousing of his insides and was also press-ganged into service.

'Give me a hand, Shorty. Get round to the shutters on the other side of the house, or you'll have no gin-god to worship here tomorrow night!'

One by one, Maisie could hear the storm shutters crashing on the sills. There was nothing subtle about her husband and his friends. Maitland yelled over the wind, 'Where the bloody hell are you, Maisie? Get that useless lubra of yours in here, quick smart. She needs to get to work and earn her bloody wages.'

Maisie almost laughed at the irony. Marjorie was at that moment in town trying to win money, because the boss didn't pay her any. She was marking a chiffa ticket with the signs that they hoped portrayed success in love and vengeance in enemies. They had struggled with the riddle and were going for the magic finger approach tonight: *eeny, meeny, miny, moe.*

'What time do you think you'll be back?' Maisie had asked.

'Don't know exact time, Missus. Gubberment want us blackfellas back by six o'clock, but mebbe I go allonga my aunties.'

Maisie knew that the whereabouts of the natives was never supervised. They were like the feral cats in town, tolerated to do a job. She would never snitch on her maid and neither would Duc. They had become an unlikely team, intent on protecting and helping one another.

Heavy footsteps thumped down the verandah and voices forced her back into the shadows, the angle of the house shielding her from view.

'Your luggers all safe, Shorty?'

'Yes. We dragged them up to the creek.'

'I sent one of my ancient ones out today.'

Shorty laughed. 'You're a bloody maniac, Maitland!'

'It's what we agreed, Shorty. Sometimes you have to be hard-nosed and let them rot if they don't pay their way.'

'Let what rot?' Maisie climbed up the steps and stopped at the drinks table. She sloshed a large glug of gin in a glass and plopped in some ice.

'I've sent one of the old luggers out to test whether she's seaworthy. Can't decide whether it warrants the expense of a refit.'

'In this weather?' Maisie's jaw dropped. 'That's insanity, Maitland! No boat could withstand this wind. I hope it's well insured.' She turned towards their guest. 'And did you, Captain Mason, also send a lugger out with every prospect of a cyclone pending, knowing that the vessel was not sound?'

Shorty stretched out in his chair. 'When to send the boats out is always a gamble, Mrs Sinclair. We're all heading out next week. Maitland is always ahead of the game. His instincts are famous. You should be proud that he has got a lugger out at this time of year. It's a risk most of us wouldn't be prepared to take. He's got guts, your man.'

Maitland settled himself in a recliner and nodded at Shorty Mason, his mouth twisted in a smirk as if at some secret joke.

An ugly truth was dawning on Maisie – the lugger would have a crew. There was far more than an unseaworthy boat at risk. 'And which crew, Maitland, have you sacrificed to the deep in this daring gamble of yours?'

'I'm not a fool, Maisie. The one I can most easily and most cost-effectively afford to lose.'

'Please don't tell me you sent a diver out too?'

'Of course. One of my Japs, and that English fellow, Cooper.'

Maisie set down her glass with great care. Her hand was steady and her palm dry, but her stomach lurched with anxiety. She didn't want to cause another lava flow to erupt from her husband, but she couldn't let the comment go. 'A hurricane is not a person, Maitland. *It* cannot be blamed. But the man who sends out innocent lives into its destructive centre most certainly can. I am struggling to understand what sort of human being could do that. Knowingly.'

She picked up a magazine, her fingers strangling the spine. Her heart lurched as she thought of Coop – as tall as a Viking, eyes the colour of liquorice, and beautiful slim fingers she dreamed might one day touch her. She tugged at a loose thread on the chair back beside her and tried to stifle the tolling in her brain. *You might never see him again.* Round and round the words repeated themselves in her mind until her head began to ache.

Maitland turned to Shorty Mason and jiggled his glass. 'She's wearing her angry-tiger face this evening,' he sneered. 'Want another drink, Shorty? You won't be going anywhere in this weather. Might as well put on your drinking boots and make a night of it.' He jerked his chin at her. 'You can stay if you want. It's not as if you have a burning assignation anywhere else.'

Maisie shook her head. 'I'm prepared to assist you in every way I can, Maitland, for business purposes, but I am not going to remain here all evening and help you and your friend drink away our profits. If you'll excuse me, gentlemen, I believe I'll forgo supper and turn in with a book. I'm not in the mood for company.'

The two captains raised themselves slightly from their seats then sank back to their drinks, shouting loudly at each other to make themselves heard above the maelstrom that was gaining momentum outside Maitland's insulated fortress.

Maisie's bedroom was a furnace, sealed up tight at a smelting temperature of over a hundred and ten degrees. The heat was like her mother – an unrelenting, impenetrable force that would not back down. It was intolerably hot, and after a couple of hours of scrambling about among the sheets she resigned herself to the fact she would never sleep. She tried not to think of her old English bedroom in the tall London house and the fresh smell of laundry starch on her cool, expensive sheets; of her own quiet, private space with her treasured possessions all around her. Eventually, tormented with worry for William Cooper's safety, she got out of bed and began to pace; back and forth, back and forth until her thoughts began to boil. Buccaneer Bay was far worse than the picture Mrs Wallace had painted for her, and she felt at that moment that if it was her punishment to live here with a sexually irresponsive husband (Doctor Shin's diagnosis), she must have done something very bad in a previous life.

The sea was running two or three times the height of the lugger.

'Help me get this suit off, JB.' Cooper turned to one of the deckhands. 'Get the main sails down!' he shouted. 'Leave the foresail. If the wind picks up, I'll try to run her back to the creek. Get your diving stuff off, Daike. You need to be able to move.'

'Why you give orders? I number-one diver.'

'Do you know how to sail a boat in a storm? Or do you just swagger about like a jerk telling everyone you're as brave as a lion while all the time you bless the boat, the deck and the sea, before you consider yourself protected enough by your little superstitious rituals to set sail?'

Daike would not look him in the eye, but Coop saw from the set of his jaw that he was a long way from happy.

Within an hour, they hit the full force of the storm. Waves broke over the decks, slamming coils of anchor chain against the sides of the lockers. Squinty emerged from the cabin, clothes wringing wet, his face disfigured by fear. 'What we do?'

'Throw out storm anchors. We ride out willy-willy,' Daike shouted back. He felt for his lucky charm through his shirt. 'When it's day to die, you die.'

'No!' Coop shouted against the wind, a look of scorn on his face. He didn't buy into that fatalistic claptrap. The gusting wind sent him lurching sideways but his feet held fast, weighted down by his determination. He worked his way across the deck to the tiller, clinging to the rail of the boat. 'Get all the rigging down and lighten the load. Just leave me the foresail. Cut the dingy and pumps loose and hack through the bulwarks with the tomahawks I saw in the cabin. If the water can flow across the decks, there'll be less resistance when we try to surf the old girl back to the creek. Lash yourself to anything fixed down and hope like hell we make it.'

Daike looked across at Coop, his hair dripping with water, and nodded to himself. One arm braced for support against the creaking boom of the mizzenmast, he began to empty his bladder off the stern of the lugger. 'I piss on you, English boy. You no brave lion. You watch me. I show you what what on lugger boat!' he shouted.

'Stupid bugger,' Coop muttered under his breath. *He's probably tossed some charm into the water to bless his pee.*

Without warning, the wind veered. Clouds whipped across the sky and dumped rain in stair rods over the *Sharky*'s deck. The lugger rolled and pitched as she fought to stay afloat. Coop grabbed at the tiller and spread his toes to steady himself against the swell. Daike was right; boots would have slipped on the water-washed deck. Coop dipped his head in private acknowledgement of the life-saving advice he'd been given.

The stubborn Japanese still had his arm draped round the mast. He was too bloody-minded to heed Coop's advice. He held on tight with both hands as they waited for the storm to reach its height.

The circling wind caught hold of the boom and ripped Daike from his post. Coop ducked down to miss the swooping beam and saw it bowl the other diver aside like a skittle.

A man overboard was not a common occurrence in pearling waters. The boat tore along, the accidental jib tugging the rudder in his hands.

'Man overboard! Listen up! Daike's overboard. He's not attached to the boat. Point at him, all of you. Whatever happens, don't take your eyes off him. Squinty, get the lifebelt and throw it to JB! JB, when we get close, chuck the belt at Daike and reel him in. Everyone else keeps pointing at him. If we lose sight of him, he's a dead duck.'

Daike was bouncing on the waves, his arms flailing helplessly by his sides as the wind and waves blew him further from the lugger. Coop saw his mouth open, shouting something, but his words were swept up to the clouds. Over and over he turned the lugger in a figure of eight, but waves humped up like rows of breaching whales and tore the rudder from his hands, driving the boat from its course. His eyes burned with salt spray and yet he continued to turn back towards the stricken diver, dodging the flying boom, hauling on the sheets, carving slow, laborious spirals.

'Come on, Coop!' JB shouted. 'Come about again. I nearly had him that time.'

Finally they came close enough. The exhausted crew pulled Daike in by the lifebelt, clutching him under the arms and heaving him onto the deck.

Coop tore a strip from his shirt and wound it round his bloodied fingers.

'Cookie, take him below and turn him on his side. Everyone else hold on tight. I'm going to run us back to the mangrove inlet we passed this morning. It might give us some shelter from this blow.'

'Righto, but you one crazy, mad English fella,' Squinty said.

Coop clamped his swollen hands on the tiller and dragged the rudder from side to side, keeping the wind trapped inside the sail as the little boat battled through the galloping waves. *If the sheet starts to flap, we're in trouble.* It became his mantra. Over and over he repeated the words, his bloodshot eyes staring alternately at the reef and the sail until he could barely focus.

The crew had terrified eyes locked on him, as if keeping him in sight would keep them safe. He fastened his thoughts on the channel they had sailed up that morning. He knew it wasn't that far. He was grateful then that Daike had doubted his ability to dive and that they hadn't gone further through the reef-strewn Neptune's Dairy. A long time after, he became conscious that the wind had eased and the towering peaks in front of him were no longer waves but trees.

Wide-eyed, Daike emerged from the cabin and stared from one to the other of the crew as if he couldn't believe he'd survived. 'Why you come for me?'

'You haven't shown me where the shell is yet, you stupid, stubborn bugger!' Coop shot back.

Just before midnight, Maisie put on her white cotton kimono and tiptoed out of her bedroom in search of a glass of water.

The drinking boots were still laced up tight on the verandah.

'Warmed up the bed, Maisie, and come to get me?' Captain Mason lurched from his chair and grabbed her from behind.

He scrumpled up one of her breasts as if he were balling up a napkin, the twisted blue veins ugly on his hand as he squeezed hard through her robe. He swung her round and planted his gin-soaked lips upon hers in a crushing kiss.

She jumped back from him, appalled. 'What on earth do you think you're doing, Captain Mason?'

Shorty Mason was too drunk to be put off. He lunged at her and bared his teeth, his breath hot and rancid on her face, and puckered his lips for another assault. His face looked grey in the lamplight, and sweat ran down the sides of his nose. She pulled back her head and tried to drag herself away but he held her fast, his hips slamming hard against her thigh.

'Maitland!' she cried. 'Make him stop!'

Maitland snorted and pointed at her with his pipe. 'Don't think you're anything special, wife. He does it to all the women.'

She wrenched herself free and fell hard on her knees, her face still fixed on her husband. Shorty Mason's hips were drawn back, posed to thrust, his trousers straining at the groin. A shudder ran through her when she saw that her distress excited him. She scrambled to her feet and stood for a moment on rubbery legs, unable to move. Slowly she backed away towards the door, feeling for the furniture behind her, her skin prickly. She only realised when she reached her room and barricaded herself in that her teeth were chattering.

Cooper limped the *Sharky* into a mangrove-lined creek to shelter from the cyclone while the sea raged beyond. It was obvious they wouldn't be able to move until at least the next day, and then only if the lugger didn't need any emergency patch-ups.

The wind roared around them and rain whipped cruelly at their salt-chafed skin. The men set up a camp among the tree roots and sat huddled, ravaged by the assault. Cookie fed them on fish he found washed up along the high-water mark. There were hundreds of maimed birds thrown up on the mud as well, but no-one had the stomach to try them.

Coop's temporary bedroom was the small, low-ceilinged cabin with its blackened rafters of hard, dark wood through which no air could penetrate. The walls were dirtied by years of pipe soot, and cockroaches popped up through the flooring like a spring-loaded army. There was no porthole. It was a room without a view, and it could not have been less appealing.

Although stifling inside, it was a better option than toughing it out on a mildewed blanket in the fetid swamp. JB had joined him in the cramped space. The rest of the crew was taking its chances with the sandflies, which hunted in relentless swarms. Their bites left suppurating lesions on ankles, forearms – anywhere tasty flesh was exposed. The wounds itched relentlessly and the temptation to scratch was maddening. Coop preferred to sweat.

He pressed his face into his pillow and squeezed his eyes shut. JB was already asleep, his breathing regular and untroubled. Coop rolled onto his side, then onto his back, and stared at the ceiling for a bit. After tossing and turning for half the night he got down from his berth and raked his fingers through his matted hair – there was no way he was going to sleep. He slipped out on deck in the early hours and lay down on a tarpaulin. He closed his eyes and tried to untangle the events that had led to their present predicament.

Captain Sinclair had abruptly changed tack to flatter him out to sea on a clapped-out lugger. He spent a long time wondering about that. Like an excited child, he'd signed a document in Captain Sinclair's office that he'd pretended he could read. Whatever Captain Sinclair was up to, he was as smart as the devil, and Coop needed to wise up.

He slapped at a mosquito and shifted his position. It was impossible to get comfortable on deck. The water smacked at the planking, unbalancing the order of his thoughts. He found himself thinking about Mrs Sinclair. He barely knew her, but her elegance and beauty did nothing to diminish her resourcefulness or strength of will, and despite her poise she truly seemed to judge others by who they were rather than how they had been born. She was different from anyone he had ever met – a finer breed of woman, and utterly out of his reach. He pressed his palms together, imagining them cupping her face and travelling south over her lithe, soft body. The blood pounded in his head, while his thoughts made him sweat.

JB emerged from the cabin, rubbing sleep from his eyes, and pulled a tin of tobacco from a sodden pocket. He rolled two cigarettes and handed one to Coop.

'We need to be careful when we get back to shore,' he said. 'I think we're being played. But I don't know yet what the game is.'

Coop lit up and nodded. 'Got to agree with you there, JB. I'm getting the feeling we weren't meant to come back from this little jaunt.'

CHAPTER 13

THE STORM ON SHORE blew itself out in the early hours. By daylight, the residents were emerging from their shelters. In the hotel bars and along the waterfront, the verandah talk was of the weather. Everyone agreed it felt a lot cooler. Storms sometimes did that.

On another verandah, the temperature was still too hot.

When they had called it a night some hours before, Shorty had borrowed a pair of Maitland's pyjamas and bunked down in the guestroom. He had now come to rout out his host. The storm shutters were still down in the mosquito room and the stifling space was dark. He undid the buttons of the pyjama jacket and peeled it off his sweaty flesh.

'I think your gamble will have paid off, Mait. A quid to a shilling that boat will have broken up at sea.'

'Here's hoping.' Maitland kicked the tangle of damp sheets to the bottom of the bed and turned his pillow over to the cool side. The relief was fleeting. His head throbbed and his tongue stuck to the roof of his mouth. With Shorty in the house, there was no possibility of dozing off again. He reached over to the nightstand for his glass and gulped the water down. 'What time did we turn in last night?'

'Damned if I know. Late, early hours . . . depends on your point of view.'

Duc's discreet cough and knock at the mosquito-room door ruptured their talk. 'You want cuppa tea or breakfast today, Boss? It being all windy-windy. I got him saucepan fella fulla porridge.'

'Is my wife up?'

'Oh yes, she talkin' Marjorie.'

'Then no. I'll go out. You coming, Shorty?'

'Think I might breakfast with your wife, Mait. See what she has to say about life.'

Duc had cranked open a couple of storm shutters but the reek of brandy and cigar smoke was still heavy on the air. Maisie hadn't slept a wink. Shivery with worry, her stomach wild with anxiety, she could not stop thinking of William Cooper. The cyclone had blown through, but the sea was still thrashing up the dunes, swamping the sand, swollen and angry. She wanted to cry out that Maitland had deliberately put the diver's life at risk and those of his crew. But who would have listened? For a moment the question overwhelmed her. She felt a terrible panic that those black eyes of his would not come back to the Bay and that somehow it was her fault. She peered down the shadowed verandah to the guestroom, where Captain Mason was sleeping off his drink. *In many ways, I'm no safer than the divers,* she thought. *Maitland doesn't care enough to protect me from his friend.* She turned and stared beyond the lattice to the lighthouse.

Did you do your job last night and keep a little boat safe? She shook her head. *I can't think about him now or I'll drive myself mad.*

'Morning, Maisie!'

She turned, startled at the sound of her Christian name, and stared at the bare-chested Shorty. 'Where's Maitland?'

'The packing shed, town, communing with the gin bottle. Who knows?'

'Where are your clothes, Captain Mason?'

'I wasn't planning on needing them just yet,' he said, and in one smooth movement he grabbed her hand. His head swooped down and he kissed her palm, lapping the tip of his tongue backwards and forwards across her flesh like a slobbering dog. It was about as pleasurable as a hospital-bed bath. She wiped her hand on the chair arm and didn't give two hoots if he'd seen her do it.

He straightened and gripped her shoulder with his massive paw. She felt her bones crunch.

'Maitland is a lucky bloke, Maisie, but you deserve better; a proper man with lead in his pencil.' He bent down a second time and stamped a rash of slimy kisses on her lips and neck.

She peeled his hand from her arm and wiped her mouth with her sleeve. 'What do you think you're doing?'

'What do you think, child bride?' The sweat was thick on his forehead, his voice breathless. 'I want you.'

'I'm married,' she said, stiffly.

He lunged at her again and ran his hand down her leg. 'Are you sure that's a valid excuse, Maisie? I can't see the certificate hanging in pride of place on your wall.' He shook his head, mocking. 'You'll change your mind eventually, and I'll be waiting when you've had enough of Maitland. I never give up and you *will* give in, I guarantee it. You won't get a better offer. It's time for you to get down off that high horse of yours and face up to what life's all about here.'

Maisie stepped back towards the door. 'I think you should go home, Captain Mason. I don't feel comfortable with you in my house. Maitland's not here and I thought we were all dedicated to perpetuating the myth that we know how to behave like gentlemen in this parody of little England.'

'Cut me some slack, Maisie. I'm only human.'

'And I am too,' she said.

'Are you, though? You're too bloody perfect, so high-principled that no-one can keep up. That's probably why Maitland blasts himself with the gin bottle every night – he can't cope with living with Saint Maisie.' He sat down at the table and thrust his spoon in his bowl. 'Have some porridge. It's not half bad.'

Maisie struggled to keep her voice level. 'Do you think I have an appetite? You've just told me that I have a totally unrealistic view of what life is like here, that no-one can live up to my expectations of them or tolerate being preached at by a newcomer. But while you chomp your way through my food, let me tell you what it's been like for me. Everyone with a white face who I've met in Buccaneer Bay believes themselves to be well bred, a slave to a British code of conduct of which they have no firsthand experience and which has been dreamed up by a generation of impostors. There is discrimination here on a scale that horrifies me, and the violence towards the native inhabitants – which is ignored and unpunished – is, to my mind, nothing short of criminal.'

His face stiffened. 'What's the matter with you, Maisie? Where's all this come from?'

She stared at him tight-lipped and thought hard about his accusatory summation of her character, and the marriage that was a sham.

'Tell you what, Maisie.' Shorty Mason got up from the table and picked up a box of Maitland's cigarettes. He flipped up the lid and took one out. He tapped the end on the back of the box then put the cigarette between his lips. 'I'll get dressed and get out of your hair. I'll come back later when you've calmed down.'

Maisie wanted to slam her fist in his patronising face. 'That's too good of you, Captain Mason. By the time you return, I'm sure Maitland will be home from wherever he's gone and be delighted to pickle you with drink.'

Shorty Mason paused at the door and said, almost gently, 'I'm sorry if I offended you, Maisie, but I think you have a very great deal to learn about the ways things are in the Bay.'

CHAPTER 14

IT WAS THE LATEST start to the pearling season that anyone could remember. Slowly, the weather was changing. Delicate blooms began to lift frail heads from buffeted stems, and butterflies rose from the earth in puffs of yellow. Weeds flourished in the garden and threatened to strangle the tender shoots. It should have felt like spring but, to Maisie, heaviness like a wet autumn in England clung oppressively round her shoulders.

In the days after the cyclone, she had tried to put William Cooper out of her mind and concentrate on the business of living with her husband. Shorty Mason's words had stung; perhaps she wasn't trying hard enough, or was being naïve about marriage. Doctor Shin thought that the difficulties more likely lay with Maitland; that he had followed a bachelor existence for so long that he was finding it hard to adjust to married life. Give him time, the doctor had said; nature not medicine has its own way of sorting things out. Despite her efforts, she thought constantly of the tall English diver – one moment daring to hope he had survived the storm, the next convinced he had not. He had become her romantic fantasy, resonating in her head every time she looked out to sea.

Two days after the blow, as the afternoon sun was sinking, the *Sharky* limped into the Bay.

Maitland's slack-jowled face was red with fury. 'What the bloody dickens!'

'Looks like that old tug of yours survived the willy-willy,' Blair said, draining his whisky. His voice was ugly. 'Impressive, mate.'

Maitland shook his head. 'Incredible.'

Maisie exhaled, hugging both arms around her body, cradling her relief.

He didn't miss the sigh. 'And what are you looking so bloody smug about?'

She hoped he wouldn't hear the joy in her voice. 'Your boat's safely home, along with your crew. That's something to be pleased about, surely?' She felt ridiculously happy.

He gave her a long, hard look. His grey eyes were cold with scorn. 'They aren't returning from a bloody cruise, Maisie. They went out to work the pearl beds and have obviously failed. I'll have to patch up the lugger and send them off again next week with the rest of the fleet. That costs money – which doesn't grow on trees by the way, despite what you've been brought up to think. And you can get to work as well. You've loafed around here long enough, enjoying my bloody hospitality.'

Maisie inhaled, struck by the damning finality of his words.

Early the following Monday morning, Maisie joined Maitland's workforce. She sat in a swivelling, sweat-stained chair in the fire that was her husband's office and ran her finger down the schooner's supply list. She pivoted around, using her foot as a rudder, and stared at the back of Maitland's bulldog neck. It was pitted with black pores, which seemed as if they could do with a good scrub.

'There's a great deal of food here, Maitland. How long do the men spend at sea?'

He remained perched on the edge of the desk and didn't turn round, which gave her an interesting look at his ears. 'A month to start with. They'll store the tinned goods in the boat's dinghy.'

Mrs Wallace had told her that men with small ears, in her modest experience, invariably possessed a venal temperament. *Mrs Wallace.* Maisie mouthed her name and almost cried out with longing. She had come to treasure her as the mother she'd never really had and the pain of her absence was still raw, like a wound that refused to heal. What advice would she hand out if she were here right now? Had she already guessed at the size of Maitland's tiny ears and been trying to warn her?

She pulled a handkerchief from her sleeve and dabbed at her eyes. 'It's all tinned goods. Is there no fresh food? Whole armadas died of scurvy in the past. And beri-beri,' she added for emphasis.

'Jesus, Maisie,' Maitland said, easing his paunch from the desk, 'I'm not running a bloody restaurant. They'll supplement what I give them with fish. And when you go out on the schooner you'll make sure they haven't hidden any of my pearls. I know I'm being done right and left, and you're going to ensure that it bloody well stops.'

'How am I expected to do that? Captain Hanson does his own shell policing. You've heard him say over and over that it's the only way he can vaguely control the onboard thefts.'

'What's your point?'

'His boats all fish the same patch and he rotates between them. I'm not supervising the opening of shell, Maitland, and will I be taken seriously as a woman doing a man's job?'

He gnawed at the tip of his pipe, his small, effeminate mouth working the smooth surface between his lips while he eyed a sarong-wearing Malay stacking shell into bins.

'I'm not suggesting you personally open the shell, Maisie,' he snapped. 'You collect what they've opened up when they row it over to the schooner. There's a wooden box that some bloke in town's just invented – the shell-opener drops the pearls in and there's a valve that makes it bloody impossible to shake them out. I have the only keys here in my office. I don't have the time to ponce about at sea, although you have nothing but time on your hands. So, you pick up and record the shell and run the slop chest. Even a *female* should be capable of that.'

Maisie thought it would be simpler just to steal the box, new invention or not, and pretend it had fallen overboard.

'What will you be doing while I am at sea?'

He flipped the lid off a tin of tobacco and began stuffing his pipe. 'Pencil and paper tallying.'

'Isn't that what I'm doing?' She thought of the number of ledgers he expected her to fill in.

'No.' The light-grey eyes screwed up with annoyance. 'Everything that came off the luggers during the lay-up was labelled with the licence number of the boat it came off. It's been stored up at the camps. Now we're off to work again, I have to reissue the gear to the lugger it came from, item by item.'

Maisie studied her husband. He was flushed as red as Mars, and drops of perspiration stood proud on his brow like blisters.

'I thought all the luggers were out to sea.'

'So?'

'So, why are you doing this if the boats aren't here anymore?'

'Residual stock. We'll keep it here or on the schooner, for repairs.'

She looked at him suspiciously. 'How many luggers am I supplying with residual stock?'

'Mine, two of Hanson's, Espinell's and a couple of Blair's.'

'Not Captain Mason's?' She had all her fingers crossed he was at sea with his luggers.

Maitland shook his head, unleashing an arc of sweat.

'And the slop chest?'

'Is the shop we run off the schooner. I told you. I'm not sure how I can explain this to you any plainer. The schooner is a floating shell repository-cum-office-cum-shop. It serves three purposes, all mutually dependent. We try to keep the luggers generally in the same area, within a few miles or so, to cut down on costs because it's expensive to transport supplies and equipment back and forth. At the moment, though, we're not all fishing the same beds. Mason's gone north of Neptune's Dairy because he says he doesn't know where the most plentiful beds are just yet.'

'But you're putting all your eggs in the same basket.'

She sensed he wanted to stamp his foot. Or better still, to slap her.

'For the moment I am. While we're at the tail end of the Wet. My crews think Cooper is the messiah, after that stunt with the *Sharky*. Give it a week or two and they'll move off to different patches. The Jap divers know where to go for the richest pickings.'

Over the past week, Maisie had heard whispers that the business with the *Sharky* had saved Maitland's fleshy hide. She was not clear quite why. 'And then what?'

'You'll sail about on the *Hornet* till you find them, Maisie.'

'Where is the schooner? I've never even set eyes on it.'

'Mangrove Point Jetty in Japtown, close to the wholesalers who supply the stock. You should take a trip there and get your face known. Running the slop chest is your job now, so don't stuff it up.'

She looked at the large balding head with its straggly, thinning moustache and button-sized ears. 'Is it really, Maitland? I thought my job was to provide you with some social respectability. How do you expect me to do that if I'm never at home?' She stood up and scooped the ledgers under her arm. 'I think I'll take this paperwork to the office at the house. The sound of your pencil cooking the books is giving me a migraine.'

For the crews at sea, six days of the week were a miserable, exhausting slog. Saturday was different in only one sense: they dropped anchor at the end of the day and didn't work again until Monday.

The fleet's rendezvous point was Shell Bay. All the designated luggers in the pearling cluster began to arrive on Saturday afternoon and, as they dropped anchor, the crews pushed out in dinghies to stretch their cramped limbs and greet friends from the other boats. The only English crew was on board the hastily patched-up *Sharky*. Coop wondered if the other white divers were raising more excitement than he was. He'd been at sea a couple of weeks and already he was struggling to remember if there was life beyond spending days on end in primitive conditions, searching for an ugly mollusc that didn't want to be found.

By sun-up the next day, the *Hornet* was in their midst. The schooner was a superb three-mast vessel, fore and aft rigged, and had been built in the shipyard at Port Fremantle. Coop pondered the expense. Captain Sinclair ran a fleet of just three luggers – as far as he could see. Living on board a vessel you could walk about on, and that boasted sixteen crew in addition to the skipper and his mate – that meant seriously big money. He must have hit the jackpot somewhere along the line.

Emerging from his confined quarters, Coop began to sweat. He knew his shell tally was a fraction of what the Japanese divers were hauling to the surface and he sensed the captain was banking on his poor yield.

He shielded his eyes from the searing light. He could see loaded dinghies casting off from the luggers, pyramids of shell ready to dump aboard the supply schooner, and compared them to his own pitiful pile. Maybe he could make his pile look a bit more impressive. He gave it an experimental poke with his foot. He still believed it was just a matter of getting his eye in, but spotting the shell on the seabed was proving to be far harder than he could have imagined. He'd kidded himself that it would be easy, and knew that Captain Sinclair was laughing behind his back. But Coop was dogged and would not give his boozed-up employer the satisfaction. He was convinced that perseverance and more practice would level the scores. He knew he could do better.

The *Sharky*'s crew loaded the shell onto the dingy, then Coop and JB rowed it over to the *Hornet*. It was far too early for Slippery Sid, the Filipino shell-opener, to be up and about. He generally did not appear on deck till late afternoon. He was still tucked up in his hammock, taking care of a hangover and snoring like an industrial machine.

For Coop, evening was the most exciting time on the pearling lugger. During the day, if it had been a good one, basket upon basket of shell was sent up to the deck, awaiting the skill of their shell-opener. Sid, it seemed to Coop, lived a mind-numbing existence, his work taking him less than an hour and a half a day; a little more if he stopped for a cup of coffee or a puff of opium. Captain Sinclair called him 'the Asian limpet', because he was clinging to a desperate job that no-one else wanted to do. The only reason the captain had him on board was to try to arrest the pilfering of his pearls. Coop knew that finding a decent pearl could set a man up for life. It was considered fair game; they would hijack the little creamy globule if they found one. After all, no-one would get hurt. It was theft without a victim. But Coop thought the captain had badly miscalculated with Sid, because he was the worst of them all. There was talk that he had a lucrative sideline in town selling the pearls he snitched. The crew despised him.

There were half a dozen other dinghies circling the schooner, waiting for the ladders to be thrown down at the appointed hour. One of the captain's clerks, dressed in a cream silk jacket and trousers, stood on the deck with his clipboard in hand, supervising the uploading of the boss's shell.

Coop looked up at him from the dinghy and snatched a worried breath. 'Is Captain Sinclair on board?'

'No, Coop. But Mrs Sinclair is in the forward hull with the ledgers.'

Slowly he exhaled, trying not to shout. '*Mrs Sinclair* is on board?'

'Yes, she's running the slop chest. Captain Sinclair gets seasick . . . or at least that's the excuse he's giving his crews.' The clerk shot him a knowing wink. 'She says she's opening it in a few minutes. You want to come on board?'

Coop and JB tied up the boat and climbed one of the ladders, joining the crews from other luggers who were already gathered on deck.

The slop chest was eagerly awaited by the men who lived on monotonous rations for weeks at a time. It was also a way for the master pearlers to fleece their crews. Alcohol, food and tobacco were sold at inflated prices, and Coop suspected Captain Sinclair's aim was to ensure that by the end of the season his crew ended up having already spent most of the money they'd earned. The white men were led downstairs amidships once the indentured crews had been served, and along a corridor by the ship's Japanese bosun.

The daily competition between divers and the crews was keen, but here, on the schooner, the men were oddly patient as they lined up to make their selections.

Maisie Sinclair was wearing a white blouse, the sleeves rolled up to the elbows. The sun shone through a porthole to stain her blonde hair gold. She sat behind a desk, a pen in her left hand. Everything they chose she recorded in two large ledgers. A fat stack of envelopes – mail for the crews – was tied up with red tape on the pristine blotter. Behind her stretched an Aladdin's cave of treats. The shelves were groaning with temptation for a homesick sailor. There were cigars, bottles of pills, tea from China and wooden boxes of spices, parcels with labels depicting dragons and bears, chocolate, tobacco, coffee and bottles of spirits. There were cans of fruit and vegetables and lumps of opium resin.

Coop dithered at the front of the queue, wondering what to say to her.

'Morning, Mrs Sinclair.' His voice sounded odd and he gave a laugh to cover it.

Maisie looked up and flapped a stray wisp of hair behind her ear. The last time she'd seen him she'd passed out cold on the jarrah wood floor. 'Mr Cooper. Is something amusing?'

'Not amusing, no. I wasn't expecting to see you, that's all.'

'So, you find it amusing that I'm here?'

'No. Just unexpected. I wasn't laughing at you.'

'I wasn't expecting to be here either, Mr Cooper, but working on the luggers was what you chose to do.' Her voice sounded brittle.

'True enough, Mrs Sinclair. Although living in a stifling cabin shared with rats, cockroaches and a grumpy Jap is not a laughing matter.'

'The accommodation is not comfortable?'

'You can't imagine, madam.'

A flush of red stained her throat. Her hand flew to her neckline, trying to pinch the edges of the collar together, and she looked around in dismay. 'Is there anything we have here that could help?' she asked. 'I see you are stocking up with supplies. Is the diet not a laughing matter, either?'

Coop had seen her discomfort before, and it intrigued him. He never seemed to catch her at ease unless she had half a bottle of gin on board. 'I've never much cared for rice or fish.'

He placed his purchases on her table: a box of fruitcake, a packet of needles and some thread, a tin of cocoa, five cans of tobacco and a couple of bottles of whisky. He watched her record the items against his name in one ledger and then the other.

'Did you find everything you wanted?' she said.

'I would have relished some fresh fruit or vegetables. Anything not condemned to old age in a tin.'

She sucked on the end of her pen then laughed lightly, as if she'd had a brainwave. 'Then I must offer you supper tonight!

I'll get the cook to roast something. It's the least I can do for my fellow countrymen. I'm not sure I can guarantee the fruit or vegetables on this occasion, but please pass the word.'

Coop looked at her, unable to keep a trace of amusement out of his voice. 'I accept with pleasure on behalf of myself and John Butcher. But I fear our number will be small. The other English divers are anchored up somewhere else. I haven't seen them for weeks. They weren't in my billet in town – I believe they were in one of the lay-up camps in Devil's Creek, but I haven't seen them since the welcome bash.'

Maisie stared up at him, her eyes dark pools of blue. She flipped her ledgers shut, her hand unsteady. 'I wonder if I might ask a favour of you, Mr Cooper?' She tapped the pile of letters. 'I still have the mailbag for the crews, which I neglected to give out with the slop chest. I know the men long for news from their families. Would it be too much trouble for you both to drop the letters for me?'

'Consider it payment for our supper, Mrs Sinclair. There may even be a letter for one of us, which would be grand. It's no trouble at all.'

It was after six, and the sea was settling to a shimmering, oily darkness. Night fell quickly from light to dark; there was no murky twilight at sea. JB rowed with long, regular strokes as they moved towards the riding light in the schooner's rigging.

Coop was first up the ladder when they reached the larger vessel's side. Maisie had put on a clean cotton blouse and skirt and a pair of heeled shoes, which were all wrong for the schooner. She tottered slightly with the movement of the boat, and threw an arm out to steady herself on the ship's rail.

He wondered if she had already been at the gin.

'Is it wise of you to put yourself in the company of two rough pirates, Mrs Sinclair?'

Again, he'd said the wrong thing. He pushed at his sleeves and wanted to bite back his words.

Attempting a blasé tone, she said, 'I am sure the pirates will exercise ample self-restraint, Mr Cooper, and that I shall be in no danger. Mr Butcher will stand by as my protector.'

'As I will, too, madam,' he said.

'I trust that you would do nothing to distress Doroth– the one who has captured your heart,' Maisie replied, and continued when observing their blank expressions. 'At home, on shore – in the Bay.'

JB shot a glance at Coop and scratched his ear.

'All hands on deck, then,' he said. 'And prepare to repel boarders!'

They sat in the main cabin in the best clothes they could muster, a ridiculous uniform for the heat and the occasion. Coop had donned a bright yellow neckerchief. JB was buttoned up to the neck and sweating. It was far too hot to be below deck eating roast meat, tinned vegetables and dumplings. Coop tucked a large linen napkin into his collar and Maisie patted her face rather too vigorously with her handkerchief. Saying grace and remembering all those lost at sea, she invited JB to carve.

'Would you tell me about life on board a lugger? I see the product of your effort in the shell collected on deck. I also see your tiny craft at anchor, which I believe is home to several men for weeks on end. I would like to understand what it is like for you all.' She turned to Coop. 'You mentioned earlier that conditions are basic.'

A putrid whiff floated in through the porthole on a faint pulse of wind. Maisie wrinkled her nose and made a poor attempt at disguising her distaste. The silence expanded as JB shook his head over the meat, producing a complicated performance involving a long thin carving knife and sharpening steel, like a samurai warrior at a training camp.

'It's not a glamorous existence, Mrs Sinclair. That shocking smell,' JB waved his carving knife at the porthole, 'is the oyster drying out. It sits on deck all day, slowly dehydrating, and by nightfall it takes a final gasp. That's what you can smell.'

Maisie smiled cheerlessly. 'I am acquainted with the smell of dead oyster, gentlemen, but I cannot pretend indifference to it. My husband brings the reek of his profession home in his clothing.' She considered for a moment, her pale eyebrows dipping. 'But he does not sail with his fleet and is a poor judge of weather conditions, it seems. Fortunately for us all, Mr Cooper, it appears you are not.'

JB looked at Coop and grinned. 'The crews won't let him out of their sight, Mrs Sinclair. They think he can walk on water. Even the fatalistic Japs are happy.'

'That's a bit of an exaggeration, JB,' Coop said. 'I was brought up by the sea. I know boats and I was born under the sign of Pisces. It's fated that I have a natural affinity with water.'

'I'm also a Pisces and yet I cannot swim,' she said.

'Then I should teach you. It's unthinkable you should be at sea and unable to swim.' He said it before he had time to think and again wished he could have bitten back his words. 'I'm sorry. I have overreached myself.'

Maisie stared at the tablecloth and felt the heat in her cheeks. She didn't care for the sea; she knew too well the fear of its ruthless strength.

The day she'd learned of it, thrashing grey water had crested with white-topped waves, and there had been a picnic on the sand behind a windbreaker. It was new, that windbreaker; a cloth construction of brightly coloured fabric, ribbed with spine-straight rods that were supposed to shield them from the wind. They'd brought it with them, rolled up tight like a sausage, and she had carried it under her arm, feeling proud that she had been given an important job. The canvas wall hadn't been tall enough to stop the wind, though, and she'd tried to crouch down, bending her spine to duck her head beneath it. Her mother had slapped her hard on the arm and told her she was slouching like a monkey.

There was someone else on the beach with them – a man who wasn't her father – and she remembered the weight of disappointment tugging her hands to her sides. Despite the wind, it was hot. Her feet had burned inside thick lace-up boots and her knitted cardigan scratched at her skin through her dress. She'd sat on a rug, legs slung wide to make a table of her dress, eating sandwiches and cake.

She smiled to herself.

Victoria sponge: two perfect circles of golden cake sandwiched together with cream and strawberry jam. Her mother had tutted and vowed to have words with the cook because the jam should have been raspberry. The two adults were drinking cook's special lemonade and leaning in close, whispering. Her mother, for once, had looked happy.

Maisie remembered getting up and shaking the crumbs off her dress. She'd wandered off towards the seashore, her head regularly swinging over her shoulder to see if her mother was watching, but she and the man were sipping their drinks and laughing. That had shocked her – the sound of her mother's laugh.

The rocks were jumping-distance apart, little pools of seawater trapped between them. She bent down and picked up a shell and listened to the tide rushing round the curvy carapace.

With the shell clutched in her hand, she sat on the sand. Placing the shell carefully beside her, she unlaced her boots and peeled down her stockings. The damp sand was deliciously cool between her toes.

Maisie flexed her feet in an attempt to recall that feeling.

She'd picked up the shell and listened in to the sound of the sea once more. The lull of the lapping waves on the sand seemed to be calling her towards the water's edge. She looked further out to where the sea roiled, as if great white horses galloped towards the shore. The noise consumed her as she waded into the waves.

Then there'd been heaving, a sore chest, sickness. The man was wringing water out of her sodden cardigan, saying kind words, and mopping at her with the tea towel from the picnic hamper. Her mother had stood by and watched.

Maisie thought now she'd been disappointed her child hadn't drowned.

'Mrs Sinclair? Are you quite well?'

'Are you a swimmer, Mr Butcher?' she said, ignoring the question.

JB paused, his cutlery clutched like weapons in his palms, the business ends pointing upwards, a lump of meat speared on his knife. Gravy trickled down the shaft onto his hand. He licked the blade and spoke through a mouthful of meat and potatoes.

'I'm more of a fixer,' he said, chewing hard. 'I'm an engineer and a poor sailor. Born and brought up in the north.' He sucked the sauce off his knuckles. 'Where was home for you, Mrs Sinclair?'

Coop parked his cutlery together as she had, vertically dissecting the plate. Her smile, a quick flex of the mouth, didn't reach her eyes. He saw that home was an uncomfortable topic for her.

'I grew up in London. My father is a High Court judge.'

'Do you miss your family?' JB said.

Mrs Sinclair said nothing – merely nodded her head – which made Coop wonder if JB had overstepped the mark with his question. The roast dinner ground on, punctuated with awkward pauses broken only by the clink of silver on china and the sound of the schooner straining against its sea anchor. Coop could sense she would retreat from them completely unless he broke the three-sided silence.

'Why not tell Mrs Sinclair what we do each day, JB? That will give her some idea what it's like on the lugger.'

JB rubbed crumbs from his mouth with the back of his hand. Coop felt a fresh flash of dismay that she would again associate him with his unsophisticated tender, that she would consider him coarse and ill-bred.

JB reached for his coffee and blew noisily into the cup. 'Work begins at daybreak.' He stacked three sugar cubes onto a spoon and hovered the bowl below the surface of the hot liquid as he waited for the crystals to dissolve. He withdrew the spoon and slurped up the sugary syrup.

Mrs Sinclair lowered a sugar cube into her own cup with a pair of silver tongs.

'The cook produces breakfast on his makeshift stove. It's really a topless oil drum with iron rods across the top to support the cooking pots,' JB said, oblivious to the scene he was causing. 'While Coop has his coffee and a smoke, I get his kit together. It's cold down below, so he wears layers of undergarments and stockings, which reach up to his thighs.' He slashed a line across his leg to mark the spot. 'On top of that, he has his heavy rubberised diving dress and lead-soled boots. All the clothes protect him from the cold and the pressure as well.'

Coop nodded. 'I dress as if for the North Pole. Captain Scott would be proud of me. Sometimes when I come up from the deep water, on my skin you can see every crease from the clothing. That's from the pressure. Even though it's freezing you still sweat a lot.'

JB laughed. 'And Coop is fussy. He washes and dries his underclothes every night.'

Coop burned with embarrassment. He kneaded his forehead with his fingers, thumbs anchored on his temples. Mrs Sinclair's head remained inclined towards JB. She was nodding, giving him her full attention. Coop stared at her profile and felt within him a longing that almost made him groan.

Mrs Sinclair turned back and for a moment they looked at each other. He thought he read something in her eyes but knew it meant nothing. The divide between them was too great. And she wasn't his.

She leaned across the table. 'After you have had breakfast, the diving begins?'

JB chattered on, explaining the safety checks and the diving gear.

'And then the diving begins?' she repeated.

'And then the diving begins,' JB said.

'I know it might seem a lot of work just to get one man underwater, but JB's job is about keeping me alive,' Coop said. 'He's on the end of a lifeline that is my only communication with the surface. He interprets my tugs on the rope that I send from the bottom of the ocean. I am really sailing the lugger from the seabed, if that makes sense. He has to stay alert – my life depends on him instantly reacting to my every move.'

'I also have to time his dives,' JB continued. 'You know about the diver's paralysis, I assume, Mrs Sinclair?'

She nodded, and explained that she had seen some of the afflicted in the Japanese hospital.

'Divers are generally pretty cautious, but a tempting patch of shell can be distracting,' JB said. 'Working at twenty fathoms is safe enough, and I only let Coop stay down for half an hour, but it takes a little bit longer to come up, in timed stages. He usually manages about six descents during a working day.'

She turned to Coop. 'Is it not very tiring walking against the current on the seabed?'

'We tend to work in slack water, Mrs Sinclair, but a Japanese diver showed me how to ride the anchor if we are prospecting rather than collecting the shell. We drop the anchor to about five feet off the bottom and sit astride it as the lugger drifts over the beds. When I see shell, I signal to JB, who lets out the anchor and I drop to the bottom and pick it up.'

She nodded, dabbed at her mouth with her napkin and cast it aside. 'You both must be keen to turn in. Please forgive me for detaining you so long.'

JB scoured his lips with the cloth. He smoothed the pleats with his fist and rolled it into a tight cylinder. He scanned the table uncertainly before poking his linen cigar through the handle of his coffee cup.

'We've had a really good feed, Mrs Sinclair. But you're right, we've an early start tomorrow, so we should get back to the cockroaches and rats.'

Coop closed his eyes and wondered how he would ever ford the chasm of social discordance between them. He balled up his napkin as she had done and pushed back his chair.

'Thank you, Mrs Sinclair, for a most agreeable evening. It has been very pleasant to dine well, and off china rather than a tin plate.'

JB opened and shut his mouth.

She escorted them to the ladder on deck. 'It has been a pleasure, gentlemen. Perhaps you would care to repeat the evening next Sunday after the slop chest is closed? Hopefully our numbers will be greater if we can hunt down the rest of your English colleagues.'

With no warning, she leaned forward and kissed both men on the cheek. Right. Left. Peck. Peck. A gesture that seemed to cause all three of them equal astonishment.

Coop had moved a fraction too soon; her lips missed his cheek and bruised the edge of his mouth. Soft, smooth, firm skin, often dreamed of. The muscles round his eyes contracted as physical desire flared through his body. It took every inch of his willpower to step back from her, to push away thoughts of pulling her mouth onto his and kissing her deeply. Cheeks inflamed once more, he turned away, his hands darting in and out of his breast and trouser pockets in search of tobacco. The distraction, the salvation from his distress, was a sharp-edged rectangle prodding his ribcage.

Mrs Sinclair had already stepped back from the physical muddle and was staring out to sea.

'Forgive me, Mrs Sinclair, I almost forgot. This was among the bundle of letters you asked us to hand out.'

He held out the cream envelope and watched the smile slip from her face as she took in the rigid, scratchy script.

CHAPTER 15

MAISIE STARED AFRESH AT the disciplined handwriting on the cream parchment envelope. She knew it well – even the inky alphabet itself was forbidden to slouch.

In the days since William Cooper had given it to her, her mother's letter had stayed hidden in her dressing-table drawer, where she had put it under a pile of clothes. It lay there like a rebuke. It was not her name on the envelope, and it had never been meant for her eyes. She took it out and fingered the narrow rectangle, nails picking at the corners, her pulse jumping. What was in there that could not have been addressed to her? The floorboards creaked and Marjorie appeared in the doorway.

'You want anything, Missus?'

Maisie clutched the letter to her chest. 'No, thank you, Marjorie. I'm going to have a lie-down in a moment.'

The maid eyed the envelope and tapped her nose with one finger, dislodging her new spectacles to the side. 'I'm allonga washing room if you want find me.' She resettled the frame on the bridge of her nose and closed the door.

Maisie found the woman's timing quite unnerving at times.

She worked her finger under the edges. The heat had dried out the glue, and the triangular seal gave up without a struggle. She pushed her hand into the tissue-lined envelope and pulled out the writing paper. Smoothing back the central fold, trying not to visualise her mother's blazing countenance, she lay back against the pillows and began to read.

Cousin Maitland,

I trust this letter finds you and my daughter in good health. We are assuming she arrived safely, although a letter from her might have been polite.

I will be brief.

Maisie's uncle, my brother Marcus, passed away shortly after she left for Australia. It was sudden and unexpected.

Marcus was fond of Maisie – although their paths rarely crossed – and he has marked that affection in his Will.

She knows nothing of the rest of it.

My brother has left her a considerable amount of money and laid down his terms for inheritance very clearly.

He has stipulated that authentic proof of your marriage to his niece Maisie be provided in the form of the original certificate of your marriage, duly signed and dated by both parties and your witnesses. This was always in place – irrespective of whom she married. However, as the named executor of his Will, I add two conditions of my own:

* *You are to provide a legally binding document stating that you will no longer pursue Maisie's father and threaten his political career.*

* *You will inform me of what happened to my son sixteen years ago, with the details corroborated by a third party.*

Yours,

Audrey Porter

P.S. We recently received an extraordinary telegraph from our daughter. Are we to understand that she is now complicit in your dealings?

A breeze slipped through the netting like a gasp and almost blew the letter from her hand. It was nearly dark outside and the mosquitos had started to whine. She had been in her room a long time, the glow from the lighthouse beam tracing an arc across the floor. Maisie pressed the cream writing paper to her face and closed her eyes. Her head was full of words.

Uncle Marcus was dead, and now there appeared to be some mystery about her brother. She tried to remember what she'd heard about him. He had died when she was a baby. Once, when she was of school age, she had tried to ask about him, but her father had cut off her questions and implored her not to talk about it. *It makes your mother sad,* he'd said. Certainly there had never been any mention of strange circumstances. Why on earth then, years later – in a letter to her husband she was never intended to see – would her mother refer to her son as if his death was never explained? And how and why was Maitland threatening her father's career when he knew nothing of English law? Confusion and despair pressed upon her.

What childish hope had she clutched at, that there might have been a hopeful message for her in that letter? Her parents hadn't received a single one of her letters even though Maitland took them from the house each week. *Ne cede malis*. Yield not to misfortunes. She felt she was standing at the cusp of a cliff side and the only way was down. Hand pressed hard to her mouth, she stifled the cry.

That Sunday, just after sunset, the sky was a mass of brilliant stars, and the ocean as black as polish. Maisie found herself a place on deck to wait for her dinner guest, and was cooling herself with a small silk fan when William Cooper came up the ladder. She had been watching the long rhythmic strokes that brought the dinghy nearer to the schooner. The week after the mistimed kiss had been an agony, the bungalow even more of a claustrophobic cage and Maitland more of a self-important power-seeking boor. Why had she decided to kiss William Cooper's cheek when a handshake would have been enough? Everything had screamed at her that it was wrong but she had gone ahead anyway. What on earth must he have thought? And tonight? She had changed her clothes twice and redone her hair until she was satisfied she looked her best, and now she was so nervous her hands had started to shake.

Maisie stood up and went over to greet him. 'No Mr Butcher this evening?' Her question was rhetorical. She knew he was alone.

'JB sends his apologies, Mrs Sinclair.'

She waited for him to go on. 'Is he unwell?'

Coop chewed his lip. 'Something he ate, I think.'

'That's a great shame. I do hope he is better soon and that it does not compromise your diving for tomorrow.' *You sound stilted*, she chided herself, *like an inadequate actor in a play*.

Coop nodded, his face blank. There was silence as they considered the fact that they would spend an evening alone together.

Below deck, he sat facing her, so close that if he would just stretch out his arm he could touch her. She pushed a dish towards him. 'Speaking of eating, Mr Cooper, last week you mentioned that you were longing for fresh food, so I have brought you some mangoes from my garden. It's not much, but it's the best I could manage.'

He picked up a green-tinged red fruit and rolled it between his palms, his long fingers cradling it like a wounded bird.

'Thank you. Although I'm not sure what to do with it.'

Why did his voice make her leg muscles feel suddenly weak? She stared at his mouth. His front teeth were crooked. She hadn't noticed that before, nor that he had a small dimple on his chin. He had reappeared in her life after the long sea voyage, thousands of miles from home, like a mirage in a sandy waste, and she was now terrified that he was not real. What was it about him that tempted her? Other than the fact he was so completely out of bounds? And she was not free.

She leaned across, blue eyes locked on black. 'You peel it and eat the fruit, Mr Cooper, and then suck the flesh off the flat stone. At least, that's what I do.'

He ran his knife down the length of the leathery skin, all rubbery like a polished lily pad. 'I wonder if I might ask a favour, Mrs Sinclair?' he said, mango juice slithering down his hand.

Maisie reached for a napkin and pushed the square of cloth towards him. Her fingers grazed his, but he did not pull away.

She felt a strange excitement she didn't understand. 'What favour might that be, Mr Cooper?'

He ran his tongue over his sun-cracked lips and kept his voice casual. 'If we are to continue to meet each week for Sunday dinner, might I persuade you to call me Coop?'

She nodded and felt slightly giddy, knowing that what she was about to suggest would unite them in some way. 'If I might persuade you to call me Maisie.'

'Maisie,' he repeated, saying her name out loud for the first time. 'Now we are on first-name terms, there is a second favour I must ask you.'

'Yes?'

He looked at her and then looked away and for the briefest second she felt his hesitation. 'Are you certain? This is fairly significant.'

'I'm intrigued. I'll be happy to help if I can.' She took a breath and when he didn't immediately continue, she added, 'Coop.'

'Do you think you could look through Captain Sinclair's papers and find out what I signed?'

Over coffee, they talked about their early impressions of life in Australia. Maisie asked him if it was all he expected it to be. He fell quiet for a little while then bent to light his cigarette. He kept his eyes hidden from view.

'Not yet. But I hope it will be. And you?'

Maisie lifted the hair off the back of her collar and wiped her neck with her hand. She'd started to wear it higher up on her head in a tight knot, yet still it slipped from its pins. She gave them a short-tempered squeeze.

'I despise the climate.'

He looked at her plainly. 'You've only just got here, Maisie. Getting all hot and bothered about something you can't alter will just make matters worse. Give it time. It's bound to get easier.'

They went on deck after that, and he did his best to lift her mood. He flicked his cigarette overboard. 'Tell me something you remember from England? That you can really hold on to.'

Maisie gazed out towards the sea. 'My father used to play a game with me when I was little. He used to make me try to catch my shadow.'

'And you never could.'

'No. It's an impossible game but it kept me entertained for hours.'

Coop leaned towards her and she could smell the sea. 'Do you miss him very much?'

'Yes,' she said. 'He's a fine, upstanding man.'

When he rowed back to his lugger, she lay awake in her bunk, her thoughts ebbing and flowing between her husband and his tall English diver.

On the point of leaving her for another week, he had kissed her cheek; there had been no clumsy mistake on this occasion. It was proper, chaste, but the touch of his mouth on her skin, his dry lips rasping her flesh, had awoken a longing in her she couldn't deny.

What went on in her head she could generally control, push down, so she could hide from what she was really thinking, but that night she couldn't fight the tide. To do what Coop requested would put a large question mark against her loyalty. If she were discovered, the repercussions would be unimaginable.

Ultimately, however, she knew she wanted to help him. She, too, had her reasons for going through Maitland's papers.

Maitland stood with arms folded, his weight straining against the lattice of the verandah railing. He was late leaving the bungalow for his lunch in town and was running through his day with Duc, speaking slowly as if dealing with the mentally impaired. Maisie watched them from behind a large oleander tree, a basket of mangoes on her hip. She wished he'd hurry up and leave.

'There's another debate at the Pearlers' Association. I'll be back at tea time.'

'Yes, Boss.'

'How many clean suits are there in my wardrobe?'

'You gettin' low, Boss. Mebbe five, ten?'

'Which?'

'Mebbe six?' he stammered.

'Not good enough!' He lashed out with the back of his hand, spinning Duc around to face him. 'It's time you learned to bloody well count! When's the steamer due from Singapore?'

Duc's eyes were bright with fear. 'Steamer in later today, Boss.'

Maitland stamped his foot. 'When today?'

Duc held up four trembly fingers. Maisie peered at her husband's face. He looked excited, like a schoolboy winning a fight. She turned away, sickened.

'All right. I'll be back about drinks time. I'll fetch the stuff off the jetty myself.'

She heard him slam the front door and watched him lumber out of the house, flicking irritably at the shell path with his cane.

When she was sure the coast was clear, Maisie went round the back of the house, set down her basket in the kitchen and tiptoed to the room next door. She sat down on Maitland's sweat-streaked chair. The home office felt different, peaceful, as if he had not yet polluted the air with his poisonous gas.

'Wot you up to, Missus?'

Maisie shot out of the chair.

'Marjorie! I almost had a heart attack.'

'You lookin' for somethin' partiklar? Probly I knows where it is.'

'Marjorie! Have you been spying on Captain Sinclair?'

'I sees stuff,' she said, and turned her back.

Search discarded, Maisie followed her onto the verandah. Marjorie picked up the conversation, her spectacles magnifying eyes that saw more than they should.

'When I does the dustin' sometimes I does practise my readin' of documents and correspondence for my English advancement.'

Maisie almost laughed. 'Why haven't you admitted this before?'

'Didn't know it was a crime, readin'.'

'No, it isn't, but going through someone's personal papers most definitely is. That's why you made me jump. But since you asked, I am particularly looking for Captain Sinclair's ledgers.'

Marjorie said, 'Seems like dat might be one rule for me and one rule for you, Missus. Reading wot ain't meant to be read by some. There's loads of them fella files. Wot you lookin' for?'

'You are right, I am being a hypocrite. I'm looking for paperwork about the English diver.'

'Dat paper's not here.'

'Are you sure?'

Marjorie gave her a long look over the new spectacles.

'I'll go and search the packing-shed office then. And while I think of it, have you come across my marriage certificate when you have been practising your English advancement?'

'No, Missus. I never seen dat document; not in dis house.'

Maisie leaned round the packing-shed door. There was no-one there, no faithful employee making careful entries into a ledger, double-checking the shell tallies, or supervising shipments. The shed was silent, yellow bright, clean. The floor was swept bare; brushstrokes stretched long and deep, curved inwards like a lobster's claw. It was out of character, and made her uneasy.

She drummed her fingers on the battered desktop, the central leg space flanked left and right by twin stacks of drawers. An inexplicable intuition sent her hand to the left, sliding the desk drawers back, one by one. She knew what she was searching for would be here.

All the same, it took her a long time to find it. It was not in the white ledger where details of divers' employment were recorded, but in the daily journal for another of Maitland's luggers, the *Clancy*, a ship that had been wrecked in the cyclone. She was sure that Maitland didn't want it found.

She put her head in her hands and a swamping tide of fury and desolation left her shaking from its force. Her husband's treachery hadn't stopped with her mail. From the window, she watched a sea eagle hover above the hot-red rock face standing guard over the beach. Its prey flailed only briefly, clamped between its claws, as if it knew there was no hope. She felt the blood draining from her cheeks, leaving her skin cold.

Coop had reason to be worried. He had effectively signed his own death warrant.

Back at the house, Maisie took her empty breakfast tray to the kitchen. Duc still did not encourage her passage across the threshold and stood guard in the doorway, blocking her path.

'What are you planning for supper tonight, Duc?' she said.

He outlined what he proposed to cook for dinner, but his windmilling arms semaphored his unhappiness. The shellfish had been caught the previous evening from traps across Mangrove Creek and had arrived in a squirming sack. They rarely went shopping. The mobile market came to the house, along with the twice-daily delivery of ice for the ice chest. That morning, the delivery was late.

'How many's we, Mem?'

'I don't know. Captain Sinclair hopes to invite the new French pearl doctor and his wife to supper, with the bishop and his wife and Miss Locke. The mayor and Miss Montague will probably join us too, and I expect Captain Mason will be here as usual. Why not cook for twelve and then there will be extra food for you and Marjorie if we are fewer.'

'Hope ice boy come soon. Or shellfish get stinky.'

'Where is it now?'

'I put 'im in wash house after I boil them fellas.'

'All right. I'll go and get it, and you can clear a space in the ice chest.'

The ice chest, which lived on the back verandah, was the only means of keeping food cool and reasonably fresh. Twice a day, the ice was raced into the bungalow from the road. It was a backbreaking but vital job in their climate. A panting employee carried the melting block with huge iron tongs and deposited it in the chest. The contents were first taken out and then put back when the new, fresh block was in place.

From the back of the house Duc was shouting, 'I cook boy in house here! I tell you ice no good!'

'I don't deal with coloureds. Where's your Missus?'

'Mem don't want talk to white-trash ice boy.'

'And I don't take orders from little brown faggots.'

Duc in his spotless singlet, a crisp white sail on a light teak deck, cupped a hand behind his ear. 'What you say?'

Maisie stepped into the fray, her voice sharp. 'Joe, isn't it? Are you a little behind schedule this morning?'

'Problem at the ice factory, Mrs Sinclair.'

'Is your problem an excuse for your tardy arrival, when we all depend on your promptness to keep our food fresh and us in good health? Did you oversleep?'

Joe took a step backwards, his hands shielding his eyes. 'I'm sorry. What more can I say? My father died yesterday. An ice block at the factory crushed his chest. I didn't want to come to work today but Mum insisted we try to be normal until we work out what to do.'

Maisie felt wretched. 'Oh, Joe. I'm so sorry. Is there anything we can do to help?'

Joe shook his sunburned face, arms straining under the weight of the ice. 'We'll be right, Mrs Sinclair. Better get this in the chest and I'll be off.'

A trail of water sparkled on the wooden floor: guilt, shame and shifting priorities shimmering in fat, accusing droplets.

Words do not evaporate like water, Maisie. If you cannot be gracious, keep your mouth shut.

She bowed her head, and prayed he could not see her face.

With the ice situation resolved, Maisie left the verandah and went down into the garden to inspect her fledgling allotment.

She was peering at a sickly fruit when Marjorie returned from chiffa business in town. Something was attacking the plants she had grown from the seed that Mrs Wallace had sent her from Gantry Creek. It was supposed to flourish in the fiery red soil, but the leaves were ragged, the fruit meagre. She suspected the goat.

Marjorie traipsed up the path. 'Word is, Missus . . .'

'What is it, Marjorie?'

'Another one of them whitey divers beeum dead.'

Maisie could hear galahs shrieking in the trees in the distance, the birds acting as if nothing had changed. But the world was spinning. The icy knife of dread shot through her chest as her eyes swerved towards the jetty. It couldn't be him. William Cooper couldn't be dead. She struggled to force air into her lungs and wrapped her arms round her body, to blanket the sound of her pounding heart. She prayed Marjorie would think the tears in her eyes were the doing of the cruel sun.

'Who told you?'

'Chinky oar fella wot brings us da fish was on da jetty pickin' up stories. He saw da lugger boat sail in with da flag thing halfway down da pole. All happened before I got allonga dere.'

'Did he see which lugger?'

'I told you before dat dem Chinky blokes like Duc can't see so good. And before you gets to asking, he can't read no boat names neither. So, don't know whether it was dat diver fella you like or not what got deaded down below.'

'I beg your pardon, Marjorie?'

'Missus.' Marjorie folded her arms across her chest. 'I'm black girl, like you know, but I got white girl's brain like you, and I ain't stupid. I got eyes. Biggum good ones now with da peepies an' all, but even before dat I could still see things. Don't need fancy spectacles for dat stuff.'

'Marjorie. If you are in any way suggesting that I have feelings for this man beyond what is right and proper, you are grossly mistaken. I am a married woman!'

I might be a married woman, Maisie thought, *but William Cooper is the man who sets my heart racing, not my husband.*

''Scuse me, Missus, I know dat. But I ain't no sneak. We's on da same side! An' I got ears too. Go where dey no shoulda go. 'Member that randy goat captain fella day after the big blow? He think that black girls can't hear no good.'

'Colour has nothing to do with it, Marjorie.'

'No, I knows you think dat but you's strange. Others think we's invisible. And deaf. So, we hear wot we not supposed to hear. Yes?'

Maisie nodded.

'Wot's it you white folks say? Walls gottum ears? Well, I is a wall dat hear the captain and those gamblin' fellas when you wants me to listen. You very happy to hear wot I had to say dat time den. Now I'm not sposed to use em.'

'Just tell me what you know.'

'Doctor Shin was on da jetty, Missus. He did da looking.'

'What do you mean?'

'Fish man said when da diver bloke was brung ashore he was covered with a blanket, his head and all, so da doctor had to look. To see wot was underneath.'

'And it was a white man.'

'Yes, Missus. Chinky fella said white face.'

'And he was dead?'

'Don't know 'bout dat. Told you, word is he beeum dead.'

Maisie tore down the verandah to the back door, flying down the steps to the garden as if pursued, and jumped on the heavy iron-framed bicycle that saw scant service. The front tyre was half-flat, and the chain was dangling off its hub. She wound the pedals backwards until the chain snaked onto the spiky teeth. She'd forgotten she knew how to do that. She'd also forgotten her hat, her gloves and her reason.

William Cooper might be dead.

She paused for a second at the junction of Vulgar Villas, her secret name for the ostentatious eyesores the Bay's new wealth called home, then pushed off for the turn to Captain Espinell's shore-side camp. She wheezed over the handlebars, wobbly legs straddling the iron frame, sweat guttering down between her shoulder blades. She had gripped the rubber-clad handlebars so tightly that her palms were tacky with gluey latex, her heat-swollen fingers bent over like claws. A vulture flapped overhead; she narrowed her eyes and followed its path, the first two fingers of her left hand welded together in a tight cross.

Please, God. Don't let him die.

Bearing down on the pedals, breath thinly restored by the short rest, she pumped over flecks of storm-exfoliated paint that littered the road, the same shade as the walls of the government hospital. Scalloped pink flakes scattered on a bright white surface. *Like confetti*, she thought. *Was there confetti at my wedding?*

She shook her head; it might have been important once.

William Cooper might be dead.

She braked with a squeal and threw her bicycle in a patch of scrubby grass. A wheel was still spinning. Round and round on a loop in her head.

William Cooper might be dead. William Cooper might be dead.

William Cooper might be dead.

She knew she was a mess; she didn't care. She dashed up the steps of the Japanese hospital and smacked through the front door with a fearful heart.

It was too quiet. She wanted bright lights and clanging bustle, brisk nurses and swinging doors. Evidence that a life was being fought for. She banged on the counter with her fist.

She thumped again, her voice booming loudly like a foghorn. 'Hello! Is anybody there?'

A nun gliding past came to a stop beside her. 'Mrs Sinclair, there is no need to shriek.' The disapproval was tight in her voice.

Maisie flushed and lowered her voice. 'Might I have a word with Doctor Shin?'

'This is really not a good time, unless you are in extremis,' the nun said. 'The doctor does not generally consult at this hour. Midday on the third Wednesday in the month is his slot for white ladies. But you know this.'

'I do know, and am quite well, thank you, but most concerned for an employee of my husband. We have heard a man has been brought in for treatment. We feel responsible for our divers' welfare. So, I am here to find out what we might do.'

'I see,' the nun said. Her head turned slightly towards a door, as if she was expecting company. 'Doctor Shin is attending to a white diving casualty at the moment, but I wouldn't know to whom the man is indentured. I shall let the doctor know you are here. You may have a long wait.'

The last time she had sat in the hospital waiting room, the agenda had been hers; today, the room was the same, the walls were the same, tall and square and pink, but now the vigil was not the same. She sat alone, despair tearing at her heart. It was too early in the day for accidents; they mostly occurred after working hours when the heat and drink inflamed tempers, when shucking knives slipped on hard carapace in overheated packing sheds. Midday was not the hour for a diver to die. Was there ever a good moment? She sat in the silent, stifling box, clutching and twisting her handkerchief, and tuned in to the silence. The day stretched out, hour after hour, a time-distorted limbo.

The smell of antiseptic in the waiting room was like poison. Maisie held onto the memory of Coop's voice, cradling it inside, wrapping the sound of him around her like an antidote. She clacked her fingernails on the chair arm, in time with the clock on the wall. It was too fast, too fast, too fast.

The *Buccaneer Star* had reported an English casualty, but she couldn't remember when. Was it this week? Or last? She breathed deeply and tried to regulate her pulse.

Albert Banks had only been at sea a few days. According to the Malay shell-opener, a sudden gust of wind had caused the boom to jibe and caught him unawares. It pitched him off the deck stool and dumped him overboard still clutching his coffee mug in his hand. Weighed down by his fourteen-pound lead boots and the plates on his chest and back, he'd dropped to his death like a stone. It was a tragic accident, the reporter had written, and could have happened to anyone. *Like Coop*, Maisie thought.

'Mrs Sinclair?' Doctor Shin appeared at the door. A muscle twitched under his left eye, fatigue kneading his face. Outside, the light had started to fade and his shadow was long in the room. He rubbed his eyes, his mouth grim.

Maisie stood up, giddy with nerves, hardly able to support herself. She saw that dry skin was flaking through the dense dark stubble on his chin. He drew back, shaking his head.

She was aware she was chewing her lip, as Coop often did, and willed herself not to shout. *Is it him?*

'I'm here representing the Bay's English community. We have lost one of our own, I believe. Might you tell me who has perished at sea so that I might pass on the news to his employer and family?' She sounded like a pompous third-rate hack, and hated herself.

Doctor Shin consulted his clipboard as if the answers to her questions were chiselled there.

'An Englishman has passed away, Mrs Sinclair, you are quite correct. He was dead before he was brought ashore and I have been conducting his autopsy, to ascertain how he died. On one of your previous visits, I believe I mentioned I was making a study of diver's paralysis – caisson disease, or "the bends" as it is referred to on the pearling boats.'

'Was he our diver, Doctor Shin? Is it William Cooper who is dead?' The questions burst out of her like a ruptured dam.

The Japanese doctor took her elbow and guided her towards the door.

'No, Mrs Sinclair. This was not your husband's diver. The crew said that the deceased was John Geoffrey Jones. I believe he was one of Captain Hanson's men, the second of his to be brought in this week. They are diving in very deep waters, beyond Neptune's Dairy, with no regard for their own safety. All these white men think about is matching the indentured divers in shell collection and they are paying for it with their lives. I said to you before that I feel the white-diver experiment will not end well.'

Maisie looked at her shoes, and pawed at the floor with a cramped, sweaty foot. She could hear the doctor's voice echoing round the tall square room with its pink walls, like the *whoosh whoosh* sound of the sea trapped in a shell.

William Cooper is alive. William Cooper is alive. William Cooper is alive.

She stumbled and fell sideways, faint with reprieve.

CHAPTER 16

MAISIE PROPPED HERSELF UP on the sofa as soon as she arrived home and began to leaf through an old copy of *Every Lady's Journal*. Doctor Shin had sent her home in his sulky and told her to stay inside and rest. Fainting in the heat was not uncommon, he said, but needed to be taken seriously. She wasn't certain that fainting with relief was an illness, but hadn't set him straight.

Duc was singing in the kitchen. It sounded like he was practising his scales; up and down, a tone at a time, again and again.

'What about Miz Locke?'

Maisie looked up at the sound of Marjorie's voice.

Marjorie, in her brown frock, was busy with her broom, sweeping up another sack-load of horticultural debris from the floor, corks wedged in her ears. Even though the Wet was said to be over, insects still penetrated the fine gauze lining the mosquito room and were impervious to any deterrent except the constant burning of joss sticks, which Duc brought back in handfuls from the emporium in Asia Place. She planted them in holders with a little tray underneath to catch the ashes. The trays were useless; pale grey ash, the colour of fish scales, blew everywhere.

Marjorie swerved her eyes towards the garden lavatory. 'She been waitin' here hours, and just gone to relieve herself in da dunny.'

'Miss Locke's our guest, Marjorie. If she's come to see me and waited here all afternoon, then she must have a very good reason to drop in unannounced. I'm sorry if it has put you out in any way. What time did she get here?'

''Bout siesta time and I'm allonga babysittering her since then while you was out.'

'It was an emergency.'

Marjorie spread her feet apart and tented her hands on the broom handle. 'Yes'um. Big 'mergency with that white man wot makes you go all moonie-eyed.'

'He's alive, Marjorie. That's what's important.'

'See dat, Missus. But she stayin' for dinner or wot?'

'Yes, Miss Locke's staying. Duc said this morning he would cook seafood with his special rice, our garden tomatoes if the goat hasn't eaten them all, and snake beans from the Japanese market. There's a lot of fish, so that should embrace the captain's extras as usual. Could you trot by the bishop and Mrs McMahon and remind them they are joining us?'

The question seemed to consume her for a second. 'Thought you don't like fish.'

'I don't particularly, but I am making an effort to get over my dislike – as I am asking you to do – by reminding the bishop and his wife about tonight. I know you would prefer not to go, but sometimes you have to swallow down things you find unpalatable.'

Marjorie rubbed her index fingers along the sides of her nose. Maisie knew the gesture; there was more to come.

'Okay, Missus. I go to the holy churches and before dat I'll remind Duc 'bout food. He'll be one mad fella, though. He'll be spectin' some other sea-boss fellas, as boss fella said they do gamblin' later and he like them fellas more better. You and me, though, we need words 'bout chiffa money.'

'Why?'

'We's now got lotta quids in that skimpies jar. Duc an' me been wonderin' 'bout doin' dat investin' he told you 'bout.'

Jane Locke returned from the squalor at the far end of the garden, sniffing anything fragrant she came across en route.

Maisie patted the chair next to her and Jane sat down. 'I am glad you came, and apologise once again for my pitiful state. When we met that time in Asia Place I was all of a lather, and today I had a fainting spell in town, so Doctor Shin has confined me to the house for a few days.'

Jane shifted forward in her seat. 'Are you anticipating a happy event?'

Maisie felt the blush creep up her neck. 'No,' she said. 'Nothing so exciting. Doctor Shin is convinced I am on the brink of collapse, although I'm sure I did nothing to make him think that. To him, I am a great white puzzle that he is struggling to fathom.'

Jane nodded sympathetically and poured out two cups of tea. She moved in a little closer and looped an arm around Maisie's shoulders. 'I think we white women all are, in some measure, which is why we must look to each other for comfort and support. Would you agree?'

Maisie glanced up at her friend. 'Most definitely. Mrs Wallace made it very plain that I should integrate myself with all the ladies in the Bay as, without their support and acceptance, I would soon find myself very lonely indeed.'

'That's not quite what I meant.'

'Is there something else I should be doing?'

Jane reassured her that, no, there was nothing else she should be doing.

'What, then?'

'Have you heard of Sarah Orne Jewett?'

Maisie started. 'My goodness! Don't tell me I forgot to visit someone?'

'No. She was an American writer who died a few years ago, in 1909, I believe. She never married but enjoyed the constant companionship of another lady who was either divorced or widowed. I can't remember which. They lived together, travelled together, did everything together, independent of the financial or emotional support of a man.'

Maisie opened her mouth to speak but nothing emerged.

Jane removed her arm and sipped her tea, and Duc continued to screech in the kitchen. He had moved on to swooping arpeggios now, and both Jane's proposal and the musical gymnastics were beyond uncomfortable.

'You are a dear friend – and I value that above anything I have in the Bay – but for better or worse, I am married to Maitland.'

Jane lifted a magazine off the table and flipped over a page. 'Forgive me. I sometimes have these moments of weakness and cause a dear friend to suffer. Ill-timed, misjudged, inappropriate, whatever you want to call them.'

Maisie waved her hand in a dismissive gesture and then touched her friend's arm, just for a second. 'You said when we had lunch that you were going to tell me how you found yourself in the Bay after your husband left.'

Jane shut the magazine and smoothed her hand over the front cover. 'It was a family conspiracy. Even if one is of age and perfectly in command of one's mental facilities, a female who has been duped by a serial liar is trapped. Family imposes its will, and in this instance, its will was for me to keep an eye on my brother – Blair.'

Maisie's eyebrows expanded a fraction. 'Blair is your *brother*?'

'My parents adopted Blair when it became clear that there would be no more children after me. They took him in when he was tiny. After my marital disgrace, my parents wanted me to move in with him and supervise Dorothea's upbringing, but I knocked that idea on the head straightaway. We might have been raised in the same household but there is no mutual affection between Blair and me. I have never felt comfortable alone in his company, and – if I'm totally honest – there is something about him that makes me uneasy. I've never told my parents the reason I put my foot down so firmly, but they were adamant that I come to the Bay and they engineered the position with the McMahons. Blair had become their life, you see – the precious son, the heir apparent. It feels a little ironic sometimes, a woman being sent to babysit a man when we are dependent on them in so many other ways.'

Maisie put down her half-empty teacup. 'I had no idea.'

Jane sighed. 'There is no reason why you should have. Life is so often pretence, Maisie. We are chameleons, adopting a different skin to blend in with our changing backgrounds. We all do it, consciously or not, and I had a good teacher in my late husband. Look at Dorothea and the lengths she goes to in order to conceal her loneliness. Quite honestly, some people are just good at disguise. My father ran a Catholic school in Melbourne, so Blair was educated there, despite not actually being Catholic himself. There was something in his adoption papers, I believe, which withheld permission for him to be christened, but I don't know the specifics. School is where he met Maitland, who was fully immersed in his religion. The two of them have been as thick as thieves ever since.'

Maisie heard the thrum of the cicadas through the lattice.

My husband never goes near a church!

'I thought they met here in Buccaneer Bay.'

'No. They've been inseparable since they were young. Blair was two academic years older than Maitland, and once he left school, Maitland was gone too, within weeks. He never finished. In fact, I recall that he was asked to leave, but I have no idea why. Anyhow, eventually Blair married a widow with a young child, Dorothea. Maitland moved here to the Bay, and a year or so later, as soon as Dorothea was legally his, Blair moved them here as well. His wife died not long after from blood poisoning, or so I believe the story goes.'

Maisie looked out at Maitland's lawn. The scorched blades were grown over with glossy new grass, lush, thick and cropped short, past evidence covered up. 'Do you doubt that is how his wife died?'

Jane stretched out her legs and cleared her throat. 'I don't know anything for certain. Blair worked for Dorothea's father for a year or so – he was a wealthy and much-respected gem merchant in Melbourne – before he died of blood poisoning in strikingly similar circumstances to his wife. Dorothea, of course, knows none of this. She has no idea she is adopted or any of the rest. I wouldn't have bothered to tell you either, except that

Maitland's past and now his present are interwoven with Blair's in some inexplicable way and, as a dear *friend*,' she gave weight to the word, 'I worry for you.'

The house was too quiet. The Chinese scales had run their course. The sun had started to sink behind the lighthouse, throwing dappled shadows through the lattice. Jane looked at her watch. 'The others will be here soon. If you wanted to know more you could always ask Maitland's mother.'

Maisie scratched her cheek, trying to decide if Jane was pulling her leg. 'Maitland hasn't talked much about his family. He's an only child and, as far as I know, he has no contact with his parents. I assumed they'd passed away.'

Jane nodded. 'His father, yes. He died on the opal fields years back. But his mother is definitely still with us. I see advertisements from her company in the newspaper from time to time,' she said. 'Pammie Sinclair invented the Correct Posture Corset. She has made quite a name for herself and travels all over the world demonstrating her garment.'

Maisie held up her hands. 'Please, Jane! I know nothing of Maitland's background, let alone that he is Catholic, and now he has a mother who models corsets! Your parents were instrumental in sending you here, and so were mine. All I know about Maitland is that his father – who I now know to be definitely deceased – was my grandmother's cousin. My parents received a letter from him – out of the blue, I think – but my mother is not Catholic. I have no idea why they were so set on him as the ideal husband and why I was sent out to him at just three weeks' notice.'

Jane stood up from the tweed-covered chair and moved towards the green box on the coffee table. 'That's soapstone, isn't it?'

'I wouldn't know,' Maisie replied, disconcerted at the key change. 'It's Maitland's.'

'Definitely a man of secrets.' Jane picked it up and stroked its smooth surface. 'My parents have one. Have you worked out how to open it?'

'I've barely noticed it.'

Jane shook the box and held it to her ear. 'It's difficult to know what's within. That he has this at all is interesting, though, don't you think?'

Maisie let her head tip back. 'I thought it was a cigarette box,' she said to the ceiling.

'It's an exercise in cunning and misplaced logic. There is no key, because there is no lock, and the hinges are not hinges. You have to think in a particular way. I never managed to open the one at home, but I do remember my father saying that guile and pressure would let you in.' Jane returned the box to the table. 'Shall we play detective and do some investigations of our own?'

Maisie rolled her head back down. 'Why are you so set on this, Jane?'

'A suspicious mind in the first place, and a very great desire to watch over a dear friend. If Maitland is not the personification of respectability he would have us believe, then I feel you should know all the facts, don't you? So that you have the measure of the person you married.'

Maisie looked into her earnest face. Jane might have private reasons for investigating Maitland, but she had a confession of her own to share. 'I agree that he is not always the gentleman he would have us believe.'

Jane pursed her lips. 'Has something happened?'

'The night of the cyclone, Captain Mason had rather too much to drink and pressed his attentions on me.'

Jane laughed. 'Yes, he's well known for it. I think he even tried it on with the bishop's wife on one occasion!'

'Maitland said so at the time, but he was there, Jane. Maitland saw that I was upset and yet he did nothing to help me. I realise that I am newly married but – surely–'

'Yes,' Jane cut over her. 'He should have intervened.'

Maisie twirled a strand of hair round her finger. 'So, maybe I could approach the corset lady, if you can find me one of her advertisements, and delve into the family archives.'

'Of course I'll help you with the address. We're bound to find it in one of your magazines. But . . .' Jane sat down again and put her hands on Maisie's arm. 'I cannot pretend that it will be plain sailing, and you will have to be prepared, possibly, for some unpleasant truths. Mothers generally lose contact with their children for a reason.'

Maisie looked beyond the shutters at a black dot on the ocean. Everything that made the world matter to her was bobbing about in a pearling boat somewhere on that great expanse of sea. 'We can't risk Maitland or Blair finding out. Maitland has a dreadful temper and is capable of despicable violence. I have proof, also, that he is intercepting my private letters.'

'Then we shall have to ensure that he no longer has access to your correspondence.'

Maisie turned her eyes on Jane. 'How do we do that?'

'All mail comes in and out of the Bay via the central post office in Asia Place. If you are prepared to ignore Doctor Shin's advice, I suggest we go now and speak to the postmistress. If the others arrive while we are out, Duc can serenade them with one of his charming tunes.'

Mrs Brightlight lived up to her name. 'Skulduggery,' the carrot-haired postmistress decreed when Maisie explained the reason for their visit. Her solid stomach was perched on the edge of the counter, round and hard like a football, her blouse falling in soft ruffles around her neck. Maisie thought she looked like a turkey, all fattened up and ready for Christmas.

Mrs Brightlight tapped the counter with a pencil. 'There have indeed been a number of letters for you, Mrs Sinclair, since you came to the Bay. The captain is very charming when he picks them up. We always chitchat about my children and the new one that's on the way.' She looked down at her stomach. 'He's very keen to have little ones of his own, he tells me. Devoted to his wife, that's what I've always thought. He says he is sparing you the discomfort of the walk to the post office, you being new to the climate and all.'

'Devoted to his own ends,' Jane said, bleakly.

'It's wicked,' Mrs Brightlight's fleshy mouth tightened, 'to cut a person off from their correspondence.'

'And do you send on the letter I write each week to England?'

'No, dear, I have never had one of those. Your correspondence amounts to the letters in and out to Gantry Creek and the magazines that come up from Port Fremantle. That's all.'

Maisie gasped, hardly daring to believe her but knowing – deep down – what Mrs Brightlight said was true.

'The Bay is a small community. Letters and parcels are what I know. Show me someone's handwriting, I can tell you who wrote the label. Like a teacher knowing which little hand has scribbled naughty words on the desk.' She tapped her pencil again on the counter, as if preparing to demonstrate her point.

Maisie was finding it difficult to understand. 'Why is he doing that?'

Mrs Brightlight talked on. 'Some people are plain dishonest. I could tell you a tale or two about dishonesty in this town.'

Maisie turned to go. That she had been tricked by Maitland was more than enough. *For now.* 'I will look forward to and value another conversation with you but it will have to wait for another time, Mrs Brightlight, when I am not quite so pressed. In future, though, please be quite clear: you are not to give my husband any parcel, package or letter connected with me, even if he brings you flowers.'

The postmistress leaned heavily on her hand and snapped the tip off her pencil. 'There will be no further cooperation from me,' she said. 'Even if he brings me every single bloom from Port Fremantle.'

CHAPTER 17

MAITLAND WAS IN HIS office. With the Wet now decidedly over, the Bay was returning to normal. The only real thorn in his side was Maisie. Having her in the house was like living with a yapping dog, constantly underfoot and nipping at his heels. *Duc's goat* this and *ice boy* that. Nag, nag, nag. Getting her out running the slop chest had been a stroke of genius, though. The weekends were once again his own. Duc was whining less too, and the food had improved.

All told, he was in a very good mood. His white suits went to the laundry in Singapore more or less every fortnight on the Blue Funnel steamship. A dozen of them could be starched and laundered for ten shillings. It was cheaper to use the Singapore cleaners, he told Maisie when she'd badgered him, and far more reliable to have them washed and pressed two thousand miles away than a couple of miles up the road in Asia Place.

He smiled to himself about the real reason – the little extra-curricular import–export business he had going on the side, bringing in opium concealed within the lid of the laundry chest. The previous afternoon, he'd picked out the sticky lumps, which he would now sell on to the divers at five-hundred per cent profit. *I am a bloody genius*, he laughed to himself. *Even bloody Blair hasn't thought of this!*

A scraping noise interrupted his thoughts. The Malay packing-shed boy peered round the door and whispered, 'Tuan, one of crew. Him pinch pearl.'

Maitland slapped his pen on the desk. 'My crew?'

'No him's crew. Tuan mayor.'

Maitland sat up in his chair. Someone had snitched one of Blair's pearls? 'And where is it now?'

The Malay scratched his bare stomach. 'I no know. But Java Boy Pete know. He say tell you. Maybe you like buy?'

Maitland's eyes narrowed. 'How big is this snide?'

'Him big fella, forty- to fifty-grain stringer, no flaws.'

'Did Java Boy Pete say where to meet him?'

The teak face relaxed. He had the answer to this question. 'Oh, him say at Seafarer's when you done finish here.'

Despite appearances, Maitland was short of ready cash. He had expanded his business interests as far as he could with bank loans, but his debts to the Chinese ship-chandlers had grown heavy. His luggers were all mortgaged to the hilt and one had just been smashed in the blow. The new schooner had yet to be paid for. He'd cashed in Maisie's dowry but the money he was wringing from her father was nowhere near enough. He should have asked for more; that was a bloody error of judgement.

Fifty-grain stringer? A sodding fortune if it was true. He'd sell it on, settle his debts and get out of the pearling game. He was sick of the stench of rotting oysters and of being kept dangling at the Pearlers' Association. There was a debate that afternoon but he thought he'd give it a miss. Blair said that war was brewing in Europe, and they should get into wool. Army uniforms was where the real money would be made. They were talking about going into it together.

The Seafarer's Rest Hotel was a rambling single-storey construction that offered 'tiered' accommodation to its multinational clientele. Maitland had a large interest in the property and had dumped the English diver and his tender in single rooms along one side of the building. A picket fence marked off a plot of land to the right side, which housed the stables, wash blocks and toilets. The left-hand yard was swept clean. The divide was intentional: whites on the left, coloureds on the right, and strictly no stepping over the line.

Java Boy Pete was lodged on the right-hand side beyond the sanitation block, in a filthy smoke-blackened square at the back of the hotel. The narrow outbuilding was enclosed in a concrete yard. It was stiflingly hot, windowless and smelled of sweat.

Maitland banged the door with the toe of his boot. 'You in there, Java?'

There was no answer. Maitland prepared to kick again, the inside edge of his foot ready to stave in the door.

'Gud evening, Tuan Sinclair.' Java Boy Pete sidled up behind him barefoot, bare-chested and saronged.

Maitland pivoted on his heel and looked at the Javanese as if he were an exhibit in a jar. 'You Pete?'

The young boy nodded. 'You got money in pockit, Tuan?'

Maitland lifted his eyebrows to his hairline.

'You buy pearl? Big as a whale.' The boy made an elaborate gesture with his arms. 'Mebbe thousand pounds? Then you sell like quick sticks for double?'

'Where did you get it?'

'No trouble 'bout that. Everyone in the Bay buy snide. I don't blab to no-one. You want see?'

The swarthy, indentured Pete was as slippery as a snake and potentially ten times as dangerous. Maitland needed time to think. The pearl masters sent their divers to the depths to haul up pearl shell. That was the day-to-day business, their bread-and-butter money. But from time to time, once in every ten thousand shells, a magnificent pearl would be found. Divers and crew were relied upon to be honest and set this bounty aside for their employers. Some did, but the desperate majority did not, and supplied the snide market with pearls that were filched from their bosses and sold on to known snide buyers or anyone prepared to resell them at a profit. Maitland knew that his own shell-opener, Sid, was a thieving crow who sold his best pearls out at sea. Likewise, someone had shanghaied this 'beaut' from Blair. But it could be the perfect solution to get him out of the Bay.

'You'd better have it. If you dragged me out here for nothing, you'll regret it.'

'I have it, Tuan. No need worry.'

Maitland felt his heart pounding with an excitement he could barely contain, but it wouldn't do to look too eager. 'I'm going up to the bar for a drink. Wait for me outside but keep out of fucking sight or the deal's off.'

He rechecked his watch and nodded again to the barman. An hour later, he frowned at the scrub and shoved himself out of his chair. The wooden steps had rotted in places and snapped at his feet like an alligator's teeth. He tripped on a plank, his flabby hands unable to break his fall. Java Boy Pete appeared at his side and hauled him to his feet.

'So, where's the snide?'

Java Boy Pete broke into a smile. 'It's in best place to hide it, Tuan.'

'Best place?' Maitland lowered his gaze to the south.

'Oh yes. Very best place. You want to sample goods?' The Malay set off towards his digs, casting furtive glances over his shoulder, like an animal checking for its master. He ran his hand through his oily hair and wiped it on the cloth covering his buttocks.

Maitland's pulse quickened as they crossed the filthy threshold. 'Lock the door,' he said.

Maitland turned to the dosshouse wall and looked over his shoulder. Reassured that no-one was watching, he wrapped the pearl in his handkerchief and placed it in his breast pocket. A snide that size would be hard to get rid of quickly, but he could afford to wait for a bit.

Some said big pearls were unlucky, but Maitland spat on all that nonsense. Java Boy Pete was not going to talk about this particular one. The boy was lying dead on his bed, his purple-black tongue lolling out of his head. Maitland had watched a fly crawl into his mouth. Old snitches, he told himself, were too unpredictable – sometimes it was advisable to crush them underfoot like irritating bugs. If anyone had seen him in that shithole, it would be a white man's word against a coloured's.

Maitland straightened his jacket and blew a few specks of dust off his lapel. He looked at his watch. He was going to be late, and cursed himself for not booking Mr Li's rickshaw to trot him home. He didn't much care for walking unless he could detour his journey to the pub. His legs were short and called upon to support too much weight. His ankles protested and his toe joints ached. And although he had constructed his life to keep walking to a minimum, tonight he had no choice.

He looked at the sky and approved his decision. It was not going to rain; last night's blow seemed to have cleared the air. He set off on foot, eager for the forthcoming evening with his drinking chums. He had forgotten to invite the new pearl cleaner, but that would keep. A hint of breeze was blowing offshore, coaxing the moisture out of the air. It had been an excellent afternoon altogether, and if he kicked on a bit, he wouldn't be too late after all. He felt almost joyful.

Dusk was creeping over the town, and a lone fruit bat squeaked overhead as Maitland sauntered towards his bungalow, past shredded scraps of paper and broken glass, untidy reminders of the cyclone. A few scrawny dogs were nosing through the filth. He was hardly interested; he was too pleased with himself. Even the southern stars had come out to light his way home, as if saluting the victor in his triumphant march. A gust of wind met him from the salmon-tinted dunes, tempting him to take a short-cut over the sand to enjoy the breeze. He paused for a moment, patted his breast pocket and gazed out to the sea. The hairs stood up on the back of his neck. There was a ripple in the air, a sound so tiny that he wasn't sure he'd really heard it.

Was someone after his snide? He glanced around, tapped the lump in his pocket and shook his head. Cockatoos were roosting in a tall dead tree, ghostly white against the darkening night sky, but there was not a soul about.

CHAPTER 18

CHARLIE LOITERED BY THE semi-deserted bar and leaned on the handle of his wheelbarrow. A gaunt figure, his mop of woolly black hair covered with a wide-brimmed hat, he melted into the shadows of the hotel, his eyes missing nothing. He sucked on his pipe and let out a long stream of smoke.

He believed that revenge could be achieved with secrecy, cunning and patience, and he had the temperament to watch and wait. He had endured enough that a few more hours wouldn't make any difference. The dusk was deepening and soon it would be dark. He slid his hand inside his dilly-bag. The junba had taken place. Bodies painted and adorned with animal fur, the Elders of his mob had overseen the secret ritual. Stamping their feet in the sunburned scrub, they had summoned the Bush Spirit to imbue the killing bone with psychic energy. Left for days to steep in a dingo's rotting corpse, the bone had become a septic dart. The Elders were glad the Kurdaitcha had started. They had seen what the captain had done. Now it was time.

Each kundela, or killing bone, was specific to the tribe. Charlie's was eight inches long and could have passed as a carpet needle in any European household. Other tribal killing bones differed in length and in what animal had given up the bone. Common to all, though, at the flattened end, a strand of human hair was threaded through the hole and glued into place with spinifex gum.

Normally, Charlie wore heavy second-hand boots. Tonight, in his bag, he had a brand-new pair of shoes. Not the kind favoured by the white man – his were made of soft emu feathers pasted together with animal blood. A silky woven net of human hair covered the upper surface. There was a hole at the top in which to insert his foot. His little toe had been dislocated during the initiation ceremony and a gap at the side allowed it to poke free. Decorated with lines of pink and white down, the shoes were primed with magic.

Charlie had tracked a man before, during his initiation, but this was personal. He wiggled his feet into his Kurdaitcha shoes and flexed his toes.

He watched the fat white man wrap something in a handkerchief and place it in his pocket. Charlie looked upwards, sniffed the air, and then wheeled the barrow back to the woodpile, avoiding eye contact with a half-caste girl who was laboriously pegging sheets on the washing line beyond the division fence. No-one would ever know who had been there. He left no footprints in the red earth.

He had abandoned his white man's clothes and now wore nothing but a pubic tassel of kangaroo skin. A ten-inch wooden stick with needle-sharp ends was thrust through his nose. On his chest and stomach, white against his ebony skin, the Banardi tribe's sacred drawing dazzled in the moonlight. He called upon the Bush Spirit to do its work and threw a pebble onto the sand.

A reddish dust clouded up, stirring up the ashes of his ancestors, long dead and as potent and fiery as a freshly cut termite hill.

The white man hesitated by the dunes as the cloud came at him, spiralling like a mini tornado towards his face. He had no time to react. The cayenne-coloured dust blew into his vision and up his nose. Sneezing, he rubbed his burning eyes and spat on his sleeve, pressing the wetted cloth into the hollow between his eyes and nose.

The man swore and rubbed his face alternately into the sleeves of his jacket, spreading brown-red stains on the brilliant white fabric. He slithered down the dunes, and lost his footing. At the bottom, he tipped the sand out of his shoes, brushed it off his cheeks and rolled onto his side, whimpering like a woman.

Charlie squatted on his haunches. Junba. The Bush Spirit was beginning its real work, twisting and tormenting the white man, calling him towards the scrub. The Aboriginal man ran his finger along the killing bone, still wrapped in its protective shroud. He was careful to avoid the needle-sharp tip.

The fat man pushed himself to his feet and stumbled on, still blinded, snapping off brittle stalks of scrub grass, tripping often on low, entangling bushes, his face scratched and lashed by whippy stems. He plunged onwards, eyelids closed, his arms outstretched like a wheedling child. Again he went down, smacking his head hard as he fell. Cheek pressed against one arm, he sobbed with frustration, his pleading fingers quivering as he reached out for help.

He scarcely flinched as the deadly-sharp pinprick plunged into his flesh, deep within the seat of his trousers.

Charlie stood up and withdrew the killing bone. Blood welled up and dyed the fabric red, like shame. The white man would be found soon enough. It was where he'd left him after the whipping, all but a hundred yards from the entrance to his home.

As the guests gathered on the verandah, Maisie knew that the supper party would be a disaster; the mix was awry. The salty smell of the ocean was strong on the air and the crickets too strident. Another headache clamped her skull. Doctor Shin had again told her to take it easy when she'd gone to see him about them, but she had not been following his advice.

Maisie inspected her nails. They were short, filed and tidy, the opposite of her scrambled thoughts.

Tonight, they were waiting for the pearl doctor and his wife, and for Maitland. Maisie wasn't sure if they had been invited this time, and Maitland was not here to consult.

Buoyed up on a tide of alcohol-induced bonhomie, Captain Mason was making the most of his friend's absence. To him flirtation was second nature, a sport; he had already run his swollen-knuckled paw up Jane Locke's leg. She was now perching on the edge of a chair, ready to hop up out of reach if the ageing captain made another lunge.

The conversation stop-started and stalled like the Bay's open-top tram.

The bishop and Mrs McMahon were discussing their dogs and drinking their whisky neat; they didn't trust the water, because they hadn't checked its source.

Blair swatted at the mosquitos, which clustered round the lamps as thick as fog. 'Have you heard from your parents recently, Jane?' Maisie asked, watching his face. Not a flicker. He looked bored, a card player good at bluffing.

'No, not as of late. I wrote to them a while back and anticipate their reply from Melbourne any day.'

Maisie got up and stared through the lattice, wondering where on earth Maitland had got to. She was unsure how to proceed and Jane was quiet, waiting for another prompt, as if something had fettered her tongue.

'And how is your study of the Indigenous population progressing?'

'I am hoping to travel north to the mission sometime soon. The bishop has kindly agreed to arrange a visit for me.' She looked over at him and smiled. 'We have found a decommissioned lugger that can take us, and I am hoping to work with the native women, many of whom are suffering from malnutrition, leprosy, and diseases we know they have contracted from the European.'

Mrs McMahon bridled. 'Not appropriate, Lockie dear, when food is about to be served.'

Maisie stared at a streak of polish on the floorboards. 'I thought I might accompany her, Mrs McMahon. My maid, Marjorie, spent time at the mission and has expressed a desire to revisit her mentors. How long did you say the journey would take, Jane?'

'Three days,' Jane said, loosening up. 'Then we thought we might take a boat across to Spikey Island, where Marjorie could interpret for us. Nothing is cast in stone, though, just yet. We're still at the planning stage, and a trip like this takes weeks to put together.'

Mrs McMahon clasped her husband's forearm. 'Are you going too, dear?'

The bishop shook his head and smiled at her.

Maisie tried to think of something witty to say but couldn't come up with a thing. She turned to Dorothea, hoping for once to unleash the girl's tongue.

'And Dorothea, what is new in your world?'

The girl gave an anxious glance at her father and studied the bottom of her empty glass. The colour in her face had risen. 'Not so very much, Mrs Sinclair. I am beginning to understand why dear Mama found the Bay so confining.'

'She must have missed her family keenly.'

Dorothea looked up. 'Did you know my mother's family?' she said, her lip jutting out miserably.

Maisie took a bottle off the drinks tray and pushed it towards her. 'Not in person, but I do understand what it is like to be parted from one's kin. That is why it made such good sense for me to come to Australia and marry cousin Maitland – to keep the family unit close.'

'Is that so, *chère madame*?' the mayor said dryly.

Maisie was feeling reckless. 'Of course. I can't believe Maitland would have kept you in the dark given you were so friendly at the Catholic school in Melbourne.'

Dorothea was pouring liquid into her glass when the bottle slid through her fingers. It clanged on the wood like a bad joke. 'Dada?'

'Rubbish,' he said sharply. 'Watch what you are doing, Dorothea. You are making a mess.'

Dorothea stole another glance at her father and buried her misery in her glass.

Maisie produced a forced laugh. 'When Maitland asked my parents for my hand, they were delighted to agree, and I am grateful they chose so well for me. What an adventure, coming out to Australia! I couldn't think of anything more exciting.'

Captain Mason was drunk, or near as made no difference. He was having trouble with his feet, and his eyes were glassy. 'Might just avail myself of the facilities, ladies and Bishop. Empty the tank, what?'

'Do what?' Mrs McMahon startled awake, having nodded off.

'Captain needs the dunny, dearest,' her husband said, patting her hand.

They sat uncomfortably side by side like patients enduring the dentist's waiting room and gulped at their drinks.

'Poor thing,' Jane said. 'It must be sad to be so lonely.'

'Is he?' Maisie asked. 'He's always here at our house, trying to catch me alone. I can't get rid of the man.'

Mrs McMahon's podgy face stretched out of the lamp-lit gloom, a turtle straining its scaly neck towards the light. 'He's been here a long time, Maisie. It's high time you learned some compassion and stopped measuring people against your rigid morals and inexperience of life. For goodness' sake, this is not England. A lack of compassion can be as vulgar as an excess of tears.' She fixed Dorothea with a look.

Maisie said nothing but felt as though she had swallowed a wasp. *Is this what I've become? A judgemental hypocrite?*

Duc stood in the doorway, his face stretched tight. He attacked the three sides of a musician's triangle with a dented metal rod; the notes resonated round the bungalow.

'Dinner is now absolutely or fish go in shitcan.'

'Might be a bit of a delay,' Captain Mason slurred. 'Just nearly tripped over Maitland outside. He's had a tumble and might need a shower.'

*

Maitland slumped in a chair and rubbed the back of his neck. His hand shook violently but he could not stop it. He had a crushing headache and little pinpricks of white light danced before his eyes. He'd told them what had happened, yet he could see disbelief plastered over their sodding sweaty faces. He wanted them all to fuck off home.

'I told you, there was someone following me. Even though I never saw him, he was there all the same. I'm not a total arse.'

'But Captain Mason has been to look outside. He says it's really too dark to see properly, but as far as he can tell there are only your footprints in the sand, Maitland,' Maisie said. 'Why would anyone want to follow you?'

He angrily jabbed a finger towards the sea. 'I took a shortcut along the beach because I was running behind and I knew you'd bloody nag if I was late for dinner. There was someone behind me, I'm telling you: hiding, disorienting me, herding me towards the bush.'

'To do what, exactly?' Blair was sitting by the drinks table, with one leg casually crossed over the other, studying the back of his hand. 'One too many at the Seafarer's, Mait?'

Maitland worked hard to keep his voice level. 'Get me a ruddy drink, Blair, and cut the cute comments.'

Blair got up, selected a bottle and sloshed a generous measure into a stubby tumbler. 'This should sort you out,' he said, plonking the glass in Maitland's palm, 'you miserable, fat bastard.'

Maitland felt stiff with an anxiety he could not explain and siphoned the liquid up between his teeth, hoping it would disengage the knot in his stomach and swamp the sour taste in his mouth. They were staring at him in the half-light, exchanging boggled-eyed looks as if he was mad. *Fuck them,* he thought. *Fuck them all!*

Mrs McMahon shot a look at her husband then leaned forward.

'Do tell, Captain Sinclair. Do you think it might have been a goblin chasing you, trying to create mischief?'

'Or a bush sprite.' Dorothea giggled. 'Trying to hex you!'

Maitland lurched from his chair and slammed his glass on the table.

'Don't cheek me, young lady. Take that smirk off your face and tell the lubra we'll eat in ten minutes, when I've had a shower and changed my clothes.'

CHAPTER 19

THE SKY SPARKLED LIKE Christmas-tree lights.

Coop turned and his eyes met hers. 'Have you ever seen stars like these?'

Maisie felt his look in the pit of her stomach. Her breath quickened.

'No, I haven't.' Her knees felt as if they might give way. She lolled back against the rail and pulled a packet of cigarettes from her skirt pocket. She held the packet towards him, his silhouette slim in the pallid light. 'Would you care for one of mine?'

Coop took the box of Chesterfields and tapped the base with the back of his hand. Two cigarettes slid forward like skiers on a slope.

'They do satisfy, you know, Coop,' Maisie said, watching his fingers.

He drew his head back. 'Sorry?'

'It's what the advertisement says in the newspaper. "They Do Satisfy." The cigarettes.'

Coop rarely smoked boxed cigarettes. He couldn't afford them, she knew.

Maisie pulled out one of the pair. She had become adept at lighting up in the dark. Cigarette clamped in furtive lips, match struck once or twice and hey, presto! Tonight was different. She was an amateur in the company of a professional.

'You might have to help me. The wind is a little tricky.'

He leaned towards her and cupped the end of the cigarette in his hands. 'Now try.' His skin was warm under her fingertips, the flame bright in the darkness.

She breathed in his tobacco scent and felt she was falling. She turned and grasped the rail like a diver on a wreck. She would not let herself feel ashamed for touching him. Below, the ocean was mottled with moon shadows, and silence stretched out like a carpet.

'Is something wrong?' Coop said.

Sunday supper had become their private affair.

Maisie had spent the past week counting down the days, allowing herself one thought of him each hour until, in her dreams, there was no restraint. In her dreams, she sailed on the seas with her dark-eyed captain, bathing herself in the luxury of him; she did not have to eke out the minutes until their Sunday was over, because their time together was not defined. Maisie knew that the fleeting freedom she felt would end the next day, when she sailed back to shore.

She was excited, confused, nervous. Tonight, she had decided she would tell him what she'd wanted to say for weeks. She would tell him that she loved him; but now that the moment was here, the words would not slip past her lips. She was not free to utter them and he was not free to hear them. So, she clamped them inside, her secret unshared.

She stood for some time smoking her cigarette, her eyes fixed on the water. 'Tell me something about you that no-one else knows.'

He half-turned next to her and raised his hand to his forehead. He said in a mock-serious voice, 'My middle name is Hereward.'

Maisie tried to hold her laughter in place. 'That's a weighty load to bear.'

'Indeed it is, Mrs Sinclair.' He grinned. 'And now the load is half yours! And what of you, Maisie? What secret can we share?'

She felt a different tremble in her legs and put a hand on the rail to support herself. 'I went through Maitland's desk.'

Their evening was drawing to a close and she felt spooked, as if an ill wind was blowing towards them. Coop leaned against her.

She saw the sweat glistening in his hair, could feel his breath on her face. Could he sense that she felt faint? 'The day we arrived in Fremantle on the steamer, you were wearing patterned socks.'

'That's an odd thing to say.'

'It was the first thing I noticed about you. It struck me that you'd completely misread the occasion.'

'My father sells socks for a living.'

'My father's a judge, but I don't wear a wig.'

'I hate anything dull. I am scared my life will be beige and flat with no contours or colour, so I wear bright socks to remind me to climb mountains.'

'Is that why you came to Australia. To find a mountain?'

'The challenge excited me.'

Maisie turned her face away and made herself say out loud, 'Enough for you to sign your own death warrant?'

'What do you mean?'

'You signed a document saying that you would only get commission when you hauled up more than two-and-a-half tons of shell. At the rate you're going on the beds you're diving, you're never going to get there.' She saw the clench of his jaw and felt him tense. 'That's bad enough.' She took a deep breath. 'What's far worse, though, is that you agreed that you will hold Maitland blameless should you be injured or killed while diving in his employ.'

He was quiet for some time, as still as stone. Eventually, he turned her back to face him and pressed her hand in his. Fleetingly, there was something in his expression that made her think she was on the brink of hearing a confession of which he wasn't proud.

'You have to help me with another favour then, Maisie.'

She pulled her hand away. 'Another?'

'You have to burn that page.'

'If he catches me,' she said after a pause, 'I don't know what he'll do.'

'You saw what I signed.'

She nodded. 'The pearl masters hatched their plan weeks ago.'

'Did you know?' His gaze seared her face.

'You're staring at me.'

'Eye contact's a good thing. You can tell when someone's lying.'

'Maitland had some of the master pearlers round for drinks a few months back, before the cyclone. Marjorie overheard them tossing coins and placing bets.'

'Go on.'

The words came out in a rush. 'The bottom line is you're too expensive. The pearlers are paying lip service to the government, counting on the fact that the Bay is too far away to police, and are working together to make sure the white-diver experiment fails. I'm guessing they were placing bets on who did what to whom to sabotage the scheme. There is no doubt in my mind that you are in the gravest danger, Coop.'

'JB will watch my back.'

'What if something happens to him?'

'Forewarned is forearmed. Isn't that how the expression goes? I promise I'll be careful, but you have to get rid of that page.'

Anxiety pinched her face.

'I know you're afraid, but that's not everything, is it?' Coop said.

Digging her nails into her palms, Maisie looked out across the vast stretch of water and thought she could make out the lighthouse. She couldn't help herself and blurted out, 'I hear you are engaged to be married to Miss Montague.'

A gust of laughter escaped Coop, but then he caught Maisie's sombre expression. He let out a low whistle.

'She told me that you'd kissed at the Welcome Dance and that after that things were understood between you.'

He looked at the deck, his face flushed. 'It's true about the kiss. She launched herself at me when I was fetching your drink. The rest, though . . . I don't know where she got that from.'

'She thinks life's a romantic novel, Coop. She's longing for something that doesn't exist and thinks she's found it in you. You are the knight who is going to whisk her away on his white horse. If she persists with the fantasy and tells her father, you will have a far worse enemy who will make Maitland look like a beginner. Blair has no scruples; he thinks he's above the law.'

Coop paused and flicked the butt of his cigarette over the balustrade. 'It can't be easy for Dorothea having no mother to turn to. The day I met her she prattled on and on about how busy her life is in the Bay, although now I suspect she spends a lot of time on her own, with her heart-fluttering stories. The reality is that she's lonely and neglected.'

Maisie listened to his words, wondering if he realised he had almost precisely described her own situation. 'What are you going to do?'

'I danced with her on a whim, and I'm going to have to deal with the consequence of that. She'll be hurt, but I must find a way to let her down lightly.'

'Yes,' Maisie said, polishing the deck with the toe of her shoe. 'But please don't ask me to help you with that.'

He drew her into him then and held her, hand cradling her head, and kissed her hard. She had dreamed of this moment, of what a kiss would feel like and how he would taste. He crushed her to him, opening her lips with his own. As her innermost self started to melt, she expected a parental admonishment to resound in her head about virtue and morals, and how far she could expect to fall from grace. But there was nothing, except her own voice whispering his name.

'Why did you marry him, Maisie?' he spoke into her hair.

She placed a hand on his cheek and thought despairingly, *Because he asked and my parents said yes.*

Maitland was dreaming. An exhausted stupor weighted his limbs like shackles and he was frightened. Did ghosts seek revenge on the living?

Something had dragged him back through the years to his schooldays, and now there he was – caught up among the furtive conclave in the lavatories.

'Come on, Maitland. Let's see your goods.'

His three assailants pinioned his arms behind him and pulled his trousers down past his knees.

'Let's unpack his crate,' one of the boys jeered. 'Look at his box of tricks.'

'What's the matter? I'm the same as the rest of you.' His shrill adolescent voice quavered.

Three pairs of eyes stared at him.

'Look, he's wet himself,' someone laughed.

'Ladyfinger!' someone else sniggered.

The door burst open. 'What the hell's going on?' It was Blair.

Maitland buttoned his trousers, his cheeks ablaze, burning hot like a bonfire. 'They'll be sorry,' he said, his voice barely audible.

'Yes,' said Blair. 'They will.'

Maitland woke with a jolt, the three boys disappearing into shadow.

'You look bloody awful,' Blair said.

'How long have you been here?'

'Long enough to see you thrashing about under the covers.'

'Doc says I've got Barcoo fever.'

'That's bad. Chlorodyne and brandy's about the only thing for it. Get Duc to soak some potatoes in vinegar overnight and then boil them up and mash them. Bland food's what you need. You got the trots as well?'

'Opposite. My belly is rock-hard and I can't stomach food. The smell makes me puke.'

'Have you been drinking contaminated water?'

'How would I know?' he said irritably. 'We use the rain tanks here in the house, but I might have picked something up at the Seafarer's.'

'When were you up there?'

'Last Tuesday. I was fine till Thursday morning, when the puking started up and Maisie began to fuss.'

'They found a body up there a few nights back.'

Maitland raised an eyebrow. 'Is that so?'

Blair picked at the edge of a fingernail. 'Trussed up like a chicken. Not pretty, apparently.'

'How'd he die?'

'Not exactly sure, Mait.' Blair leaned in close, his thin, colourless lips close to Maitland's ear. 'But the doc said he had some "unusual" injuries.'

Maitland sipped his drink and pushed back against the pillows. 'What's more unusual is why, after six years of putting myself forward, do the blokes suddenly think I'm fit to head up the Association?'

'Extraordinary General Meeting because I'm standing down and going off to Europe for a bit with Dorothea. I need to get her away from here.'

'That's a bit sudden, isn't it? You never mentioned you were thinking of a trip.'

'I wasn't till last night when Dorothea announced her engagement to your bloke Cooper.'

Maitland stared at him. 'When did that happen? He's been on the lugger for weeks.'

'At that bloody dance, she says. I'm taking no chances. She's over twenty-one, so doesn't need my permission to get married, but we can't let them anywhere near each other. She's got another three years until she's twenty-five, and won't see any of her trust money until then. You hear what I'm saying? That's three more years I'm to grind out. I'm not going to let it slip through my hands, so I'm getting her out of the way, and you need to step up plans to get rid of him.'

'Where are you thinking of going?'

'Paris, London, New York. Wherever we do business. That fancy new steamer the *Atticus* pulls in here soon, so it seemed a good time to go.'

Maitland squeezed his glass and took another mouthful. 'Why are you really off on a trip, Blair? The start of the season's not a wise time to be away.'

'They're sending a government chap up from Perth to look at what's going down here with the white diving blokes. Check tallies and progress, that sort of thing. Visit their pet project.'

Maitland nodded, draining the last of his drink. 'So, I'm the one with his head on the block if the government bloke smells a rat.'

Lines deepened across Blair's forehead. He cracked his finger joints, one by one. 'A few of the white divers are dead already and I've just dealt with another.' He pushed his hat off his forehead with the whisky bottle. 'I fixed that stupid bugger Jack Morris, with his Navy references and his sodding Admiralty staging manual. I paired him up with that old cronk Ropin, who's too old to still be alive, let alone go to sea. Sent them about thirty miles off the coast saying there was tons of shell down deep. The silly git nearly bit my hand off.'

Maitland elbowed himself up the bed. 'Then what?'

Blair necked some whisky from the bottle. 'The tender's too addled to understand his signals. He said Morris was up and down all day, yanking on his lifeline, so he kept hauling him up.'

'Staging him?'

Blair let out a scoffing laugh. 'What do you think? Even if he understood the principle of rest stops, the old bugger can't count to ten without using his fingers.'

'How'd he croak it?'

'Bends. Blackout. *Bonne nuit*. Buried him out at sea.'

Maitland leaned over the side of the bed and retched again into the bucket, then wiped his mouth with the back of his hand. 'What now?'

'You need to fix that bastard Cooper,' Blair went on. 'We need to spread the damage among us. I've done one and Hanson's seen to two of his. Send a message to Sid. Maisie can tell him something or other when he brings over the shell for the tally next weekend. Get him back to shore and you fix up what needs to be done.'

'No, it's better I see Sid myself. I can't risk his loose tongue when he's been at the grog. I'll run the slop chest on the *Hornet* next weekend. Want to come?'

'Can't leave Dorothea. I can't trust the stupid girl not to elope.'

It was just before dusk on Monday evening when she came back from the schooner. Maisie walked along the shell-grit path that snaked through the garden and paused to watch the sun sink; a ball of orange-red fire that brought her husband uncomfortably to mind. *Maitland in a rage*, she thought grimly. The air was shrill with sounds from the bush; chirping cicadas giving up for the night, the frogs that started croaking at the same time each evening, and the mosquitos that whined non-stop in her ears. There were no background sounds at sea, only the gentle slap of waves on wood. She stopped at the foot of the verandah steps, waiting out the moment before she went in and became someone else.

A movement through the lattice caught her eye. Maitland lay in bed in the mosquito room, the habitual glass of whisky snug in his palm. It was that time of day. She'd sent for the English doctor on Friday morning and she half-expected Maitland to be better by now. He had someone with him, but she couldn't tell who it was from the bend of his back or the spread of fabric across his shoulders. Maitland was smiling but it didn't mask the gauntness of his face; he had lost weight, was diminished somehow. She watched him roll over onto his side and retch. She stepped out of sight behind a bush, seen only by a passing bird that was dipping and swooping high and low, chasing the fading sunlight.

Maitland's glass crashed to the floor, the noise making her start. She eased forward to get a better look. He lay still, his face a pale blur, shiny with sweat. Had he not been so ill, she would have found his appearance faintly ludicrous. His striped silk bed jacket gave him the look of an expensive deckchair. She stood motionless in the charcoal twilight, watching the tableau.

Maitland's visitor stood up from his chair and stretched stiffly. He pushed fever-matted hair from the sick man's temples and sat on the bed. Then he began to unbutton Maitland's pyjama jacket and run his fingers over his chest.

Maitland groaned out loud. 'What's happening to me?'

'Shush, Mait.'

Maisie could see the visitor clearly now, the harsh angles of his medieval face unusually soft, hands continuing their gentle stroking southwards, down the curve of her husband's neck, the slope of his shoulder, past his navel.

Maitland stretched out, suspended in a sort of trance, his eyes half-closed, lips open. The man kissed his eyelids, licking the moisture from sweaty flesh in slow, deliberate circles. Round and round, caressing, soothing with his touch. One hand slipped inside the band of the silky trousers to continue its work, the other tightened its grip on the bedpost, tendons quivering as he kept his weight off the sick man.

Maisie saw the haze in her husband's eyes, heard his breath puffing softly between his parted lips and then the cadence changed. His breath came in short ragged bursts, faster and faster like a wheezing racehorse. Faster, faster, panting, gasping, and then he began to shake; a terrible shaking that convulsed his entire body.

As he finally reached his climax, Maitland shouted out the name of his lover, lost in his own rapture. She had heard him call it out the night of her wedding, but not from her bed: it hadn't registered then.

Blair.

CHAPTER 20

IN THE PACKING SHED, Maisie sat on Maitland's chair and swivelled towards the lighthouse. She stared at it, hardly blinking. She knew so little about homosexuality. It was against the Church and the law in England, and it was punishable with prison. That was the sum of all she knew. Her father had been involved in the trial and appeal of a homosexual writer and said that same-sex love created *practised liars of the poor devils*. She shook her head. After their afternoon tea at Maisie's house, Jane had loaned her a copy of *The Bostonians*, encouraging her to read Henry James' tale of the romantic friendship between two women. It occurred to her that while Jane might have been offering more than platonic friendship, she hadn't lied to conceal her feelings.

Blair and Maitland were married men and they were both practised liars. Maitland had brought her out to Australia to give credence to his lie. More than revulsion or even pity, she felt cheated. Not because her husband preferred a man to her – she had witnessed the look on their faces – but he had never once looked at her in that way. She had seen the coldness behind his eyes when they met. Maitland was in love with Blair Montague and had stolen her chance of finding happiness with someone else. Surely she deserved more? She balled her fists and covered her face with her arms. Tears welled up and slid down her cheeks.

Visions of Coop crowded in and her longing overcame her. He was her oasis in the middle of all this madness. In her mind she watched him as he spoke, the way words formed on his lips and his mouth changed shape as he clamped his cigarette between them. The way his kisses felt on her skin. She pressed her fists into her eyes until her eyeballs ached.

She sat in Maitland's chair for a long time. Very slowly she lowered her hands and unclenched her fists. She rested them on the desk, frightened at the ferocity of her anger.

Maisie starched her resolve when she woke on Thursday morning. She sat up in bed and pulled out the latest letter from Mrs Wallace from under her pillow. The older woman's tone had been bland and her thoughts written down in the order she thought them, but the content had shaken up the fight in her. *You still tell me so little of your husband, Maisie. I feel I know no more about him than you did the day we talked about him in Port Fremantle. You seem to be managing your household help and have made some friends, which is a good thing. Jane Locke's exaggerated offer of friendship is not unusual in small communities. I suspect there are many lonely ladies who look to their female friends to fulfil the role of the husband they don't have. It might not be your choice but you certainly are in no position to judge, having the financial support and companionship of a fine man. I'm also not surprised to hear your fruit and vegetable idea was unsuccessful. Unless someone invents a solution to long-term storage of perishable goods, I fear we are doomed to shop for fresh produce every other day, if you can't make a success of growing your own. Speaking of growing: in your next letter, I want you to tell me all about Maitland and what you are doing to help him grow his business. I can't picture the man, so please tell me what he looks like and what he does every day in that bleak little town you describe so well. What did you do for Easter, dear? It was so late this year being April. Can you get lamb in your tiny outpost? I am sure Maitland was able to get you a leg of lamb for Easter Day, as it's such an English tradition.*

Maisie thought of Maitland's cold grey eyes, and kicked down the sheets. He hadn't even bothered to turn up to the meal.

She got out of bed, straightened her spine and began to dress. She had Duc hitch the bad-tempered nag to the sulky and smacked its reluctant, elderly flanks all the way to the post office.

Mrs Brightlight was on her knees, poking about under the counter. She stood up and smiled. 'Something came for you on the steamer the other day, dear. I put it away so the captain wouldn't know about it but, in all honesty, I haven't actually seen him for a bit. There's talk he's laid up in bed with the Barcoo fever.'

'Yes, we've had the doctor out. He's not very well at all.'

'Pass on my regards for a speedy recovery, will you? I wouldn't wish the Barcoo on anyone, however badly they've behaved with their wife's correspondence.'

Maisie turned to go, preoccupied with thoughts of the sick man at home. An unfamiliar shape in the window blocked the ocean from view. A vast steamship lay at anchor in the bay. 'It's the *Atticus*,' the postmistress said, following her gaze. 'It came in on last night's tide and is here for a few days – at least until Monday, they say.'

The ship sat so high out of the water they could see it in Asia Place.

'It doesn't look safe,' Maisie muttered.

'No, it doesn't, dear. Wouldn't catch me on something like that! Now, don't you be going off without your letter. Give me two seconds to fish it out.'

She hobbled to the cupboard. 'It's from PS Corsets Ltd, in Melbourne. I wouldn't have thought you'd need one of those heavy-duty corsets here, dear, you being a slim little thing! Anyway, here it is. If you go ahead and place an order, it's going to take about a month for it to get here. I wouldn't waste my money if I were you.'

Maisie reached for the letter and concentrated on the steadiness of her hand. 'Thank you, Mrs Brightlight. I've been expecting this for a while. I'll let you know what I decide to do.'

By the afternoon, a hundred thoughts were fizzing in her head like blowflies. She felt unsettled, irritated by the constant hum of insects, nauseated by the briny stench of the mudflats, damp and lethargic. Maitland's illness had her tied to the house and yet she still hadn't got round to burning the ledger page that bore Coop's signature. The impact of her husband's homosexual encounter had consumed her in the packing shed and it had soon become too dark to look for it. The entire ship's log was now in her desk drawer, hidden under a pile of papers.

Maisie knew she needed to think about survival – both for herself and for Coop – but not now. She didn't have the energy.

Instead, she allowed herself to become distracted with the soapstone box. Maitland had concealed so much from her; what further revelations might be hidden inside? She pressed each of the two hinges, twisted and shook it, then repeated the whole process with the box upside down. It remained stubbornly shut. Short of hitting it with a mallet, she couldn't think how else to open it up.

'Maisie?'

Her head flew up like a gundog at the sound of a shot. She relaxed upon spying the familiar feminine face. 'I'm sorry, Jane,' she said. 'Today has been a bit hectic.' She shook the box. 'Still can't open it and to cap it all, today I went to the post office and checked with Mrs Brightlight to see if I had any post. Maitland's mother has written to say she's coming up on the next steamer.'

Jane moved further into the room. 'Goodness. I don't think either of us was expecting a visit, were we?'

'I don't know what I thought, but it's not so surprising that she would want to visit her son, is it? Or meet his wife of several months?'

'No, of course not. How is he, by the way?'

Maisie's head was starting to ache. 'He's feverish and bad-tempered, although he's well enough to entertain his friend Blair and stand me down from schooner duty this coming weekend. Let's discuss other topics. Talking about Maitland is too depressing. What brings you over today?'

Jane told her that she had been reading a newspaper article by a Professor of Anthropology at Sydney University. 'He's been writing about Aboriginal sorcery and I think it's possible that Maitland has been boned.'

'Why on earth would you think that? The doctor told him he had Barcoo fever! He didn't give him any treatment but said the fever would run its course soon.'

'It's not a medical procedure; it's an Aboriginal method of retribution meted out for a wrong. Do you remember when we came to supper here, and Captain Mason found Maitland in a confused heap on the cliff path, covered in red dust?'

Maisie lit a cigarette and took a long pull. She had given up pretending not to smoke in the house. 'Yes, I do.' It was hard to forget the white suit smeared in red stains and the fuss everyone made.

'Do you also remember he said he thought he'd been followed, although he never saw who it was?'

'Yes, and everybody thought he'd drunk too much and imagined it. He was fine for a couple of days after that but then he took to his bed and started to vomit. What makes you think that Maitland might have been telling the truth?'

'I don't really know. I've been reading about the bush spirits, how they are said to give a person the feeling that they are being stalked. Is there anything that Captain Sinclair might have done in the past that could cause an Aborigine to seek revenge?'

Maisie felt coloured by his guilt. 'Would you like a list? I can think of one particular incident, but it was ages ago. Maitland punished our gardener shortly after I arrived here because he watered the lawn with bore water. When Maitland came home and saw what had happened, he flayed Charlie with his stockwhip.'

Jane kept her voice steady. 'Did Charlie have a dilly-bag?'

'It's strange you should ask that. Doctor Shin persuaded me to look inside for what he called my "cultural education".'

'Do you remember what was in the bag, Maisie?'

Maisie stubbed out her cigarette. 'Not absolutely. There were a few pebbles. Doctor Shin said they were healing stones. And there were some animal bones, I think, but I can't . . .' She trailed off, the connection sparking in her brain.

'I think there is a real chance that Maitland has been both cursed and boned. First, the stones would be wrapped with paper bark and strands of your husband's hair. Particular curses would be sung into them. Then small personal artefacts belonging to your husband might have been gathered over time and "sung" again with Aboriginal magic.'

'Sung?'

'Like a repetitive religious chant. Except in this case, it's a curse.'

'And the bones?'

'It depends how they were used. Some think bone-pointing is said to inspire psychological terror in the victim to the extent that he is willed to death. But it can be overcome, depending on the ability of the victim to resist the mind willing him to die.'

'What about the other ways they're used?'

'A toxic dart. Inserted where the original violation occurred.'

'An eye for an eye, so to speak.'

'Yes, but literally, Maisie.' Jane took her hand. 'This isn't just tribal nonsense. I think you should prepare yourself. Aborigines always avenge a wrong – even if it takes years.'

'Cooee! Are you there, Mrs Sinclair?'

The two women flew apart like flushed pheasants.

'What are you two up to?' Dorothea Montague said, poking her head around the door. 'You look as thick as thieves.'

'We are wondering what to wear to the Turf Club bash,' Jane said, the lie smooth.

Dorothea accepted the explanation Jane gave her without blinking. The annual two-day meeting at the Turf Club at the end of the month was a huge event. Stockmen from the surrounding stations would descend on the town; horses would race, fit after weeks of training. Gambling was big business and large sums of money were lost and won. The Race Ball afterwards and the Sunday picnic on the beach, which wound up the whole event, were high points in the Bay's social calendar.

'What fun! Is Uncle Maitland running a horse in the two-day chase? Have you chosen your outfit yet, Mrs Sinclair?' Dorothea said, her face rapt.

'No, not yet. Maitland isn't currently in full spirits, and it isn't at all clear whether he will be fit enough to attend.'

'Dada says he has the Barcoo fever.'

'That's what the doctor thinks.'

Dorothea had already lost interest and was back to the ball. 'And Miss Locke, shall you attend with the bishop and Mrs McMahon?'

'We haven't given it much thought, to be honest. It isn't for a little while yet and we are not great gamblers at the Residence, as you know. The bishop takes a very dim view of those who fritter away hard-earned money.'

'But you were just discussing your outfits! You distinctly said you were deciding what to wear. So you must be going,' Dorothea whined.

Maisie had seen the jut of her jaw, thrust out like a rib. 'You may not even be here yourself, Dorothea,' she said. 'Your father was telling Maitland the other day that he's thinking of taking you to Europe very soon.'

'Really?' Dorothea clapped her hands loudly, her face alight. 'Would it be very rude of me, Miss Locke, to ask for a private moment with Mrs Sinclair?'

Jane got to her feet and turned towards the back verandah. 'Of course not.' She shot an amused look at Maisie. 'I need a moment with Marjorie in any case. She promised to tell me what she knows about Aboriginal juju.'

After Jane vanished through the door, Dorothea sat on the rattan sofa, ankles crossed, squeezing her handbag to her chest.

Maisie watched her friend leave the room and kneaded her forehead. Her headache was flourishing and Dorothea strained her patience at the best of times. 'You had something you wanted to discuss, Dorothea?' Maisie waited for her to say something, and gave up. 'How are your wedding plans coming along?'

Tears appeared in the baby-blue eyes. 'Oh, Mrs Sinclair. I am beside myself with grief. I told Dada about our engagement last Sunday. It seemed the perfect moment, at supper. He was so relaxed over his food and his newspaper and all the things that make him content.' She folded her arms over her bag. 'I told him about William and me, and I was about to mention where I would want to send for my wedding dress when he shouted at me. It was perfectly dreadful! He was incredibly horrid and sent me to my room! Maybe he has now relented, though, as he was trying very hard to be nice to me this morning. But I was cross and wasn't listening. So, maybe the trip is his way of saying he is happy about the wedding, and is taking me to Europe to choose my dress. What do you think? That must be it. Oh, Mrs Sinclair, I knew he couldn't be cross forever.' Dorothea lowered her voice. 'However, that's not what I really came to see you about. I have a conundrum.'

Maisie's heart sank. Her chances of speaking to Jane again before she left were now non-existent. 'What is your conundrum, Dorothea?'

'Well, I know everyone thinks I am stupid,' she began.

Maisie clamped her hand under her chin to stop herself from nodding.

Dorothea had her head down and, rummaging in her bag, didn't appear to notice. She pulled out a piece of paper and pointed at the columns on the document she'd retrieved. 'When Dada was so very nasty, I went through Mama's box of papers as I always do when I need to cheer myself up, and I found something that I really don't understand.' She handed the page to Maisie. 'Tell me what you think.'

Maisie studied it, uncomprehending. 'What am I looking at, Dorothea?'

'The dates. I can't understand them. If Mama and Dada got married on this date,' she stabbed at the third column, 'they were married in 1892 and yet I was born in 1890. It doesn't add up.' She stabbed again at the column and pursed her lips. 'So, why I am here, Mrs Sinclair, is to ask you what the two-year difference between the date my parents got married and my birthdate means, exactly.'

CHAPTER 21

COOP TOOK A SWIG of sour tea. The sun on the sea shimmered like sequins and the glare hurt his eyes. It was seven in the morning and already it was hot. He was conscious of sweat beginning to trickle on the back of his neck and his thighs chafed against the itchy wool of his long johns. He had expected to find at least a thousand pounds' worth of pearl in his first month, but in the six weeks since the *Sharky* had sailed from the Bay he'd found a grain of baroque and a few bits and pieces worth nothing very much. It wasn't just him; no-one had brought up anything. The beds they were fishing were useless.

'There's big shell in twenty-fathom beds, Coop,' Daike said.

'They're the wrong side of Neptune's Dairy.'

Daike drummed his smooth chin with his forefinger and tilted his head at Sid, considering. Sid's legs were skinny, gnarled like bark, and his knees were covered in ugly sores from shell grit, which had ground into his flesh. The daily opening of the oyster shell was a messy business. It had to be cleaned of barnacles with a blunt tomahawk before it was opened, and the operation left shards of sharp, scrunchy residue on the wooden deck.

'Maybe we go back shore quick smart for Sid knees. They look bad. Then after we go Neptune's Dairy.'

'Can we do that?'

''Course. We run boat. We say what goes.'

'Maybe we should ask Sid what he wants to do.'

'You can. I try ask him 'bout. He no like me much.'

Coop saw that Daike was right about Sid's legs. He'd picked at a sore below his knee and a trickle of blood was dripping down his leg. It was streaked with yellowy pus. 'What did you say to him?'

'I say did legs hurt bad? He say me to shut up. Now I go dive.'

Sid, wearing a grubby singlet and shapeless flannelette shorts, was cleaning his teeth using salt water and his finger, his weather-lined face impossible to read. He had a pile of shell still to open from the night before. The boss had told him not to leave any shell unopened overnight, to lessen the risk of theft, but Coop had seen that Sid was lazy. He liked to have packed in work before the last catch of the day came up in the late afternoon, and started on the more serious business of his sundowner. On his watch, the crew had generally pumped out the bilge and washed down the decks before the sun began to sink.

Coop eased himself onto the deck stool and picked at the dried soap on his rubber cuff. He wrinkled his nose. JB had boiled up something disgusting to lubricate the narrow openings to his diving dress. His wrists were dry and the skin had started to flake.

'What you thinking about, Coop?' JB asked.

'Sid's knees.'

JB glanced over at the shell-opener, shielding his eyes from the sun. 'And?'

'I'm wondering whether we should go back to the Bay and get them patched up.'

'You've got stuff in your bag of potions that would do the trick.'

'I know.'

'It's her, isn't it?'

'I might see her if we go back, JB. It killed me that the boss was on the schooner instead of her last weekend.'

JB plunged his fork into his breakfast rice and flicked it over the side. They had all become superstitious since the cyclone. 'Can't guarantee it, though, if she's playing nurse to some biddy in town like the boss said. And you're playing with fire, matey.'

JB's words were not the balm he was hoping for. 'Is she playing nurse, though? And he looked half-dead. Something's up, I'm sure of it.'

JB prodded at a lump of fish on his plate and scowled. 'Like what?'

'I did something stupid, JB. Signed a paper in the boss's office without getting you to read it first. I asked her to burn it.'

'Jesus, Coop,' he said in a hard voice. 'Why didn't you tell me?'

'Because I knew you'd go mad.'

'Jesus, Coop. What if he catches her at it? He'll skin her alive.'

'That's why I need to see her. To make sure she's okay.'

'Jesus, Coop.'

'I wish you'd stop saying that. I know I've messed up in every possible way.' He closed his eyes and pressed a palm against his forehead.

'Does she know you can't read?'

Coop hung his head. 'I'm so far beneath her already, JB. What chance would I ever have if I told her?'

JB stared at him, assessing. 'So, here's what we do. You dive today and then we start back to shore tonight. I'll make something up during the day and convince the boys I need the quack. And don't forget you owe me, Coop. Big time.'

'There's holes on sea floor, Coop, and big currents,' said Daike. 'Bottom is lottsa dead shell. You sure 'bout this?'

'We might get lucky.'

'Big risk for paralysis. This not for no-experience white boy. More dangerous than anything in ocean.'

Coop had his own misgivings that he was unwilling to admit. 'It'll be fine,' he said, and hoped he was not wrong.

'Things mebbe go wrong with air hose if you fall in hole.'

'You sound like you're scared, Daike,' Coop threw back at him.

'I no scared. Told you before. But I scared for you. Big tides big problem.'

'I have JB on my lines. Don't worry.'

'Even if I no worry, you big fool all same.'

Coop sat on the roof of the cabin and scratched at the stubble that stood proud on his lip like a spiked black comb. He only shaved once a week now, to protect his skin from the sun. Every Sunday, though, before he saw Maisie, he scraped his chin and cheeks smooth.

JB tinkered with the air compressor, which he'd bolted to the deck. Coop's shell tally was frustratingly low, and diving the Deeps was, he knew, a reckless gamble with the bends. He'd heard about the white divers who'd already died. But after weeks of failure, there was no point in holding back. JB would have Coop's lifeline in his hands, would stage his ascents and would do everything he could to keep him safe.

'When Daike comes up, JB, I'm going down until I hit a patch of decent shell. Give me an hour on the bottom.'

JB rummaged in the canvas bag he had tied to his waist. It contained the nuts and bolts of his job. 'All right,' he said, extracting a screwdriver, 'but you're going to stage twice on the ascent. No heroics. You're going to play it by the book.'

Coop nodded. 'No heroics. Now, help me get my gear on.'

The tide was a lot stronger than he had foreseen, and it seemed to Coop that the lugger was getting ahead of him. Half-walking, half-running, he pulled hard on his lifeline and signalled to JB to slacken off the rope. Imperceptibly, the vessel slowed. Coop, bent under the constant burden of disappointment, began to walk a grid over the seabed, hunting out the elusive shell. Eyes trained on the bottom, he trudged through clumps of clustering sponge and patches of seagrass, which floated in the rippling water like tendrils of lank hair. After about forty minutes, to his relief, he began to find shell, nestling on the floor or hidden among the coral or lurking in the weed. He stuffed his neck-bag like a pirate hoarding treasure. It was the best patch of shell he had found in weeks and he whistled happily to himself as he stowed his swag. It was a myth that you had to conserve air. As long as the air came down the hose, he could have sung a blooming opera. He signalled to JB that he wanted to change direction. The oysters were still difficult to 'see' but he knew he was getting better.

JB tracked Coop's progress through the movement of the coir rope, feeling instantly when he stooped to pick up the shell in the depths below, working out the direction he was moving from the ballooning air bubbles that clustered on the surface. JB checked his watch and peered into the water. He wanted Coop to come up, but the diver signalled straight back that he wasn't ready and JB should slacken off the lines.

JB turned his ear downwards, as if listening for the signal he had felt through his fingers would make it clearer. He shook his head and tried to concentrate. His head felt fuzzy. Goodness knew he'd been working all hours. Coop was underwater for long enough each day, but his own schedule was punishing. He'd been up at dawn and while Coop ate breakfast, he checked over the diving equipment, washed the hard helmet's face-glass in soapy water before he'd polished it to a window cleaner's sparkle. Next he plumbed the seabed with a lead line attached to a plug of putty. If the portent on the putty was good – sand, shell and stone – he knew they might have at least a chance of finding shell.

Getting Coop into his work suit was no mean feat, either. He washed it inside and out with saltwater most days. Coop sometimes had to pee in the suit and left yeasty smells and salty residue in his rubber shroud. JB sluiced off anything that might rot the fabric and never ate before Coop went down below, in case food smells from his hands on Coop's suit attracted sharks. This morning, unusually, Sid had handed him a plate of food and he had scoffed half of it down before realising he'd broken his own golden rule.

Normally he was thorough. Every three or four days, he inspected the fabric and seams of the dress, and kept rubber cement and pre-cut pieces of canvas for patches in his workbag. Like a Red Indian interpreting smoke signals, his ability to interpret Coop's tugs kept the unspoken lines of communication open, yet right now he was falling asleep on the job.

He gave his head a shake and chastised himself. He had to concentrate, and he washed down the thought with another big gulp of tea, hoping it would wake him up.

Sid smirked as he watched JB's knees give way. He picked another shell off the deck and prised it open with his tomahawk.

Twenty fathoms under the sea, Coop waited for the pinch of the lifeline to stop. For a few minutes, nothing happened. It was unlike JB to ignore his communications. The ominous tightening of his air pipe scared him and the tune died on his lips. He tugged more insistently on the rope, wondering what JB was playing at. He should be paying out more line as he moved about. There was no way it should be tight. As the tide dragged the lugger away, the lifeline squeezed Coop's lungs as flat as a plate. He wasn't getting enough air.

Heart thrashing, throat as papery as an old book, Coop fought down the panic. Both his lifeline and air hose were stretched tight, and he had no way of slackening them. He had to convince JB to move the lugger overhead. He tried not to think of the stories that circulated round the Seafarer's bar of gruesome end-of-career moments. Divers hauled up with heads so swollen from the pressure they had to be cut out of their helmets; divers smothered to death when something snapped the air hose; divers stung by rays or consumed by man-eating fish; divers crippled by the bends, compressed and squeezed as they were hauled from the depths by panicked tenders.

A moray eel thrust its dog-like head from its coral cave and edged forward, its razor-toothed jaws agape. Coop released a stream of bubbles from his outlet valve. The eel, momentarily spooked, slunk away. Above his head, a tiger shark circled.

Crouched below the boat, held fast in the silence, Coop knew that a wrenching pull would eventually tear his air hose from his helmet. His silvery companion was still in the vicinity. It loomed above him, circling and waiting, the outline of its tailfin and flash of its black eyes, dead like a china doll, clear through the water. He was forced to face facts. JB was not going to help him.

Daike sat on the diving stool, half-watching Coop's stream of air bubbles, and puffed steadily on his pipe. Getting through Neptune's Dairy was always a big risk. He had a wife and sons in Japan, five boys born at regular intervals, pushed out every eighteen months: five future divers in a row. He hadn't seen them for years, but news of home came regularly. They were growing up, proud and fearless, like their father. Daike was also a realist. The *Sharky* had been drifting about for a few weeks now, working the shallower beds, but the results had been disappointing. He knocked the pipe bowl on the decking and checked it was empty. They would negotiate the boiling reef waters of Neptune's Dairy first thing in the morning. The deeper water had shell in the quantity that had made him top diver for the past two years. Risk and reward – it was what had made his reputation.

He stood up and parked his pipe on the stool, and called to JB. 'Coop been down too long. Get him up.'

JB was silent.

Daike crabbed along the deck, his lead-weighted boots thudding tremors on the planking, loud enough to wake the dead.

JB didn't stir. He was slumped, unconscious, over the bulwark, the taut ropes burning weals into his flesh. Coop's air bubbles were still in the same place, but the lugger had drifted at least twenty feet.

'Both anchors astern, Squinty!' he shouted. 'Coop's rope fouled up.' He shook JB to rouse him, but the tender was sleep-heavy and deaf to his entreaties. Daike threw coils of line and air hose overboard, hoping the extra lengths would release the tension from Coop's tethers.

'Sid, you take tiller. Keep boat steady.'

'Can't do that,' Sid said. 'Got finish shell.'

'I go down. See what's what. You help fix my helmet.'

Sid sat cross-legged on the deck and didn't move. 'You no listen, Jappy boy. I got work.'

'Coop save your life in big blow. Now mebbe die, Sid. You no care?'

Sid rolled his eyes. 'I no there, 'member?'

Daike reached down and yanked him to his feet. Leaning in close he growled, 'You done something to JB? Yes? You mebbe biff him?'

Sid sprang for his tomahawk. 'I no frighty you.'

'Think you knife me?' Daike sneered and feinted with his right hand.

'I no biff him.' Sid's eyes involuntarily flicked towards JB's empty cup, a slow malicious smile spreading across his face.

Daike swung with his clenched fist and caught him on the jaw. 'You bloody bastard.'

Sid grunted and put his hand to his face, the razor-sharp tomahawk falling from his fingers and clattering onto the deck. A startled expression flared in his bloodshot eyes as Daike's fourteen-pound lead boot smashed into his ankle and felled him like a feeble sapling. He crumpled at both knees and toppled backwards over the gunwale into the ocean, leaving a crimson streak of blood on the deck.

Squinty stared over the side at the stricken shell-opener. 'What you want I do, Daike? Get boat hook and pull him up?'

Daike had his eyes trained on a dark fin that was slicing through the water towards the Filipino. Sid was struggling in the water, flailing with his arms and screaming insults at the crew. The shark glided in an arc and didn't hesitate, attacking Sid from the front. 'Help me!' he screamed, kicking out at the fish with his good leg.

Squinty wiped the sweat off his brow with his arm. 'You no want help him?'

The dark grey shark now had Sid clamped between its jaws. They saw the look of horror on his face as the shark pulled him under, leaving a spreading red stain on the ocean's surface.

'Too late. Him shark meat now. More better we help Coop.'

Squinty gripped the side of the boat and stared at the swirling red water. 'You unfeeling fella, Daike.'

'He one bad man, Squinty. What you want me say?'

Squinty straightened up, sweat dripping down his forehead. 'You get Coop, okey-dokey? We lose too much time. You tender fix on helmet quick smart. I take tiller, sail boat steady. Like you say Sid do.'

It was impossible to hurry in the bulky diving costume, and the minutes sped away too fast. Daike stepped carefully over the side of the boat and onto the ladder of four-inch-thick coir rope.

He nodded to his tender, who leaned over to fit the weights over his chest and back, then placed the domed brass helmet onto the corselet and screwed it into place. Daike had tried to convey the urgency of the situation to his man, but his tender was playing by the rules. Deep down, Daike knew he was right; safety checks meant the difference between life and probable death. And he had his family to think of. A few more profitable years and he could go home. The tender tapped the top of his helmet and handed him a short-bladed knife. If Coop was caught fast, he would have to cut him free.

Daike didn't trust motor-driven compressors. He nodded at the two Manilamen on his air pump who began to grind the pump-wheel. He found the hiss of the life-supporting air into his helmet reassuring. Taking a last look at his tender, he threw himself backwards into the water, plummeting to the dark-green depths in a stream of fizzling bubbles, his lifeline paying out as he sank towards the ocean floor. Walls of lacerating coral loomed towards him. He hadn't expected that, and fiddled with his air-escape valve to regulate his buoyancy and slow his descent.

Coop's predicament was apparent. His airline and lifeline were both fouled on the coral, held fast by the weight of the boat. Daike jammed his boots into the sand to keep himself steady. Coop's eyes were wide in the glass, his face contorted with fear. He chopped at his windpipe with the edge of his hand. He was running out of air.

Daike turned towards the steep coral cliffs and back to Coop and weighed the odds. Coop was caught on the edge of an underwater precipice. The cliffs descended into water that seemed to have no bottom, and the tide was strong. If he made it over the coral, there was no guarantee he would be able to free Coop's lines. He also ran the risk of getting snagged himself, or sucked down into the swirling water. There was only one thing he could do: he would cut Coop loose and hope they could surface before the white man ran out of air.

He scissored his fingers in front of his mask and Coop dipped his head, showing he understood. With a single slash of his knife, the lifeline was severed, leaving the knotted loop round Coop's chest. Daike slid his left hand under the rope and held on tight. He closed his own air valve to trap air in his suit and motioned for Coop to do the same. Then he severed the rubber air hose from Coop's copper helmet and signalled to the tender on deck to heave them up. He knew the rapid ascent was dangerous. The bends or suffocation? Coop might survive one but certainly not the other. Released from their restraints, the two divers shot to the surface like a couple of champagne corks.

The tender hung over the ladder, hands trembling. Daike was already on board, sitting on the cabin roof, puffing on a cigarette. Coop was dangling off the ladder, his hands bent over a rung, his knuckles white with effort. They were all dreading what they would find when the helmet came off. Would the pressure have swollen his head and forced the eyeballs from their sockets; would he be alive but wish he wasn't? The brown joints of Squinty's fingers crackled as he flexed them and unscrewed Coop's faceplate.

'Bloody hell, that was close. I thought I was a goner,' Coop said, eyes tiny black dots in his chalk-white face.

*

Daike discussed their options over the evening's fish and rice. Without a shell-opener on board, they were a man down. He considered they were two days' sail from the Bay.

'We go back and pick up new sheller?' he'd asked the other men. 'What you think?'

'I open shell,' Squinty said. 'I know how do it.'

The others were dubious. A man hacking shell with a blunt-edged tomahawk and a pair of revolving eyes did not seem hugely sensible in a confined space. Squinty banged his plate on the deck.

'I know what you thinking. I can see perfect good close up. You want lose more time for shell?'

'We can all help,' JB offered.

Coop agreed. 'We can all help. I vote we push on through Neptune's Dairy tomorrow morning to the rich shell beds and get on with the business of making money.'

'We need think slowly. Not rush,' Daike said. 'You had one big shock.'

Coop clasped his hands behind his head to disguise the tremor in his fingers. Stomach-churning fear would have been a closer description, but the tight band across his chest was not unfamiliar. 'It's not the first time I've had a sticky moment, but I'm alive. In my mind there's no decision to make. We push on tomorrow.'

'I no so sure,' Daike reiterated.

Coop gave his arm a playful punch. 'And I still think you're scared.'

'I no scared of nothing, so I too vote yes,' he said, checking his charm was safely under his vest.

*

The trouble started in the small hours. Coop moaned and grabbed his left leg. The pain in his knee joint made him gasp.

'What?'

'Something doesn't feel right. It hurts.'

JB rolled onto his side and poked his head over the edge of the bunk. His head banged like a piston and he still felt groggy. 'Where?'

Coop flinched. 'Knee.'

'Get up and walk around. Jiggle your leg about. You're probably just stiff. Don't panic. I'll sort you out a tot to drink.'

JB found Daike on deck massaging his gum with a finger. 'What's up with your face?'

'Stone in rice busted tooth. Deep dive make hurt.'

'Is the pain bad?'

Daike nodded. 'I also worried 'bout Neptune's Dairy.'

'I thought you agreed to push on tomorrow.'

Daike clamped his jaws together and rubbed his face. 'I sit here and think. Is crazy risk. Boat not fix up properly after storm.'

JB looked him in the eye. 'So, you want to go back.' It was not a question.

'I worried too 'bout Coop. He got bends, JB?'

'Don't know, Daike. I'm getting him some grog, then we'll see. You want some?'

'No thirsty. More better I think what do for best.' He hunched and flexed his shoulders. Pains in these joints could mean the onset of the bends. All was well; he'd been lucky so far.

Coop hobbled round the cabin, moaning. 'Is the rum coming soon, JB? This hurts like hell.'

'I'm here, Coop,' JB said, pushing the pannikin of spirits into his hands. 'Get it down you. And for God's sake, keep moving your leg.'

Coop's face was as pale as a moonstone, his speech thick.

JB beckoned Daike to the far end of the lugger. 'If it is the bends, we have a couple of options.' He stuck up a finger. 'One, we could make a dash back to the Bay and let Doctor Shin take care of him, and hope he doesn't die on the way.'

Daike frowned. 'It two days away even if weather good, JB.'

'I know. So, that leaves option two.' A second finger sprang up. 'He's got to go back down, right now. We'll bring him up slowly and hope for the best.'

'But it middle of night!'

'I know that, mate, but do say if you have a better plan.'

They leaned Coop against the rail, and between them they shoved him into his diving suit. It was like dressing a child; he was watching the process with wide staring eyes, yet his limbs were not coordinated enough to participate.

Daike looked at him then back at JB. 'This bad idea. He don't know what happening.'

'Can you suggest anything better?' JB snapped.

'Yes. Number-three plan is I go too. Hold his hand like baby.'

'Jesus, Daike. Last thing we need is two divers with the bends.'

Daike fingered the charm under his singlet. 'Coop one whole lot of bother, and stupid geezer, but he my friend.'

JB and Daike agreed on plan four: they would take Coop down to the ocean floor and keep him there for an hour. They had no idea if that was enough or too little time. Daike wouldn't be able to see Coop's face for signs of distress in the pitch dark, but if he sensed he was getting worse he would tug on the lifeline and JB would stage them up and dash back to the Bay. If Coop seemed better they would do exactly the same thing but not dash back to the Bay.

It was a nightmare.

The two divers, joined together, twirled to the ocean floor whipped round by the swirling current. Daike held onto the disabled diver as Coop moved in and out of consciousness. Daike peered continually into Coop's face glass, tapping the mask, poking his arms, keeping him awake. He beat out the minutes on his leg with his fist. It was as pale in the water as the white man's skin.

A tug on the lifeline, and the hour was up. Instinctively, Daike looked up towards the end of the rope and saw that daylight was shafting through the water, the solid black mass of the lugger's hull marking the distance to the surface. It could have been the moon. They would stage twice, taking twenty minutes at each stop, and then Coop would be up and out of the water. Daike touched his hand to his chest and felt for his charm, then tugged twice on the rope.

CHAPTER 22

IN THE GREY EARLY morning, JB assembled the rest of the crew on deck and pointed at the sky. Daike and Coop were sprawled on deck, exhausted. It was six o'clock and the humid air was already suffocating.

'I don't much like the look of those clouds,' he said.

'Wind from east. Is bad,' Squinty piped up.

'I think we should head back to the Bay. Daike and Coop have been up all night and most likely have the bends. What do you think?'

He heard a low moan and scrutinised Coop's face. 'You okay, mate? Any pains?'

Coop shook his head. 'Not me. All good.'

'Daike?'

Daike was sitting on his own away from the others, his hand cupping his jaw. 'I think we go back and doctor check Coop. Is better we get new shell-opener too. Before we go Neptune's Dairy.'

*

Doctor Shin was looking forward to going home. He lit a cigarette and squeezed back his shoulders. Hunching for hours over the post-mortem table had locked his muscles solid, tendons clamped tight like an oyster's shell. That morning, one of the diver patients had cut his throat with the tine of his breakfast fork, slashing away at his neck after his tray had been cleared. Attempted suicide had become commonplace, so the nuns now cut up the food and left the knives off the trays. This poor fellow, paralysed from the waist down, had been no surprise to the doctor. *I'd have done it too.*

There was now another chap waiting who'd been brought in that afternoon with a member of the same crew. He'd sent the white diver home with instructions not to work for a few days, but he knew he was wasting his breath. None of the English divers had listened to his advice and almost half of them had perished in their first few weeks in the Bay. Doctor Shin looked at his watch, and looked at the sky, his heart sinking. There was a storm coming. Another puff on his cigarette and a final gulp of tea would see him through until home time. If the man were dead, he'd cover him up and conduct the autopsy in the morning. He went over to the washbasin and began to scrub his hands.

The nun went ahead of him down the dark corridor and pushed open the treatment-room door. She glanced over her shoulder. 'Do you need me to stay, Doctor Shin?'

He shook his head and walked to the couch, peeling back the blanket, with conflicting emotions. He might be going home later than he'd have liked, but at least this one was alive. He studied the man's face; he was in his mid-thirties and looked in good shape. Black stubble peppered his face like gunpowder and his hair stood up, stiff with salt. His eyes were squeezed shut, his teeth clenched. A plug of blood had dried on the man's cheek, close to his right ear. He went through his checklist. If the man was suffering from the bends, he should take a closer look and move the man's head towards to the acetylene jet. The eardrum itself appeared clean; a good sign. He checked his nostrils and they too were clear.

He pulled down the blanket a little further, towards the waist, and fingered a circle of wrinkly flesh close to the collarbone. He'd seen that before, when a diver had been squeezed to death by the weight of the water at great depth. His helmet and corselet had clamped the life from his body like a vice. He tapped his pen on his clipboard and reminded himself that the man on the table was not a corpse.

'Can you tell me where you have the pain? Can you move your arms and legs?'

Laid out on the examination table, Daike opened his eyes. 'I haven't got the bends, Doctor Shin. I've got the bloody toothache!'

Tuesday was one of those sweltering evenings with storms blanketing the sky. Distant flashes of lightning jumped between the tumbling clouds, and thunder rumbled behind the pindan cliffs. Jane had visited Maisie in the afternoon, clutching a thin letter from her parents. They were both disappointed. Somehow, Jane said, she had expected it to be a plump affair, sides and sides of writing paper covered in informative script on the education and adolescence of her adopted brother and his young friend Maitland Sinclair. It was only a paragraph long.

'What do your parents say?' Maisie asked.

'My father says that if I can spare some time and pay them a visit, he will tell me in person what he can recall of Maitland Sinclair's time at the Catholic school.'

'And Blair?'

'No mention of him. I told you that he is the apple of their eye.'

Maisie picked at a loose piece of skin on her cuticle.

'You'll make it sore, Maisie.' Jane eyed the bloodied flap. 'I know you are dying to ask if I shall go, and the answer is yes, I will. They have wired me the money for the trip already. Blair is taking Dorothea to Port Fremantle on the *Atticus*. She was boasting of it at coffee after church. I, too, have booked a passage. From Fremantle I'll journey on to Melbourne by train. I leave tomorrow.'

Maisie stifled a sigh.

'I know it's sudden, but the opportunity was quite literally there on our doorstep. I'll be back in a month at most,' Jane said.

'Tourist and spy?'

'Something like that,' Jane said, darkly.

Maisie was scarcely listening to what Marjorie was saying. Above her head, the last puff of her cigarette smoke hung in the fading sunlight, suspended in the airless room like an accusation. Jane would be gone tomorrow. The first friend she had ever had apart from Mrs Wallace, and it was entirely her fault. Maisie knew that Jane didn't want to go. She wanted to press on with her Aboriginal research project, but she'd made light of it, saying that she needed time away from small-town politics and wanted to catch up with her parents.

Tomorrow was also the day Maisie's mother-in-law would arrive, and Maitland was not making the recovery that the British doctor had anticipated. She hadn't even been able to sail out on the schooner this weekend to reprovision the fleet. Maitland had hauled himself up from his sickbed, groaning and looking utterly frightful, and insisted – insisted! – on going himself. She had no idea what that was all about. Pearl theft seemed an unlikely reason, but he wouldn't be deterred. She'd tried to tell him he was too ill to go but he'd pushed past her concern, not even bothering to reply. He'd looked even worse on his return the night before, and had barely risen from his bed since. She shuddered, and squeezed the thought of Maitland from her mind. She ached for the few hours she'd been denied with Coop. She shut her eyes, wondering where he was and if he was doing a better job of burying his feelings than she was. She put her hand on her heart and allowed herself a moment to wallow.

'You goin' to tackle that paperwork or wot, Missus? I can't do cleanin' round that mess.'

Maisie snapped up her eyelids and got to her feet. The desk on the east verandah was a litter of paper; she hadn't been on top of her correspondence for days, nor had she yet removed the incriminating page from the *Clancy*'s ledger.

She fanned her face with the blotter, sweeping it in an extravagant arc to create some air. Marjorie was still talking, her voice low and confidential. She and Duc had come up with a plan to invest the chiffa money. Maisie had no idea they had won so much and chastised herself again. She had let so many things slip.

'So's wot we think is that we buy old lugger fella on beach and go fishing. It's that dummying wot I told you 'bout. But we ain't allowed,' Marjorie said.

'How is that going to work?'

'All them Jap fellas doin' it, makin' a packit. You got them licences for dat lugger, that's wot we thinkin'.'

'You two want to buy the *Clancy* with the chiffa money – is that what you are saying?'

'Yes, Missus.'

'You'll need a crew.'

'You want I fetch you gin drink? Mebbe big large fella with ice, like you prefer?'

'Are you suggesting that I pay the crew with my share?'

'As I said time before, Missus. You now startin' to pick up wot I puttin' down.'

'Bring me the drink, Marjorie, but I can't think about dummying now. Not with the captain so poorly. But I promise I will think about it soon. And I need a knife, to perform a little operation. Can you ask Duc to lend me one of the really sharp ones from the kitchen?'

Marjorie stopped in her tracks. 'Why you want 'im knife? You no go cutting you'self or some sick fella?'

'No. I need a knife to cut something out of something.'

Marjorie aligned the sheets of paper on the desk in a neat stack. 'Duc no let you have 'im kitchen knife. More better you use one of Boss's knives.'

'What do you mean?' asked Maisie, the blotter paused mid-sweep.

'Boss have whole box of knives in pantry cupboard. You want I get 'im?'

Maisie was up on her feet, shaking her head. 'No, it's fine. You do the drink. I'll go and look myself.'

*

The box was similar to a carpenter's wooden toolbox. She pulled it towards her and lifted the lid. It contained fifteen or twenty knives, all of different sizes with various handles, all sheathed. She selected one at random and pulled it out of its leather cover. The blade was about five inches long and was marked on one side, *Harrison Riddle & Co, West Smithfield.* Maisie put it back in its protective casing, then took out another. This one had a curved scabbard and the hilt was bound with leather. The handle appeared to be made of ivory or perhaps bone. She carried on, pulling them out and putting them back until she had sorted through the entire collection. *Here's a question for his mother*, she thought. *When did Maitland start this charming hobby?*

She pushed the box back onto the shelf, and turned towards the garden. A stiff breeze had sprung up and she turned her face towards it, the air curling round her head like a poisonous snake. She glanced up at the sky; a few spongy black clouds had started to gather as the daylight faded and a few drops of rain plopped fatly on her face. She didn't give the weather much thought. The cyclone season was over and the rain, if it amounted to anything much, might perk up the tomatoes.

She selected the least offensive looking of the knives and went back to her desk. The house was quiet; there was no roar from the lion in his lair. She sat alone in the same chair she used to write her weekly letter to her parents, and sipped her drink. The ice had shrunk to splinters. She shook the glass, smashing up the last of the shards against the sides, then she downed the liquid in one burning swallow and felt empowered.

The *Clancy*'s ledger was hidden in her drawer. Maitland was uneasily asleep, but she still found herself looking around warily as she pulled out the leather folder and flipped through the pages. It was a mixture of navigational record and narrative account; compass settings, shell tallies and day-to-day musings recorded side by side, dated and signed by the author. She came to the damning evidence and, glancing about her to ensure she was still alone, ran the razor-sharp blade as close as she could to the spine and pulled the page free. Without pausing, she struck a match and lit a corner of the yellowing page. When it had burned halfway down, she dropped it in her ashtray.

Tomorrow was a new day. She vowed that she would do better and keep on top of things. Pulling a clean sheet of paper from a desk drawer, she began to write notes. She would see Doctor Shin if Maitland was no better. She would consider what Marjorie and Duc wanted to do with the chiffa money. She would catch up on her correspondence. She would have a last cup of tea with Jane and ask her to drop a letter off at Gantry Creek for Mrs Wallace. She would meet her mother-in-law from the coastal steamer and bring her back to the house.

And she would try not to think about Coop.

She closed the ledger and smoothed her hand over the surface. Her fingers left dark oily indentations on the white cover like a thief's footprints in the snow. Maisie angled her head to one side and cradled her jaw in her hand. All ships kept a ledger. Daily life on the Fremantle to Buccaneer Bay coastal hopper would be recorded in the ship's log. The captain who had married her would have made a record in his ledger, signed and dated with his name. He might still have her marriage certificate or, at the very least, know where she could lay her hands on it. She went straight to the drinks table, and dropped three fat ice cubes into a large gin martini.

CHAPTER 23

MARJORIE SAT AT THE kitchen table, bashing a lemongrass stalk with a small mallet. A clump grew in the garden and Duc often used the lemon-tasting stems to flavour his cooking.

'Is Wednesday. You forgotten you goin' to tea with them ladies at the bishop's place this afternoon, Missus?'

Maisie put her breakfast tray beside the sink. She felt a burn of indigestion rise up towards her throat. She'd gobbled down the egg and toast far too fast and the acid reflux was fighting to get out. She swallowed hard and forced down the bile.

'I completely forgot. I might not even be back by then.'

'Where you goin' then, all day long?'

'I have things to do.'

'You wanta send a note sayin' you gone walkabout?'

'I can't do that. What would they think?'

Marjorie hunched her shoulders.

Maisie looked at her watch and decided she had time. She had two visits to make before her mother-in-law arrived on the evening steamer. It docked late, on the afternoon tide, and Maisie had cabled that she would meet her on the jetty and bring her back to the house. She had also planned to check with the captain and his log.

'I think it will be all right, Marjorie. I'll make sure I'm back for lunch and then I can do the tea with the ladies. After that I have to go out again. Did you remember Maitland's mother is arriving on the steamer?'

Marjorie clapped her hand over her mouth and leaned her large cotton-clad frame against the doorjamb. 'Captain Boss's mother comin' here? 'Course I remember. I ain't the one with the dodgy memry. I's put her in da guestroom down der end of mosquito room, furthest end from da kitchen.'

'Thank you, Marjorie. I don't know what I'd do without you.'

'Wot she gonna be like, d'you think?'

Maisie hadn't ever imagined Maitland with a mother. 'I have no idea, but we must make her very welcome. Would you please remind Duc she'll be here for supper?'

Marjorie removed her apron and stood up. 'Why's you think I bashin' this stringy stalk fella? Duc ain't got a bad memry either. He's cookin' up sommat from Miz Beeton cookbook of yours. How you gettin' about today by-an-by?'

'I hadn't thought. The sulky, probably.'

'Moody mare don't like wind. It gettin' up. Think we's getting a blow.'

'I thought the cyclone season was over.'

'You look at barometer fella? Him's droppin'.'

'How do you know how to read the barometer?'

'Missus, I keep tellin' you: I mebbe black girl but I got white girl's brain. I watch Boss. He tap glass and when da number goes lower he clap his hands. So, I's tellin' you: big blow's comin' mebbe later. You take bike or you walk. More safer.'

*

Afternoon tea with the ladies out of the way, Maisie was already on the jetty as they lowered the gangway into place. This had seemed like a good idea, but now she was not so sure. Flushed by nerves, she grabbed hold of the high rope sides and climbed up to the ship. The conversation with the captain would be difficult to engineer, but she had rehearsed what she was going to say.

Half the white faces of Buccaneer Bay seemed to be aboard, accepting complimentary drinks from the Steamship Company and catching up on gossip. The fortnightly arrival of the steamship was not to be missed. The captain took centre stage; a born performer, relaxed and comfortable in the spotlight.

Maisie snaked her way through the throng and planted herself in front of him. For some moments the captain seemed unsure. His gaze did not leave her face as he patted his inside pocket in search of cigarettes.

'Has someone offered you a drink, madam?'

'No. Thank you, I'm fine.'

Moving fractionally to his side without conceding her position, she scanned the room. The McMahons were clustered round a young officer in white uniform, both heads nodding as one at whatever he was saying. Mr Beckingsale, the bank manager, looked miserable, his dumpy wife hanging hotly on his arm, and Shorty Mason was propped at the bar, swigging back something red in a cocktail glass. The bartender polished a section of the counter with a fluffy white cloth and kept his opinions to himself.

The captain touched her arm and Maisie swung back knocking into his drink, slopping some clear liquid on the carpet.

'I'm so sorry. How clumsy of me.'

'Are you sure I can't offer you a drink?'

'Well, maybe a small one.' *To settle my nerves*, she thought.

The captain snapped his fingers and a Malay waiter appeared through the crowd. Maisie took a glass off the tray and nipped at the drink, eyes darting about, a nervous antelope at a waterhole. *Gin. Perfect!*

'Are you on board by yourself?' the captain said.

Maisie patted her hair with her spare hand to conceal her embarrassment. 'Yes. My husband's unwell but sent me on his behalf.'

'I am sorry to hear that.'

'Do you not recognise me, Captain? I sailed up from Port Fremantle with you some months ago, and you married me in the dining room to Maitland Sinclair?'

The captain nodded at her two or three times as if the movement were stirring his brain into action, then banged his chest with his fist like a gorilla in a zoo.

'Of course,' he said. 'It was quite a party.'

Maisie took a slightly larger glug of gin. 'And did you make a note of it in the log that you had married us at sea?'

'Well, we weren't at sea exactly,' he said, a little flummoxed.

She laughed and rested her hand lightly on his arm. 'But I'm sure you recorded it in the log?'

The Beckingsales had formed a line to his side. 'Probably. Yes, I'm sure I would have recorded the event.'

'Might you be able to check?'

He appeared slightly vexed and gestured at the bank manager and his wife. 'I could, yes, but not at this moment. You can see I am entertaining.'

She smiled in apology. 'My husband has been left some money, Captain. To claim it, he needs his original marriage certificate – but the thing is, we seem to have mislaid it. We have had some modifications done to the bungalow and I tidied all the paperwork away and – this is rather embarrassing – because I am so scattered, I can't find the papers anywhere. We wondered if you might be able to help.'

The captain's eyes softened. 'Yes, I could make you a copy of the entry if I can find it, but it wasn't a legally binding ceremony. Maitland said it would do well enough until the resident magistrate came back after the Wet. It was more of an excuse for a party, I understood. You'd need to ask the RM for a copy of the actual certificate when he performed the civil marriage.'

Maisie drained her glass and laughed, a hollow sound even to her, and patted her hair again. She was careful not to let the words slide into one another. 'I did tell you I was scattered, Captain! I should have thought of that myself. Oh, and I almost forgot to mention – the main reason I'm here is that I am meeting Maitland's mother. Might you know who she is?'

'Well, that's easy. Mrs Sinclair's standing right behind you,' he said.

She spun round and, feeling herself redden, dashed a hand across her cheek. 'Mrs Sinclair?'

Maitland's mother was tall and elegant in her cream-coloured dress, her eyes the same grey as his, but hers were lively, intelligent and warm. 'Please, call me Pammie. Is everything all right? You look a mite rattled.'

Maisie put her hands to her face and yet she could do nothing to stop the heat creeping across her cheeks. She held out a hesitant hand and suggested a drink at the bar.

'How about if we go back to your house so I can catch up with Maitland? It's why I've come, after all. And to meet you, of course.'

Maisie put down her glass. 'Whatever am I thinking? You must be longing to change your clothes and see your son. He is not very well at the moment, but the doctor assures us he'll soon be on the mend.'

'I'm sorry to hear that,' Pammie said. 'Have you informed him that I am coming?'

'No, I haven't.' Maisie turned towards the double doors. 'I wanted it to be a surprise.'

Maisie led her mother-in-law into Maitland's room and stood guard beside the bedhead. She mimed drinking a cup of tea, but Pammie shook her head. Maisie dropped her hands, hot fingers dangling at the end of leaden arms, then turned to the man in the bed and shook his shoulder.

'Look who's here, Maitland!' Maisie said, her voice unnaturally bright.

Maitland rolled his feverish eyes towards the door.

'It's me, Maitland. Your mother.' Pammie moved over to the bed and sat down.

Maitland shifted his legs away from the edge and clutched at the sheet. His face was grey, skin flushed with fever, eyes dim and weak, but recognition was written there in stark cold letters. 'What're you doing here? Come to crow?'

Pammie took a cigarette and box of matches out of her bag and reached over to the bedside table for the ashtray. She lit up and puffed smoke into the air. Very calmly, as if she were settling down to read her son a bedtime story, she said, 'I've often wondered how you've fared since you fled without a word, my entire savings in your short pockets.'

Maitland flinched. 'It wasn't me.'

'Well,' she said through the thick purple-grey smoke, 'I don't know who else it could have been.' She got up from the bed and went over to the dressing table. For a tall woman, she walked in small strides – her bottom firmly restrained by a wonder of structural engineering – and picked up a hairbrush. She rubbed the silver back with her thumb. 'I see you have the dressing-table set your father had sent over from England. Funny, isn't it, how it disappeared from the house at the same time you did. Maybe the thief sent it to you to dilute his guilty conscience.'

The spite in Maitland's eyes flattened. 'I didn't ask you to come. I don't want you here. Bloody go away.'

'I want some answers after all this time.' Pammie replaced the brush on the table. 'Such as how exactly your father died.'

Maitland thrashed his legs about under the covers, threw out his arm and swept the water jug off the table.

Pammie came back to the bed and stubbed out her cigarette. 'You are too old for tantrums, Maitland. Sleep if you must, but do mind that we'll return to this discussion in the morning, once you are rested and have a handle on your temper.'

She left the room, remaining as tall and straight as when she entered. Maisie was two steps behind, doing her very best not to slouch.

'I'm sorry,' she said through her teeth. 'He's not well and in a great deal of pain.'

'Maitland should have told me he was married.'

'He probably thought I was irrelevant.'

Pammie Sinclair stopped and turned, eying her with suspicion. 'Oh?'

Maisie immediately regretted her indiscretion, and said quickly, 'All the men here lead a clubby sort of life. Wives are expected to fit in round them. It's a different life to what I was expecting, and I'm not sure I'm built for the heat. I sometimes think . . .' She broke off, not certain how to complete her sentence.

Pammie inclined her head towards her son's bedroom. 'Maitland's father, Paul, was like that too. He didn't want the responsibility of a wife but socially he thought he ought to have one. Now, do you know what I think?'

'What might that be?'

'You should show me to my room and let me change for dinner.'

The two women sat in the near-dark, side by side on a cane-backed sofa, and spoke softly. Maitland, asleep in his room, was not necessary to their conversation but he was their common ground.

'When did you last hear from Maitland, Mrs Sinclair?'

'Pammie, please!' She offered Maisie a stern frown that held no harshness. 'Twenty years ago, in my estimates. He'd been working the opal fields at West Cliffs with Paul, who would have been your grandmother's cousin. Paul kept in vague touch, but I never heard a thing from my son. I'd packed them both off there after Maitland finished school – he was probably livid with me.'

'I understood that he hadn't actually finished at the Catholic school.'

'You'd be right. I don't suppose he told you the details.'

Pammie got up and went over to the drinks table. She poured herself a large slug of scotch and turned back to her daughter-in-law. She settled herself against the cushions and got down to business. 'What were you discussing with the captain, Maisie, earlier on? When we met on the ship?'

Maisie recounted the story while Pammie sipped at her drink, back ramrod-straight. She could almost have dusted the ceiling with her hair. There were no exclamations of surprise, no frowns, no slouch of the spine, no censure. Maisie's own mother would not have approved of the corset lady, she thought.

'Let me be sure I have got this correct,' Pammie said. 'Maitland wrote to your parents at the end of last year and, on the strength of that letter, you were sent away to marry my son. Your uncle has now passed away and left you his money, but in order to claim it, your uncle stipulated that your husband, whoever he might be, must prove that he legally married you. That, to me, sounds like your uncle had his head screwed on and was looking out for your best interests, Maisie. The captain told you this evening that the ceremony he conducted on board was a piece of theatre and that you should have had the wedding ratified in the court-house by the resident magistrate. Only, Maitland never bothered to legalise the arrangement. Is that about it?'

It was not hard to see why Pamela Sinclair had got on in business.

'Yes,' Maisie said. 'But I think there is a little more to it than that.'

'Oh?'

Somewhere in the bungalow, floorboards creaked.

Pammie frowned. 'Is anyone else here, besides us?'

'Just Marjorie and Duc.'

Pammie edged a little closer. 'Go on with what you were saying.'

'A while back I came across a letter my mother had written to Maitland. It wasn't addressed to me and I'm not proud to say that I opened it – but I did, mostly because I hadn't heard a word from my parents since I arrived in Australia. I learned that Maitland had been intercepting our correspondence, so they had not heard from me either, even though I was writing each week. My mother suggested that he was in some sort of arrangement with my parents and made a bizarre comment about my brother, who I always understood to have died as a baby.'

'What did she say exactly?'

Maisie closed her eyes and pictured the words. '*You will inform me of what happened to my son sixteen years ago, with the details corroborated by a third party.*'

Pammie ran a finger round the rim of her glass. 'I will ask Maitland about that in the morning, and if there is anything to uncover, rest assured I'll winkle it out of him. What I find most puzzling is that your parents sent you here to him – a second cousin your mother barely knew and had never met. I'm not even sure Maitland was aware of your existence. Paul would have known, of course. He came to Australia nearly forty years ago and that's when he and I met. Your mother must have run into him in England, though.'

Maisie chewed her lip. 'Why did he come out to Australia in the first place?'

'Paul had a string of debts in England but he was a great charmer. He took me in at the start, led me to believe that he was wealthy and well connected – and, stupid young girl that I was, I fell for it. Give him his due, though, he always had a great belief that his ship would come in and that he would make enough money to send Maitland back home to meet his grandparents. His son was his greatest achievement. Paul adored him and was wholly convinced that all would be forgiven, because he had produced another male Sinclair.'

Maisie wondered about absolution and was not certain it was a given. 'And did they forgive him, eventually?'

'It's hard to know. Paul did go back to England for a spell when his father died, but he left Maitland here.'

'When was that?'

'Years back. Fifteen or sixteen years. Something of that order. Although Paul and I were estranged, he did write to me before he went. He was good like that.'

Pammie looked Maisie up and down and pulled her chair nearer. She leaned forward and clasped the girl's hands. 'Your mother must have had very good reason to send her only child away. It's not a natural thing to do.'

'You did.'

'Yes, I did. But he was never on his own – he had his father with him. I sent him away to get him out of Melbourne. Maitland didn't leave school in the usual way after final examinations and so on; he was asked to leave and it devastated him. The Catholic Church was his life, you see. He adored all the prayers and singing, the music, the bells and the–' Pammie search for her words. 'Sense of order that his faith gave him. He was always ambitious – in a good manner – and wanted to work his way into a position of trust and authority within the Church. It was both his dream and career plan.'

Maisie knew that the craving for acceptance had not lessened any. 'What happened?'

'Maitland was taken on as an altar boy at our church. Do you understand what that is?'

'I don't know anything about Catholicism.'

Pammie sat back in her chair and crossed her ankles. 'Along with two other boys, he assisted the priest at liturgy and also helped him prepare for it. There were a great deal of things to do, such as filling the pitcher for the washing of hands, replacing the charcoal in the censer, putting out the cups for the wine and cutting bread for communion. The three boys naturally spent a good deal of time alone with the priest. He was instructing them in Bible studies. They adored him, those boys, and Father Patrick loved them. He'd take them back to the presbytery – his home – for afternoon tea after Bible study, which they considered a huge honour. We all did. One Sunday afternoon, though, some desperate soul needed his confession heard and pushed his way into the presbytery. He caught the priest with his trousers down.'

Maisie had to ask. 'Was he with Maitland?'

'Not on that particular occasion, but he had been.'

The wind howled round the house and banged a door, snapping off the conversation. A moment passed before Maisie could think what to say. She lifted her drink to her lips and raised her other hand to the glass to steady it. 'How old was he?'

'Young. Fifteen or sixteen. I was appalled, although his father wasn't especially shocked. He himself jumped both ways – it was common in the privileged English country-house circuit he moved in, before his parents packed him off to Australia. But in a small community, folk are not so accepting, nor do they forget or forgive. Father Patrick received a weak slap on the wrist from Rome and was given a few hundred Hail Marys as his punishment. He was moved up north and told to ignore his unnatural urges, and the boys were expelled from school. Maitland was destroyed, utterly heartbroken that his hopes of entering the priesthood were in tatters. Paul took him off to the opal fields after that to get him away.'

Maisie shook her head, trying to imagine Maitland with a broken heart. 'I had no idea. He's never shared any of this with me.'

'Even his love of religion?' Pammie said.

'He never goes to church.'

Pammie drew herself up even straighter. 'No?'

Maisie looked away in the direction of Maitland's bedroom and squeezed her lips together, feeling suddenly close to tears. 'No. I would say that turning his back on his faith has given him licence to do exactly what he wants without accountability to anyone. His behaviour is despicable and he tells so many lies it would need a very robust priest to act as his confessor. There's no-one in the Bay who remotely wants to take him on and now I find myself responsible for a very sick man who is not my husband, and I'm finding that a bit hard to deal with.'

Pammie placed her glass gently on the table. 'What has changed by you finding this out, Maisie? You say that everyone thinks Maitland is your husband, so continue with that deception. No-one is going to know any different.'

Maisie patted her sleeve to locate her handkerchief. 'If it ever comes out that I have been living with a man out of wedlock, no decent man is ever going to want me.'

'No-one knows the truth of your situation, and if the worst happens and Maitland were to die, you can present yourself as a grieving widow.'

Maisie blew her nose, unconvinced. 'Blair Montague knows the truth of what's going on here. He's complicit in everything Maitland does and is bound to know our wedding was a sham. He probably even suggested it in the first place, and I know it would give him great delight to see me publicly pilloried.'

'Blair Montague is here?'

'He's the mayor.'

Pammie was very still. The light from the lighthouse flitted across her face, a tangle of memories illuminated in her eyes. She swallowed the last of her drink and stubbed out her cigarette.

'Maitland always believed that Blair was the one who discovered Father Patrick with the boy. It makes no sense at all that they should be here together.'

'Unless, of course, Blair was jealous,' Maisie said, 'and blew the whistle on purpose.'

Later that evening, when Pammie had turned in, Maisie called an emergency meeting in the kitchen.

Duc was setting the bread for morning while getting his vocal chords around a new tune he had picked up in Asia Place.

Maisie saw no point in prevaricating. 'We are all going to take turns nursing the captain. He's getting worse and I don't want him left alone.'

Marjorie pulled her spectacles up her nose. 'I ain't touchin' him.'

'I want you to sit with him, that's all. If he wakes up and needs anything, you can come and fetch me. Or his mother, now she's here.'

Marjorie scowled. 'What 'bout Duc? His howling like a kangaroo dog not exactly peaceful for sick boss fella.'

'He'll take his turn after you. I'm sure you'll keep the noise down to a dull roar, won't you, Duc?'

Duc grinned.

When Maisie opened the bedroom door, the stench of sickness hit her like a wall. For a moment she wavered and then was conscience-stricken at her hesitation. *This is what I wanted to do once upon a time*, she thought. *Tend the sick, whoever they are. So, nurse-volunteer Maisie Porter, pull back your shoulders and walk right in.*

Maitland lay on the bed. His eyes were wide open, this man who had robbed her of everything. His breathing was shallow and raspy, like the sound of grating carrots.

She tried for a lightness of tone, a breezy nurse style. 'How are you feeling, Maitland? Are you pleased that your mother is here?'

He looked grey and filmed with sweat, stunned almost, but didn't speak.

In the next few hours she did everything she knew to make him comfortable in that hot, stinking room. She wrung out a washcloth and sponged the fever from his skin, whispering over and over that he was going to get well.

A little before midnight, Maitland began to moan.

She crouched by the bed and leaned in close but could make no sense of his words. 'What is it, Maitland? Are you in pain?'

Faint with fatigue, Maisie sat by the bed and took his wrist. She watched the clock on the nightstand and began to count. She shook her head and started again. She must have made a mistake; his pulse was far too fast. She lifted his head and smoothed his pillow, and listened to the boom of the waves breaking on the rocks. Pity was the last thing she'd expected to feel and yet there it was, its noise filling the room. She put her hands over her ears and blocked out the sound.

The sky was still dark when Marjorie poked her head round the sick-room door. 'You want me take my turn, Missus?

Maisie swallowed hard. 'No, Marjorie, we have got beyond that now. I think you must go to the hospital and ask Doctor Shin to call.'

CHAPTER 24

When Maisie finally lay in bed, sleep would not come. Light flickered through the lattice, but it wasn't from the lighthouse. She had come to like the dependability of its beam and knew its pattern. Round and round every eight seconds. She wondered vaguely if all lighthouses pulsed at the same rate or whether they were different, like fingerprints. Coop would know, she thought, wherever he was.

Coop.

What would he say when he found out that she was living with a man who wasn't her husband? A man who was a homosexual and had been molested by a priest? She grimaced. Could Maitland be sent to prison? In the Bay if the law was inconvenient, everyone ignored it. No. There was no way he would be sent to prison.

Somewhere near dawn she got up and poked about under the bed for the chamber-pot, feeling for the familiar smooth shape in the dark. She eased herself down onto the rigid china and cradled her head in her hands.

The despair of the evening had lifted slightly and she felt oddly comforted by Maitland's mother. She reminded her of

Mrs Wallace: a practical, sensible pioneering woman who took life in her stride. Mrs Wallace had told her she would have to grow a strong backbone, and Maisie realised that now was the time.

Standing, she peered through the lattice and followed the light. It seemed to be bobbing along the shell path from the house to the packing shed. She heard the sound of a cough. *It must be the night-pan collector*, she thought, *going back to his cart.* She turned her head and listened again but there was nothing else. The strange light had disappeared.

She got back into bed and flapped the sheet. Her skin was so hot she thought it might scorch the linen. The storm had blown through and frogs were now croaking happily in the stillness, but it was no cooler. Somewhere in the bungalow a door closed and floorboards creaked. Perhaps it was Maitland's mother wandering about in the unfamiliar house or looking in on her son. Maisie got up again and slid her feet into her slippers. The light was back, bouncing up the path, stopping, starting and moving away until only a faint glow filtered through the lattice.

Someone was in the garden.

Maisie edged her way down the verandah and hesitated by the steps. Walking about in the dark was perilous. Early on, when she had not long been in the Bay, she had almost stepped on a tangle of whip snakes, entwined like twisted seaweed, and from then on nocturnal expeditions to the garden lavatory had ceased.

Holding her wrap tight around herself, Maisie wished she'd brought a lamp. Concentrating on the bobbing light, she didn't watch where she was walking and banged her toe hard against a chair leg. She cried out in pain.

A whisper from the garden. 'Maisie, is that you?'

'Coop?' She sensed the nod of his head and smiled into the dark.

'I was worried when you didn't come this weekend for the slop chest, so I came to check all was well.'

She turned her head and checked along the verandah. Reassured there was no-one about, she pushed open the door and went down to the garden.

He was leaning against a tree, his shirtsleeves rolled up, a cigarette between his finger and thumb. Fanned by the faint breeze, the tip glowed, and it was this, she supposed, that she had seen from the house, tracking up and down the path. She felt her body straighten as if she were being laced up in one of her discarded corsets.

'I don't understand why you aren't at sea. You can't just pop back on a whim for a cup of tea and a slice of cake.'

He peered at her, tipped his chin towards the ocean. 'My lines got fouled on the coral.'

She stood still, not daring to move. She knew if she touched him, she would be lost. He threw his cigarette away, its butt tracing a glowing arc as it flew into the flowerbed. He leaned towards her and brought his arm around her back, circling her waist, pulling her in. *He smells of the sea,* she thought, *and I am drowning.* He turned his lips onto her neck; she could feel his breath and then the tiny kisses. She let her hands drop but did not push him away.

Longing tormented her. It was embedded so deeply and painfully it throbbed in her veins. 'Please don't, Coop. You've got to go. We might be seen. Maitland's in the house and his mother's here too.' *Even though I know I am perfectly entitled.*

'I've been here for hours. Everyone's asleep.'

He pressed against her. She could feel his body – hard now – and still she did not move.

'This is wrong,' she said. *And yet this is consuming me.* She suddenly felt very at sea. She breathed in slowly, feeling the way with her words. 'Tell me what happened to your lines.'

'Daike cut me free but we came up too quickly. JB was fussing, so we sailed back to the Bay yesterday and dropped by the Japanese hospital and got ourselves checked out.'

His face was close now. She concentrated on his eyes, the black eyes that set her on fire, afraid of what his mouth might say. 'And the doctor gave you the all clear?'

'Yes. But we lost Sid, our shell-opener.' He cupped his hand round the back of her head, his unshaven chin scratching her cheek. 'I came to the house this morning to tell the boss we're a man down and find out what he wants to do. Your maid told me he's even worse than he was on the schooner.'

Maisie pushed backwards and pulled herself free. 'He's very poorly. That's why his mother is here from Melbourne. We're not at all sure that he's going to get better.' Her lie was ill-prepared but Coop didn't appear to notice.

'How do you feel about that?'

Coop's face held something but she could not say what, and desolation sliced through her. She took another step back, certain his dark eyes would see into her soul. 'That's an unfair question, Coop.'

His fingers found her hand and she felt him tug. 'I'm sorry. You're right. Let's walk to the lighthouse, get away from here for a while.'

He strode away, holding her hand in the dark, pulling her behind him. The sharpness of the crushed shells cut through the soles of her slippers and the hem of her nightdress dragged in the sand like a brake. Once or twice she stumbled as she stepped on uneven ground. A mist was rolling in from the sea and settled on her eyelashes; she felt them clumping into pointed spikes.

She stopped and wiped her eyes. 'This is far enough. We don't want to disturb the lighthouse-keeper. His wife is an invalid.'

A flash of light from the beacon briefly illuminated the spot where they stood. 'I can't bear to be away from you,' he whispered.

Tears caught in her throat. 'Please don't, Coop.' Maisie stopped for a moment, waiting for him to comment, but when he said nothing she changed the subject. 'Sid wasn't a diver, so what happened to him?'

'He fell overboard.' Coop scratched the side of his nose. 'And met with a shark.'

Maisie brought a hand to her chest. 'That's a desperate way to die.'

'Mmm. It is.'

She couldn't read his expression in the dim light, but his tone was not sincere. 'I'm not hearing heartfelt grief.'

'He was not easy to like. He tried to kill me.'

'What do you mean?'

'Sid slipped a mickey in JB's tea. I got snagged on the coral because JB was unconscious and had it not been for Daike watching the pattern of my air bubbles on the surface, I would no longer be here.'

A lump of dread lodged in her throat. 'Why would Sid do that?'

'I think your husband told him to, and it has everything to do with the document I signed in the packing shed. Six out of the twelve English divers who came are already dead. I'm still here, more by luck than anything else, and another chap has just chucked in the towel and gone back to Fremantle.'

'You've been sacrificed for the government bet,' she said bitterly.

'I'm not giving in, Maisie. I came here to make money and I'm damned if I let myself be cheated out of it.'

Maisie narrowed her eyes and stared out to sea. A faint shimmer on the horizon pushed its way through the mist. 'You can't dive for the pearlers here anymore. They've had one pop at you and they won't stop.'

'There has to be one honest pearler in the Bay who'll take me on.'

'I destroyed your page, Coop, but I heard Maitland and Blair Montague talking. A government official is coming soon to see how their white experiment is getting on and the two of them are counting on your paperwork to prove their point. Do you not see we have made things worse? Without your damning evidence they will have no alternative *but* to kill you.'

CHAPTER 25

MAISIE WALKED DOWN THE verandah towards the front door, her heels on the wooden floor drilling the silence. Before the sun was up, Coop had gone back to the lugger – once more out of reach, like the shadows she'd tried to catch as a child.

She felt guilt where there should have been none. Everything was upside down.

Doctor Shin stood on the other side of the screen, his medical bag clutched in his hand. He looked bowed, stiff, as if he hadn't stood straight for a thousand years.

'Doctor Shin,' she said, pulling open the screen. 'Thank goodness you are here. Maitland is in the mosquito room, yet perhaps you would prefer some refreshment first?'

He shook his head. 'I should like to examine the patient, Mrs Sinclair. That is why you summoned me in the small hours, after all, is it not?'

'Yes, of course. Whatever am I thinking? I'll show you where he is.'

She led the doctor down the corridor and opened the bedroom door. It still smelled sour, acrid, as if someone had upturned the chamber-pot. Maitland looked like he was asleep, lying with his face towards the open lattice, a pudgy hand slack on the bedclothes.

Pammie came into the bedroom carrying a platter of fruit for Maitland's breakfast. She set it down beside the bed and positioned herself at the bedhead, her back pressed against the wall as if she was trying to distance herself from the scene. She nodded in acknowledgement of Maisie and the doctor.

Doctor Shin put his bag on the floor and knelt by the bed. Maisie saw a frown cross his face as he put two fingers on Maitland's neck and took his pulse. The brevity of his examination was not what she was expecting.

'Is everything all right, Doctor?'

There was a tinge of sympathy on his face. 'I am very sorry, Mrs Sinclair. Your husband has passed away.'

For some moments, the doctor's announcement made no sense. She sat on a chair and stared at Maitland's face, fully expecting him to open his eyes and say something mean. 'I don't understand,' she said.

Pammie leaned forward and straightened the ashtray on the nightstand. 'He was absolutely fine last evening and first thing this morning when I looked in on him. Everyone's been taking turns all night to sit with him because Maisie was so worried. It's impossible that he's dead. The British doctor saw him several times and was certain he was getting better.'

Doctor Shin swallowed hard and sat on the rumpled bed. A muscle clenched in his neck. 'The message that was left for me at the hospital said Captain Sinclair had the Barcoo fever. I doubt that was an accurate diagnosis. I have not seen a single case in the Bay in years, and it is more commonly expected where a water source might be contaminated. It would be a more convincing argument had he spent an extended period in the bush. It is a pity that you did not send for me sooner.' He rolled his eyes, and stowed his hands in his pockets.

'If it wasn't the Barcoo fever, what do you think he died of, Doctor?' Maisie said.

'For the symptoms described – nausea, vomiting, fever, pain and the general look of his mottled skin – I would hazard a guess at sepsis, but I wouldn't like to say for certain without conducting an autopsy. I could do so, if you would like, but it wouldn't change the facts. He is still dead.'

Maisie looked at her mother-in-law and took in the shocked white of her face, the fallen corners of her mouth. The fluffy face of motherhood might not have been her forte, but she had still just lost her only child.

'I think he's suffered enough,' Maisie said.

Pammie waved a hand in the air and spoke so quietly Maisie had to strain her ears to hear her. 'Maitland's dead. There's no need for a medical witch-hunt. The doctor's right; it won't alter the facts.'

Doctor Shin cleared his throat. 'You will need to inform the undertaker, dear madams. The burial must take place tomorrow before the flesh starts to putrefy in the heat. If his condition was contagious, and I cannot be sure that it wasn't, you would be putting the household at risk.'

Maisie twisted the ring on her wedding finger and set off towards the door, touching Pammie lightly on the shoulder as she drew level.

'I'll go straightaway, Doctor, and Pammie – would you sit with him until I get back? I'll ask Duc to bring you some tea.'

*

The next day, in the afternoon, Maitland was buried in the hot, red earth of the Bay's cemetery, in the corner section reserved for the whites. An ancient horse-drawn hearse, conveying the brass-handled coffin, was driven by the night-pan collector, who did extra duties in the afternoon for the town's undertaker. Beside him, a large Malay sat smoking a calabash pipe. A small procession led by the two Mrs Sinclairs followed the hearse. It came to a halt beyond a row of ornate tombstones bearing inscriptions to Japanese divers who had died on the shell beds. Last to arrive was Bishop McMahon – sweat-shiny and flustered – with Mrs McMahon, dressed in black-watch tartan, hanging on his arm, and weeping with copious abandon. She clutched a tartan handkerchief that matched her dress. A small group of Aboriginal people had clustered in a far corner, and Maisie was sure she had spotted Charlie wearing his full tribal gear before he vanished into the scrub.

It made her sad to think that their free-roaming race was dying out. Jane was right. The white man's legacy was a terrible thing.

The bishop preached sternly about the perils of drinking tainted water, and Mrs McMahon wailed throughout. Despite the heat, he read the whole burial service until, after an uncomfortable half-hour, Maitland's coffin was lowered into the ground.

Maisie stood, head bowed beneath the relentless sun, and barely listened to the bishop's voice. She felt an ache in her heart so deep and profound it almost bent her double. But it was not for Maitland, this terrible pain. For him there was nothing. *Coop*, she whispered, and started to cry.

After the service, the house's east verandah was half-filled with people talking in quiet church voices. A shaft of bright sunlight lit up the table where Duc had laid out his feast on top of a stiff white tablecloth; he had produced his best work for boss fella's last supper. Marjorie, in her floral frock, was moving among the mourners with plates of finger food, eyelids cast down and her mouth artistically drooping at the corners, trapping the smirk on her face. *Deception is so easy*, Maisie thought, *among this army of deceivers*. She knew Marjorie felt nothing for Maitland.

Coop, come to pay his respects, had taken off his jacket and was talking to a red-eyed Mrs McMahon, whose necklaces chimed sharply against the crockery as she swooped backwards and forwards to grab the cakes.

Pammie slid forward on her chair and nudged Maisie hard in the ribs. 'Are you going to say something to thank people for coming?'

'Do you think I should?'

'Yes, if you can take your eyes off that tall man next to the tartan feeding frenzy for a couple of minutes.'

Maisie felt her face burn. 'I'm sorry. Mr Cooper is one of Maitland's divers. I was thinking about what is going happen to the fleet.'

Pammie wore an expression Maisie had often masked her own with: silent disbelief. Maisie knew she had been studying Coop in the dark wool suit with intense concentration, as if she was trying to memorise his details. The way he chose the smaller items to make them easier to eat. The way he pursed his top lip when he drank from his glass to stop the ice tipping over the top. And when Mrs McMahon dropped a bacon-wrapped oyster on the floorboards, the way he bent his knee to pick it up as if he were about to propose marriage to her. Pammie had seen it all.

Maisie pulled herself together and got to her feet.

*

'That was a nice little speech you gave, Maisie,' Pammie said when the mourners had gone.

Maisie put her head in her hands. 'I've just walked the path to damnation with the lies I told and now I have to organise a headstone for Maitland and perjure myself further.'

Pammie nibbled on a sandwich. With a corset that tight, there was no room for much beyond a crumb in her stomach. 'It seems to me you have an opportunity to perpetuate the myth of your marriage, if you call him a loving husband and simply record the dates of his birth and death. No-one would expect any more than that.'

Maisie pushed away a plate of leftovers. 'Then that's what I shall do.'

Pammie glanced at her, a frown dissecting her forehead. 'What are your plans, though? Will you go back to England?'

'I don't know. I have a lot to settle up here first. What about you? I'd like it if you stayed.'

'I can't stay here in this soul-sapping climate. I'll go back to Melbourne and pick up where I left off. I have a successful business and make good money; it's what I do. You will think me a most unnatural mother, I'm sure, but I confess I came here to understand what happened to my husband in the opal fields, not to rekindle a relationship with our son. I told you, I think, that Paul always kept in regular touch but then, all of a sudden, his letters stopped. If he had been ill, I feel certain I would have known and I hoped that Maitland might have had something to tell me about that.' She sagged momentarily with disappointment. 'But whatever Maitland knew, he took his secrets with him.'

'Not unnatural, no. I have an unnatural mother and you are in no manner her counterpart. As for Maitland, you should at least take his personal effects back with you. They don't belong to me. I've always hated the hunting pictures. The silver brushes I might keep, though, if you didn't mind too much, because they came from my family in England. There's also a soapstone box. Perhaps you might like that?' She got up from her chair and went to the huge dark desk at the far end of the verandah. The box was at the back of a drawer, an Aladdin's lamp waiting for its secret command.

Pammie let out a small gasp as Maisie set it down on the table. 'Gracious! That's Paul's. I haven't seen it in years. He used to hide his winnings in there . . . till Maitland discovered how to open it, that is.'

'Do you know how it works?'

'It's a Chinese riddle of sorts. It's not a box, although it looks like one.' She turned it upside down and squeezed the underside between her thumb and forefinger, dragging it sideways like a slide. The bottom of the box pulled out part-way then stopped. There were two items in the ingenious hiding place: an enormous pearl and a letter.

CHAPTER 26

MAISIE DIDN'T KNOW WHO else to consult. The manager was a dull, blotchy-faced Scot who spoke to her with deliberate slowness as if believing her incompetent.

He gave her an incurious smile. 'Mrs Sinclair?'

'Mr Beckingsale, my husband has just passed away. I need to ascertain what our position is financially.'

'Do you have authority to enquire?'

'I am his widow. I would think that gives me sufficient authority to enquire.'

'It is an unusual request.'

'My husband is dead,' Maisie said. 'I have already told you that, Mr Beckingsale, and he didn't make a will. If I am to survive financially, I must know where I stand, and the nature of your dealings with my husband.'

Gerald Beckingsale folded his arms over his crisp white shirt. 'We have advanced your husband money several times over the years, and each time it has been repaid without difficulty.'

'That is a relief to hear,' Maisie said.

The bank manager wrapped his arms a little more securely round his middle and blinked once, raising his eyebrows over the top of his spectacles. His eyes were not benign.

Maisie was uneasy. 'I sense a "but", Mr Beckingsale.'

'Our best security has always been your husband's integrity and the rising price of pearl shell. Until now, both have been above reproach. The thing is, this last time we loaned him a large sum of money against the stock and holdings of Sinclair Marine Trading. All his pearl-fishing equipment, boats, schooner and so on, are mortgaged.'

'Is that not the same arrangement as for any other pearl fleet?'

'Yes, it is, but he is – I'm sorry, was – not meeting his repayments. The regular income from England is what is propping you up at this time.'

Maisie felt she was not keeping up. 'From England?'

'Yes. The monthly amount he receives wired from London.'

Maisie looked beyond the window at the long wooden jetty. She paused before she answered, struggling with the tense. 'From whom did he receive the monthly payment?'

The bank manager's hands had moved to a filing cabinet behind his desk. He leafed through the paperwork and paused, a finger against a name. 'A Judge George Porter provides a generous monthly stipend. In addition, a large single payment was wired to your husband last November from the same account.'

Maisie looked back at the jetty and squinted. The morning sun had gathered force, the heat slowing the trade, unlike the gathering tempo of her pulse. She turned away from the glare of light and shut her eyes.

'There is an additional monthly income from England that you may find of interest,' the bank manager went on.

There was a long pause as Mr Beckingsale bent again over his filing cabinet and stirred his files with his hands, like an alchemist making gold.

He revealed that her mother also sent money to Maitland every month. It didn't make any sense. She felt destabilised and pulled at the neck of her blouse, worrying her fingers round the top button.

She opened her eyes and asked him coldly, 'Would you please prepare me an exact statement of our financial affairs? The monthly amount coming in, and what is owed and to whom? A complete record.'

The bank manager stood and wiped his fingers on his trousers. He looked at her with cold, sharp eyes, weighing his decision. He held out his hand, and his grip was as limp as spinach. 'Very well, Mrs Sinclair. I will provide you with Captain Sinclair's monthly monetary comings and goings relating to this bank. But I should point out there will be other accounts with the ships' chandlers, chits with the tradespeople and so on in Asia Place. Short of knocking on doors, I am not sure how you will discover what you owe, and to whom. Eventually your creditors will come to you, I imagine, when they run out of patience for their money. I would advise that we keep the nature of this conversation private. We do not have an established protocol for dealing with widows.'

Maisie walked to the door, feet blazing in her thick soles. 'When you have the paperwork ready, please send a message and I will come in personally to collect it.'

He didn't see her out.

Maisie wrapped the pearl in a handkerchief and took it to the pearl-skinner's shop. Most pearls needed cleaning to get rid of surface imperfections before they were ready to sell. Pierre Fornallaz ran his jewellery and pawnbroking business from a single-fronted shop in Asia Place, and had come to the Bay with a reputation as the best pearl cleaner in Australia. He twirled the huge pearl between his thumb and forefinger.

'It's a gamble, Mrs Sinclair. This pearl has a significant surface imperfection. Maybe the crinkle can be cut away. Maybe it goes all the way through. You might end up with nothing. It's your choice.'

'I think we have to try. My husband was a gambling man. He would have been excited by the risk.'

Mr Fornallaz pointed to a seat. 'All right. You sit and watch so you cannot accuse me of treachery if the pearl is no good.'

Maisie sat in the chair opposite his work table, feeling the perspiration begin on her brow. She wasn't sure if it was the horrible heat inside or terror-ridden anticipation that was making her so uncomfortable. A lot was riding on the quality of this pearl.

'A pearl is like an onion, Mrs Sinclair,' Mr Fornallaz said. 'It is made up of many layers folded over each other. If there is a rotten bit of onion flesh, you can sometimes cut it away and the rest is fine to eat. Sometimes, the rotten flesh goes all the way through and you have to throw it away. A pearl is just like that.'

He screwed a jeweller's eyeglass onto his eye and picked up a three-cornered file, the handle of which was made of a champagne cork. Maisie thought it a primitive tool for the delicate operation he was about to perform, but back and forth he gently stroked the surface of the pearl like a violinist arcing his bow. Pearl dust began to fall on the green felt tabletop.

'What do you think, Mr Fornallaz?' Maisie asked.

'Patience, please,' he said, rotating the pearl. 'I cannot rush or I will ruin what may lie beneath.'

While he worked, Maisie gazed over his shoulder at a picture that hung on the wall. She had no idea what it was supposed to depict and couldn't concentrate on the garish sweeping brush-strokes. There was too much on her mind.

Time passed. Maisie sensed the change in Pierre Fornallaz's bowing and focused on the black, waxed moustache above his mouth.

'You have a beautiful pearl, Mrs Sinclair.' Mr Fornallaz held the pearl out for her to examine. 'It has a lovely gold tint, which is rare. Most of the pearls from the waters round the Bay are milky white. This is unusual and will increase its value, presuming you are wanting to sell?'

'I have no choice, Mr Fornallaz. Could you find a buyer for me? I wouldn't know where to start or what it's worth.'

His face was sympathetic. 'I was sorry to hear of your husband's passing, Mrs Sinclair. If you are to take over his fleet, however, you must begin to learn about the value of things or people will cheat you.'

'I hadn't thought about carrying on with his business. Is it possible for a woman to run a pearling business?'

His eyes widened. 'I'm sorry if I spoke out of turn. I assumed that you would, and I think the Bay assumes that you will. You have been running the slop chest most efficiently, I hear. Mr Beckingsale from the bank has a high opinion of you. He thinks you have a head for money matters.'

Maisie didn't know what to say. It felt peculiar to think they had been discussing her. 'It is too soon to make definite plans, Mr Fornallaz. I am not sure what I am going to do.'

He rolled the pearl in his palms. 'This will fetch a lot of money if you are patient and wait for the right buyer. In the meantime, the season is barely started. If you are going to continue to harvest pearl shell, my advice would be to get your divers working hard, now, while the market is strong.'

Maisie sat on the bed and stared at the crowded rail of white suits. She had no idea what to do with them, nor with the twenty pairs of white leather shoes, seventy or so silk shirts and dozens of ties.

'Mebbe you cut off der buttons, Missus. All dem pearls got to be worth something.'

'That's a good idea, Marjorie. Do you know anyone who might like the clothes?'

The maid rolled her eyes. 'My mob don't wear dat fancy stuff. Thought you knew dat. Wot about white diver fella?'

'He's too tall,' she said.

Marjorie lifted up a trouser leg, as if measuring its length. 'Dat true enuff. What you want to do with him trunk-box fella?'

'I'm sorry?'

'Dat box under his bed with da holy clothes and wot not.'

Maisie's mouth was dry, the saliva not doing its job. 'Show me.'

Marjorie knelt and pulled out a curved-top box, similar to her own cabin trunk. Justifying her snooping, she said, 'Part of my English advancement, readin' everything I can, even Caflick litrature.'

Maisie lifted the lid on the trunk. Folded neatly on the top, wrapped in calico to protect them from the jaws of silverfish and moths, was a black cassock and surplice. She lifted them out and smoothed over the folds with her palm. Underneath the clothing were religious books: a hymnal, the Book of the Gospels, a lectionary and sacramentary and a leather-bound Bible. She discovered a rosary with its smooth black beads in a soft cotton pouch and a heavy silver crucifix in another. There was a fat wad of sheet music and full scores for the Mozart and Verdi requiems with tenor passages underlined in pencil, and a pair of silver candlesticks with their tall slim candles, religious pictures painted on the wax.

She sat very still, her shoulders slumped, and tried to process her feelings. She'd known nothing about Maitland until a few days ago, that he'd once loved music, singing and God. She couldn't imagine him young and fresh and pious; what he had become blackened his memory and sickened her heart. 'We'll take them to the Catholic church, Marjorie. They were obviously very important to Captain Sinclair and I am sure he would want them to have a good home.'

Pammie appeared in the doorway. 'Take what?'

Maisie showed her the box. 'See for yourself.'

Pammie lifted out the Bible and flipped through the well-thumbed pages, the tips of her fingers tracing the embossed religious illustrations. 'Maitland won this Bible at Sunday school, Maisie. He came first in the Bible-study competition year after year. He loved all the stories and could quote long passages from memory.'

Maisie said nothing and Pammie went on. 'I should have fought harder for him and found him another school in another state. What does that say about me? That I was too caught up with my own needs and didn't care enough about my son?'

'Maitland had his own demons that had nothing to do with what you did or didn't do. He turned his back on his religion, and what he became – well, that was his choice.'

Pammie's head dropped to her chest. Grim-faced, she knelt beside the box and began to put back Maitland's belongings, as if she were packing his things for a trip. Eventually she got to her feet and said, 'Let's go and sit on the verandah, Maisie. There's something else I have to tell you.'

*

It was another scorching day, wetly oppressive, and there would be no downpour to cool the air. A flock of black cockatoos streaked noisily overhead, a dark smudge on an innocent blue sky.

Duc banged a tray on the table and fiddled with the cups. 'You want I bring cake? I make scones you like with recipe from Mem Beeton.'

Since Maitland's death, Duc had gone out of his way to be helpful. Perhaps he had realised he was now dependent on her for the roof over his head, or that she was on the point of enabling him to realise his dream. Whichever it was, he was more eager to please than ever.

'We're fine, Duc, and thank you. I couldn't have managed without you lately and I want you to know that I am very grateful.'

He looked at her with a broad grin, his eyes sparkling with joy. *At least someone's happy*, she thought.

Pammie's hand shook a little on the coffee pot. 'I read Paul's letter. The one in the soapstone box.'

Maisie gave her a small nod of support. 'Did it answer your questions?'

Pammie waited for Duc to leave. 'Ten years back, he took his own life. He'd been ill for a while and knew he wouldn't recover, so from somewhere or other he got hold of a large quantity of opiate and knocked it back with a bottle of whisky.'

Maisie sat very still. 'Was Maitland with him at the time?'

'Yes, as far as I know. Paul's letter never reached me and yesterday we find it among Maitland's affairs. Even an amateur sleuth could reason that Maitland must have been around Paul at the time and stole the letter.'

Maisie agreed. 'He did have a taste for other people's correspondence.'

Pammie dropped a sugar lump in her coffee and gave it a brisk stir. 'Knowing what happened to him ends a decade of puzzlement, but there's a great deal more that is not so easy to fathom. The letter was also a confession of something he had done in England for which he was seeking absolution.' Her face stiffened. 'He was asking me to be his confessor.'

'What on earth had he done?'

Pammie took a sip of coffee. 'There's no easy way to say this, Maisie. When Paul went back to England for his father's funeral he got himself into serious financial trouble. I told you that my husband was a serial gambler and it seems he had markers all over London. I think when Maitland read what Paul had written, he hatched a plan to use what he found out to extort money.'

'I don't understand,' Maisie said.

Pammie drained her cup. 'I'm sorry, I'm not explaining this at all well. Paul got involved in a high-stakes gambling syndicate and ran up a frightening debt that he simply could not pay off. He promised to settle up when his father's estate had been formalised, but his debtor would not let him off the hook so lightly.'

The question rose up inside her. 'He told you who it was?'

Pammie went still. 'Yes. It was your father. He did ultimately wipe Paul's debt but he named his own chilling price.'

Maisie's voice sank to a whisper. 'What did he have to do?'

'He had to kidnap a baby.'

She forced herself to speak. 'Whose baby did my father ask him to take?'

Pammie studied her hands, now motionless in her lap. 'His own. Paul stole your father's baby son.'

Maisie felt light-headed. Her mind was racing, trying to picture Maitland's father, the fast-living, gambling charmer who one day found himself so pressured with debt, he could set out and steal a baby. Her breath came out in a laboured gasp. 'Why would my father ask him to steal his own child?'

Pammie pulled the letter from her pocket and held it out. 'It doesn't say.'

She stared at the sheet paper and for a second was mute. An image of her father – respected upholder of the laws of England – burned like a judgement in her mind. 'What did Paul do with the baby? Where did he take him?' she said.

Pammie looked up at her face. 'He was too frightened to write it down, but he says he told Maitland.'

It was not hard to imagine the rest. 'So, Maitland demanded money from my father to not expose him?'

'Yes, I think that must be about it,' Pammie said.

Maisie's mind chattered on, joining up the desperate dots, completing the monstrous picture. 'And Maitland said he would tell my mother where her son was if she handed me over with a nice fat dowry, a regular monthly income and enough china to sink a ship.'

She thought back to her conversation with her father before she boarded the SS *Oceanic* to Australia.

Why am I being sent away, Father?

It's your mother's wish. And my own.

Paul's letter fluttered from her fingers. 'My parents agreed to Maitland's demands and I was the trade-off. I see now that being their daughter for nineteen years counted for absolutely nothing. My position in their affections was never secure. The truth is, Pammie, I was sacrificed by them both; by my father to keep his secret and by my mother to find her son.'

CHAPTER 27

COOP HAD BEEN DITHERING for days, wondering how long to wait before he called on her. The crew was badgering him. Delay cost money, they said. The cyclone had blown through and they had to know what was happening with their jobs now the boss was dead. Given the circumstances, though, he couldn't just barge in and demand answers. The cable office was picking up news that the *Atticus* had gone missing, somewhere this side of Port Fremantle. It gave him the excuse he'd been looking for.

He pulled open the screen door and knocked on the lintel. Maisie was sitting on the verandah, silhouetted against the wall like a paper doll. She raised her blue eyes and, as always when she saw him, swatted at her hair. The familiar gesture twisted his heart so tight his chest hurt.

'Coop, the very person! I was just thinking about you and the crew.'

'Oh?'

'Do you know about dummying?'

'Of course. Why?'

'How quickly could you fix up the *Clancy*?' she said. 'It's the only way I can get you all out to sea and diving again. I can lay my hands on the money to do her up, but the bank says I can't trade until Maitland's affairs are settled. The indentured crew's permits are attached to the lugger and only whites can hold the permits, so . . .' She paused. 'If you take on the boat, you can continue to dive, with me as the silent backer.'

'You've been busy.'

'You said you came to make money. I'm trying to at least make that work for you. Maitland owed you that.'

He felt a frisson of foreboding. 'What are your plans now?'

'I don't know what I'm going to do. I have personal business in England to attend to – business that I don't believe can be dealt with through letter or cable. I'm thinking about going home.'

'Can you delay?'

She shook her head. 'Let's walk along the cliff. I fancy taking a look at the ocean.'

He guided her through the storm-ravaged garden, his left hand a gentle rudder at her back. From the coastal path, they saw that the water was high, still angry after the blow. The jetty stuck out to sea, an undulating wooden carpet on its rickety stilts, and Coop marvelled at how it was still standing.

There was a bench halfway along the path; no-one knew why it was there. They sat on it and gazed out to sea.

'There's talk in town that the *Atticus* has gone missing, Maisie. That's what I came to tell you. I didn't know if you'd heard.'

She twisted to look at him. 'That's not possible. It's supposed to be unsinkable!' Tears welled in her eyes. 'The mayor and Dorothea were on board. The silly thing told her father that you two were engaged. He was planning to take her to Europe, to get her away from here.' She slumped forward, head cradled in her hands, and sobbed. 'My dear friend Jane was on board too. On a meaningless errand. If she is dead, it will be my fault. I may as well have made her walk the plank.'

Coop put his arm around her shoulders and handed her his handkerchief. 'Missing doesn't necessarily mean she's dead.'

She shook her head and blew her nose. 'They said that about Captain Oates and that was proven to be a lie.' She turned and looked him in the eye. 'I have to get away from here, Coop. Buccaneer Bay is not my home and now Maitland has gone I have no need to be here. I need distance and time away so I can think about what I'm going to do.'

Coop saw the look in her bloodshot eyes, and the certainty that she would leave him made him frantic. His heart was battering so hard he could barely get out the words. 'There's always hope, Maisie. Your friend could have got off the ship.'

'It's a consoling notion, but not very likely.'

They remained on the bench for a long time, sitting close and watching the sea. A pair of sea eagles hung in the air, circling, diving, their claws stretched out to land.

Her silence made him uneasy. He moved a little closer to her and regretted that he hadn't changed his clothes. He'd been wearing the same things for days.

She was looking where one of the buttons on his shirt was missing and he realised that his skin was visible where the fabric gaped open. She put her fingers against the cloth, pressing down, closing the space. 'You're not very good with buttons, are you? You almost lost one at the Welcome Dance. I wanted to sew it tight, so it would be safe.'

He covered her hand with his own. It felt warm and soft, as fragile as a small bird in his palm.

'What's really wrong?' he said, gently.

'Secrets I can't tell. Things that are not mine to share.'

'We all have things we keep hidden, Maisie.'

She disentangled her fingers. 'Like you not being able to read?'

He pulled back sharply, waiting for the shaking in his chest to subside. 'How long have you known?'

'Since the time on the *Hornet* when I asked you to hand out the crew's mail. A letter on the top of the pile was for JB. You didn't recognise his name.'

'I should have told you but I was scared . . . scared you would think less of me.'

She put a hand on his arm and gave it a squeeze. 'I would never think less of you, Coop. You are one of the most noble and generous-hearted people I know, but I have to go home.'

He saw the tightening of her fingers. 'What is it that you're not telling me?'

'I can't say, I'm sorry. You would despise me if I did, and I couldn't bear that from you.'

He raked his hands through his hair, sudden tears burning his eyes. 'Whatever it is, I could never hate you, Maisie. I can't imagine anyone ever hating you. I'd love you forever if you would only let me.'

She shut her eyes and hung her head. 'The water's too rough.'

He was floundering, battling with the sides of his mouth, forcing himself not to cry. His voice felt scratchy in his throat. 'When you're at sea, you can't change the way the wind blows. You have to adjust the sails.'

She hesitated a little, her voice distant. 'I have to make a future for myself, but right at the moment I can't see what that might be. It's as though my sails are flapping and I'm not sure which way the wind will blow me.'

He clasped her to him, wishing the tide would turn and take them both with it, but her hands were on his chest, pushing him away.

'You've lost interest in the sinking ship, haven't you?'

'No, Coop, I haven't, but with Maitland gone and his business mortgaged to the hilt and now Jane missing, I can't think how I'm going to manage on my own.'

He took her face between his hands and pressed it gently, kissing a different part of it as he spoke each word. 'You don't have to, Maisie.'

CHAPTER 28

COOP'S NEWS ABOUT THE *Atticus* brought Maisie into town. She stood on the jetty where the vast ship had berthed. The cyclone had blown through but the sea was as wild as she had ever seen it. White-topped waves blurred with the low grey clouds, and the horizon had disappeared. The storm had blown along the mangrove-lined shores and twisted its way through the jumble of buildings in Asia Place, felling the least robust like skittles and relieving the courthouse of its roof.

She'd seen the ship from the post office over a week ago, as tall as a mountain. How could it be that it had gone missing? It was as ridiculous as saying Big Ben had been lost.

It was the Chinese who began the whispers. They had intuition in these matters, Duc said. They could sense the truth as accurately as sniff the air for rain.

The *Atticus* was safe and sheltering at Gantry Creek, riding out the storm till the weather had cleared. Or, she had met with a mishap to her propeller or suffered minor disablement. Either way, it was good news. They'd hear from her soon enough. A few days here or there was nothing on the north-west coast.

As Blair Montague was on board, the resident magistrate appointed himself stand-in mayor. The *Atticus had* suffered minor disablement, he said, as a result of the vessel pitching about in high seas. That was the reason they'd not heard.

It was seized upon as the perfect explanation and kept spirits high throughout the morning. Mrs Brightlight, he said, would post up any news, as soon as there was anything to tell.

Mrs Brightlight's post office was crowded out. Noon-time came and went.

By mid-afternoon, the waiting crowd turned fractious as anxiety gained momentum. Didn't the *Atticus* have Marconi wireless apparatus? If so, why had no message been received to put everyone's mind at rest? It was days since she'd sailed. Arguments broke out. Somebody must know something.

Mrs Brightlight shooed the residents outside to wait. As soon as she had news, she said, she would let them know. In the meantime, why not trot over to the cable station? They might know something more.

At the cable station, Wayne Ramsey explained that the wires were down. That was why there was no news. It might take a day, he said, now they knew where the problem lay, before the men they'd sent out could rejoin the wire. He jiggled the key to prove his point. There was nothing there. But he would keep trying the *Atticus* call sign and as soon as he heard the merest crackle he would let Mrs Brightlight know. Early days, though. No need to panic.

Late in the afternoon Mrs Brightlight laid bare the grim news, writing the words in capital letters on a black-bordered page she kept for divers' death notices. She hung it on the board outside.

THE *ATTICUS*. MISSING FOR A DAY AND STILL NO NEWS.

In the Seafarer's bar that night, the harbour master had his say. 'I told the captain about the falling barometer and the heavy seas, and he said it had been dropping for three days but not sharply enough to cause any concern and he was going straight out to sea. He'd already missed the morning tide, he said, and wasn't prepared to delay a full day. He wasn't going to wait for the evening tide or see what the weather was doing. Wind is wind, he said, and the *Atticus* was powerful enough to sail through the squalliest of squalls.

'I told him that wind needs respecting but he repeated the ship could sail through anything. Out-manoeuvre it, I think he said, and there were watertight doors between every section of the ship. Even if it took on water, it simply could not sink. I said he was talking like a man who knew nothing of the north-west, and he said he knew better than me.

'He wasn't even the regular captain and didn't know the waters round here. He was standing in for Captain Stovell, who's on leave down south.'

Sometime the next morning, a wire came through from Gantry Creek. The *Atticus* was not sheltering there but a steamer had been reported heading towards Port Fremantle. It was most likely that the *Atticus* radio antenna was damaged in the cyclone, but all was well. The vessel was unsinkable. The Steamship Company said so.

Mrs Brightlight wrote out a new notice and hung it on her board.

DAY TWO. THE *ATTICUS*. EN ROUTE TO PORT FREMANTLE?

Coop was not so certain. She had not been heavily laden, he said, and was riding too high on the water. It was more likely that the *Atticus* had been overwhelmed by the cyclone and capsized. He wanted Maisie to be prepared.

Maisie shut herself in the house and stared through the lattice, willing the *Atticus* back to shore.

The resident magistrate sent a cable to the Premier in Perth, demanding a full-scale search. There were prominent Bay citizens on board. What was he proposing to do to help? Every steamer within five hundred miles should be drafted in.

The search went on for days.

By the morning of the tenth day, optimism began to fade. The first artefact of disaster – a cabin door painted white on one side and polished on the other, still hinged to its broken stile – had washed up on shore. No-one doubted its provenance or that it spoke of a violent separation from the ship. The word *Atticus* was stencilled above the lock. After the door, other items were found: a leather cushion from the first-class lounge, a billiard cue and the seat of a wicker chair; a lifebelt found its way back to land.

The finality of their discovery – reported by message at Mrs Brightlight's hand – left doubt in no-one's mind.

DAY TEN: *ATTICUS* OVERWHELMED AT SEA. LOST WITH ALL HANDS.

The knitting circle cancelled its weekly meeting 'out of respect'.

Doctor Shin lit a candle at the Buddhist temple and drank sake to the lives of those who had perished at sea.

Bishop MacMahon scheduled a Special Seafarer's Service and Mrs MacMahon, clad in her funereal black-watch tartan, pumped out 'Abide with Me' on the organ.

Maisie sat in her house and sobbed.

Jane's death left a heavy mark on Maisie.

Whatever secrets Jane had been hoping to discover – the truth about Blair and Maitland – had cost her her life. Both men were dead. Their secrets buried with them. It had all been a pointless waste.

Day after day Maisie sat motionless on a cane recliner and watched the poinciana leaves flitter across the verandah and settle in fluffy piles at her feet.

Marjorie leaned on the handle of her broom. 'You better lift you feet if you want I sweepum up, Missus.'

Maisie shook her head. 'What's the point? More will blow in and then more and then more. What's the point of anything?'

'Time you snapped out of wotever it is you's botherin' 'bout. Bin weeks since dat boat went down. Wot's done's done. Ain't nothin' you can do to fix it. You's got commitments.'

'Doctor Shin says I've had a nervous collapse.'

'You done bin tol' me dat before, Missus. Seems like a handy excuse if you don't mind me sayin'.' Marjorie pulled a letter from the sagging pocket of her apron and slapped it on the table. 'Right enuff you's collapsed on a chair but you ain't the nervous type. Best cure for you is get yourself washed and brushed. Mrs Wallace is payin' you a visit.'

Maisie sat up. 'Have you been reading my letters?'

'I bin readin' my own letters, actually. You bin mopin' 'bout with a face like a fifty-shillin' racehorse so long Duc and me decided to get our own medcin to fix you up. Mrs Brightlight gived me da address of dat woman you used to write to every week 'fore you gave up your letter-writing habit. Duc's gone to fetch her in da sulky and I've bin put her in da mosquito room where boss fella used to sleep. So, you better get yourself tidy quick smart 'cause she'll be here 'fore you know it.'

Maisie listened to Marjorie's heavy tread on the floorboards and heard a door bang somewhere in the house.

She made herself get up. Marjorie was right. Since the *Atticus* went down, her life had become so shapeless, the routine that had once driven her on was now barely familiar.

When she reached her room, she saw that Marjorie had chosen a clean dress for her to put on and had laid it out on the back of a chair. Her shoes had been newly polished and placed side by side, underneath the cane seat upon which she'd placed a folded handkerchief. She felt her chin begin to wobble. Lost and miserable, she sat down on the bed and for the first time in weeks, allowed the tears to fall.

On the verandah an hour or so later, Maisie held out a shawl.

'Are you warm enough, Mrs Wallace? It's been cool here in the evenings for a couple of months. Since the beginning of July, in fact.'

Mrs Wallace – that comforting, solid presence – had arrived in a whirl of turquoise gingham, and was as forthright in her views as ever.

She swivelled round in her chair and raised her eyes above the steel rims of her spectacles. 'This isn't a scene from a Jane

Austen novel, dear, where we talk about the weather and pussy-foot around what's really wrong with you because you have an over-delicate disposition. So let's be clear. When exactly did your backbone collapse? Marjorie tells me that you have fallen into a slump and are letting things slip.'

Maisie saw that the sky was getting dark through the lattice, and her temples had begun to thump. She let the shawl slither to the floor. 'Since events bent me out of shape.'

Mrs Wallace scrabbled in her handbag and extracted a hanky. 'That sounds like self-pitying twaddle to me.'

'It's too hard here. Everything's too hard. I've had enough of the heat and the flies and Maitland's debts and deceit. I can't forgive myself for the fact that I killed the first real friend I've ever had and that secrets eventually come out however much you think they are buried. I'm going to sell up when Maitland's affairs are settled and go back to England. I feel like a trapped bird, Mrs Wallace. The bars of my cage are red desert and sea. The only way in and out is the fortnightly steamer. It's suffocating me.'

Mrs Wallace spat on a corner of her hanky and removed her spectacles. 'You have responsibilities here, Maisie. People depend on you. Have you become so selfish that you would turn your back on them because you feel your wings have been clipped?'

'Pardon me?'

She began to polish the glass. 'Marjorie and Duc, for starters, and your lugger crews and divers. The merchants in Asia Place are owed money, as is the bank. Going back home seems to me the coward's way out. And where would you go? Do you think your mother would welcome you back, given all the trouble she took to send you here?'

Maisie was momentarily lost for words. 'She couldn't wait to see the back of me.' She hesitated and then went on. 'You started to tell me something months back in Port Fremantle, but you stopped yourself and changed the subject. Is there something you know and are not telling me?'

Mrs Wallace put a hand to her chest. 'Your mother was keen on someone else for a while.'

'Yes, I remember that conversation. I assumed it was someone she'd known before she married my father and you changed the subject. I'm guessing now that she was married.'

'Yes. She'd been married for a few years and you would have been about two, I think.'

Maisie wasn't sure where this was leading. 'Go on,' she said.

'Your father was working very long hours at his courts of law, making a name for himself, and your mother was on her own with a young baby – you – and she was lonely. She became – shall we say – *close* to a work colleague of your father and the friendship developed.'

'Was she in love with him?'

Mrs Wallace replaced her spectacles and sank back on the chair. 'Oh, yes. Head over heels. But he was married too, and nothing could ever come of it. Your father found out, of course, and when your mother told him she was expecting a child, he refused to believe it was his. He insisted she give it up for adoption but she wouldn't hear of it.'

Maisie's curiosity was spiked with incredulity. 'How do you know all this, Mrs Wallace?'

'I was there, dear. I nursed your mother after the little boy was taken.'

'Didn't her family wonder what had happened to the baby?'

'Your father gave out that the baby had died. They even conducted a funeral for him with an empty coffin and burial ceremony. It almost broke your mother.'

'Why, then, did she send me away?'

'I don't know for certain. But I suspect she never forgave your father, and you are the very spit of him. Maybe you were too much of a reminder of what he had done and she wanted to punish him. What I do know is that your mother didn't send you away without knowing you would be safe and looked out for a thousand miles from home.'

Maisie sat very still, trying to take it all in. Even now, she struggled to understand how her father could have been so cruel.

Mrs Wallace brushed some fluff off her sleeve. 'Your mother and I stayed in contact – at Christmas and so on. She knew I was over in England last year and asked me to travel with you to Australia. That's why everything was arranged so quickly after she received Maitland's letter. My passage was already booked and I couldn't afford to wait. So, in a very roundabout answer to your question, I don't think you going back home would be in anyone's best interest.'

Through the lattice, Maisie caught a glimpse of Marjorie as she tried to duck from view. She got up from her chair and said, loudly, 'Do you know what, Mrs Wallace? I believe my backbone has got over its slump. Tomorrow we go back to work.'

CHAPTER 29

MAISIE FOLDED THE BROADSHEET and laid it on the desk. The Wet was in full swing. After months in the Japanese hospital, Charles Harvey had succumbed to diver's paralysis. Coop was now the last of the imported English divers still in the Bay to have survived the experiment.

The comments in the newspaper recorded the white public's bewilderment and outrage. *'How is it possible that white men have lost out to the Asiatics?'* demanded one correspondent. *'The Japanese sabotaged the divers,'* claimed another. A third attacked the pearling industry, insisting the white divers must have been given *'unsuitable boots and faulty equipment in a bid to shanghai the experiment'*. Not one considered the possibility that the Japanese divers were just better at finding and hauling up shell.

Beyond the lattice, Maisie could hear Marjorie laughing. She had a beautiful laugh, deep and unrestrained, and Duc was laughing with her. It was good to hear some happiness in her home. They never failed to cheer her up. She cast a glance at Coop, who was slumped in a cane recliner, smoking a cigarette. From time to time she looked in his direction, but her eyes could not hold his. He seemed lost in his thoughts and she tried to imagine what he might be thinking.

They'd been silent for some minutes but Maisie was not ill at ease. Their silences were comfortable and fond, like memories they were yet to collect.

She pushed back her chair a little. 'It's not just the Japanese that the newspaper is targeting. They launched a scandalous attack on the Indigenous people a few days ago too.'

Coop hid his thoughts in his whisky glass. 'What did it say?'

'The editor called on the new mayor to rid the town of all Aborigines. He says that the whole race is an idle nuisance – "a drunken, disease-infested menace" was what he actually said in print. He seems to think the government is right behind him.'

'I wouldn't worry. No-one's going to take him or the government seriously. Every household I can think of employs at least one Aborigine, and most have a Chinese cook as well.'

'You would think so, but there have been no letters of protest to the editor and only one of support, from Bishop McMahon – which I find somewhat disappointing given that Jane was such an advocate of Indigenous rights.'

Coop leaned back and took a long pull on his cigarette. 'The leading whites will stir themselves if they think they're going to lose their domestic help. It won't have anything to do with protecting native rights, though. It'll be more to do with not being inconvenienced.'

Maisie laughed. 'When did you become so cynical?'

He shifted in the chair. 'Since Duc told me this morning that he's had his application for a car licence turned down. The mayor made a point of telling him personally.'

'He shouldn't need permission from anyone. Duc earned that car with his own money. Licences are routinely stamped over the counter at the council offices, and Mrs Brightlight says it won't be long before she is going to be able to issue them at the post office.'

'I know. What the mayor's really saying is that an Asian shouldn't be allowed to own a car.' Coop's eyes seemed to focus on the world outside the window for a long second. 'What did Marjorie have to say about this latest grand scheme to expel Aboriginal Australians from the town?'

'In her opinion, her people will never be accepted in "white-fella" Australia, even though they lived here long before Captain Cook planted the British flag in Botany Bay. She says the ways her people are tormented will never change – not even a hundred years from now. As long as white men are in charge, they'll never be left alone. And I trust her instincts because, at the end of the day, she really is the one at the receiving end.'

'It's not going to just blow over, that's for certain.' There was a dark tone to his voice.

Maisie pushed at a pin in her hair. 'Why do you say that?'

Coop ground the stub of his roll-up into the ashtray. 'You see the Aborigines on the streets blind drunk, or begging for tobacco and food. Or they camp outside the welfare office waiting for their benefit money. Give them something and next thing you know, they've given it away. So they're always broke and hungry. The whites don't want to accept responsibility for the situation they've put the locals in, so if they shove them all out of sight – well, problem solved.'

'Aborigines see things differently to you or me. If one of Marjorie's mob were to bang on our back door and say he was hungry, she would be obliged to feed him. She calls it "kinship stuff". And the Aborigines are not the only people lolling around on the streets, by the way. Most of the indentured crews are drunk throughout the lay-up season.'

He cleared his throat. 'Let's not argue, Maisie. I'm not defending the whites. We agree that something needs to be done about racial unfairness. It's a real problem for the pearling industry. The Japanese are just better suited to diving for shell, whatever your newspaper says. There's no simple solution to any of this, though. It's going to take years of negotiation by people more skilful than you or me.' There was no anger left in his voice, no lingering bitterness. 'Let's talk about something cheerier. Have you heard from Mrs Wallace?'

'Yes, she says she's bringing her husband Arthur to walk me down the aisle in lieu of my father, and that she wouldn't miss it for the world. She can't spare us her boys, though, as they're busy on the farm. It's a pity because I would have loved to have met them.'

They didn't say anything for a while, and she wondered if he'd heard her. A gust of wind blew in through the lattice, carrying with it a puff of dust, and sent a drying leaf flittering across the floorboards. Coop stretched out and trapped it under his boot.

'You're darned lucky to have Mrs Wallace. Not everyone would up sticks and leave their family for a month, even for a blood relative. I don't know how you'd have coped if she hadn't been here when the *Atticus* went down.'

The thought of Mrs Wallace and her blustery kindness made Maisie shake her head. The grief of Jane's loss had almost engulfed her. It was still there months later, waiting beneath the surface.

Maisie drank some tea, then got up from her chair and walked over to the lattice. She felt wobbly on her feet, like she'd been drinking, and clung to the wooden screen for balance. She forced herself to stand up straight and pushed her shoulders back. Coop didn't need to worry himself over how upset she still was about Jane.

She concentrated on the view. It hardly seemed possible that a year had passed since she'd last looked out on the same scene. The *Clancy* lay on its side on the tidal mudflat, picked clean of its rigging like a bleached bone, waiting for the full tide to rid it of its vermin. She let her gaze move past the lugger to the water of the Bay. The sea shone like molten jewels, but it was beauty spiked with danger. For a moment she saw Jane's face, and thought about the others who had been lost with her. But there was no point dwelling on what was gone, she reminded herself. Jane herself had taught her that.

Coop tapped his foot on the floorboards. 'What about your parents? What news from England?'

Maisie frowned. Her head had begun to throb. The last thing she wanted to think about was her parents. Just that morning, a starchy formal note had arrived. Written in her mother's black, rigid script and signed without any expression of affection, it had waspishly declined Maisie's invitation to the wedding.

His people are in trade. And he's your employee! What can you be thinking? If you were still living under our roof you would not be allowed to entertain such madness. It would be tantamount to consorting with the chauffeur. Could you imagine being married to Prebble? We simply would not permit it.

Damn you, Mother, she thought. She was almost glad that Coop couldn't read. Accidents of circumstance did not dictate one's worth as a person. More than the unwarranted attack on Coop, though, she was hurt that even though she had released them from their financial commitment to Maitland, her parents still didn't care to be involved with her life. So many times she had wanted to ask her mother about the paternity of her brother and why her father had done what he did, but she had not had the courage to begin. She understood with perfect clarity that they would never know what had happened to their little boy and she would never know her brother. They were bound together, her mother and father, and were clinging to a veneer of respectability, rather than walk away from the mistakes they had made.

She crumpled up the reply she had begun, threw it in the wastepaper basket and reached for the teapot. 'My parents are not coming to the wedding.'

'Did you really expect them to?' Coop said. His dark eyes were hooded, an alien expression on his face.

Maisie lifted the lid of the teapot and stirred the dark brew. 'I suppose I hoped that they might, but they said they'd send something as a wedding gift – when they'd had time to consider what might be suitable.'

Coop put his glass on the coffee table and slid it away. He looked hesitant. 'In their letters, they never mention me, do they? And that's why you never read them out. I will always be working-class to them, the wrong side of the chalk line. I can't do anything to change that. It's who I am. They remind me why I left England in the first place. I'm better off here in the Bay, where no-one gives a toss where you come from. Here I'm William Cooper the diver, whose business is pearl shell. That's all anyone cares about.'

She turned away, pulled a handkerchief from her dress pocket and began to blot her clammy hands. 'My parents' views are very different to mine, Coop; I don't know how many times I need to say that. I do have some better news, though. Pierre Fornallaz has sold the pearl.'

He was fussing with his glass again, sliding it a few inches to the left and then to the right. A deep frown wrinkled his forehead. 'When were you going to tell me that?'

'Don't get cross! I only heard from the bank today that all Maitland's outstanding debts are cleared and, if I want, I am free to trade again under Sinclair Marine.'

Coop continued to move his glass but didn't pass comment.

Maisie felt a little cold hand squeezing at her heart, and clutched her handkerchief between trembling fingers. 'Aren't you pleased for me?'

'Yes, of course, but what comes next?'

'Duc is spending a lot of his time in Asia Place with his ear to the ground. He's talking about investing in the wool business. Apparently he once overheard Maitland say that was where the smart money would be made if war comes to Europe. So, I'm going to invest my uncle's money in wool too. When your father comes for the wedding, you should tell him to think about army uniforms instead of socks.'

Coop stood up and raked his fingers through his hair. 'He isn't coming either, Maisie.'

'I'm sorry. That's a dreadful blow. You must be devastated.'

'Like you, I'm not that surprised if I'm honest. He can't afford to be away from the business for three or four months, travelling here and back. And after what's happened with the *Titanic* and then the *Atticus*, well, understandably he's not keen on boats just at the moment. He sends his fond wishes for our happiness, though.'

'I think you should still tell him about the investment opportunity. If war does break out, he'll be much more in the thick of it than us. I'll help you write to him, if you'd like?'

'Don't worry, I'll ask JB to help me when I go back to the Seafarer's tonight. He always seems to get the words just right with my dad.'

Maisie pressed her clenched hands into her lap. The rejection had come out of nowhere like a sudden wind, and blown her off balance. 'What's going on, Coop?'

He began to jiggle the coins in his trouser pocket. 'We're poles apart, you and me. You've created the beginnings of a commercial empire, Maisie. For nine months of the year, I roll up my sleeves and dive for pearl shell. The more I pick up, the more I earn. That's the extent of it.'

She *had* to make this better. 'My only ambition is to be your wife.'

'When I can't read? When the only work I know how to do means using my hands? Maybe your parents are right, and I should remember I'm a working-class man. I'm not in your league and shouldn't fool myself I ever could be. Maybe it would be for the best if I just walked away.'

He was staring at her so bleakly that knots of dread tightened in her stomach. 'Where has this come from? Are you saying that you don't want to marry me? You've changed your mind?' The words burst out of her mouth like bubbles. She hardly knew what she was saying.

Coop held up a hand, his long expressive fingers stretched wide. 'How could you even think that? I've longed to marry you from that first moment on the ship when I saw you at the lifeboat drill. It's just – I don't know how to say this . . . Sometimes when

I look at you, my heart leaps with glorious hope for our future. Then I remind myself where you come from and who I am, and it sinks with despair. Maisie, I'm scared to death that one day you'll wake up and realise you've made a terrible mistake, and it will be *you* who has changed *your* mind.'

She made herself wait before she spoke. The one thought she could hold onto, amid the panic, was that she couldn't lose him; that it was up to her to make him understand.

'Yes, we're from different backgrounds, but we're absolutely *not* mismatched. Who you are is far more important than where you hail from. We're fighters, Coop. This is the best decision of my life.' She held out her arms as if inviting him to dance. 'Come, my love. Let's take a walk up to the lighthouse. It's too hot in here to think straight.'

They followed the crushed-shell path towards the beacon, Maisie clutching Coop tight to her side. She could feel his heart racing against the top of her arm, his skin damp through his shirt. When they reached the bench, she turned to him and looked deep into his eyes for a very long time, stroking his sunburned face with the back of her hand and whispering the things that people in love say to each other.

'Let's go a bit further,' she said after a time, 'while we still have the light.'

He looped his arm around her waist and they walked on together, her head against his shoulder, towards the horizon and the future.

AUTHOR'S NOTE

In July 2013, Perth in Western Australia was cold and wet.

At 2200 kilometres north of Perth, Broome is not the sort of place you visit on the spur of the moment, but sometimes we do impulsive things.

From the moment I arrived, Broome had a romantic feel about it – a remote, rugged outpost with a past woven through with colourful characters and adventurous tales of hard-hat divers battling through cyclones to wrest pearl shells the size of serving platters from the depths of the Indian Ocean.

On every street corner, the town of Broome celebrates the industry that put it on the map. There are museums devoted to pearl-shell diving, a historical society, bus tours to take and pearl farms to visit. Diving memorabilia is everywhere.

At Gantheaume Point, the lighthouse dominates the coastline where Anastasia's Pool was fashioned from a rock pool by the lighthouse keeper for his arthritic wife.

At the Japanese cemetery, over 900 Japanese men are buried and other sections of the cemetery are dedicated to Chinese, Muslims and Christians.

Between 1910 and 1912 in Broome, I learned, there were some 500 diagnosed cases of beri-beri, with almost one hundred deaths. In the case of the diver's paralysis (the bends) there were close to 200 deaths between 1910 and 1914, and from drowning approximately 700 deaths between 1887 and 1935.

I wanted to know more about Broome's pearl-fishing industry.

The pearling industry in Western Australia stretches back to the mid-nineteenth century, with Broome emerging onto the scene in the mid-1880s. Mother-of-pearl was in worldwide demand for use as buttons, cutlery handles, watch-faces and inlay for marquetry. The rich beds of pearl oysters (*Pinctada maxima*) off the beaches of the north-west coast provided a ready supply of the sought-after shell.

By the turn of the twentieth century, Broome was a town of enormous wealth derived almost entirely from pearl-shell fishing.

The pearling industry drew migrants from across Asia – divers from Japan and Malaysia as well as the Chinese, Timorese (Keopanger), Filipino and other nationalities as deckhands and general labourers. In its heyday, in the first decade of the twentieth century, Broome had built a reputation not only as the centre of the mother-of-pearl industry but also as a rough and rowdy outpost in the north-west back of beyond – akin to a sort of Asian Wild West.

And yet in 1912, a deep sense of foreboding hung over the town. At that time, the racial composition of workers in the pearl industry, from official figures (Pearl and Pearl Shell Fisheries, Government Statisticians' Office, Government Printer, Perth), on 309 pearling vessels read as follows: whites, 223; Aboriginal people, 67; Chinese, 4; Japanese, 1148; Keopangers, 0; Malays, 716; Manilamen, 128; other, 102; for a total of 2098 Asiatics.

To understand the source of this deep unrest, I turned to books and periodicals of the time.

When the six states federated into the Commonwealth of Australia in 1901, at the very heart of its thinking was the restriction of Asian immigration to its shores. The Australian government passed an act in the same year – its *Immigration Restriction Act* (more widely known as the White Australia policy). There was national consensus that white Australians needed protection from the invading yellow hordes from the north, and politicians demanded that all coloured indentured labour was to be expelled from the pearl-fishing industry.

Up in Broome – far removed geographically from Canberra – laws, if they were inconvenient, were largely ignored. No-one ever travelled north to police them. The pearl bosses were not concerned and carried on as usual.

But the Australian government was determined. By 1911, the Federal Parliament had decided to appoint a royal commission to conduct a thorough investigation into the pearling industry. The commission was led by Fred Bamford – the member for Queensland – whose staunch, oft-repeated views on White Australia were well known. The commission did concede, however, that it could not complete its investigation before the pearlers made their staffing arrangements for the 1914 season, so the deadline for cessation of the employment of coloured labour was extended by a year – to the end of 1914.

The pearling masters began to panic.

Pearling relied on a non-white workforce. If it was no longer available, it would spell ruin – for the industry as a whole, and more particularly for the profits of the controlling white pearling masters.

There had never been more than a handful of white divers employed in the industry, and the pearling bosses knew that the coloured divers, especially the Japanese, picked up more shell. They were also more tolerant of the conditions under which they worked on the luggers (small diving boats), which were crammed with equipment and stores. It was cramped on board and for up to three months at a time, working every day except Sundays from sun-up to sunset, divers hauled up shell from the ocean bed. The conditions were so brutal that Europeans, the pearling masters argued, would not be able to stand them.

In addition, coloured wages were lower than those paid to Europeans. The indentured crews cost half as much to feed, rice and fish being their staple food, and if they became difficult to handle, permits could be cancelled and the troublemakers sent packing.

Added to this soup of discontent, February 1912 also marked the beginning of what would come to be known as the 'White Experiment'.

To prove that the pearl-fishing industry could be manned by white labour, twelve experienced Royal Navy divers, some with their own tenders, were brought out from England to introduce the face of white diving to Broome.

Almost overnight, pressure was put on the most prominent pearlers to literally buy in to the experiment.

An article appeared in Perth's *Sunday Times* on 4 February:

WHITE DIVERS FOR THE PEARLING INDUSTRY

An Interesting Experiment

An important step in the direction of settling the vexed question of white divers versus Asiatics was taken on Feb. 1 with the arrival of 12 experienced divers from England with the necessary tenders.

It will be remembered that the Pearlers' Association of Broome, in order to thoroughly test the question of whether white divers are capable of performing the arduous work of finding pearl shell in deep water, arranged to set apart a certain number of luggers, to be manned by white divers and tenders, these men to be employed for a sufficient time to decide the point beyond the shadow of a doubt.

In order that none but the best and most experienced men should be obtained, the matter was placed in the hands of Messrs. Siebe, Gorman and Co., the celebrated manufacturers of diving gear, in conjunction with a committee of Broome pearlers now resident in London, and the 24 men now arrived are those chosen by the selectors.

The whole of these interesting immigrants are ex-naval divers, that is, men who have not only a practical experience of the work under all conditions, but who also have a thorough knowledge of its scientific aspect. They are, in addition, imbued with all the traditions of a service which imposes so high a standard of duty that the idea of shirking or evading either danger or responsibility is an impossibility. Under such conditions as these, the experienced body of men may be relied upon to give the Pearlers' Association loyal and active support in their attempt to solve the problem that lies before them, and it only remains for the association, on the other hand, to see that the test is carried out under absolute fair working conditions, and that no unconscious bias in favour of the Asiatic diver is allowed to interfere.[1]

It seems clear that the British divers – in their desperation to succeed – pushed the boundaries of safety, often diving for too long without taking the necessary decompression stops when returning to the surface. Another difficulty facing the white divers was that they were not being shown where and how to find shell. Marine Engineer Jim Low, whose job was to ensure the smooth running of the engine-driven compressors on the white divers' luggers, wrote variously to his sister that:

One of the white divers one of Siebe Gorman's crack men died of paralysis last week, he wouldn't work to the scientific method and refused to be recompressed after the attack. He was of the old school who had made a name for himself in the diving world, recovering treasure from wrecks, went with the McMillan expedition through Central Africa bringing up specimens out of the deep potholes somewhere or other and now has finished up here.

Tomorrow I go out again with another engine and air compressor to start two more of the white men but I am going to keep them near Broome this time . . . I have never seen or heard of the last crowd I was out with since I left them nor has anyone else. They are off quite on their own somewhere or other. Their engine must be going all right or the Malay child has killed them all, one or the other.[2]

And again he wrote to his sister:

Two of the white divers has got 'fed up' and shook the sand of Broome from their feet; there is now only five left. I am afraid 'white diving' is doomed.[3]

The Pearler's Wife is set against this background – which is true. The characters, however, and incidents in the book are all imaginary.

1. 'White Divers for the Pearling Industry', the *Sunday Times*, 4 February 1912
2. Low, James Galloway, Letters 1904–91, Battye Library, ACC 2612A (listing: MN681). Letter from Jim to his sister Jane, 21 June 1912
3. Low, James Galloway, Letters 1904–91, Battye Library, ACC 2612A (listing: MN681). Letter from Jim to his sister Jane, 4 July 1912

ACKNOWLEDGEMENTS

WRITING A BOOK IS like building a house; you need expert guidance at every important stage in the process. I have been lucky to have found the very best.

Thank you to my editor and dear friend, Salomé Jones of Flourish Editing, for making this book publishable. You are everything I could hope for in an editor, Salomé, and I couldn't have done this without you.

Thank you to Isobel Dixon at Blake Friedmann for responding to my submission material on a sunny Sunday afternoon in June. I am so grateful to you, Isobel, for taking a chance on me and for suggesting that your wonderful, talented colleague Hattie Grunewald would be an expert pair of hands for my book. You were certainly not wrong.

Thank you also to my publishers, Beverley Cousins at Penguin Random House in Australia and Lynne Drew at HarperCollins in the UK, who made brilliant (also terrifying!) suggestions to improve the manuscript and have taken such good care of the book.

Thank you to my husband Harry, who has read (and re-read) countless drafts, always with a critical eye but never without encouragement.

Thank you to Philippa Donovan at Smartquill and to my reading group for your constructive criticism, and especial thanks to my niece Madeleine and my sisters: Jo, for reading the entire manuscript on her mobile phone, and Sarah, for suggesting the trip that sparked it all off!
Most of all I want to thank the divers of Broome – without whom there would have been no story to tell.